THE DEATH
SCULPTOR

About the author

Born in Brazil of Italian origin, Chris Carter studied psychology and criminal behaviour at the University of Michigan. As a member of the Michigan State District Attorney's Criminal Psychology team, he interviewed and studied many criminals, including serial and multiple homicide offenders with life imprisonment convictions.

Having departed for Los Angeles in the early 1990s, Chris spent ten years as a guitarist for numerous rock bands before leaving the music business to write full-time. He now lives in London and is the *Sunday Times* bestselling author of *The Crucifix Killer*, *The Executioner* and *The Night Stalker*.

Visit www.chriscarterbooks.com

Also by Chris Carter

The Crucifix Killer
The Executioner
The Night Stalker

CHRIS CARTER

THE DEATH SCULPTOR

**SIMON &
SCHUSTER**

London · New York · Sydney · Toronto · New Delhi

A CBS COMPANY

First published in Great Britain by Simon & Schuster UK Ltd, 2012
A CBS Company

First published in paperback in 2013

Copyright © Chris Carter, 2012

1 3 5 7 9 10 8 6 4 2

Simon & Schuster UK Ltd
1st Floor
222 Gray's Inn Road
London WC1X 8HB

www.simonandschuster.co.uk

Simon & Schuster Australia
Sydney

Simon & Schuster India
New Delhi

A CIP catalogue record for this book is available from the British Library

Paperback A ISBN 978-0-85720-303-8
Paperback B ISBN 978-0-85720-302-1
Ebook ISBN 978-0-85720-304-5

Typeset by Hewer Text UK Ltd, Edinburgh
Printed and bound in Great Britain by CPI Group (UK) Ltd, Croydon, CR0 4YY

This novel is dedicated to all the readers who have entered the competition to become a character in this book, and especially to the winner, Alice Beaumont, from Sheffield. I hope you all enjoy it.

Acknowledgements

Writing is regarded by many as a lonely profession, but I am far from alone. I am very fortunate to have the help, support and friendship of some incredible people. My friend, and the best agent an author could ever hope for, Darley Anderson. Camilla Wray for helping me shape a simple draft into a finished novel, yet again. My fantastic editor at Simon & Schuster, Maxine Hitchcock, for being so fantastic at what she does, and for all the support, suggestions and guidance from the first word to the last. Emma Lowth for her expert eye and advice. Samantha Johnson for listening and for being there. Everyone at the Darley Anderson Literary Agency for all their hard work in every aspect of the publishing business. Ian Chapman, Suzanne Baboneau, Florence Partridge, Jamie Groves and everyone at Simon & Schuster UK – you guys are the best. Thank you also to all the readers and everyone out there who have so fantastically supported me and my novels from the start.

One

'Oh my God, I'm late,' Melinda Wallis said, springing out of bed as her tired eyes glanced at the digital clock on her bedside table. Last night she'd stayed up until 3:30 a.m., studying for her Clinical Pharmacology exam in three days' time.

Still a little groggy from sleep, she clumsily moved around the room while her brain worked out what to do first. She hurried into the bathroom and caught a glimpse of her reflection in the mirror.

'Shit, shit, shit.'

She reached for her makeup bag and started powdering her face.

Melinda was twenty-three years old and according to an article she'd read in a glossy magazine a few days ago, a little overweight for her height – she was only five foot four. Her long brown hair was always tied back into a ponytail, even when she went to bed, and she would never go outside without at least plastering her face with foundation to hide her acne-riddled cheeks. Instead of brushing her teeth, she quickly squirted a blob of toothpaste into her mouth just to get rid of the night taste.

Back in the room, she found her clothes neatly folded on a chair by her study desk – a white blouse, stockings, a knee-length white skirt and white flat-soled shoes. She got dressed in record time and sprinted out of the small guest-house in the direction of the main building.

Melinda was attending the third year of her Bachelor of Science in Nursing and Caretaking degree at UCLA, and every weekend, to fulfill her job-experience curriculum, she worked as an in-house private nurse. For the past fourteen weekends she'd been working for Mr. Derek Nicholson in Cheviot Hills, West Los Angeles.

Just two weeks before she was hired, Mr. Nicholson was diagnosed with advanced lung cancer. The tumor was already the size of a plum stone and it was eating away at him fast. Walking was too painful, sometimes he needed the help of breathing apparatus, and he spoke only in a barely audible voice. Despite his daughters' pleas, he declined to start chemotherapy treatment. He refused to spend days locked inside a hospital room and chose to spend the time he had left in his own house.

Melinda unlocked the front door and stepped into the spacious entry lobby before rushing through the large but sparsely decorated living room. Mr. Nicholson's bedroom was located on the first floor. As always, the house was eerily quiet in the morning.

Derek Nicholson lived alone. His wife had passed away two years ago, and though his daughters came to visit him every day, they had their own lives to attend to.

'I'm sorry I'm late,' Melinda called from downstairs. She checked her watch again. She was exactly forty-three minutes late. 'Shit!' she murmured under her breath. 'Derek, are you awake?' she called, crossing to the staircase and taking the steps two by two.

Derek Nicholson had asked her on her first weekend at

the house to call him by his first name. He didn't like the formality of 'Mr. Nicholson'.

As Melinda approached his bedroom door, she caught a noseful of a strong, sickening smell coming from inside.

Oh, damn, she thought. It was obviously too late for his first bathroom break.

'OK, let's get you cleaned up first . . .' she said, opening the door, '. . . and then I'll get you your breakf—'

Her whole body went rigid, her eyes widened in horror and the air was sucked out of her lungs as if she had been suddenly propelled into outer space. She felt the contents of her stomach shoot up into her mouth and she vomited right there by the door.

'God in heaven!' Those were the words Melinda had intended to say as she moved her trembling lips, but no sound came from them. Her legs began to give way under her, the world began to spin, and she held on to the doorframe with both hands to steady herself. That was when her horrified green eyes caught a glimpse of the far wall. It took her brain a moment to understand what she was seeing, but as it did, primal fear and panic rose inside her heart like a thunderstorm.

Two

Summer had barely started in the City of Angels and the temperature was already hitting 87°F. Detective Robert Hunter of the Los Angeles Robbery Homicide Division (RHD) stopped the timer on his wristwatch as he reached his apartment block in Huntingdon Park, southeast of downtown. Seven miles in thirty-eight minutes. Not bad, he thought, but he was sweating like a turkey on Thanksgiving Day and his legs and knees hurt like hell. Maybe he should've stretched. In fact, he knew he should stretch before and after exercising, especially after a long run, but he could never really be bothered to do it.

Hunter took the stairs up to the third floor. He didn't like elevators, and the one in his building was nicknamed 'the sardine trap' for a reason.

He opened the door to his one-bedroom apartment and stepped inside. The apartment was small but clean and comfortable, though people would be forgiven for thinking that the furniture had been donated by Goodwill – a black leatherette sofa, mismatched chairs, a scratched breakfast table that doubled as a computer desk, and an old bookcase that looked like it would give under the weight of its over-crowded shelves at any minute.

Hunter took off his shirt and used it to wipe the sweat off

his forehead, neck and muscular torso. His breathing was already back to normal. In the kitchen, he grabbed a pitcher of iced tea from the fridge and poured himself a large glass. Hunter was looking forward to spending an uneventful day away from the Police Administration Building, and the RHD headquarters. He didn't get many days off. Maybe he'd drive down to Venice Beach and play some volleyball. He hadn't played volleyball in years. Or maybe he could try to catch a Lakers game. He was sure they were playing that night. But first he needed a shower and a quick trip down to the launderette.

Hunter finished his iced tea, walked into the bathroom and checked his reflection in the mirror. He also needed a shave. As he reached for the shaving gel and razor, his cell-phone rang in the bedroom.

Hunter picked it up from his bedside table and checked the display – Carlos Garcia, his partner. Only then he noticed the small red arrow at the top of the screen indicating that he had missed calls – ten of them.

'Great!' he whispered, accepting the call. He knew exactly what ten missed calls and his partner on the phone that early on their day off meant.

'Carlos,' Hunter said, bringing the phone to his ear. 'What's up?'

'Jesus! Where were you? I've been trying you for half an hour.'

A call every three minutes, Hunter thought. This was going to be bad.

'I was out, running,' he said, calmly. 'Didn't check my phone when I walked in. I only saw the missed calls now. So what have we got?'

'A hell of a mess. You better get here quick, Robert. I've

never seen anything like this.' There was a quick, hesitant pause from Garcia. 'I don't think anyone has ever seen anything quite like this.'

Three

Even on a Sunday morning, it took Hunter almost an hour to cover the fifteen miles between Huntingdon Park and Cheviot Hills.

Garcia hadn't given Hunter many details over the phone, but his evident shock and the slight trepidation in his voice were certainly out of character.

Hunter and Garcia were part of a small, specialized unit within the RHD – the Homicide Special Section, or HSS. The unit was created to deal solely with serial, high-profile and homicide cases requiring extensive investigative time and expertise. Hunter's background in criminal-behavior psychology placed him in an even more specialized group. All homicides where overwhelming brutality or sadism had been used by the perpetrator were tagged by the department as 'UV' (ultra-violent). Robert Hunter and Carlos Garcia *were* the UV unit, and as such, they weren't easily rattled. They had seen more than their share of things that no one else on this earth had seen.

Hunter pulled up next to one of several black-and-white units parked in front of the two-story house in West LA. The press was already there, crowding up the small street, but that was no surprise. They usually got to crime scenes before the detectives did.

Hunter stepped out of his old Buick LeSabre and was hit by a wave of warm air. Unbuttoning his jacket and clipping his badge onto his belt, he looked around slowly. Though the house was located in a private street, tucked away in a quiet neighborhood, the crowd of curious onlookers that had gathered outside the police perimeter was already substantial, and it was growing fast.

Hunter turned and faced the house. It was a nice-looking two-story red-brick building with dark-blue-framed windows and a hipped roof. The front yard was large and well cared for. There was a two-car garage to the right of the house, but no cars on the driveway, except for more police vehicles. A forensic-unit van was parked just a few yards away. Hunter quickly spotted Garcia as he exited the house through the front door. He was wearing a classic white hooded Tyvek coverall. At six foot two, he was two inches taller than Hunter.

Garcia stopped by the few stone steps that led down from the porch and pulled his hood down. His longish dark hair was tied back into a slick ponytail. He also promptly spotted his partner.

Ignoring the animated herd of reporters, Hunter flashed his badge at the officer standing at the perimeter's edge and stooped under the yellow crime-scene tape.

In a city like Los Angeles, when it came to crime stories and reporters, the more gruesome and violent the offence, the more excited they got. Most of them knew Hunter, and what sort of cases he was assigned to. Their shouted questions came in a barrage.

'Bad news travels fast,' Garcia said, tilting his head in the direction of the crowd as Hunter got to him. 'And a potentially good story travels faster.' He handed his partner a brand new Tyvek coverall inside a sealed plastic bag.

'What do you mean?' Hunter took the bag, ripped it open and started suiting up.

'The victim was a lawyer,' Garcia explained. 'A Mr. Derek Nicholson, prosecutor with the District Attorney's office for the State of California.'

'Oh that's great.'

'He wasn't practicing anymore, though.'

Hunter zipped up his coverall.

'He was diagnosed with advanced lung cancer,' Garcia continued.

Hunter looked at him curiously.

'He was pretty much on his way out. Oxygen masks, legs weren't really responding the way they should . . . The doctors gave him no more than six months. That was four months ago.'

'How old was he?'

'Fifty. It was no secret he was dying. Why finish him off this way?'

Hunter paused. 'And there's no doubt he was murdered?'

'Oh, there's absolutely no doubt.'

Garcia guided Hunter into the house and through the entry lobby. Next to the door there was a security-alarm keypad. Hunter looked at Garcia.

'Alarm wasn't engaged,' he clarified. 'Apparently, arming it wasn't something they did often.'

Hunter pulled a face.

'I know,' Garcia said, 'what's the point of having one, right?'

They moved on.

In the living room, two forensic agents were busy dusting the staircase by the back wall.

'Who found the body?' Hunter asked.

'The victim's private nurse,' Garcia replied and directed Hunter's attention to the open door in the east wall. It led into a large study. Inside, sitting on a vintage leather Chesterfield sofa, was a young woman dressed all in white. Her hair was tied back. Her eyes were raspberry red and puffed up from crying. Resting on her knees was a cup of coffee that she was holding with both hands. Her stare seemed lost and distant. Hunter noticed that she was rocking her upper body back and forth ever so slightly. She was clearly in shock. A uniformed officer was in the room with her.

'Anybody tried talking to her yet?'

'I did,' Garcia nodded. 'Managed to get some basic information out of her, but she's psychologically shutting down, and I'm not surprised. Maybe you could try later. You're better at these things than I am.'

'She was here on a Sunday?' Hunter asked.

'She's only here on weekends,' Garcia clarified. 'Her name is Melinda Wallis. She goes to UCLA. She's just finishing a degree in Nursing and Caretaking. This is part of her work experience. She got the job a week after Mr. Nicholson was diagnosed with his illness.'

'How about the rest of the week?'

'Mr. Nicholson had another nurse.' Garcia unzipped his coverall and reached inside his breast pocket for his notebook. 'Amy Dawson,' he read the name. 'Unlike Melinda, Amy isn't a student. She's a professional nurse. She took care of Mr. Nicholson during the week. Also, his two daughters came to visit him every day.'

Hunter's eyebrow arched.

'They haven't been contacted yet.'

'So the victim lived here alone?'

'That's right. His wife of twenty-six years died in a car accident two years ago.' Garcia returned the notebook to his pocket. 'The body is upstairs.' He motioned to the staircase.

As he took the steps up, Hunter was careful not to interfere with the forensic agents as they worked. The first-floor landing resembled a waiting room – two chairs, two leather armchairs, a small bookshelf, a magazine holder, and a sideboard covered with stylish picture frames. A dimly lit corridor led them deeper into the house, and to the four bedrooms and two bathrooms. Garcia took Hunter all the way to the last door on the right and paused outside.

'I know you've seen a lot of sick stuff before, Robert. God knows I have.' He rested his latex-gloved hand on the doorknob. 'But this . . . not even in nightmares.' He pushed the door open.

Four

Hunter stood by the open door to the large bedroom. His eyes registered the scene in front of him, but his logical mind was having trouble comprehending it.

Centered against the north wall was an adjustable double bed. To its right he could see a small oxygen tank and mask on a wooden bedside table. A wheelchair occupied the space by the end of the bed. There was also an antique-looking chest of drawers, a mahogany writing desk, and a large shelf unit on the wall opposite the bed. Its centerpiece was a flat-screen TV set.

Hunter breathed out but didn't move, didn't blink, didn't say a word.

'Where do we start?' Garcia whispered by his side.

Blood was everywhere – on the bed, floor, rug, walls, ceiling, curtains, and on most of the furniture. Mr. Nicholson's body was on the bed. Or at least what was left of it. He'd been dismembered. Both legs and both arms had been ripped from his body. One of his arms had been hacked at the joints into smaller pieces. Both of his feet had also been separated from his legs.

But what baffled everyone who entered that room was the sculpture.

On a small coffee table by the window, the victim's

severed and hacked body parts had been bundled up and arranged together into a bloody, twisted, incomprehensible shape.

'You've gotta be kidding me,' Hunter whispered to himself.

'I'm not even going to ask. 'Cos I know you've never seen anything like this before, Robert,' Doctor Carolyn Hove said from the far corner of the room. 'None of us have.'

Doctor Hove was the Chief Medical Examiner for the Los Angeles County Department of Coroner. She was tall and slim with deep penetrating green eyes. Her long, chestnut hair was tucked away under the hood of her white coverall, her full lips and petite nose hidden under her surgical mask.

Hunter's attention moved to her for a couple of seconds and then to the large blood pools on the floor. He hesitated for a moment. There was no way he could walk into that room without treading on them.

'It's OK,' Doctor Hove said, motioning him and Garcia inside. 'The entire floor has been photographed.'

Still, Hunter did his best to circumvent the blood. He approached the bed and what was left of Mr. Nicholson's body. His face was caked in blood. His eyes and mouth were wide open, as if his last terrified scream had been frozen before it came out. The bed sheets, the pillows and the mattress were ripped and torn in several places.

'He was killed on that bed,' Doctor Hove said, coming up to Hunter.

He kept his attention on the body.

'Judging by the splatters and the amount of blood we have here,' she continued, 'the killer inflicted as much pain as the victim could handle before allowing him to die.'

'The killer cut him up first?'

The doctor nodded. 'And the killer started with the small, non-life-threatening pieces.'

Hunter frowned.

'All his toes were cut off, together with his tongue.' Her stare moved back to the revolting body-part sculpture. 'I'd say that was done first, before he was dismembered.'

'He was alone in the house?'

'Yes,' Garcia answered. 'Melinda, the student nurse you saw downstairs, spends the weekends here, but she sleeps in the guesthouse above the garage you saw up front. According to her, Mr. Nicholson's daughters came by every day and spent a couple of hours with him, sometimes more. They left last night at around 9:00 p.m. After putting him to sleep and finishing up in the house, Melinda left Mr. Nicholson at around 11:00 p.m. She went back to the guesthouse and stayed up until three-thirty in the morning, studying for an exam.'

It wasn't hard for Hunter to understand why the nurse never heard anything. The garage was all the way up front and about twenty yards away from the main building. The room they were in was right at the back of the house, the last one down the corridor. Its windows faced the backyard. They could've had a party in here and she wouldn't have heard it.

'No panic button?' Hunter asked.

Garcia pointed to one of the evidence bags in the corner of the room. Inside it was a piece of electric wire with a click button at the end of it. 'The wire was snipped.'

Hunter's attention focused on the blood splatters all over the bed, furniture and wall next to it. 'Was the weapon found?'

'No, not yet,' Garcia replied.

'The spit-like blood pattern and the jagged edge of the wounds inflicted indicate that the killer used some sort of electrical sawing device,' Doctor Hove said.

'Like a chainsaw?' Garcia asked.

'Possibly.'

Hunter shook his head. 'A chainsaw would be too noisy. Too risky. The last thing the killer would've wanted would be to alert anyone before he was done. A chainsaw is also a harder tool to control, especially if your aim is precision.' He examined the body and the bed for a while longer before moving away from it and approaching the coffee table and the morbid sculpture.

Both of Mr. Nicholson's arms were awkwardly twisted and bent at the wrist joints, forming two distinct, but meaningless shapes. His feet had been cut off and bundled together in a peculiar way with the arms and hands. All of it was held in place by thin but solid pieces of metal wire. Wire had also been used to attach a few of his severed toes to the edges of the two pieces. His legs had been laid flat side-by-side, and formed the base to the sculpture. Everything was covered in blood.

Hunter circled it slowly, trying to take every detail in.

'Whatever this is,' Doctor Hove said, 'it's not something anyone can put together in a couple of minutes. This takes time.'

'And if the killer took the time to put it together,' Garcia added, moving closer, 'it's gotta mean something.'

Hunter took a few steps back and stared at the macabre piece from a distance. It meant nothing to him.

'Do you think your lab could create a life-size replica of this?' he asked Doctor Hove.

Under her surgical mask, she twisted her mouth from side to side. 'I don't see why not. It's already been photographed, but I'll call the photographer back in and ask him to get a snapshot from all angles. I'm sure the lab can get it done.'

'Let's do it,' Hunter said. 'We're not gonna figure this out here and now.' He turned towards the far wall and froze. It was so covered in blood that he almost didn't notice it. 'What in the world is that?'

Garcia's stare moved to Hunter and then back to the wall. He breathed out a heavy sigh.

'That . . . is everybody's worst nightmare.'

Five

Doctor Hove pulled down her surgical mask and faced Garcia. 'He doesn't know?'

Hunter's eyebrows arched.

Garcia unzipped his coverall and reached inside his pocket for his notebook once again. 'Let me talk you through what we know, but for you to fully understand it, I have to take you back to yesterday afternoon.'

'OK.' Hunter was intrigued.

Garcia read on. 'Mr. Nicholson's oldest daughter, Olivia, came by at around 5:00 p.m. Her younger sister, Allison, arrived half an hour after her. They had dinner with their father and kept him company until about 9:00 p.m., when they both left. After that, Melinda, the nurse, helped Mr. Nicholson into the bathroom, and then tucked him into bed, as she had done every weekend night. It took him about thirty minutes to fall asleep. She never left his side.' Garcia indicated the chair on the other side of the bed. 'She sat over there. She had some of her study books with her.' He flipped a page on his notebook. 'Melinda then turned off the lights, emptied the dishwasher downstairs, and at around 11:00 p.m. retired to her room in the guesthouse.'

Hunter nodded and his attention reverted back to the wall.

'I'm getting there,' Garcia said. 'Melinda remembers locking all the doors, including the backdoor in the kitchen, but she can't say the same about the windows. When I got here earlier this morning, two of the ones downstairs were unlocked, the one in the study and the one in the kitchen. LAPD First Response said they didn't touch anything.'

'So chances are they were open all night,' Hunter said.

'Most probably, yes.'

Hunter glanced over at the sliding glass balcony doors.

'Those were left ajar,' Garcia explained. 'Apparently this room can get a little stuffy, especially during summer. Mr. Nicholson didn't like air conditioning. The balcony overlooks the backyard and the swimming pool. The problem is, the entire wall outside is covered in Morning Glories – as you probably know, the most-common climbing plant in California. The wooden trellis that supports it is strong enough for a person to climb it. Gaining access into this room from the backyard wouldn't be difficult.'

'Forensics will be going over the backyard and balcony as soon as they are done with the house's interior,' Doctor Hove added.

'At around midnight,' Garcia continued, still reading from his notebook, 'Melinda realized she'd forgotten one of her study books here in the room. She came back to the house, opened the front door and made her way up the stairs.' Garcia guessed Hunter's next couple of questions and offered an answer before he spoke. 'Yes, the front door was locked. She remembers using the key to unlock it. And no, she didn't notice anything strange when she came back into the house. No noises either.'

Hunter nodded.

'Melinda came upstairs again,' Garcia moved on, 'and

because she didn't want to disturb Mr. Nicholson, and she knew exactly where she'd left her study book . . .' He pointed to the mahogany writing desk pushed up against the wall . . . 'on that desk, she never turned on the lights. She just tiptoed into the room, grabbed her book, and tiptoed back out again.'

Hunter's stare moved back to the bloody wall next to the bed and his heart skipped a beat as Garcia's account of what had happened finally started to make sense.

'Melinda slept through her alarm this morning,' Garcia carried on. 'She got up, got ready as fast as she could, and rushed back in here. She said she opened the front door at 8:43 a.m. She checked her watch.' Garcia closed his notebook and returned it to his pocket. 'She came straight upstairs, and as she entered the room she was greeted not only by what you see here, but also by that message from whoever was in the room.' He indicated the wall again.

Among all the splatters, written in large blood letters were the words 'GOOD JOB YOU DIDN'T TURN ON THE LIGHTS'.

Six

An awkward silence took hold of the room. Hunter took a couple of steps towards the wall and studied the words and the lettering for a long moment.

'What did the killer use to write this with, a piece of cloth soaked in blood?' he asked.

'That would be my guess as well,' Doctor Hove agreed. 'But the forensic lab will have a better idea in a day or two.' She turned away from the wall and faced the bed once again. Her voice trembled with distress. 'This defies belief, Robert. It's beyond any case I've ever worked on. The killer spent hours in here, first torturing, then dismembering the victim. Not only that, but he then went on to create that thing.' She pointed to the bloody sculpture. 'And still found time to leave a message like this behind.' She looked at Garcia. 'How old is that girl again? The student nurse?'

'Twenty-three.'

'You, better than anyone, know that she'll need months, maybe years of psychological treatment to get over this, Robert, if she ever does. The killer was in here when she came back for her book. If she had reached for that light switch, we'd have two bodies, and she'd probably be part of that grotesque thing.' She indicated the sculpture again.

'Her nursing career is over before it had begun, her psychological stability shaken forever. And the nightmares and the sleepless nights haven't even started yet. And you know first hand how destructive that could be.'

Hunter's insomnia was no big secret. He had started experiencing it at the age of seven, just after cancer robbed him of his mother.

Hunter was born an only child to very poor working-class parents in Compton, an underprivileged neighborhood of South Los Angeles. With no family other than his father, coping with his mother's death proved to be a very difficult and lonely task. He missed her so much it was physically painful.

After the funeral he started fearing his dreams. Every time he closed his eyes he saw his mother's face. He saw her crying, contorted with pain, begging for help, praying for death. He saw her once fit-and-healthy body so drained of life, so fragile and weak, she couldn't sit up on her own strength. He saw a face that once had been beautiful, with the brightest smile he'd ever seen, transformed during those last few months into something unrecognizable. But it was still a face he never stopped loving.

Sleep became a prison he'd do anything to escape from. Insomnia was the logical answer his body found to deal with his fear and the ghastly nightmares that came at night. A simple defense mechanism.

Hunter had no reply for Doctor Hove.

'Who in the world is capable of something like this?' She shook her head in disgust.

'Someone with a lot of hate inside,' Hunter said quietly.

Everyone's attention was diverted from the room by the loud shouts coming from downstairs. A female voice that was fast becoming hysterical. Hunter looked at Garcia with concern.

'One of the daughters,' he said and quickly started moving towards the door. 'Keep this door shut.' He exited the room, cleared the corridor in no time and reached the stairs going down. Standing at the bottom, being obstructed by two police officers, was a woman in her early thirties. Her wavy blonde hair was long and loose, falling halfway down her back. She had a heart-shaped face with light green eyes, prominent cheekbones and a small, pointy nose. The expression on her face was of pure desperation. Hunter got to her before she managed to break free from the officers.

'It's OK,' he said, lifting his right hand. 'I'll take it from here.'

The police officers let her go.

'What's going on? Where's Father?' Her voice croaked with fear and anxiety.

'I'm Detective Robert Hunter of the LAPD,' Hunter said in the calmest voice he could muster.

'I don't care who you are. Where is my father?' the woman said, trying to push past Hunter.

He subtly stepped back, blocking her path. Their eyes met for an instant and he gave her a delicate headshake. 'I'm sorry.'

She closed her tearful eyes and brought a hand to her mouth. 'Oh, God. Daddy . . .'

Hunter gave the woman a moment.

She paused and stared at Hunter as if something had suddenly dawned on her. 'Why are you here? Why are the police here? Why is there crime-scene tape everywhere?'

Since Derek Nicholson's doctors diagnosed his illness four months ago, his family had, in a way, been preparing themselves for his departure. His death was expected, and didn't come as a real surprise to his daughter. Everything else did.

'I'm sorry, I didn't catch your name,' Hunter said.

'Olivia, Olivia Nicholson.'

Hunter had already noticed the faint, whiter patch of skin around her ring finger. She was either a recent widow, or a recent divorcee. Most widows in America are reluctant to get rid of their wedding rings and discard their husband's name quickly. Olivia also looked too young to be a widow, bar some sort of tragedy. Hunter's educated guess was – divorcee.

'Could we maybe talk someplace more private, Ms. Nicholson,' Hunter suggested, gesturing towards the living room.

'We can talk here,' she replied defiantly. 'What's happening here? What's all this?'

Hunter's stare moved to the two officers at the bottom of the stairs, who were listening attentively. Both quickly got the hint and moved away, towards the front door. Hunter's attention returned to Olivia.

'Your father's illness didn't take him.' He waited for Olivia to fully absorb his words before continuing. 'He was murdered.'

'What? That's . . . that's ridiculous.'

'Please, let's have a seat somewhere,' Hunter insisted.

Olivia breathed out as tears returned to her eyes. She finally gave in and followed Hunter into the living area. Hunter didn't want to put her in the same room as the young nurse.

Olivia sat in the light-brown armchair next to the window. Hunter took the sofa opposite her.

'Would you like a glass of water?' he offered.

'Yes, please.'

Hunter waited by the door while an officer fetched them two glasses of water. He handed one to Olivia, who drank it all down in large gulps.

Hunter took his seat again, and in a steady voice explained that in the early hours of the morning someone had gained access to the house and to Mr. Nicholson's bedroom.

Olivia couldn't stop shaking or crying and, understandably, was questioning everything.

'We don't know why your father was murdered. We don't know how the perpetrator entered the house. At the moment we have a truckload of questions and no answers. But we'll do everything we can to find them.'

'In other words, you don't have a clue what happened here,' she fired back angrily.

Hunter kept silent.

Olivia stood up and started pacing the room. 'I don't understand. Who'd want to kill my father? He had cancer. He was . . . already dying.' Her eyes filled with tears once again.

Hunter still said nothing.

'How?' she asked.

Hunter looked at her.

'How was he murdered?'

'We'll need to wait for the coroner's autopsy examination to positively identify cause of death.'

Olivia frowned. 'So how do you know he was murdered? Was he shot? Stabbed? Strangled?'

'No.'

She looked perplexed. 'So how do you know?'

Hunter stood up and approached her. 'We know.'

Her eyes moved back to the staircase. 'I wanna go up to his room.'

Hunter gently placed a hand on her left shoulder. 'Please, trust me, Ms. Nicholson. Going into that room won't settle any of the questions you have. It won't ease your pain either.'

'Why? I want to know what happened to him. What aren't you telling me?'

Hunter hesitated for a moment, but he knew she had the right to know. 'His body was mutilated.'

'Oh my God!' both of her hands shot to her mouth.

'I know you and your sister were here last night. You had dinner with your father, right?'

Olivia was shaking so hard she could barely nod.

'Please,' Hunter said. 'Let that be the last memory you have of your father.'

Olivia exploded into desperate sobs.

Seven

Hunter and Garcia got back to their office on the fifth floor of the Police Administration Building in West 1st Street in the middle of the afternoon. The PAB was the new operational headquarters for the LAPD, substituting the nearly 60-year-old Parker Center building.

After hearing the news, Captain Barbara Blake had also come in on her day off and was waiting for both detectives with a parade of questions.

'Is it true what I heard?' she asked, closing the door behind her. 'Someone dismembered the victim?'

Hunter nodded and Garcia handed her a bunch of photographs.

Barbara Blake had been the Robbery Homicide Division captain for the past three years. Handpicked by the ex-captain himself, William Bolter, and sanctioned by the mayor of Los Angeles at the time, it didn't take her long to gain a reputation for being a no-nonsense, iron-fist captain. Blake was an intriguing woman – stylish, attractive, with long black hair and cold dark eyes that could make most people shiver with a simple stare. She wasn't easily intimidated, took shit from no one, and didn't mind upsetting high-powered politicians or government officials if it meant getting the job done.

Captain Blake flipped through the photographs, the look on her face growing more worried with each picture. As she got to the last one, she paused and held her breath.

'What in God's earth is this?'

'A . . . sculpture of some sort,' Garcia answered.

'Made of . . . the victim's body parts?'

'That's right.'

Silence ruled the room for the next few seconds.

'Is it supposed to mean anything?' Captain Blake asked.

'Yes, it means something,' Hunter said. 'We just don't know what yet.'

'How can you be so sure it means something?'

'Because if you want someone dead, you walk up to them and shoot them. You don't risk the time it takes to do something like this unless the whole act has a meaning. And usually, when a perpetrator leaves something that significant behind, it's because he's trying to communicate.'

'With us?'

Hunter shrugged. 'With somebody. We'll need to figure out its meaning first before we know.'

Captain Blake's attention returned to the picture. 'So that would mean that this wasn't random. The killer didn't just put this thing together in a burst of sadistic inspiration right there and then?'

Hunter shook his head. 'Very unlikely. I'd say the killer knew exactly what he would do with Derek Nicholson's body parts before he killed him. He knew exactly which body parts he needed. And he knew exactly what his horror piece would look like when finished.'

'Great.' She paused. 'And what does *this* mean?' The captain showed them a picture of the bloody message left on the wall.

Garcia ran her through the whole story. When he was done, Captain Blake was uncharacteristically lost for words.

'What the hell are we dealing with here, Robert?' she finally said, handing the pile of photographs back to Garcia.

'I'm not sure, Captain.' Hunter leaned against his desk. 'Derek Nicholson was a prosecutor for the State of California for twenty-six years. He put a lot of people behind bars.'

'You think this could be retaliation? Who the hell did he send to prison, Lucifer and the Texas Chainsaw Massacre gang?'

'I don't know, but that'll have to be our starting point.' Hunter looked at Garcia. 'We need a list of everyone Nicholson has put behind bars – murderers, attempted murderers, rapists, whoever. Let's prioritize by anyone who has been released, paroled, or made bail in the past . . .' he thought about it for a moment, 'fifteen years . . . and also by severity of crime. Anyone he put away for any type of sadistic crime comes first.'

'I'll get the research team on it,' Garcia confirmed, 'but it's Sunday. We won't get anything until maybe tomorrow evening.'

'That's fine. We'll also need to crosscheck whatever names we get with a list of their immediate family members, relatives, gang members, or whatever; anybody who could be capable of going after Derek Nicholson for revenge on someone else's behalf. There's a chance this could've been indirect retaliation. Maybe the person Nicholson sent to prison is still there . . . maybe he died in prison, and somebody on the outside is after payback.'

Garcia nodded.

Hunter reached for the pile of photographs and spread

them out on his desk. His stare settled on the one with the sculpture.

'How did the perpetrator put that thing together?' the captain asked, joining Hunter by his desk.

'He used wire to hold the pieces in place.'

'Wire?'

'That's right.'

She bent over and studied the photograph again. A sudden chill ran the length of her body. 'And how do you suppose we'll figure out what this thing means? The more I look at it, the more freaky and incomprehensible it seems.'

'The forensics lab will create an exact replica for us. We might bring in one or two art experts and see if they can make anything of it.'

In all her years in the force, Captain Blake had seen the most unimaginable things when it came to killers, but nothing like this. 'Have you ever seen or heard of a crime scene like this one?' she asked.

'I know of a case where the killer used the victim's blood as paint to create a canvas,' Garcia offered, 'but this is in a league of its own.'

'I've never heard or read about anything like this,' Hunter admitted.

'Could the victim have been random?' Captain Blake asked, glancing through the notes Garcia had jotted down. 'I mean, it looks to me that the sadism of the act, and the creation of that grotesque thing, is what was most important to the killer, not the victim himself. The killer could've picked Nicholson because he was an easy target.' She flipped a page on Garcia's notebook. 'Derek Nicholson had terminal cancer. He was weak and practically bedbound. Totally defenseless. He couldn't have screamed for help if the killer had given him a megaphone. And he was alone in the house.'

'The captain has a point,' Garcia agreed, tilting his head from side to side.

'I don't buy that,' Hunter said, moving away from his desk and approaching the open window. 'Derek Nicholson was an easy target, I agree, but there are plenty of easier targets in a city like Los Angeles – tramps, homeless people, drug addicts, prostitutes . . . If the victim made no difference to the killer, why risk breaking into an LA prosecutor's home and spend hours doing what he did. Also, he wasn't *that* alone in the house. His nurse was in the guesthouse above the garage, remember? And as we know . . .' he tapped the photograph that showed the message on the wall, '. . . she walked in on the killer. Thankfully she didn't turn on the lights.' Hunter turned and faced the room. 'Believe me, Captain, this killer wanted this victim. He wanted Derek Nicholson dead. And he wanted him to suffer before he died.'

Eight

Instead of playing volleyball in Venice Beach or catching a Lakers game, Hunter spent the rest of his day carefully studying all the crime-scene photographs, with one question coming up all the time.

What in the world did that sculpture mean?

He decided to go back to Derek Nicholson's house.

The body, together with the morbid sculpture, had been taken to the coroner's office. All that was left behind was a sad and lifeless house full of grief, sorrow and fear. Derek Nicholson's last few hours alive were splattered all over his room, and it all spelled only one thing – terrifying pain.

Hunter stared at the message the killer left on the wall and felt an empty hole grow inside him. The killer took Derek Nicholson's life, and in the process devastated three others – both of Nicholson's daughters' and the young nurse's.

The forensic team had lifted at least four different sets of fingerprints from the house, but analysis would take a day or two. They'd also collected several hair and fiber samples from the room upstairs. Hours of sieving through it, the backyard and trellis on the outside wall of Derek Nicholson's room gave them nothing. There were no signs of forced entry. No windows had been broken, no latches damaged, no doors or locks tampered with, but then again, Melinda Wallis, the weekend nurse, couldn't remember if she'd locked the backdoor. Two of the windows downstairs had been left unlocked overnight, and the balcony door that led into Mr. Nicholson's room was left ajar.

Hunter had tried talking to Melinda Wallis, but Garcia had been right, she was psychologically shutting down. Her brain was struggling to cope with the shock of discovering Derek Nicholson's body inside a room bathed in blood, but more than that, her mind was doing its best to shelter her from the knowledge that she had been only a hair away from death.

Hunter spent all of his time back at the house studying the room upstairs, looking for clues that he might've missed earlier on. He didn't find anything the forensics team hadn't already found, but the savagery of the scene was more than disturbing. It was like the killer had made a point of splashing blood all over the room.

The message left on the wall wasn't part of the original plan, but a last-minute act of cocky defiance. The entire scene seemed like a display window for the killer's anger and senselessness, and that bothered Hunter.

Night had already fallen by the time Hunter got back to his apartment. He closed the door behind him and rested his tired body against it. His eyes scanned the dark and lonely living room, and in his mind he debated if staying in tonight was such a good idea.

Hunter lived alone, no wife, no girlfriends. He'd never been married, and the relationships he had never lasted that long. The pressures that came with his job and the commitment it demanded always seemed too much for most to understand. He didn't mind being by himself. Living alone didn't bother him either. But after spending most of the day surrounded by death and walls stained with blood, the loneliness of his small apartment was the last thing he needed.

Los Angeles nightlife is amongst the liveliest and most exciting in the world, with a spectrum of choice that goes from luxurious and trendy nightclubs, where A-list celebrities hang out, to themed bars and dingy, sleazy underground venues, where the freaks come out to play. Whatever mood you find yourself in, you're sure to find a place in LA to suit it.

Hunter made his way to Jay's Rock Bar, a dive just two blocks away from his home. It was one of his favorite drinking spots, with a great Scotch selection, a jukebox overflowing with rock music, and friendly, full-of-life staff.

Hunter sat at the bar and ordered a double dose of 12-year-old GlenDronach with two cubes of ice. Single-malt Scotch whisky was his biggest passion, and though he had overdone it a few times he knew how to appreciate its flavor and quality instead of simply getting drunk on it.

Hunter had a sip of his whisky and allowed its smooth hazelnut, oaky flavor to fully develop in his mouth. The bar was busy enough, and after what he had seen today he was glad to be amongst people laughing and enjoying themselves.

A group of four women sitting at the table closest to Hunter were discussing the worst pick-up lines they had ever been approached with.

'I was in a bar in Santa Monica one night,' the short-haired blonde one said, 'and this bald-headed guy came up to me and said –' she put on a baritone voice – '"Baby, I'm no Fred Flintstone, but I can make your Bedrock!"'

Two seconds of stunned silence from the group was followed by loud laughter.

'That's just plain lame,' the youngest-looking of them said. 'But I got something that'll beat that. Last weekend, I was in Sunset Boulevard, and someone came up to me in broad daylight, in the middle of the street and said: "Honey, your name must be Gillette, 'cos you're the best a man can get."'

The group laughed again.

'OK, OK,' the long-haired brunette said, 'that one has got to take the medal. I've never heard anything so bad in all my life.'

Hunter agreed and smiled to himself. That had been the first time he'd smiled all day.

'Another one?' Emilio, the young Puerto Rican bartender asked Hunter, nodding at his empty glass.

Hunter's attention moved from the four women to Emilio, and then to his glass. He felt tired, but he knew that if he went back home now he wouldn't fall asleep. He barely slept anyway. His insomnia made sure of that.

'Sure, why not.'

Emilio poured him another double dose and dropped one more cube of ice in his glass. Hunter watched it crack as it hit the light brownish liquid. A man sitting at the end of the bar in a battered gray suit coughed a throaty, smoker's cough and Hunter's mind went back to Derek Nicholson and the case. Why kill someone who was already dying of lung cancer? Someone who was already condemned to such a painful death? One, maybe two more months at the most, and his cancer would've finished him off anyway. But the killer couldn't . . . wouldn't allow that to happen. He wanted to be the one delivering the fatal blow. The one looking into Nicholson's eyes when he died. The one playing God.

Hunter had a sip of his drink and closed his eyes. He had a bad feeling about this case. A really bad feeling.

Nine

In a city like Los Angeles, violent crimes aren't uncommon. In fact, they are pretty much the norm. It's not surprising that on average LA coroners are as busy throughout the year as any ER doctor. Work piles up like snow, and everything has to follow a schedule. Even with an urgent request, it was a whole day before Doctor Hove was able to start the autopsy on Derek Nicholson's body.

Hunter had managed to get only four hours of sleep. In the morning his eyes felt gritty, and the headache lurking at the base of his skull was typical of a sleep hangover. Experience told him that there was nothing he could do or take to get rid of it. It'd been part of his life for over thirty years now.

Hunter was getting ready to leave for the PAB when Doctor Hove called saying that she was finally done with Derek Nicholson's autopsy.

At 7:30 a.m., he covered the seven miles between his apartment and the LA County Department of Coroner in North Mission Road in seventeen minutes flat. Garcia had arrived just a minute before him and was waiting for Hunter in the parking lot. He was clean shaven and his hair was still wet from his shower, but the bags under his eyes belied the fresh morning look.

'I've gotta tell you, I'm not looking forward to this,' Garcia said, greeting Hunter as he stepped out of his car.

Hunter looked at him curiously. 'Have you ever looked forward to anything when you walk into this building?'

Garcia stared at the old hospital turned morgue. The building was architecturally impressive. Its façade was a stylish combination of red brick and light-gray lintels. The sumptuous steps that led to its main entrance added another touch of elegance to a structure that could easily be mistaken for a traditional European university edifice. A beautiful shell for a building that sheltered so much death.

'Point taken,' Garcia admitted.

Doctor Hove met both detectives by the staff entrance door on the right side of the building. Her hair was tied back into a conservative-looking bun. She had no makeup on, and the whites of her eyes showed just enough red to suggest that she hadn't had a good night of sleep either.

They greeted each other with simple head bobs, and in silence Hunter and Garcia followed her into a long and brightly lit corridor. At that time in the morning, there was no one else around, which, coupled with the bland white walls and the squeaky-clean vinyl floors, made the place look and feel much more sinister.

At the end of the hallway, they took the steps going down to the basement and onto a shorter and not so well-lit corridor.

'I used our special autopsy theater,' the doctor said as she came up to the last door on the right.

Special Autopsy Theater One was usually used for post-mortem examinations of bodies that, for one reason or another, could still pose some sort of public threat

– infection with highly contagious viral diseases, exposure to radioactive materials and/or locations, chemical-warfare agent contaminations, and so on. The room had its own separate database system and cold-storage facility. Its heavy door was secured by a six-digit electronic lock combination. The chamber was also sometimes used during high-profile murder investigations – a security provision to better prevent sensitive information from reaching the press and other unwanted parties. Hunter had been in it plenty of times.

Doctor Hove punched the code into the metal keyboard on the wall and the heavy door buzzed open.

They all stepped inside a large and winter-cold room. It was lit by two rows of florescent lights that ran the length of the ceiling. Two steel tables dominated the main floor space, one fixed, one wheeled. A blue hydraulic hoist stood next to a wall of fridges with small, square, mirror-polished doors. Both examination tables were covered by white sheets.

Doctor Hove put on a new pair of latex gloves and approached the one furthest from the door.

'OK, let me show you what I found out.'

Garcia shifted on his feet in anticipation while Hunter reached for a surgical mask. He wasn't afraid of contamination, but he hated the distinct odor that came with every autopsy chamber – as if something rotten had been scrubbed to high heaven with strong disinfectant. A stale scent that seemed to beckon from beyond the grave to haunt those still living.

'The official cause of death was heart failure ...' Doctor Hove said, pulling the white sheet aside and revealing the dismembered torso of Derek Nicholson, '... induced by loss of blood and probably sheer pain. But he held on for a while.'

'What do you mean?' Garcia asked.

'Skin and muscle trauma indicate that he'd lost his fingers and toes, his tongue, and at least one of his arms before his heart stopped beating.'

Garcia took a deep breath and shook off the uncomfortable shiver that hugged his neck.

'We were right about the saw-like instrument used for all the amputations,' the doctor continued. 'Definitely something very sharp with a serrated edge. But the blade's teeth weren't as fine as one would expect. And the distance between them is certainly larger than usual when compared to the instruments usually reserved for clinical amputations.'

'A handheld, carpenter's saw, maybe?' Garcia asked.

'I don't think so.' The doctor shook her head. 'The consistency of the cuts is too uniform. There's some hacking, but mainly when the cutting instrument hit bone, which isn't surprising, especially given that I'd expect the victim wasn't sedated at all. Toxicology will test for any trace of drugs found in the victim's blood, but that will take a day, maybe two, but without anesthesia the pain would've been unbearable. Even being held tight, the victim would've shrieked and writhed incessantly, making the amputation job much harder.'

Garcia sucked in a cold breath through clenched teeth.

'But keeping the victim alive shouldn't have been a concern. The perpetrator could've just chopped his arms and legs off in whichever way he wanted.'

'But he didn't,' Hunter said.

'No he didn't,' Doctor Hove agreed. 'The killer wanted the victim alive for as long as possible. He wanted the suffering. The cuts were well and properly performed.'

'Medical knowledge?' Hunter asked.

'Despite the fact that nowadays anyone can spend a few hours on the Internet and acquire detailed instructions and diagrams on how to perform an amputation, I'd say the killer has at least basic knowledge of medical procedures and anatomy, yes.' Her stare focused on the second autopsy table. 'He sure as hell knew what he was doing. Have a look at this.'

Ten

Something in Doctor Hove's demeanor and tone of voice concerned both detectives. They followed her over to the second examination table.

'I have no doubt everything that happened in that room was planned, and very well planned.' She pulled back the white cover sheet. The macabre sculpture left behind by the killer had been dismantled. Derek Nicholson's severed body parts were now carefully arranged on the cold metal slab. They'd all been washed clean of the blood that had encrusted them before. 'Don't worry,' the doctor said to Hunter, noticing his concern. 'The lab took enough pictures and measurements to create the replica you wanted. You'll get it in a day or two.'

Hunter and Garcia's stare stayed on the body parts.

'Did you make anything of the sculpture, Doc?' Garcia asked.

'Nothing at all. And I had to dismantle that thing myself.' She coughed to clear her throat. 'I swabbed under the finger-nails. No hairs or skin. Just regular dirt and excrement.'

'Excrement?' Garcia pulled a face.

'His own,' Doctor Hove confirmed. 'During tremendous pain, the kind that'd come from an amputation without anesthesia, the subject will undoubtedly lose control of his bladder and bowels. And that's the strange thing.'

'What is?' Garcia questioned.

'He was clean,' Hunter said. 'When we got to the crime-scene, the bed sheet should've been saturated with urine and feces. It wasn't.'

'Because of his illness and his lack of mobility, going to the bathroom wasn't such a mundane task anymore,' Doctor Hove took over again, 'his nurses helped him to it, but when they weren't there, he wore adult diapers.'

'Yeah, we saw the package in one of the drawers,' Garcia said.

'Forensics found a pair of dirty ones wrapped in a plastic bag inside the trashcan downstairs.'

Garcia's eyes widened. 'The killer cleaned him up?'

'Not so much cleaned him up, but someone did dispose of the dirty diaper.'

No one said anything for several seconds, so Doctor Hove moved on. 'The reason I believe the killer has knowledge of medical procedures is because I found these.' She pointed to the upper portion of one of the severed arms, just around where the cut had been made. 'I only saw them when I washed the blood off the arms and legs.'

Hunter and Garcia stepped closer. The faint outline of a black marker pen could be seen on the rubbery-looking skin. It created an incomplete circle going around the arm just about where the cut had been made.

'In complicated medical procedures such as amputations, where the incision point needs to be very accurate, it is not uncommon for doctors, or whoever is performing the surgery, to mark the correct location with a pen.'

'But so would someone who found the information in a book, or over the Internet, as you said, Doc,' Garcia countered.

'That's also true,' she agreed, 'but check this out.' She walked back to the first examination table and Derek Nicholson's torso. Hunter and Garcia followed. 'During an amputation, it's vital that all major blood vessels, like the brachial artery in the arms and the femoral artery in the legs, are properly tied off, or else the patient will bleed out in no time.'

'They weren't tied off,' Hunter said, bending down to have a better look. 'I checked it at the crime-scene. No suture, no knot.'

'That's because the killer didn't use a thread to stop the blood flow, as most doctors would. The brachial artery in the right arm was clamped. The marks can be seen under a microscope. He used medical forceps.'

Hunter straightened up his body. 'Only in the right arm?'

Doctor Hove adjusted her surgical cap. 'That's right. And the reason is probably because the victim's heart gave in before the killer could amputate anything else. The fact of the matter, Robert, is that the killer prolonged the victim's life and suffering for as long as he could. But to do that without a surgical team to help him, he had to perform the cuts as quickly and as cleanly as possible, and contain the hemorrhaging as best as he could,' Doctor Hove concluded.

'And you're sure there's no chance he could've used a professional saw like the ones used here at the morgue?' Garcia pushed.

'No,' she replied, reaching for the Mopec autopsy saw on the worktop behind her. 'Portable autopsy saws use small, circular blades with extremely fine teeth.' She showed them the instrument. 'The finer the blade's teeth, the more accurate the cut, and the easier it is to cut through tougher surfaces like bones and muscles in full rigor mortis.'

Both detectives quickly examined the saw and its blade.

'But an autopsy blade isn't wide enough. You need something that transcends the entire width of the body part being amputated. Circular saws also leave a very distinct cut pattern, smoother than most.'

'And that's not what we have,' Hunter guessed.

'Nope. We have a friction pattern. Two very sharp blades, side-by-side, moving back and forth in opposite directions to create a sawing action.'

Hunter handed the autopsy saw back to her. 'You mean . . . something like an electric kitchen carving knife?'

'You're kidding,' Garcia interjected.

'That's exactly what I think the killer used,' Doctor Hove said. 'A large, powerful, electric kitchen carving knife.'

'Will those cut through bone?' Garcia asked.

'The most powerful ones will cut through a frozen joint of beef,' the doctor said, 'especially with brand new blades.'

'Do we know if the victim had one in the house?' Garcia asked.

'If that's what the killer used,' Hunter said. 'The knife didn't come from the victim's kitchen. The killer brought it with him.'

'How do you know?'

'Because not having the amputating instrument with him would suggest that the amputations were unplanned and that the killer came into the house unprepared.'

'And that's something this killer certainly wasn't,' Doctor Hove said. 'And that reminds me. To keep the pieces of his sculpture together, the killer didn't use only metal wire, he also used a super-fast bonder, like superglue.'

'Superglue?' Garcia almost chuckled.

The doctor nodded. 'Perfect for the job, really – easy to

use, dries in seconds, easily adheres to skin and creates an extremely firm hold. But what gets me is that this seems like a totally pointless killing.'

'Aren't they all?' Hunter commented.

'True, but what I mean is that there was very little achievement in killing this victim.' She walked towards a chart on the west wall that itemized the weights of the deceased's brain, heart, lungs, liver, kidneys and spleen. On the counter next to it there was a plastic bag filled with several of the victim's organs. She reached for it and lifted it up. 'Cancer had pretty much obliterated his lungs. He probably would've survived another week, maybe two. And this kind of lung damage means pain, a lot of it. He was already dying and going through unimaginable suffering. Why kill him like this?'

No one said anything.

No one knew what to say.

Eleven

Los Angeles County District Attorney Dwayne Bradley was a tough-as-nails man who displayed no patience for anyone who even contemplated breaking the law. At sixty-one, he'd been a prosecutor for thirty years, and the Los Angeles DA since his election in the year 2000. Upon being sworn into office, he told his staff to show no fear in pursuing the criminal element, and to seek justice always and at all costs. Dwayne Bradley lived by that rule.

Bradley was short and stocky, with just enough white hair left to cover his temples. His chubby cheeks went bright pink and jiggled ferociously whenever he argued a point. His temper had the shortest of fuses, and if gesticulation was the name of the game, Dwayne Bradley certainly was a champion at it. In short, he looked like an overexcited Mafia Don who'd decided to go straight.

This morning, instead of driving to his office in West Temple Street, he made his way to the PAB and into Captain Blake's office. He'd been there for five minutes when Hunter knocked at the door.

'Come in,' the captain called from her desk.

Hunter stepped into her office and closed the door behind him. 'You wanted to see me?'

'It was I who wanted to see you,' Bradley said from the corner of the room.

If Hunter was surprised by the DA's presence, he didn't show it. 'DA Bradley,' Hunter greeted him with a polite head nod, but no handshake.

'Detective.' Bradley returned the gesture.

Hunter's stare moved to Captain Blake for a couple of seconds before reverting back to the DA.

'Well, I'm not here to waste your time or mine with bull-shit,' Bradley said, cutting straight to the chase. 'We're all very busy and I appreciate that.' He paused for effect – force of habit. 'Derek Nicholson. You have been appointed as the lead detective in his murder investigation. An investigation that I will be *personally* overseeing.' He tilted his head in the direction of the file on Captain Blake's desk. 'I read your initial report, detective. I also saw the crime-scene pictures.' Bradley started pacing the room. 'In thirty years as a prose-cutor I've never seen anything quite like that, and I've seen a lot of sick shit, believe me. That wasn't murder. That was an atrocity without precedent. A cowardly, deranged act of unimaginable violence by some scumbag who isn't fit to call himself human. And I, for one, want the death penalty for that motherfucker. Hell, I'll bring back the fucking guillotine just for this sack of shit. And I'll be sitting pretty and smiling when his head hits the floor.' His cheeks were starting to go pink. 'And what the hell was that freaky thing he left behind?'

No one answered.

'Now, the crime-scene photographs show a totally chaotic scene, totally consistent with a rage outburst of immense proportions. But your report suggests the whole thing was premeditated and thought through. You're saying the killer planned to lose control?'

'He didn't,' Hunter said.

Bradley frowned. 'Didn't what?'

'Lose control.'

Bradley waited but Hunter didn't say anything else. 'Do you have a speech impediment? Are you capable of forming full sentences?'

'Yes.'

'Yes, what?' Bradley looked at Captain Blake as if asking 'Is this really the person you're putting in charge of this investigation?'

'Yes, I am able to form full sentences.'

'So please, burst a nut. Form as many as you like and do develop on your statement of a moment ago.'

'Which statement was that?'

'You've got to be fucking kidding me.' Spit was starting to accumulate at the edges of the DA's mouth. 'The one where you said that the killer did not lose control.'

Hunter shrugged. 'The perp used an unusual weapon to dismember the victim, possibly an everyday household electric carving knife. Before doing that, he used a marker pen to plot the incision lines on the victim's arms and legs. After at least one of the amputations, the killer used medical clamps or forceps to tie off the arteries and restrict the bleeding, prolonging the victim's life for several minutes. To create his sculpture, he needed several pieces of metal wire and a super bonder – superglue. And there was no blood anywhere else in that house except in that bedroom.' Hunter allowed his suggestion to hang in the air.

DA Bradley was still looking at him with the same 'I don't get your point' look on his face.

'The perp had all of that equipment with him,' Captain

Blake explained. 'He entered that house completely prepared to do what he did. Also, with the tremendous distribution of blood at the crime scene, there was no way the perp wasn't completely covered in it when he finished. The lack of any blood traces anywhere else in the house suggests that the killer got changed before leaving the bedroom. Probably stuck his blood-soaked clothes into a plastic bag.' She tucked a strand of loose hair behind her ear. 'Despite the chaotic state of the crime scene, there is nothing chaotic about our killer, Dwayne. It was all planned, to the last detail.'

Bradley took a deep breath and ran a hand over his mouth. 'Derek was a friend as well as a colleague.' His tone had changed in a flash. He now sounded like he was addressing a jury with his opening remarks. 'I'd known him for over twenty years. I had dinner and drinks in his house many times, and he in mine. I knew his wife. I know his daughters. I'm the one who will accompany them to the morgue for the official identification.' A muscle tensed in his jaw. 'And they still don't know all the sadistic details of their father's murder. They don't know about the sculpture. And I'm not sure if they should know. It would destroy them inside.' His gazed moved around the room before returning to Hunter. 'Derek was an excellent prosecutor and a devoted family man. We all felt saddened and robbed of an extraordinary person when he was diagnosed with terminal cancer of the lung just a few months ago, but this . . .' His eyes stole a new peek at the file and photographs on Captain Blake's desk. 'This beggars belief.'

If DA Bradley was expecting anyone to make some sort of comment, he was disappointed.

'Barbara told me that your first line of investigation is to check on all offenders Derek put away over the years,' he said after a brief pause.

'Something like that,' Hunter agreed.

'Well, that's exactly where *I* would start, so maybe your brain isn't the size of a pea after all.' Bradley unbuttoned his suit jacket, reached inside his pocket for a card and handed it to Hunter. 'That's my best researcher.'

Hunter read the name on the card – Alice Beaumont, Los Angeles County District Attorney's Bureau of Investigation.

'She's brilliant when it comes to digging into anyone's life. A computer genius. She has access to all our archives, and then some. Alice can help you find whatever file you need regarding any of Derek's prosecutions.'

Hunter slotted the card into his jacket pocket.

'I hope you're not one of those who feel intimidated by working with a female who's brighter than you.' DA Bradley smiled.

Hunter smiled back.

'Now, what concerns me the most,' Bradley said, back in his super-serious tone, 'is that over the years Derek put a lot of trash away. Many of them dirtbags caught by you.' His gaze moved from Hunter to Captain Blake. 'Or by another detective from your division, Barbara. The process is simple. You catch them. We prepare the case. We take them to court. A judge presides, and a jury of twelve jurors convicts. Do you see where I'm going with this?'

Captain Blake said nothing.

Hunter nodded. 'If Derek Nicholson's murder was payback, then he's only one link in a long chain.'

'That's correct.' Beads of sweat were starting to form on

the DA's shiny forehead. 'If what we have here is retaliation for Derek being the prosecutor in an old case, then you better catch this crazy fucker soon. Because if you don't . . . we can expect more bodies.'

Twelve

While the sun baked the day in a cloudless blue sky, the AC blasted cold air into the cockpit of the metallic silver Honda Civic that had just turned into Interstate 105, heading west. The trip shouldn't have taken them more than twenty-five minutes, but Hunter and Garcia had been sitting in stop-and-start traffic for thirty-five minutes, and they were still at least another twenty away from their destination.

Amy Dawson, Derek Nicholson's weekdays nurse, lived in a single-story, three-bedroom house with her husband, two teenage daughters, and a noisy little dog called Screamer. The house was tucked away in a quiet street behind a row of shops in Lennox, southwest Los Angeles.

Amy had been hired as Nicholson's nurse just a few days after he was diagnosed with his illness.

As Garcia finally turned into Amy's road, the dashboard thermometer showed the outside temperature to be at 88°F. He parked his car across the road from her place and both detectives stepped out into a humid and stuffy day, the sun stinging their faces.

The house looked old. Rain and sunlight had caused the paint to fade and crack around the windowsills and the front door. The iron-mesh fence that surrounded the property was rusty and bent out of shape in places. The small front yard could certainly have used a little attention.

Hunter knocked three times and was immediately greeted by a barrage of barks coming from deep within the house. Not the strong, ferocious kind of barks that would scare away a burglar, but the squeaky, annoying kind that could give anyone a headache in minutes. And Hunter already had one.

'Shut up, Screamer,' a female voice called from inside. The dog reluctantly stopped barking. The door was opened by a black woman with a round face, cat-like eyes and cornrows on her head. She was around five foot five, and her plump figure overstretched the thin fabric of her summer dress. Amy was fifty-two, but her kind face bore the signs of someone who'd lived longer and seen more than her share of suffering.

'Mrs. Dawson?' Hunter asked.

'Yes?' Her eyes squinted behind thin reading glasses. 'Oh, you must be the policeman who called earlier?' Her voice was hoarse but delicate.

'I'm Detective Hunter and this is Detective Garcia.'

She checked their credentials, smiled politely, and pulled the door fully open. 'Please come in.'

As they did, Screamer started barking again from under a table. 'I'm not gonna tell you again, Screamer. Shut up and go inside.' Amy pointed to a door on the far end of the living room and the tiny dog dashed through it and disappeared down a small corridor. A freshly baked cake smell came from the kitchen and perfumed the entire house. 'Please make yourselves at home.' She gestured towards the small and dark living room. Hunter and Garcia had a seat in the mint green tufted sofa, while Amy took the armchair directly in front of them.

'Would you care for some iced tea?' she offered. 'It's mighty warm out there.'

'That would be great,' Hunter replied. 'Thank you very much.'

Amy walked into the kitchen and moments later returned carrying a tray with an aluminum jug and three glasses.

'I can't believe anyone would want to harm Mr. Nicholson,' she said as she served the drinks. Sadness coated her words.

'We're very sorry about what happened, Mrs. Dawson.'

'Please call me Amy.' She gave both detectives a feeble smile.

Hunter smiled back. 'We appreciate you taking the time to talk to us, Amy.'

She stared down at her drink. 'Who would want to hurt a terminal-cancer patient? It just makes no sense.' Her eyes found Hunter's. 'I was told it wasn't a burglary.'

'It wasn't,' he replied.

'He was such a nice and kind man, who I know is now in much better hands.' She looked up towards the ceiling. 'May he rest in peace.'

Hunter wasn't surprised that Amy didn't seem distraught. She hadn't been told about the sordid details of the crime. Hunter had also checked her background. Amy had been a nurse for twenty-seven years, eighteen of those dedicated to helping patients with some form of terminal cancer. She did her job to the best of her abilities, but inevitably all of her patients passed away. She was used to dealing with death, and she had learned long ago to keep her emotions in check.

'You were Mr. Nicholson's nurse on weekdays, is that correct?' Garcia asked.

'Monday to Friday, that's right.'

'Did you use the same room as Melinda Wallis, the nurse that took over from you on weekends?'

Amy shook her head. 'No, no. Mel used the guesthouse above the garage. I used the guestroom inside the house. Two doors from Mr. Nicholson's room.'

'We were told that Mr. Nicholson's daughters visited him every day.'

'That's right, for at least a couple of hours. Sometimes in the morning, sometimes in the afternoon, sometimes in the evening.'

'Did Mr. Nicholson have any other visitors recently?'

'Not recently.'

'At any time?' Garcia pushed.

Amy looked pensive for a moment. 'When I first started, yes. I remember only two separate visitors during my first few weeks in the house. But as soon as the most severe symptoms began to manifest themselves, then he had no more visitors. Mainly because Mr. Nicholson himself didn't want to see anyone. He also didn't want anyone to see him looking the way he did. He was a very proud man.'

'These visitors, can you tell us any more about them?' Garcia asked. 'Do you know who they were?'

'No. But they looked like lawyers, you know, very nice suits and all. Probably work colleagues.'

'Do you remember what they talked about?'

Amy looked at Garcia with a touch of indignation. 'I wasn't in the room, and I don't listen to other people's conversations.'

'I apologize, that wasn't what I meant at all,' Garcia backpedaled as fast as he could. 'I was just wondering if maybe Mr. Nicholson mentioned anything.'

Amy offered Garcia a feeble smile, accepting his apology.

'The truth is, not very much is ever said when visitors come around to see cancer patients. No matter how talkative people are, they tend to lose their ability to make conversation when they see what the disease has done to their friend, or family member. People usually just stand there, mostly in silence, trying their best to appear strong. When you know someone is dying, it's hard to find words.'

Hunter said nothing but he knew exactly what Amy Dawson meant. He was only seven when his mother was diagnosed with glioblastoma multiforme, the most aggressive type of primary brain cancer. By the time her doctors discovered it, the tumor was already too advanced. Within weeks she went from being a smiling, full-of-life mother, to an unrecognizable, skin-and-bones person. Hunter would never forget the image of his father standing by her bed with tears in his eyes, but unable to utter a single word. There was nothing he could say.

'Do you remember their names?' Garcia pushed.

Amy thought about it for a long, hard moment. 'My memory isn't very good anymore, you know? But I remember thinking that the one who came first must've been a really important man. He came in a very large Mercedes with a driver and all.'

'Could you describe him?'

She tilted her head from side to side. 'Older, chunky fellow with chubby cheeks. He wasn't very tall, either, but he was very well dressed. Liked to move his arms around a lot.'

'DA Bradley?' Garcia suggested, looking at Hunter who gave him a 'probably' nod.

'Yes,' Amy said with a hint of a smile. 'I think that was his name, Bradley.'

'How about the second visitor, can you remember anything?'

Amy searched her memory. 'Slimmer and taller.' She looked at Hunter. 'I'd say he was about your height, could've been around the same age too. He was quite attractive. Nice dark-brown eyes.'

Garcia took notes. 'Anything else you can remember about him.'

'I think he had a short name. Something like Ben, Dan, or Tom, maybe.' She hesitated, taking a breath. 'Yeah, something like that, but I can't be sure.'

'Amy,' Hunter said, leaning forward and placing his empty iced-tea glass on the coffee table between them. 'I'm sure you and Mr. Nicholson had several conversations, especially given that you spent so much time with him.'

'Sometimes, at the beginning,' Amy admitted. 'But as the weeks went by, his breathing worsened. Talking was an effort. We talked very little.'

Hunter nodded. 'Did he tell you anything that you think can help us? Anything about his life? Anything about one of his cases? Anything about someone in particular?'

Amy frowned and shook her head. 'I was just his nurse. Why would he confide in me of all people?'

'In the last few weeks you spent more time with him than anyone else. Even his daughters. Nothing at all comes to mind?'

Hunter understood the intrinsic need human beings have to talk to each other. Talking has a psychological soul-cleansing effect, and that need is heightened exponentially when someone is certain of his or her death. Because she spent so much time alone with him and was caretaker to Derek Nicholson, Amy Dawson would've seemed like the oldest and best of friends. Someone he could talk to. Someone he could confide in.

Amy looked away for a moment, focusing her stare on the window to Hunter's right. 'Once he said something that got me wondering.'

'And what was that?'

Her eyes stayed on the window. 'He said that life was a funny thing. It doesn't matter how much good you've done throughout it, or how many people you've helped. Your mistakes are what haunt you until your dying days.'

Neither Hunter nor Garcia replied.

'I told him that no one was free from mistakes. He smiled and said he knew that. And then he said something about making his peace with God, and telling someone the truth.'

'The truth about what?' Garcia asked, scooting to the edge of his seat.

'He didn't say. I never asked. It wasn't my place. But it was certainly something that was eating him inside. He wanted to clear his conscience before it was too late.'

Thirteen

Hunter had arranged to meet both of Mr. Nicholson's daughters that afternoon. Olivia, the older of the two, whom he'd met in Mr. Nicholson's house, had asked him to come over to her place in Westwood. Her sister, Allison, would meet them there.

Hunter and Garcia arrived at 4:35 p.m. The two-story house was modest by Westwood standards, but still, larger and more expensive-looking than most Angelinos could ever hope to afford. They climbed the few red-brick steps in front of the house and followed the short pathway through a well-kept front yard where summer flowers were already blooming. There were two cars parked in front of the two-car garage, a red BMW 3-series, and a brand-new-looking tuxedo-black Ford Edge.

Hunter rang the doorbell. They waited almost a minute before Olivia herself opened the door. She was wearing a black sleeveless knee-length dress and black shoes. Her hair was tied back into a neat and conservative ponytail. Her face was hidden behind heavy makeup, but even so, the signs of a sleepless night spent crying were clear.

At the sight of Hunter and Garcia, her eyes filled with tears again, but with some effort she held them there.

'Thank you for agreeing to see us so soon, Ms. Nicholson,' Hunter said.

'I told you,' she replied, putting on a brave smile. 'Call me Olivia. Please come in.'

They followed her into an anteroom decorated with a lot of taste and elegance. Vases, flowers and furniture came together to create a comfortable greeting space. Olivia guided them into the first room on the right – her study. The room was spacious, with the entire south wall taken by a floor-to-ceiling bookcase. The decoration was just as elegant as the anteroom, but unlike outside, where the clear skies and the sun drew a smile on everyone's faces, the mood inside was solemn. The place was dark and suffocating, helped by the shut windows and drawn curtains. The only light came from a pedestal lamp in one of the corners.

Standing by an imposing partner's desk was a woman in her late twenties. She was also dressed all in black. As both detectives entered the room, she turned and faced them.

Allison Nicholson was striking, though skinny. She had straight black hair that came down to the top of her shoulders and very dark, soulful eyes that were far more knowing then they ought to have been at her age. Hers, too, were red from crying.

'This is my sister, Allison,' Olivia said.

Allison's eyes moved from Hunter to Garcia, but she stood still. No offer of a handshake.

'These are Detectives Hunter and Garcia, Ally,' Olivia said, moving closer to her sister.

'We're very sorry for your loss,' Hunter said. 'We know how difficult this is for both of you and we appreciate your time. We won't take much of it.' He reached inside his pocket for his black notebook. 'If we could ask you just a few quick questions?'

Their silence prompted Hunter to continue.

'You both visited your father on Saturday last, is that correct?'

'Yes,' Olivia answered.

'Can you remember what time you got there and what time you left?'

'I got there before Ally,' Olivia said. 'I had a few things to do in the afternoon. We're opening a new store.'

Hunter knew Olivia owned Healthy Eats, a chain of healthy-food stores with several shops downtown and around greater Los Angeles. Allison on the other hand had followed in her father's footsteps. She was a prosecutor.

'I got there at around four-thirty or five o'clock,' Olivia continued. 'Ally . . .'

'I got there at around five-fifteen,' Allison took over.

Hunter waited.

'We sat around with Dad as we usually do, chatting, or trying to,' Allison continued. 'On the weekends Levy usually cooks.' She nodded at her sister. 'I sometimes help.' She shook her head. 'I'm not very good in the kitchen.'

'Did you cook on Saturday?' Hunter asked Olivia.

'Yes. Then we all ate together.'

'How about Melinda Wallis, the nurse?' Garcia asked.

'Mel always ate with us. She's a lovely person, very caring.'

'What time did you leave?'

'Levy left a couple of minutes before me,' Allison said. 'I left around nine o'clock.'

Olivia nodded.

'Do any of you remember seeing anyone in the street,

around your father's house? Anyone or anything that caught your attention?'

'I don't remember seeing anything,' Allison replied first.

'Neither do I,' Olivia agreed.

'We talked to Amy Dawson this afternoon. She mentioned something about your father having two visitors about three-and-a-half months back. Did your father mention anything about that? Do you know who they were?'

Olivia and Allison looked at each other for a moment.

'I know that DA Bradley visited Dad at the house when he first fell ill,' Allison said.

'Yes, we figured that,' Garcia commented. 'But apparently there was someone else.' He quickly checked his notes. 'Slim, about six foot tall, same age as your father, brown eyes, does it ring any bells?'

Olivia shook her head.

'Half of the male prosecutors in the DA's office could fit that description,' Allison noted.

'Your father didn't mention anything about having someone visit him a few weeks ago?'

'Not to me,' Allison said.

'Me neither,' Olivia tagged. 'And that's strange, because Dad did mention when DA Bradley went over to visit him.'

Hunter returned his notebook to his pocket. 'Mrs. Dawson also told us that your father said something about making peace with someone, telling someone the truth about something.'

Both women frowned.

'Do you know anything about that?'

'Truth about what?' Allison asked.

Garcia shrugged. 'That's what we'd like to find out.'

'About a case he prosecuted?'

'We don't know. That's all the information we have.'

Silence took over for several seconds.

'I don't remember Father saying anything about making peace with anyone,' Olivia said. 'Is Amy sure that's what he said?'

Hunter and Garcia nodded.

Olivia looked at Allison.

'Dad never said anything to me either.'

There was one more question Hunter wanted to ask them, but he needed to choose his words carefully. He tried to sound casual. 'Was your father into modern art?'

By the look on their faces, Hunter couldn't have asked a more surprising question.

'Like sculptures, for example,' he added.

Their confused looks intensified.

'No,' Olivia said before looking at Allison. Then they both said in unison.

'Mom was.'

Fourteen

If Hunter's question had surprised Allison and Olivia, their answer had certainly had the same effect on him.

'Why do you ask?' Olivia enquired, her eyes squinting a fraction.

Hunter held her gaze. He had to come up with something good. Neither of Mr. Nicholson's daughters knew about the sculpture left behind by the killer, and the psychological trauma that that knowledge would bring would haunt them forever.

'Something we found in your father's room,' he replied matter-of-factly. 'We think it might be a piece of a broken sculpture or something like that.'

'In my father's room?'

Hunter nodded. 'It might've been left there on purpose.'

Those words seemed to suck the oxygen out of the room. Both women tensed.

'Left there by the killer?' Allison asked.

'Yes.'

Olivia's eyes filled up with tears once again.

'What is it?' Allison pushed. 'Can we see it?'

'The forensics lab has it. They're running it through a few tests,' Hunter replied calmly and with conviction. 'But you said your mother liked sculptures. Modern art sculptures?' He swiftly steered the subject back to where he wanted it.

'Yes,' Olivia replied, wiping a tear from her cheek. 'I guess you can say that. Mom loved pottery. A hobby she picked up in her later years.' She indicated a medium-sized vase on the coffee table, holding a bouquet of yellow-and-white flowers. 'That's one of hers, and so are the ones in my entrance room.'

Both detectives acknowledged it.

'But Mom also liked creating sculptures.' Allison this time. She turned and pointed to a piece sitting on one of the bookshelves. It was about ten inches high and it portrayed two androgynous-looking figures. The first was standing with its legs apart. Both of its arms were stretched out in front of its body pointing down. The second figure, identical in shape to the first one, was directly in front of it, but it looked as if it was falling backward. Its stiff body reclined at forty-five degrees. Its arms also stretched out in front of its body, holding on to the arms of the first figure.

'Do you mind if we have a look at it?' Hunter asked.

'Please do.'

Hunter picked it up and studied the piece for a moment. It was made out of clay, with a wooden base.

'Trust,' he whispered.

'What?' Garcia's eyes moved from the piece to Hunter.

'Trust,' he said again. 'I'll catch you if you fall.'

Olivia and Allison looked at him surprised. 'That's exactly right,' Allison said. 'Mom made me one just like it. Dad has one too. It means that we could always trust each other. That we'd always be there for each other, no matter what.'

'It's a very nice sculpture.' Hunter placed it back on the shelf.

'This piece you found in Dad's room,' Olivia said. 'What was it made of?'

'Some kind of thin metal alloy,' Hunter lied again. 'Could be mainly bronze.'

Garcia bit his lip.

'So it wasn't from one of Mom's sculptures. She only used clay.'

'Did she create many pieces?'

'Vases – a few. Sculptures – only six, I think.' Olivia looked at Allison for confirmation. She nodded. 'As Ally said, she's got one the same as mine in her apartment. The other four are in Dad's study.'

Fifteen

Hunter saw no use in taking up any more of Olivia and Allison's grieving time. But their revelation aroused his curiosity, and before the day was over, he wanted to go back to Derek Nicholson's house and have a look in the study and at the four other sculptures by Lindsay Nicholson, Derek's deceased wife.

'Your poker face in there was impressive,' Garcia said as they got back into his car. 'A piece of thin metal left behind by the killer that could've come from some sort of sculpture? Inventive. *I* was starting to believe it. But tell me something, what if their mother had created metal sculptures as well?'

'Chances were that she wouldn't have,' Hunter replied, buckling up.

'How do you know?'

'Most sculptors, especially amateur ones, like to stick to the same material for their pieces. Something that they're comfortable with. The few who move from one substance to another very rarely go from a malleable one like clay to something as hard as metal. It requires a different sculpturing technique.'

Garcia looked at his partner and pulled a surprised face. 'I never took you for an art buff.'

'I'm not. I just read a lot.'

Hunter had only gone into Derek Nicholson's study very briefly. That was the room Melinda Wallis was sitting in when he got to the house for the first time yesterday morning. In the evening, when he revisited the crime scene, he would focus all his attention on the room upstairs.

It took them only ten minutes to drive to Cheviot Hills from Olivia's place in Westwood. They unlocked the door and stepped into a house that Hunter was sure one day had been home to a happy family. Now, that building was forever tainted with the stains of a brutal homicide. Every single happy memory that those walls once held completely erased by one act of unthinkable evil.

The air inside the house was warm and stale, and it carried a distinct mixture of unpleasant smells. Garcia rubbed his nose, cleared his throat a couple of times and allowed his partner to lead the way.

Hunter opened the door to a long, wood-paneled room where bookshelves lined two of the walls. The space was reminiscent of a court-of-law judge's chambers, with a large twin desk, comfortable armchairs and the musty odor of old, leather-bound books. They spotted the four sculptures Olivia had mentioned straight away. Two were on the bookshelves, one was on Derek Nicholson's desk, and one was on a side table next to a whisky-colored leather armchair. Unconventional-looking as they were, however, none of them even remotely resembled the grotesque piece left behind by the killer.

'Well, at least we know that the killer wasn't trying to mimic any of these,' Garcia said, placing the sculpture he was holding back down on the side table. 'God knows *what* he was trying to do or mimic.'

Hunter had looked at all the sculptures and was now studying some of the books on the shelves. Almost all of them were criminal-law related, but a handful were about pottery and ceramics. Two of them were about modern sculpture. Hunter pulled one out of the shelf and flipped through its first few pages.

'Do you think his murder could really be related to what he said to his nurse?' Garcia asked. 'Something about making his peace with someone and telling them the truth about something?'

'I'm not sure. But I know we all have secrets, some more important than others. One of Derek Nicholson's secrets was so important to him . . . it bothered him so much, that he didn't want to leave this life without clearing things up, without "making his peace".' Hunter used his fingers to draw quotation marks in the air.

'And that's gotta mean something, right?' Garcia said.

'It's gotta mean something,' Hunter agreed. 'But we don't know if he did or not. Make his peace, that is.'

'According to his nurse, he told her about this *making his peace* business sometime between her first and second week here. Since then, other than the weekend nurse and his two daughters, it looks like he'd only talked to two other people.'

Hunter nodded. 'DA Bradley and our mysterious, six foot tall, brown-eyed visitor.' He replaced the book on the shelf and reached for the second volume on sculpture. 'Maybe the DA knows who he is. I'll try to talk to him tomorrow.'

'The weekdays nurse used the room upstairs,' Garcia commented. 'But Melinda had the one above the garage outside. It's no coincidence the killer picked a weekend night for the murder, is it?'

'No.' For no reason Hunter's eyes darted towards the ceiling and then the walls. 'Somehow the killer knew the habits of this house. He knew when people came and went. He knew Derek Nicholson's daughters would visit him for a few hours every day and then leave. He knew when he would be alone and the best time to strike. He might've even known that the burglar alarm wasn't usually engaged, or that Derek Nicholson didn't like air conditioning and the balcony door that led into his room would probably have been unlocked at this time of year.'

'So that means that the killer staked out the house,' Garcia said. 'And not for just a day.'

Hunter moved his head as if pondering Garcia's words.

'You think it's more than that, don't you?' Garcia asked.

Hunter nodded. 'I think the killer has been in here before. I think the killer knew the family.'

Sixteen

'So, do you know what the problem is?' Andrew Nashorn asked the mechanic, who was hunched over the inboard engine pit inside the cabin of his midsized sailboat.

Nashorn was fifty-one years old with a full head of light brown hair, a thick chest and arms, and a swagger that told everybody that he still knew how to handle himself in a fistfight. The scar above his left eyebrow and the crooked nose came from his early boxing days.

Nashorn spent the entire year waiting for the official start of the summer. It's true that in Los Angeles, and most of southern California, summer is an almost endless season, but those first few official weeks were considered by many boat owners as the best for sailing. The winds were kinder and practically unceasing. The ocean calmer than ever. The water was clearer, and clouds seemed to go paint the sky somewhere else for a couple of weeks.

Nashorn always filed for his two-week holiday at the beginning of every year. The period was always the same – the first few weeks of summer. He'd been doing so for the last twenty years. And for the last twenty years his vacation had been exactly the same, he'd pack a few clothes, some supplies, his fishing gear, and disappear into the Pacific for fourteen days.

Nashorn didn't eat fish; he didn't like the taste of it. He fished simply for sport, and because it relaxed him. He'd always throw his catch back into the water as soon as he unhooked it from his line. He used only circle hooks, because they were kinder to the fish.

Despite having many friends, Nashorn always sailed alone. He'd been married once, over twenty years ago. His wife, Jane, suffered a heart attack in their kitchen one afternoon while he was out working. It happened so quickly she never managed to get to the phone. They'd only been married for about three years. Nashorn never even knew she had a heart condition.

Jane's death devastated him. To Nashorn, she simply was the one. From the first day they met, he knew he wanted to grow old with her, or so he hoped. The first two years after her death were torturous. More than once Nashorn thought about ending his life so he could be with Jane again. He even had a special bullet set aside for the occasion – a .38 hollow point – but that day never came. Little by little, Nashorn managed to step out of his dark depression. But he never remarried, and since then, not a day went by that he didn't think of her.

Officially, summer had started yesterday, and Nashorn had planned to set sail this afternoon, but when he tried engaging his 29 h.p. diesel engine, the motor coughed and rattled a few times before stalling. He tried it again, but the engine just wouldn't start. Some sailors might've considered taking off with a dead engine – after all, it was a sailboat – but that would've been careless, and careless was something Nashorn was not.

He was lucky, though. He was about to call Warren Donnelly, his usual mechanic, when another mechanic, who had just finished servicing the boat right next to his, heard the engine coughing like a dying dog and asked if Nashorn needed any help. That saved Nashorn at least a couple of hours, maybe more.

The mechanic had been looking over the small engine for just over five minutes now.

'So,' Nashorn said again, 'how bad is it? Can it be fixed today?'

Without looking up, the mechanic lifted a finger, asking for one more minute.

Nashorn moved closer, trying to look over the mechanic's shoulder.

'There's a crack in your lube-oil pump,' the mechanic finally said, in the calmest of voices. 'You've been leaking oil for a day, maybe two. Some of it has dripped onto the fuel-injection nozzle and clogged it.'

Nashorn looked at the mechanic with a blank stare. He knew very little about engines. 'Can you fix it?'

'The oil pump can't be mended, the crack is too big. You need a new one.'

'Oh, you've gotta be kidding.'

The mechanic smiled. 'Fortunately, that's one of the most common oil pumps around. They don't crack that easy, but it happens. I think I might have a spare one somewhere in my bag.'

'Oh, that'd be awesome.' Nashorn lips broke into a half smile. 'Could you check?'

'Not a problem.' The mechanic moved back from the engine pit and checked the large toolbox by the steps. 'I guess it's your lucky day. I've got one. It's not brand new, but it's in good condition and it will certainly do the trick.'

Nashorn's half smile turned into a full one.

'But before changing the pump, I need to clean the oil mess and unblock the fuel-injection nozzle. It shouldn't take more than ten minutes, fifteen tops.'

Nashorn checked his watch. 'That'd be just awesome. I can set off before sundown.'

The mechanic returned to the engine pit, and using an already-stained cloth, started cleaning away some of the oil that had dripped onto the fuel line.

'So, are you sailing far?'

Nashorn walked over to the fridge and grabbed two beers. 'I don't know yet. I don't really plan anything. I just try to go with the wind. Beer?'

'No thanks. I had too many of those over the weekend.'

Nashorn twisted the cap off one of the bottles, had a sip and returned the other one to the fridge. 'This is the only vacation I take in the year. Two weeks away from everything.'

'And you can't wait to get started, right? I know exactly what you mean. Me, I can say that I haven't had a vacation for . . .' The mechanic paused for a second and then laughed, sadly. 'Wow, I can't even remember the last time I had a vacation.'

'You see, I couldn't do that. It would drive me nuts. I need these two weeks to myself.'

'Oh shit!' the mechanic interrupted, jerking backwards. Liquid squirted up from the engine and onto the floor.

'What happened?' Nashorn moved forward, looking worried.

'One of the high-pressure fuel-injection lines disconnected.'

'That doesn't sound good.'

The mechanic looked around quickly as if searching for something. 'I need to get a clamp to fix it back in place. Can you do me a favor and hold this hose just like this while I grab a pressure clamp.'

'Sure.' Nashorn put his beer down and held the hose in place as the mechanic showed him.

'Don't let go of that, I'll be right back.'

Nashorn kept his finger and his attention firmly on the thin dark rubber pipe. He could hear the mechanic rummaging through the toolbox behind him. 'This isn't gonna delay you fixing the engine is it?'

No reply.

'I'd really love to set sail before nightfall.'

Silence. The rummaging had stopped.

'Hello . . . ?' Nashorn twisted his body awkwardly to look back.

At that exact moment the mechanic swung a metal wrench around as if it were a baseball bat. Time went into slow motion for Nashorn. The wrench collided with his face with a chilling cracking sound. His jaw fractured in one, two, three places. The skin started to rupture at the base of the jaw, and did so all the way to his chin, exposing flesh and bone. Blood splattered high into the air in all directions. Three of Nashorn's teeth shattered and were violently projected against the wall. A large bone splinter broke loose from his fractured jaw and perforated his gum, just under the now-missing first molar, its tip touching the exposed nerve left there by the missing tooth. Pain darkened his eyes. The hit was so powerful and well placed that Nashorn's body was catapulted backwards; his back slammed against the engine, his head against the wooden panel above it.

Nashorn's vision blurred instantly. Blood flooded his mouth and trickled down into his throat, blocking his airways and making him gasp for air. He tried to speak but the only sound he could muster was a pitiful, gurgling noise. Just before he lost consciousness, he saw the mechanic standing high above him, still holding the wrench.

'You . . .' the mechanic said with an evil smile. 'I'll take my time with.'

Seventeen

Hunter got to the PAB at 8:33 a.m., just minutes after Garcia.

'Goddamn, did they get you too?' Garcia asked.

'The reporters outside, you mean?'

Garcia nodded. 'Are they camping outside or what? I got out of my car and instantly had three of them shouting questions at me.'

'Our victim was a prosecutor, who was dismembered in his own house, on his deathbed three days ago. That's the stuff TV series are made of, Carlos. They could kill each other to be the first to get an insight from someone working the case. It will only get worse.'

'Yeah, I know.' Garcia poured Hunter and himself a large cup of coffee each from the machine on the corner. 'Any luck with those?' he asked, handing his partner a cup and nodding at the books under Hunter's arm.

Hunter had taken all the modern art and sculpture books he could find in Derek Nicholson's study home with him last night.

'Nothing.' Hunter put the books down on his desk and took the cup. 'Thanks. I also spent half of the night searching the net, reading about any and every Los Angeles sculptor I could find. Nothing there either. I don't think our killer is trying to reproduce an already-existing piece.'

Garcia returned to his desk. 'Me neither.'

'I'll drop by DA Bradley's office today,' Hunter continued. 'I want to ask him if he knows anything about Nicholson wanting to make his peace with someone before dying, and if he has any idea who the other man who visited him was.'

'Isn't it easier to call?'

Hunter made a 'maybe' face, but he hated having to ask questions over the phone, regardless of who was on the other end. Face-to-face meetings allowed him to observe the movements, reactions and facial expressions of the person he was talking to, and to a homicide detective, that was invaluable.

The phone on Hunter's desk rang. He checked his watch before picking up the receiver.

'Detective Hunter.'

'Robert, I just got the first batch of results back from the lab,' Doctor Hove said. Her voice sounded a little heavier than usual.

Hunter fired up his computer. 'I'm listening, doc.'

'First let me tell you that the lab has done a great job with the replica you asked for.'

'Is it ready?'

'Yep, they worked overnight. It's on its way to you now.'

'That's great.'

'OK,' Doctor Hove proceeded. 'Forensics lifted five sets of fingerprints from the crime scene and other locations throughout the house – kitchen, bathroom, staircase handrail . . . you know the drill. As expected, no joy there. The fingerprints are confirmed to have come from the two nurses, both of the victim's daughters and the victim himself.'

Hunter said nothing. He wasn't really expecting anything to come from those.

'The hairs retrieved from most of the same locations as the fingerprints were also matched to the same five people,' Doctor Hove continued. 'I don't think we'll need to DNA-test them. Analysis on some of the fibers found is still going on. The ones they've already analyzed came back as cotton, polyester, acrylic . . . the most common fibers found in everyday clothes. Nothing that will lead you anywhere.'

Hunter rested an elbow on his desk. 'Any toxicology results yet, doc?'

'Yes, I had to push for them, though. The lab is overworked.' She paused for just a split second. 'And here is where it gets interesting. And positively more evil.'

Hunter grabbed Garcia's attention with a quick hand wave and motioned him to listen in on his extension.

'What does the test say, doc?' Hunter asked.

'OK, we know that to prolong the victim's suffering the perp clamped the brachial artery of the amputated right arm using medical forceps, keeping the victim from bleeding out. But even so, something was baffling me from the start.'

Hunter pulled out his desk chair and had a seat. 'The victim's fragile condition.' He didn't phrase it as a question.

'That's right. The victim was already in the very late stages of terminal pulmonary cancer. His body was as weak as a 90-year-old man's. His resistance to pain, his stamina, had all been reduced to a fraction of what it should've been.

A person in those conditions should've died of shock after losing a finger. He lost five of them, all ten toes, his tongue and an arm before dying.'

Hunter and Garcia exchanged a long worried look.

'As I expected,' the doctor continued, 'he wasn't sedated, but he was drugged to his eyeballs. Toxicology found high levels of a few drugs, but that was expected due to the victim's ill health. But some of the high-level drugs are just plain wrong.'

'Like what?'

'OK, we found high levels of propafenone, felodipine and carvedilol.'

Garcia looked at Hunter and shook his head. 'Hold on, doc. Easy with the chemical jargon. Chemistry wasn't my strongest subject in school, and school was years ago. What are those?'

'Propafenone is a sodium-channel blocker. It works by slowing the influx of sodium ions into the cardiac muscle. Felodipine is a calcium-channel blocker, and very big on controlling high blood pressure. Carvedilol is a beta-blocker. It blocks the binding of norepinephrine and epinephrine to beta-adrenoceptors. The combination of those three drugs will also, most certainly, inhibit the body's production of adrenaline.'

Garcia's frown was so intense his forehead looked like a prune. 'You did hear when I said that chemistry wasn't my strongest subject in school, right, doc? OK, neither was biology. Pretend I'm a seven-year-old kid and tell me all that again.'

'In a nutshell, that's a very strong cocktail of drugs to slow anyone's heart rate down, control blood pressure and inhibit the production of adrenaline by the adrenal glands.

As you know, adrenaline is released whenever a person senses danger. It's the fear and pain hormone. It increases heart rate and dilates air passages, getting the subject ready to fight or flee.'

Garcia still looked a little puzzled.

'So the killer reduced the victim's blood flow,' Hunter said, 'and sedated his production of adrenaline.'

'That's exactly right,' Doctor Hove said. 'When the body senses danger or feels pain, like when having a finger, toe or tongue cut off, adrenaline is released and the heart speeds up, pumping more blood to the affected area, brain and muscles. Those drugs wouldn't allow that to happen. They'd keep the heart in rest pace, if not even slower. That way, smaller amounts of blood were distributed throughout the victim's body. He would've bled a lot less than expected. But none of those drugs have a sedating effect.'

'Meaning he would've felt all the pain,' Garcia caught on. 'But held on for longer.'

'Correct,' the doctor agreed. 'When a victim is severely cut, but no vital organs are damaged, there are mainly two ways the victim can die. Bleed to death, or the heart gets overworked to such an extent that it fails. In an unorthodox way, this killer addressed both of those problems with his drug combination. He didn't want the victim to die too soon. And he certainly wanted the victim to feel as much pain as he could endure. But without a surgical team to help him, the killer would've had to work a lot faster to be able to perform the amputations and contain the hemorrhaging before the victim bled out. Well, his cocktail of drugs helped him a lot.' She paused, dwelling on the severity of her own words. 'I think all this strengthens our suspicion that this killer knows medicine, Robert. And I'd say he knows it well.'

Eighteen

Hunter and Garcia placed their receivers back in their cradles at the same time. Hunter laced his fingers, rested both elbows on the arms of his chair, and sat back.

'OK,' he said, facing his partner. 'I know this is a long shot, but since all three of the drugs toxicology found are prescription only, let's start checking with drugstores and pharmacists to see if anyone has sold all three in one go. I mean, all in the same prescription to the same person. Who knows, we might get lucky.'

Garcia was already reading through the email they'd just received from Doctor Hove, noting down the names of all three medications.

'How are we doing on that list of criminals Nicholson put away?' Hunter asked.

'We haven't got it yet, but the team is working on it.'

'Tell them we'll need to reprioritize it. Check if anyone on that list has any previous medical education, worked in a hospital, care home, maybe even a gym.'

Garcia's eyebrow twitched.

'Gym instructors and personal trainers must know first aid,' Hunter explained. 'If any of the people on that list knows so much as how to properly put on a Band-Aid, I want to know.'

There was a knock on the door.

'Come in,' Hunter called from his desk.

The door was pushed open by a petite and very pretty woman in a dark business suit. She had long, straight, dyed blonde hair and deep-brown eyes. In her right hand she held a black leather briefcase. There was no doubt she was a lawyer, or worked for one.

'Detective Hunter?' she said, looking straight at him.

'Yes, can I help you?' Hunter stood up.

The woman stepped forward and offered her hand.

'I'm Alice Beaumont. I work for Los Angeles District Attorney's office. Directly with DA Bradley himself. He said you could use my help on the Derek Nicholson investigation.' She shook Hunter's hand with a firm and self-assured grip.

Garcia frowned.

Hunter studied the woman in front of him for a moment. Her eyes were full of intelligence – both the university and street kind. Hunter noticed that she had expertly and subtly allowed her gaze to run around the room. It took her less than two seconds to take in her entire surroundings. There was something vaguely familiar about her.

'DA Bradley gave me your card,' Hunter said. 'But maybe I misunderstood him. I thought he said that *if* we needed your help, I would give you a call.'

'Trust me, detective, you need my help.' Her tone was as confident as her posture. She turned and faced Garcia. 'You must be Detective Carlos Garcia.'

'The legend himself,' Garcia joked, shaking her hand.

Alice didn't smile; instead, she walked over to Hunter's desk, placed her briefcase on it, flipped the top open, and retrieved several sheets of paper that'd been stapled together.

'This is a list of all perpetrators Derek Nicholson sent, or helped send, to prison over the years.' She handed it to Hunter. 'There are some really nasty people on that list. It's been prioritized by severity of crime; ultra violent and sadistic ones come first. Also by those individuals who have been released, paroled, or made bail recently.' Her gaze circled from Hunter to Garcia. 'I've already checked. None of the violent criminals he put away have been released – either on probation or in any other way. None has escaped either. The files of the ones who have committed minor offenses and have either served their sentences, or were granted early release for whatever reason, don't read like the type of people who would be capable of such a crime.'

'You'd be surprised what people are capable of,' Garcia said, moving towards Hunter to have a look at the list. 'Especially the ones who don't look the type.'

'You've read these files?' Hunter asked.

'The most relevant ones, yes.'

'Who stipulated their relevance, you?'

Alice didn't reply.

Hunter held her gaze for a moment before flipping through the pages. There were over 900 names on it. 'You said that none of the violent criminals on this list have been released recently. How recently are we talking?'

'Past year.'

'We need to go further back than that,' Hunter countered.

'That won't be a problem. How far back would you like?'

'Five years, to start with, maybe ten.'

'Give me a computer with a fast Internet connection and a few minutes and you'll have it.'

'I need to know what each and every person on this list was prosecuted for.'

'It says right there next to their names and ages,' Alice said with a tiny amount of prickliness in her voice while she nodded at the list.

Hunter's eyes didn't move from her face. 'It says *homicide*, *aggravated homicide*, *armed robbery*, and so on. We need to know exactly what they did and how they did it. What weapons were used? Was the crime scene bloody? Was the perpetrator violent because he lost control, or because he enjoyed it? We need real specifics.'

'Again, not a problem. Just give me a computer.'

'We also need to cross-reference the names on this list with any family member, relative or gang member who is on the outside, and who'd be crazy enough to seek revenge on behalf of the inmate.'

'Not a problem.'

Hunter's eyes moved to the list, then to Garcia, and then back to Alice. 'You're very confident. You think you're that good?'

A smile lit up her face for a brief second. 'I'm better,' she replied without hesitation. 'Get me a computer and I'll go to work right now.' She pointed to the list in Hunter's hands. 'But for now, that can give us a start.'

For a moment no one spoke.

'Us . . . ?' Garcia asked.

'DA Bradley wants me to help you as much as I can. That sort of puts us in a team, doesn't it?' Her stare returned to Hunter.

'Ms. Beaumont,' Hunter said, putting the list down on his desk. 'We're the Homicide Special Section of the Robbery Homicide Division. This isn't Club Med. We know that DA

Bradley is keen to get results, and so are we. We appreciate your help, and this list can give us a good start, you're right. But I have no authority to add anyone to this investigation without consulting my captain. For starters, she's not very keen on civilians being involved in any of the department's investigations.'

Alice smiled and walked over to the pictures board where all the crime-scene photographs had been pinned up. She had a sensual walk. Slow and easy, as if she knew men liked to watch her move.

'Don't be so modest, Detective. You *do* have the authority to bring anyone you like into your team,' she replied in a non-aggressive way. 'I checked. In here, you call the shots and everyone listens. But in any case, DA Bradley has talked to Chief of Police Martin Collins, who, in turn, has talked to your "not very keen" captain. She didn't have much of a choice. And I'm afraid that neither do you. DA Bradley always gets what he wants.'

Hunter was seasoned enough to know that protesting wouldn't make a sand grain of difference. He hated people butting into his investigations, dictating what he should and should not do, hence his reputation for not exactly sticking to protocol all the time; but the LAPD had a chain of command, and he was a long way down it. Sometimes he had to go along to get along, and this sure as hell was looking like one of those times. He said nothing.

Alice's eyes browsed the pictures on the board for just a moment. 'Oh my God,' she whispered in a weak breath and quickly turned away.

Hunter's stare was fixed on her.

'I knew Derek well,' she said in a more tender voice. 'I helped him in tens of cases. I helped him put away many of the names in that list. He was a good man who didn't deserve any of this. I want to help. And I know I can because I'm the best at what I do. Please give me a chance to help you catch the son of a bitch who did this to Derek.'

Nineteen

Before Hunter could say anything, there was a new knock at the door.

'Busy here this morning,' Garcia joked before calling out. 'Come in.'

'Sorry, sir,' a male voice replied from outside. 'Not enough hands.'

Everyone in the room frowned. Garcia stepped up to the door and pulled it open.

A rookie officer, barely out of his teens, was standing outside in a crisp, straight-out-of-the-bag police uniform. Both of his arms were wrapped around a large package, covered by thick black plastic sheets held in place by duct tape.

'Forensics lab just delivered this for you, Detective.'

'OK, thanks. I can take it from here,' Garcia said, reaching for it. The package was a lot lighter than it looked. Its base was flat and easy to grab hold of. 'Over by the board?' Garcia asked Hunter, after allowing the door to close behind him.

'Yeah, I think that'll do.' Hunter cleared a space on a small table and pushed it closer to the pictures board. Garcia carefully deposited the package on it.

'What is that?' Alice asked, moving around to the other side.

'A life-sized replica of this,' Garcia replied, pointing to the photograph on the board.

Hunter saw Alice hold her breath for a beat. 'Have you ever worked this closely with a homicide investigating team?' he asked.

'No,' Alice replied firmly. No embarrassment.

Hunter took a penknife out of his pocket and flicked it open. 'As I said before, this isn't Club Med.' He skillfully cut through the duct tape. 'You can stay if you want. But this will be no picnic.'

'I hate picnics.' Alice stood her ground.

Hunter and Garcia pulled down the black plastic cover, letting it drop to the floor. For a long moment, the only sound in the room came from the pedestal fan behind Garcia's desk. Doctor Hove was right; forensics had done a fantastic job in replicating the morbid piece, despite the short amount of time. The replica was done in white plaster, cast over a light wooden base, no color finish, but it still made the hairs at the back of Garcia's neck stand on end, and it had knocked the air out of Alice's lungs.

Hunter found it hard to tear his eyes away from it. Images of the real thing flashed at the back of his mind like fireworks, going off every few seconds. With it, his subconscious brought back the same sensations he experienced two days ago when he walked into that crime scene for the first time. He could smell the pungent odor of that room. He could see the blood splattered all over the walls and floors, and the way it trickled down from the human flesh sculpture. For a second he could even see the bloody words painted onto the far wall 'GOOD JOB YOU DIDN'T TURN ON THE LIGHTS'.

'Do you mind if I pour myself a glass of water?' Alice

said, finally breaking the silence. Her words seemed to have interrupted some sort of group trance. Hunter and Garcia blinked almost at the same time.

'Please do,' Hunter replied, folding his arms over his chest. His attention was still on the piece. He walked over to the other side to look at it from a different angle.

Garcia moved a few steps back, as if trying to see a bigger picture.

There was nothing there. The piece resembled nothing else they'd ever seen. It didn't trigger anything in either of their minds.

'That has got to be the most grotesque thing I've ever seen,' Alice said, after downing a glass of water as if to put out a fire inside her. 'And judging by the way you two are looking at it, you have no idea what it means, do you?'

'We're working on it,' Hunter replied.

She refilled her glass. 'Well, I know someone who might be able to help.'

Twenty

Silver Lake is a hilly neighborhood, east of Hollywood and northwest of downtown Los Angeles. The place is inhabited by a wide variety of ethnic and socioeconomic groups, but it is best known for the eclectic gathering of hipsters and creative types that live there, as well as a significant LGBT community. The neighborhood is also home to some of the most famous modernist architecture in North America, and that was exactly where Hunter and Alice were heading.

Alice owned a red Corvette, and she drove it like a boy racer trying to prove a point; crisscrossing lanes without signaling, cutting in front of traffic, and accelerating as if trying to outrun a tsunami every time a traffic light went yellow. Hunter sat beside her in the passenger's seat. His seatbelt securely fastened.

'Ms. Beaumont, if we go any faster we might travel back in time,' he said, as she hooked onto West Sunset Boulevard.

She smiled. 'Am I scaring you?'

'The way you drive would scare Michael Schumacher.'

Another smile. 'I'll tell you what. If you stop calling me Ms. Beaumont and call me Alice, I'll slow down.'

'That's a deal, *Alice*. Now please take your foot off the gas before we end up in 1842.'

They reached Silver Lake in just under fifteen minutes.

'Don't be alarmed,' Alice said, as she parked in front of Jalmar Art Gallery. 'Miguel is a bit eccentric.'

Hunter grabbed the replica created by the forensics lab from the backseat and followed her inside.

Miguel Jalmar was an art collector, gallery owner and connoisseur extraordinaire when it came to modern sculpture. Passionate about art from a very young age, he was still in his teens when he started collecting.

'Alice, darling,' Miguel said in a high-pitched voice, putting down the book he was reading and leaping from his chair as soon as Alice and Hunter walked into his gallery.

Miguel was in his mid-forties, tall, slim, with straight midnight-black hair that came all the way down to his chest. Immaculately dressed in a D&G suit, he had a chic three-day beard and smelled of expensive cologne. He hugged Alice as if he'd just found his long lost sister, before kissing her on both cheeks.

'Thanks for seeing us at such short notice, Miguel,' Alice said, breaking away from his embrace. 'We really appreciate it.'

'Darling, anything for you, you know that.' The high-pitch had vanished from his voice, but not the femininity. His eyes moved to Hunter and his eyebrows arched in a curious way. 'And who is this? More importantly, where have you been hiding him?'

'This is Robert Hunter. He's a friend of mine.'

Hunter smiled and nodded at Miguel.

'Robert Hunter . . . ? Now that's a strong, masculine name. I like that. And by God, look at those broad shoulders and those biceps. I bet you work out like a bodybuilder.'

So that's what Alice meant by 'eccentric', Hunter thought.

'Oh,' Miguel's attention moved to the package Hunter was carrying, 'is that the piece you'd like me to have a look at?'

'That's the one.'

'Well, follow me into my office.'

Miguel's office was a clash of eras. Modern art and antique pieces mingled together in a way that shouldn't have worked, but did. Sculptures of all shapes and sizes were absolutely everywhere. There were masks on the walls, zebra-print rugs on the floors, and a black leather couch with a tiger throw and leopard cushions.

'Let's put it over here,' Miguel said, pointing to a coffee table. He removed the two statues that were standing on it. Hunter placed the package down and took off the black plastic cover.

'Oh, my!' Miguel reached inside his suit pocket for his glasses. 'Wow. This is . . .' He paused and looked at Hunter questioningly. 'Did you create this, darling?'

'No, it wasn't me.'

'OK, in that case this is simply grotesque.' Miguel walked around it, studying the piece from every angle. He paused and cringed. 'Do these represent human body parts?'

Alice nodded. 'I guess so.'

'I've never seen anything so sick and horrendous in all my life. But one thing is for sure . . . it's very creative. I have to give the artist that. This is one of those crazy, "what-the-hell-is-this" pieces that could win the Turner Prize in London. Hell knows what those judges look for.'

'Have you ever seen anything like it?' Hunter asked.

'Only in nightmares, darling.' Miguel had crouched down and tilted his head to one side. He was looking at one of the feet at the edge. 'Who's the artist?'

'Not sure we can call him that,' Alice commented, but immediately regretted it.

Miguel looked up at her.

'We don't know,' Hunter cut in, 'but I'd really like to find out.'

'Are you a collector?'

'I guess you can say that,' Hunter said, matter-of-factly. 'I'm just starting, though.'

'Maybe we should get together one night and talk about art and . . . other things.' Miguel smiled. 'I would really like that. I would gladly give you a few tips.'

'It's a very intriguing piece,' Hunter said, moving the subject along. 'In your experience, Miguel, what do you think the artist is trying to say?'

Miguel returned his attention to the piece. 'Well, I'm in two minds. I'm inclined to say that, whoever the artist is, this is not his first piece.'

'Why not?'

'The way it's put together, the crazy imagination and creativity of it all strikes me as . . . someone who has a great deal of experience in sculpting. Someone who doesn't care what others think, who isn't afraid to show his art, whoever it might offend. But on the other hand, the sculpture was done in cast, which simply screams amateurism. No one does anything in cast anymore. And if he wants to sell this, he might consider adding some color. Maybe some blood red to go with the theme.' Miguel stood up, took a few steps back and rested his hands on his hips. 'But he is a daring, defiant artist who isn't scared of breaking conventions. And I like that. He's clearly telling us something here.'

'And what do you think that is?' Alice asked.

Miguel returned his glasses to his pocket. 'The way that

the artist has simply toyed with the human body, rearranging it in his own way – he's challenging creation.' He shrugged. 'Hell, this is so bold that, in his mind, he might even be challenging the creator himself.'

Alice felt a shiver run down her spine. 'Miguel, you're saying that this artist thinks he's God?'

Miguel nodded. His attention didn't shift from the strange piece. 'That's exactly what that's telling me, darling. I am God and I can do whatever I want.'

Twenty-One

On his way back to the PAB, Hunter dropped by the Los Angeles District Attorney's office in West Temple Street. He was lucky; DA Bradley had just come out of a three-hour-long meeting with a team of attorneys.

Bradley's office was the size of a small apartment. Long, pristine bookshelves lined two of the walls. The other two were covered in diplomas, awards, certificates and framed photographs depicting the DA doing all sorts of important things – shaking hands with politicians and celebrities, posing with lawyers at bar meetings, standing behind podiums during speeches, and so on.

Hunter was shown into the DA's office by his PA, a very young and attractive brunette dressed in an elegant and tight-fitting black suit. Bradley was sitting behind an imposing mahogany pedestal desk, unwrapping a sandwich that could probably feed three people.

'Detective,' Bradley said, motioning Hunter to have a seat at one of the three fine leather armchairs in front of his desk. 'Do you mind if I eat while we talk? I've had no lunch today.'

'It doesn't bother me.' Hunter shook his head, taking the chair on the left.

Bradley took a mammoth bite of his sandwich.

Mayonnaise, ketchup and mustard dripped down onto the wrapper.

'She's nice, isn't she?' Bradley spoke while he chewed.

'Excuse me?'

'Alice,' Bradley clarified. 'The girl I sent over to you. She's a fine piece of ass, isn't she? And she's as bright as diamonds. Hard combination to find these days. But don't you go getting any ideas. She's totally out of your league.'

Hunter said nothing, and watched as the DA used a paper napkin to wipe away a blob of mustard at the corner of his mouth.

'So,' Bradley continued, 'what do you have for me, Detective? And please form full sentences.'

'I'll try. I've got a few questions for you.'

The DA looked at Hunter. That certainly wasn't the answer he was expecting.

'We're piecing a few things together.'

'OK, ask away, Detective.' Bradley took another bite of his sandwich and chewed with his mouth open.

'I was told that you visited Mr. Nicholson in his home a few months ago, after he was diagnosed with his illness.'

'That's right. I drove down to his place after I left the office. I wanted to let him know that if he needed anything, he could count on me. He'd been with this office for twenty years. It was the least I could do.'

'Do you recall exactly when that was?'

Bradley twisted off the cap on a bottle of Dr Pepper and drank half of it down in large gulps. 'I can easily find out.' He stared at Hunter skeptically.

'Could you, please?'

Bradley reached for the intercom on his desk phone. 'Grace, I dropped by Derek Nicholson's house a few weeks ago. Do you have an entry in my schedule? Could you check and tell me what day that was?'

'Sure, DA Bradley.' There was a short pause, sound-tracked by the clacking of a keyboard. 'You visited Mr. Nicholson on the seventh of March. That was after hours.'

'Thanks, Grace.' He nodded at Hunter.

Hunter wrote it down on his notebook. 'Around that same time someone else visited Mr. Nicholson in his home. Do you know anything about that? Do you know if it's someone from your staff, someone he was good friends with, perhaps?'

DA Bradley chuckled. 'Detective, I have over three hundred able-bodied prosecutors working for me, and about the same number of people working for the office in various other capacities.'

'About six foot, around the same age as Mr. Nicholson, brown hair . . . if it was someone from your office I thought he might've mentioned it to you.'

'No one has mentioned anything to me about visiting Derek, but I can easily enquire around and find out.' Bradley reached for a pen and wrote something down on a piece of paper. 'Derek was a nice and decent person, Detective. Everyone got along with him. Judges loved him. And his circle of friends went beyond this office.'

'I understand, but if his other visitor was someone from your office, I wouldn't mind asking him a few questions.'

Bradley studied Hunter for a long silent moment before chuckling derisively. 'Are you saying that you think some-body from this office could be a suspect, Detective?'

'Without information everyone is a suspect,' Hunter replied. 'It's right there in the detective's manual. We gather information and use it to eliminate people from the suspects list. That's usually how this works.'

'Don't be a goddamn smartass. That crap might be funny to your monkey friends, but not to me. I'm running this goddamn investigation, so you better show some respect, 'cos if you don't, your next job will be walking the dogs from the K9 unit while they take a dump, you hear me?'

'Loud and clear, but I'd still like to know if this other person who visited Mr. Nicholson is someone from this office.'

'OK,' Bradley said after a new pause. 'I'll check and let you know. Is there anything else, Detective?' He consulted his watch.

'Just one more thing. Did Mr. Nicholson ever mention anything to you about making his peace with someone? Telling someone the truth about something?'

A muscle twitched on Bradley's jaw and for a quick instant he stopped chewing. 'Making his peace with someone? What do you mean?'

Hunter told the DA what Amy Dawson had told him.

'And you think that this man who visited him a few months ago was the person he was referring to?'

'It's a possibility.'

Bradley wiped his mouth and hands on a new paper napkin, sat back in his leather swivel chair, and regarded Hunter for a moment. 'Derek never mentioned anything to me. Not about making his peace with anyone, or telling anyone the truth about anything.'

'Do you have any idea what he could've been referring to?'

Bradley's eyes jumped to his wall clock and then back to

Hunter. 'It's a messed-up world we live in, Detective. You, better than anyone, can vouch for that. We, as state prosecutors, try our best to maintain order in our society by trying to make sure that the individuals who aren't fit to live in it are put away. We deal with evidence that is given to us by detectives like yourself, forensic scientists, technicians, our own investigators, witnesses, etcetera. But we are also human and, as such, we're bound to make mistakes. The problem is, when those mistakes occur, due to the nature of what we do, they tend to incur dramatic consequences.'

Hunter shifted on his seat. 'You mean, either the wrong person gets sent to prison or the right one walks free.'

'It's never as simple as that, Detective.'

'And was Mr. Nicholson ever guilty of one of these "mistakes"?'

'I can't answer that question.'

Hunter leaned forward. 'Can't or won't?'

Bradley's stare changed into something harder. 'I can't because I don't know the answer.'

Hunter studied Bradley's poker face.

'But I can tell you that anyone who's been a prosecutor for long enough would've experienced at least one of those situations. I've lost count of how many times I've come across an accused man who was as guilty as water is wet, and because of some technicality, because of some idiot at the lab, or some rookie cop who fucked up at the arrest or at the crime scene, contaminating evidence, the sack of shit walked free.'

Hunter had been in that situation many times, but he knew that the opposite was also true. There would always be cases where an innocent person served time, or, worse, received the death penalty for something he or she didn't do.

'We've all been there, Detective. And Derek Nicholson was no exception.'

Twenty-Two

Hunter spent the rest of the day back in the office. His mind was swirling with questions, but he couldn't stop chewing over what Miguel Jalmar had said.

Was that really it? he thought. Was that what this killer was trying to tell them with that sculpture? Could he be so arrogant, so delusional, to think he was God? To think that he could do whatever he wanted without being stopped?

Hunter knew that the answer to that question was a resounding 'yes'. It happened a lot more often than most criminal-behavior psychologists would like to admit. Some call it the 'homicidal God complex'. In most cases it's triggered by the moment a killer realizes that he or she has a power usually attributed only to God – the power to decide who lives and who dies. The power to become the supreme ruler of death. And that power can be a thousand times more addictive than any drug. It elevates their frequently damaged egos to heights they'd never imagined. And at that moment, it equates them to God. Once hooked, it is more than likely they'll come back for more.

The sculpture was back by the pictures board, and Hunter still couldn't stir his attention from it for more than a minute or so. It was starting to play with his mind.

Alice was tucked away in the corner, working on a laptop. Her task was to break down the list of perpetrators Derek Nicholson had put away into several separate categories. After his meeting with DA Bradley, Hunter also asked her to compile a new list – all the cases Derek Nicholson should've won but lost because of a technicality, or a mistake by someone involved with the arrest or the collection of evidence. He needed to know who the victims were, if they blamed Nicholson for losing the case, and if they were capable of any type of retaliation.

Garcia had spent the entire day checking with drugstores and pharmacists. So far, none had sold a prescription for all three of the drugs used by the killer to reduce Derek Nicholson's heart rate. The problem was, Garcia discovered, obtaining any of those drugs through illegal Internet outlets was as easy as ordering candy.

Hunter checked his watch. It was getting late. He got up and approached the sculpture for what seemed like the hundredth time. 'Carlos, do you still have your digital camera here with you?'

'Uh-huh.' Garcia opened his top drawer and pulled out an ultra-slim, cellphone-sized camera. 'Why?'

'I don't know. I wanna photograph this thing from different angles.' Hunter nodded at the sculpture. 'See what I get.'

'Not really convinced by what the expert told you?'

'Maybe he's right. Maybe the killer *is* delusional enough to think he's God. After all, it was his decision, not God's, to end Derek Nicholson's life. And that's a mind-boggling power to come to terms with. But I still think we're missing something, somewhere. The problem is, the more I look at this thing, the less sense it makes. Maybe the camera eye can help.'

'I guess it's worth a shot,' Garcia said, moving towards the board.

'OK, let's start from here,' Hunter indicated a spot directly in front of the sculpture. 'Let's take three pictures – one standing up in a downward angle, one leveled with it, and one from a crouched position sort of looking up. Then take a step to your left and do the same again. Let's go around it once.'

'OK.' Garcia started clicking away, the glare of his camera flash filling the room every couple of seconds.

From her desk, Alice flinched a little too abruptly.

Hunter noticed it. 'Are you OK?'

Alice didn't reply.

'Alice, are you OK?' Hunter persisted.

'Yes, I'm fine. Camera flashes sort of bother me a little.'

Hunter could see that it was more than a little. She looked rattled, but he decided not to ask.

Garcia had taken about seventeen pictures when Hunter saw something that took his breath away and made him shiver.

'Stop,' he called out, lifting his hand.

Alice raised her eyes from her laptop.

Garcia stopped clicking.

'Don't move,' Hunter said. 'Take another picture from that exact position, don't move an inch.'

'What . . . ? Why . . . ?'

'Just do it again, Carlos. Trust me.'

'OK.' Garcia took another picture.

Hunter's heart skipped a beat as adrenaline rushed through his veins. 'No way,' he whispered.

Alice got up and approached them.

'One more, Carlos.'

Garcia pointed the camera at the sculpture and fired away.

'Jesus!'

'What's going on, Robert?'

Hunter paused and looked at his partner. 'I guess I just found out what the killer wants to tell us with that sculpture.'

Twenty-Three

Andrew Nashorn's eyelids moved in slow motion as he gathered all the strength left inside him to force them open. Light burned at his eyes like a stun grenade, despite the room being lit only by candles. No shape made sense; everything was just one enormous blur.

His mouth felt desert-dry. He coughed, and the pain that shot up from his jaw seemed to compress his head like a vice, filling it with so much pressure he thought it would explode. He was so dehydrated that his lips had chipped, and his glands could barely produce any saliva anymore. He tried forcing them, compressing the glands underneath his tongue by pushing its tip against the roof of his mouth, just like he used to do when he was a kid. He hadn't forgotten how, and was rewarded with a couple of slimy drops. As they reached his throat, it felt as if he were swallowing a mouthful of broken glass. He coughed again, this time a desperate dry cough, and the pain in his throat and jaw fireballed, engulfing his entire skull. His eyelids fluttered, and Nashorn thought he'd pass out, but something deep inside him told that, if he did, he would never open his eyes again.

He fought the pain with all he had, and somehow managed to steer away from unconsciousness.

God, he needed a drink of water. He'd never felt so weak and drained of life.

Nashorn had no idea how long he'd been awake for, but things were finally coming back into focus. He could make out the outline of a small Formica table with two chairs, and a small L-shaped bench built into the wall against the corner. Two old and deflated cushions served as backrests.

'Uh . . . ?' was the only sound Nashorn could utter through the pain of his broken jaw. He knew that place, and he knew it well. He was inside his own sailboat.

He tried moving but nothing happened. His arms didn't respond, and neither did his legs. In fact, nothing did. He couldn't feel his body at all.

A desperate panic started to gain momentum inside him. Nashorn forced himself to concentrate, searching for any kind of sensation anywhere – fingers, hands, arms, toes, feet, legs, torso.

Absolutely nothing.

The only thing he could feel was the nauseating headache that seemed to be eating away at his brain, chunk by chunk.

Feeling defeated, Nashorn allowed his head to drop down. Only then he became aware that he was naked, sitting down on a wooden chair. His arms were hanging loosely by his sides. They weren't restrained. His legs didn't seem to be, either, but he couldn't see his feet, as his knees were slightly bent back, hiding the bottom half of his legs under the chair seat. What he did see, to his horror, was a pool of blood coming from beneath the chair. His feet seemed to be resting in it. He tried moving his body forward so he could look down at his own legs, but his effort produced nothing. He didn't move an inch. Nothing in his body responded to his command.

Out of the corner of his eye, Nashorn saw movement and his breathing held tight.

A person stepped out of the shadows, walked around the chair and stopped directly in front of him.

Nashorn's gaze found the person's face. His eyes narrowed questioningly for an instant. It took him only a moment to recognize who it was. The mechanic who came to have a look at his faulty engine.

'It must be really weird not being able to feel your own body,' the mechanic said, looking straight into Nashorn's eyes.

Nashorn breathed out, and involuntarily let go of the terrified but weak groan that had hatched in his throat.

The mechanic smiled.

'Uhhh, ahhhg.' Nashorn tried to speak, but without the power to articulate his jaw, the best he could do was mumble unintelligible sounds.

'Sorry about your jaw. I didn't mean to break it. I was supposed to hit you at the back of the head, but you turned around right at the last minute. It's my loss though, because now you can't speak, and I really wanted you to.'

If fear had a smell, Nashorn was drenched in it.

'Let me show you something, I wanna see how you feel about it, OK?'

Nashorn tried to swallow again. He was so scared, he didn't notice the pain this time.

The mechanic pointed to a piece of dirty cloth that was covering something on the small bar slightly to the left of Nashorn's field of vision.

His attention shifted to it.

'Are you ready?' the mechanic asked and waited a few seconds just to up the tension. 'Of course not. No one is ever ready for this.'

With a quick pull, the dirty rag dropped to the floor.

Nashorn gasped and his eyes widened in sheer horror.

Set on the bar, completely covered in blood, was a pair of human feet.

The mechanic paused, enjoying the moment. 'Do you recognize them?'

Fear and tears filled Nashorn's eyes.

'Let me help you with that, then.' The mechanic pulled a thirty-by-twenty-inch mirror from behind the bar, held it up, and tilted it just enough so Nashorn could see his legs reflected in it.

He finally understood why there was so much blood under his chair.

Twenty-Four

Alice's eyes were squinting at the replica sculpture. The expression on her face was a mixture of confusion and surprise. She had no idea what Hunter had seen.

Garcia still hadn't moved. His questioning eyes had shifted from the replica to Hunter, and then to the digital display window at the back of his camera. He flicked back and forth through the last three pictures he'd taken, looking at each one carefully. He saw nothing different.

'OK, I'm officially confused,' he said. 'What did you see, Robert?' He looked at Alice and saw the surprise stamped all over her face as well. 'What *did* you see that the rest of us didn't?'

'You'll have to see it for yourself. I'll show you.' Hunter walked over to his desk and retrieved an LAPD standard-issue Maglite before crossing to exactly where Garcia was still standing. He clicked the flashlight on, held it at waist height and pointed it at the sculpture.

Garcia and Alice turned to look at it. Their confusion thickened.

'OK, and . . . ?' Alice asked.

'Don't look at the sculpture,' Hunter said. 'Look at the wall behind it. At its shadow.'

Simultaneously Garcia and Alice looked at the wall.

Confusion was replaced by surprise.

Alice's jaw dropped open.

'You've gotta be kidding me,' Garcia said.

The shadow that the sculpture cast when a light was shone on it from that particular angle formed two distinct shapes. Two distinct shadow puppets.

'A dog and a bird?' Alice said, stepping closer. She turned and looked at the replica again. 'What the hell?' From where she was standing, the bundled-together body parts looked nothing like a dog or a bird. No wonder no one had seen it before.

Hunter placed the flashlight on the bookshelf just behind him, keeping its beam at the same height and angle. The shadows shifted a little but were still there. He stepped closer to the wall to have a better look.

'So the killer dismembered the victim to create shadow puppets?' Garcia asked. 'It makes even less sense now.'

'He's communicating, Carlos,' Hunter replied. 'There's got to be a hidden meaning behind those images.'

'You mean . . . like a riddle within a riddle? First the sculpture, now the shadow puppets; who knows what will come next. He's given us a jigsaw puzzle?'

Hunter nodded. 'And he wants us to piece it together.' His eyes studied the shadows for a moment longer. He then turned and looked at the cast replica before walking over to the pictures board and retrieving two crime-scene photos of the original sculpture. After analyzing them for a long while, he faced the wall once again. 'What kind of bird do you think that is?' he asked.

'What . . . ? I don't know. A dove probably,' Alice said.

Hunter shook his head. 'A dove doesn't have that kind of beak. That one is longer and rounder. That's a bigger bird.'

'And you think that was intentional?'

Hunter looked back at the sculpture. 'The killer went through a lot of trouble to put this thing together. See the way he severed this finger just at the joint?' He indicated it on the cast replica and then on a photo. 'He then bent it in a specific way just to create that beak? That wasn't by chance.'

'A dove is probably the easiest shadow puppet anyone can create,' Garcia added. 'Probably the first one anyone learns. Even I know how to make one.' He laced his thumbs together, spread his fingers outward while keeping them tightly together, and flapped them like wings. 'See? Robert is right. That's not a dove.'

Alice paused and studied the shadow puppet for a few seconds. 'OK, so if you're right about the beak, then it can't be an eagle or a hawk either. Both of their beaks bend sharply down at the tip, like a hook.'

'That's right,' Hunter agreed.

'It could be a crow,' Garcia said.

'That's what I was thinking,' Hunter said. 'A crow, a raven or even a jackdaw.'

'And you think the type of bird will make a difference?' Alice asked.

'It will.'

'So then, maybe that dog isn't a dog either,' Alice pushed. 'It looks like it's howling at something. The moon, maybe?'

The dog-looking shadow puppet had its head tilted up, with its mouth semi-open.

'That's right. It could be a dog, a wolf, a jackal, a coyote . . . we don't know yet. But those two figures are there for a reason, and we need to find out exactly what they are to understand their meaning. To understand what the killer is trying to tell us.'

Everyone returned their attention to the wall and the shadow images.

'You checked Derek Nicholson's backyard, right?' Hunter asked Garcia.

'Yeah, you know I did.'

'Do you remember seeing a dog house?'

Garcia looked away for a moment while pinching his bottom lip. 'No I don't.'

'Me neither,' Hunter said and checked his watch. He walked back to his desk and started rummaging through the various notes and scraps of paper on it. It took him a minute to find what he was looking for. He reached for his cellphone and dialed the number on the piece of paper in his hand.

'Hello,' a tired female voice answered.

'Ms. Nicholson, this is Detective Hunter. I'm sorry if I'm disturbing you, I'll be as brief as I can. I just need to ask you a quick question concerning your father.'

'Yeah, sure,' Olivia replied, sounding a little more alert.

'Did your father own a dog?'

'Sorry . . . ?'

'Did your father have a pet dog?'

There was a quick two-second pause while the question registered with Olivia.

'Um, no . . . he didn't.'

'Did he ever have one? Maybe when you were younger or after your mother passed away?'

'No. We never had a dog. Mom liked cats more than dogs.'

'How about a bird?' Hunter could almost hear Olivia frown.

'A bird . . . ?'

'Yes, any sort of bird.'

'No we never had a bird either. In fact, we never really had a pet in our house. Why?'

Hunter rubbed the point between his eyebrows with the tip of his finger. 'Just checking up on a few things, Ms. Nicholson.'

'If it helps, my dad used to have an aquarium with a few fish in his office downtown.'

'Fish?'

'Uh-huh. He used to say that watching them swim around was psychologically soothing. It calmed him down before, during and after a big trial.'

Hunter had to agree with that statement. 'OK, thank you very much for your help, Ms. Nicholson. I might be in touch again soon, if that's OK.'

'Of course.'

He disconnected.

'Nothing?' Garcia asked.

'No dogs, no birds, no house pets, just a few fish in an aquarium in his law office. The connection is somewhere else.'

Right at that moment, Captain Blake pushed the door to their office open. She didn't knock. She never did. She was in such a rush she didn't notice the shadow puppets on the wall.

'You're not going to believe this, but he did it again.'

Everyone frowned.

The captain nodded at the cast replica. 'We've got another one of those.'

Twenty-Five

Marina Del Rey is just a stone's throw away from Venice Beach, near the mouth of the Ballona Creek. It's one of the largest man-made small-boat harbors in the United States, and home to nineteen marinas. It can hold up to 5,300 boats.

Even at that time of night, with sirens and flashing police lights, it took them forty-five minutes to overcome the traffic and cross from the PAB to the harbor. Garcia drove.

They made a left into Tahiti Way, and took the fourth right to reach the parking lot just behind the New World Cinema, where several police vehicles were blocking the walkway access to Dock A-1000 in Marina Harbor. A large crowd had already gathered around the police perimeter. News vans, reporters and photographers seemed to be everywhere. To get closer Garcia had to slowly zigzag around all the cars and blast his siren at several pedestrians.

As they stooped under the crime-scene tape, the officer in charge approached them.

'Are you from Homicide?' The officer was in his late forties, about five eight, with a shaved head and a thick mustache. He spoke with a husky voice, as if he was fighting off a cold.

Hunter and Garcia nodded and showed the officer their credentials. He acknowledged them and turned to face the walkway access. 'Follow me. The boat in question is the last one all the way to the left.' He started walking towards it.

Hunter and Garcia followed.

The lampposts that lit the long walkway were few and far between, shrouding the whole path with shadows.

'I'm Officer Rogers with the West Bureau. My partner and I were first at the scene,' the officer continued. 'We were responding to a 911 call. Apparently somebody had their stereo on full volume for quite a while, blasting out loud heavy-metal music. Someone from one of the neighboring boats decided to go knocking to ask if the music could be turned down. She knocked, got no reply, so she boarded the boat. The lights were off, but the cabin was lit up by a few candles. Like setting the mood for a romantic dinner, you know what I mean?' Rogers shook his head. 'Poor woman, she ended up walking into the worst nightmare of her life.' He paused and ran a hand over his mustache. 'Why would anyone do something like that to another human being? That's the sickest fucking shit I've ever seen, and I'll tell you, I've seen some disgusting crap in my life.'

'She . . . ?' Hunter asked.

'Excuse me?'

'You said *she* ended up walking into the worst nightmare of her life.'

'Oh yeah. Name is Leanne Ashman, twenty-five years old. Her boyfriend owns that yacht right there.' He pointed to a large white-and-blue boat. The name on its freeboard read *Sonhador*. It was harbored two spaces from the last boat.

'Boyfriend not around?' Hunter asked.

'He is now. He's with her in his yacht. Don't worry, there's an officer with them.'

'Did you talk to her?'

'Yeah, but just to get the gist of what happened. Better if I leave that kind thing to you Homicide dicks.'

'So she was on her boyfriend's boat alone?' Garcia asked.

'Yep. She was preparing a romantic dinner – candlelight, champagne, soft music, you know what I'm talking about? He was coming over later tonight.'

They reached the last boat. Crime-scene tape blocked the entrance to the walkway plank leading onboard. Three other officers were hanging around the area. Hunter read the expression on their faces as pure anger.

'Who turned off the music?' Hunter asked.

'What?'

'You said that there was loud heavy-metal music playing. There's none now. Who turned it off?'

'I did,' Rogers replied. 'The stereo's remote control was on a chair by the cabin door. And don't worry, I didn't touch it. I used my flashlight to press the button.'

'Good work.'

'By the way, the song was on a loop – track number three on the CD. I noticed it before turning it off.'

'The song was on a loop?'

'That's right, playing over and over again.'

'And you're sure it was only one song, not the entire CD?'

'That's what I said. Song number three.' Rogers shook his head again. 'I hate rock music. The devil's soundtrack, if you ask me.'

Garcia looked at Hunter and gave him a slight shrug. He knew how much his partner enjoyed rock music.

Rogers adjusted his cap. 'So, who would you like us to allow up here?'

Hunter and Garcia frowned.

'Forensics, of course, but anyone else? Any other detectives?'

Hunter subtly shook his head. 'I don't follow you.'

'Well, soon this place will be heaving with angry cops.'

Confusion was still stamped across both detectives' faces.

'The victim,' Rogers explained. 'His name was Andrew Nashorn. He was one of us. He was an LAPD cop.'

Twenty-Six

Hunter and Garcia slipped on a brand new pair of latex gloves and plastic shoe covers. They both pulled out their Maglites before crossing the gangplank onto the boat. As they boarded, Hunter paused and looked around the deck. He saw no footprints, no blood drippings or splatters, no signs of any struggle.

Garcia was already on the phone to the Operations office, requesting that a basic file on Andrew Nashorn be sent to his cellphone. A more detailed file could wait until later.

From starboard, where he was standing, Hunter could see more police vehicles with flashing lights arriving at the parking lot. Rogers was right, there was nothing that would rattle a police officer in the United States more than a cop-killer. Police bureaus in LA had their differences, sometimes even a little rivalry. Some departments didn't really care for each other, and some of their detectives and officers didn't see eye to eye. But every cop, every department, every bureau would come together like the closest of families whenever someone with a badge was murdered. Rage would spread through every police station in Los Angeles like celebrity gossip in Hollywood.

'If this really is the same killer,' Garcia said, coming off his cell. 'The shit will hit the *jet engine*, Robert. First a DA's prosecutor, and now a cop? Whoever this killer is, he's got balls.'

Garcia was right, and Hunter also knew that the pressure on them and their investigation, and the need for answers, was about to increase a hundredfold. As he turned towards the boat's cabin, he heard footsteps coming from the board-walk outside.

'I came as fast as I could,' Doctor Hove said, flashing her credentials at the three officers at the foot of the gangplank. Before boarding, she too slipped on a pair of latex gloves and shoe covers. 'What have we got? Does it really look like the work of the same perp?' She pulled her loose chestnut hair back and tied it up in a ponytail before tucking it under a surgical cap she'd retrieved from her bag.

The initial priority on a crime scene was always the forensic investigation, but Doctor Hove knew that, when-ever possible, Hunter liked to get a feel for the scene with the body *in situ*, before it was disturbed in any way.

'We haven't gone down to the cabin yet,' Hunter said. 'We've been here less than two minutes.'

Just like Hunter, Doctor Hove paused and looked around the deck. She carried her own Maglite. 'OK, let's go look at this.'

Five narrow wooden steps led them down into the boat's small cabin. The door was open, and the weak light inside came from six stick candles. They had pretty much burnt down to the end.

No one entered the room. All three of them gathered at the two last steps that led into the cabin.

For several seconds no one said a word. Their eyes taking in the horrifying picture before them. As with the first crime scene, it was hard to know where to start. The place was bathed in blood. Large pools covered most of the floor, and thick, runny splashes decorated the walls and the sparse furniture; but this time there were several footmark-like disturbances around the entire area.

An unpleasant sour smell seemed to hit everyone at the same time, and as if by mutual agreement, their hands moved to their faces to cover their noses.

'Sweet Jesus,' Garcia whispered. His unblinking stare was locked on the far end of the room. 'He took off the head this time.'

Twenty-Seven

All eyes followed Garcia's gaze.

Next to the kitchenette right at back of the cabin, a naked male body sat on a wooden chair. It was headless, armless and caked in blood. His knees were slightly bent, placing his lower legs just under the chair's seat. His feet had also been severed at the ankles.

Hunter was the first to spot the head. It was sitting on a low coffee table, just behind a pot plant. Nashorn's mouth was wide open, as if the last terrified scream was still to come out. His now-milky eyes had sunk deeper into his skull, indicating that he'd been dead for over an hour. But the stare was still in them. A long, distant, disbelieving and frightened stare. The stare of someone who knew he would die an agonizing death. Hunter followed it. It ended at what they were dreading. A new sculpture created with the victim's body parts. It was sitting on a tall breakfast bar against the corner.

It took Garcia and Doctor Hove a few seconds to notice it.

'Oh shit!' Garcia whispered, focusing his flashlight on the sculpture.

'I guess the answer to my previous question is – *yes*, it's got to be the same perpetrator,' the doctor said.

Hunter moved the focus of his Maglite to the floor, and one by one they entered the room, being careful to avoid the blood pools as much as they could. Hunter picked up a strange, stinging smell in the air. He knew he'd smelled it before, but with the cocktail of scents inside that cabin, it was impossible for him to identify it.

'OK to turn on the lights, doc?' Garcia asked.

'Uh-huh.' She nodded.

Garcia hit the switch.

The ceiling light flickered twice before coming on. Its intensity just slightly stronger than the candles.

Doctor Hove crouched down by the door, her attention on the first large pool of blood. She dipped the tip of her index finger in it, and then rubbed it against her thumb to check for viscosity. Its strong, metallic smell burned at her nose but she didn't even flinch. Standing up, she walked around the outer perimeter towards the chair and the decapitated and dismembered body.

Hunter made his way to the coffee table where the head had been left. Intense, unsettling fear was etched all over the victim's face, while streaks of splashed blood colored it like war paint. Hunter bent over and examined the mouth. Unlike the first victim, Nashorn's tongue hadn't been cut off. It had recoiled back, almost touching the tonsils, but it was still there. There was enormous damage to the left side of the face. An exposed fracture showed at the jaw, with a piece of bone, a quarter of an inch wide and covered in blood, protruding through the skin.

'Rigor mortis hasn't really started yet,' the doctor said. 'I'd say he's been dead for less than three hours.'

'That's because the killer wanted us to find the victim fast,' Hunter said.

Doctor Hove looked at him curiously.

'The officer first at the scene said that the stereo was on, blasting rock music.'

'The killer left it on?'

'Who else?' Garcia said. 'He wanted to call attention to the boat. He knew someone would soon complain, come knocking or something.'

'That's right.' Hunter doubled back to the cabin's entrance. Just like Officer Rogers had said, a small, black remote control sat on a chair by the door. 'The officer said track three was on a loop.'

'Just track three?' The doctor looked around and found the stereo at the back, on the small bar.

'That's what he said.'

'Let's hear it,' she said.

Hunter queued song three and pressed play.

Extremely loud music filled the boat. First a bass guitar, then a drum beat, quickly followed by keyboards. A few bars later vocals and electric guitars kicked in.

'Damn that's loud,' Garcia said, covering his ears.

Doctor Hove winced.

Hunter turned it down, but let it play.

'I know this song,' the doctor said, frowning and searching her mind.

Hunter nodded. 'It's a rock band called Faith No More. It looks like our killer has a sense of humor.'

'Why?' Garcia asked.

'This is one of their most famous songs,' Hunter explained. 'Quite old – late 1980s I think. It's called "Falling to Pieces". And the chorus talks about someone falling to pieces and asking to be put back together again. Metaphorically, of course.'

Garcia and Doctor Hove looked at each other.

'Here it comes,' Hunter said. 'You can listen to it yourselves.'

Instinctively Garcia and Doctor Hove turned towards the stereo and listened. When the chorus finished, Hunter pressed stop.

Silence took over for an instant.

'How did you know that?' the doctor asked. 'And don't tell me that you read a lot.'

Hunter shrugged. 'I like rock music. I used to love this album.'

'This guy's gotta be deranged or something,' Garcia said, taking a step back. 'How sick does anyone have to be to do something like this . . .' he lifted his hands and looked around the place, '. . . and have a sense of humor about it?'

Neither Hunter nor Doctor Hove said a word.

Twenty-Eight

The long silence was interrupted by footsteps and voices coming from outside. Hunter, Garcia and Doctor Hove turned and faced the cabin's entrance. A second later two forensic agents dressed in white, hooded coveralls and carrying metal briefcases appeared at the door.

'Can you give us a minute, Glen,' Doctor Hove said, lifting her right hand before the agents entered the cabin.

Glen Egan and Shawna Ross stopped by the steps.

'We just want to check a few things in here first,' the doctor continued. 'You can start up on the deck if you want.'

'No problem, doc.' They turned and went back up to the deck above.

'Deranged or not,' Doctor Hove continued. 'This killer knows what he's doing.' Her attention had returned to the mutilated body on the chair. 'This time he used needle and thread to close both brachial arteries and contain the bleeding, and it looks like he did a good job too.' She looked under the chair. Both of Nashorn's legs had been bandaged at the ankles, where his feet had been cut off. 'And for some reason, the killer dressed the leg wounds.'

Hunter moved closer to have a better look. 'That's strange,' he commented, and all of a sudden caught another noseful of the strange, stinging smell.

'Yes, that's very strange,' the doctor agreed.

Garcia retrieved the CD from the stereo and placed it in a plastic evidence bag. The CD case was on a shelf together with other CDs. Garcia quickly looked through them. They were mostly from rock bands from the eighties and nineties.

Hunter finally moved towards the new sculpture. It was even more sinister and creepy than the first one.

This time the arms had been severed from the body just below the shoulders, and then again at the elbow joints to produce four distinct pieces. Both forearms had been bundled together with wire, inside wrist against inside wrist, and placed in an upright position. The hands were opened outwards awkwardly, palms up, giving the impression that they were ready to catch a flying baseball. The thumbs were twisted out of shape, clearly broken. All the other fingers were missing. They'd been severed at the knuckles and tightly bundled together two by two, using wire and a strong bonding agent to form four separate pieces. But the killer made the pieces look almost identical by carving them into strange figures – chunky and round at the top, curved at the center, and skinny at the bottom. They were then placed on the breakfast bar, about a foot away from the hands. Two of the figures were standing upright. The other two were lying down, one on top of each other.

'So what you think that is this time?' Garcia asked, stepping closer. 'A crocodile?'

Doctor Hove's eyebrows arched, surprised. 'This time . . . ? You figured out what the first sculpture means?'

'We haven't figured out its meaning yet,' Hunter said.

'But we now know what the sculpture is supposed to create,' Garcia added.

'Create . . . ?'

Garcia stole a peek at Hunter before pulling a face. 'The sculpture creates shadow puppets on the wall.'

'I'm sorry?'

Garcia nodded. 'Yep, you heard it right, doc,' he confirmed. 'Shadow puppets. Quite neatly done, too. The one from the first crime scene cast a dog and a bird shadow onto the wall.' He paused. 'Or something to that effect.'

Doctor Hove looked like she was waiting for one of the detectives to burst out laughing.

Neither did.

'We discovered it by chance,' Hunter said. 'Just minutes before we got the call to come to the marina. We haven't had a chance to properly analyze it yet.' He quickly ran Doctor Hove through what had happened back in his office.

'And it looks like a dog and a bird?'

'That's right.'

Her green eyes moved to the sculpture on the breakfast bar. 'And you're sure that wasn't just a fluke?'

Both detectives shook their heads.

'The images are too perfect for it to have been a fluke or a coincidence,' Hunter said.

'So now you have to figure out what this dog and this bird mean?'

'Exactly,' Garcia said. 'The killer is playing charades with us, doc. Giving us a riddle within a riddle. Something that could mean absolutely nothing. He could be laughing at us right now. Making us go around in circles trying to figure out if there really is a meaning behind Scooby-Doo and Tweety Bird. Meanwhile, he's off on his dismembering rampage.'

'Wait.' Doctor Hove lifted a hand. 'The images look like cartoons?'

'No they don't,' Garcia clarified. 'I apologize for my crap sense of humor.'

The doctor looked at Hunter and pointed at the sculpture. 'So if you're right, that thing should give us another shadow puppet.'

'Probably.'

If there were a device inside that boat cabin that could measure tension, its gauge would have gone through the roof.

'OK, let's check it out right now, then,' the doctor said, her curiosity so intense it was almost visible. She clicked her flashlight back on before walking over to the light switch and flicking it off.

Hunter and Garcia also turned their Maglites back on. They spent the next few minutes going around the sickening sculpture, illuminating it from all sides and checking the shadows it projected against the wall.

They got nothing – no animals, no objects, no words.

That was when Hunter's gaze went back to Nashorn's head on the coffee table. Something about the way it had been positioned caught his attention. It was looking directly at the sculpture, but from a low, diagonal angle, looking up at it.

'Let me try something.' Hunter turned his Maglite back on and repositioned himself, directing his flashlight beam back at the sculpture but from the exact same angle as Nashorn's stare.

'Maybe the killer is showing us how to look at it.'

'By positioning the victim's head?' the doctor asked, looking a little dubious.

'Who knows? I wouldn't put anything past this monster.'

They all paused and contemplated the strange shadows that were now cast onto the wall behind the sculpture.

Doctor Hove's entire body tingled as if it'd been electrified, turning her skin into gooseflesh.

'I'll be damned.'

Twenty-Nine

There must've been at least a dozen police vehicles parked around the lot behind the New World Cinema building in Marina Harbor. The curious crowd that had gathered was now substantial, and the number of news vans and reporters had doubled in the last hour.

'Excuse me,' a young woman in her mid-twenties asked the mechanic, who was standing towards the back of the crowd, leisurely observing the police and media circus unfold. 'Do you know what happened here?' She spoke with a Midwestern accent. Maybe Missouri or Wisconsin. 'Has a boat been stolen?'

The mechanic chuckled at the woman's naivety and turned to face her.

'I don't think you'd get this many cops and TV vans around here just for a stolen boat. Not even in Los Angeles.'

The woman's eyes widened a fraction. 'Someone was murdered?' Her voice lifted with excitement.

The mechanic held the suspense for a moment and then nodded. 'Yeah. Inside that last boat right at the end of the dock.'

The woman went on tiptoe in an effort to catch a glimpse of the boat. She saw nothing other than the backs of the heads of fellow curious onlookers. 'Have they brought the body out yet?' she asked, moving from side to side, still trying to see something.

'I don't think so.'

'Have you been here long?'

The mechanic nodded. 'I guess you could say that.'

'Gee, I wonder what happened.'

The mechanic had read somewhere once that most people were fascinated with death. The more vicious and gruesome, the more they wanted to know about it and the more they wanted to see. Some scientists attributed it to a violent primal instinct – dormant in some, but very active in many. Some psychologists believed it was related to the obsession humans have with trying to understand death and what happens afterwards.

'I heard he was decapitated,' the mechanic said, testing the woman's morbid curiosity.

'No way.' She got more agitated, going up on the tips of her toes and craning her neck like a meerkat as she tried to see beyond the crowd.

'That's what I heard,' the mechanic continued. 'And that the whole boat was washed with blood. Pretty sick, apparently.'

'Mother of God,' the woman said, bringing a hand to her mouth.

'Yeah, welcome to LA.'

She looked disgusted for a couple of seconds, until her eyes caught a glimpse of a police officer just ahead of them. She then bounced on her toes with enthusiasm like a kid who'd just been told she'd be going to Disneyworld for the first time. 'Oh, there's a cop, let's go ask him.'

'No, I'm OK. My work here is done. I've got to go anyway.'

'I can't believe you're not curious.'

'I don't think there's anything that cop can tell me that I don't already know.'

The woman frowned at the words but seemed too excited to give them much thought. 'Well, I'll ask him anyway. I wanna know.'

The mechanic nodded and stepped back into the crowd.

The woman pushed through and approached the officer.

Neither she, the officer, nor anyone else in the crowd noticed the tiny bloodstains on the mechanic's trouser hems.

Thirty

It was close to 1 a.m. when Hunter finally got back to his apartment. He desperately wanted a shower. There was so much blood inside that boat cabin that, despite his protective-wear, he felt as if his skin, even his soul, had been stained by it.

He closed his eyes, leaned head first against the white tiles, and allowed the strong, hot shower jet to massage the tense muscles of his neck and shoulders. He slowly ran a hand through his hair. The tips of his fingers grazed the deep, ugly scar on his nape and he paused, feeling the rough, lumpy skin. A reminder of how determined and deadly an evil mind could be. Not that Hunter needed any reminding. Though it happened a few years ago, his encounter with the monster the press called the Crucifix Killer was as fresh in his mind as any memories of a minute ago. The painful scar on his nape forever telling him how close he and Garcia had come to death.

The problem was, no matter what he did, no matter how fast or hard the police worked, they just couldn't catch them quick enough. As soon as they tracked down one manic killer and sent him to prison, two, three, four more were already roaming the streets. The balance was tipped the wrong way. Ironic how the City of Angels seemed to attract more evil than any other city in the USA.

Hunter had no idea how long he stood there, but by the time he'd pushed the memory aside and turned off the water, his tanned skin had gone a dark shade of pink, and his fingertips looked like prunes.

He dried his body, wrapped himself in a clean white towel and returned to his living room. His drinks cabinet was small, but held an impressive connoisseur's collection of single-malt Scotch whisky. He needed something strong but soothing and comforting. He didn't search for long, making his choice as soon as his eyes rested on the bottle of Balvenie 15-year-old single barrel.

Hunter poured himself a generous dose, added a tiny drop of water, and dumped himself in the black leatherette sofa. He tried his best not to think about the case, but the images of everything he had seen in the past few days had nowhere else to go. They kept on spinning around and tumbling over themselves inside his head. They'd just found out about the images behind the first sculpture, but before they'd even had a chance to try and figure out the real meaning of those images, the killer had given them a second victim, a second sculpture and a second set of images that, at first look, made even less sense than the original one. He had no idea where to start.

Hunter had a long sip of his whisky and concentrated on its robust flavor. The higher alcohol content gave the malt a bit of extra muscle, without affecting its rich, fruity taste.

A few minutes and another dose later and Hunter was beginning to relax, when his cellphone rang.

Instinctively he checked his watch. 'You've got to be joking.' He snapped the clamshell phone open and brought it to his ear. 'Detective Hunter.'

'Robert, it's Alice.'

Hunter's brow creased. 'Alice . . . ? What's going on?'

'Well, I was just wondering if maybe you'd like to go get a drink.'

'A drink . . . ? It's almost two in the morning.'

'I know that.'

'So you probably also know that this is Los Angeles, where pretty much every boozer closes at two.'

'Yeah, I know that too.'

'Well, doesn't that defeat the idea of going for a drink at this time?'

A short pause.

'Maybe you could invite me over and we could have a drink in your apartment?'

Hunter frowned at the phone. 'You want to come to my apartment and have a drink?'

'Well, I'm just around the corner. I could be there in . . . two minutes or less.'

Reflexively Hunter's gaze moved to his living-room window. He hadn't had time to check, but he was sure Alice Beaumont didn't live around this part of town. Two minutes from his apartment in any direction was pretty much slap-bang in the middle of nowhere, or gangtown.

He hesitated.

'I think I found something, Robert,' Alice said.

'Found what?'

'I think I might know what those shadow puppets mean.'

Thirty-One

Hunter changed into an old pair of jeans and a white T-shirt, the cotton fabric stretching thin against his broad shoulders and hugging his torso like a second skin. Around his living room, papers, magazines and books were strewn just about everywhere. He thought about tidying it up a little, but before he had a chance to start, there was a knock at the door. He reached for his Heckler & Koch USP .45 Tactical pistol, checked the safety, and secured it tightly between the waistband of his jeans and his lower back before approaching the door.

Three new knocks.

'Robert? It's me, Alice,' she called from outside.

Hunter undid the lock and the security chain and pulled the door open halfway.

Alice Beaumont stood at his doorway holding a black leather briefcase. She had lost the ponytail from earlier in the day, and her loose blonde hair shone, even in the dim light of Hunter's hallway. She certainly didn't look like a lawyer now. Her conservative suit had been substituted by skintight blue jeans, a black cotton blouse cut low at the front, and square-heeled, black knee-high boots. Her makeup was still subtle, but it now carried a hint of daring. Her perfume was floral and provocative.

Hunter regarded her in silence.

'Is it OK if I come in, or shall we talk out here in the hallway?'

'Yeah, sorry.' Hunter stepped to his right and showed her inside. The apartment was in semi-darkness. Only the desk lamp on Hunter's breakfast table was on.

Alice looked around the small room. It didn't take her long to cover the entire area with her eyes.

'Nice . . . cozy,' she said. There was no sarcasm in her voice. 'Could do with a little tidy up, though.'

Hunter closed the door behind him and moved past her. 'Shouldn't you be sleeping?'

Alice chuckled. 'After everything that happened today? The discovery of the shadow puppets? You guys rushing out of the office on a possible second homicide from the same killer?' She shook her head. 'There was no way I could get my mind to disconnect.'

Hunter couldn't argue with that. His eyes moved away from her face.

Alice waited but Hunter said nothing else.

'Your captain was right, wasn't she? He did it again.'

Hunter nodded.

'Another sculpture?'

Hunter nodded.

Alice let go of a tight breath. 'I could really use a drink.' She placed her briefcase on the floor.

'I'm afraid I don't have much of a selection. Scotch or beer. That's all the choice you get.'

'Beer will do just fine.'

Hunter grabbed a cold one from the fridge, unscrewed its top and handed it to her.

Alice stared at the bottle for a beat and then back at Hunter. 'Could I have a glass?'

Hunter pointed to the cupboard above the sink. 'Suit yourself.'

Alice opened it and found two mugs, one tall Coca-Cola glass, four shooters and half a dozen whisky tumblers. She reached for the tall glass.

They returned to the living room and Hunter poured himself a new measure of Scotch.

'You said you think you know what the shadow puppets mean. I'm listening.'

Alice had a sip of her beer. 'OK, after you and Carlos left the office, I couldn't stop thinking about the sculpture and the shadow puppets. What you said made sense, that understanding the meaning behind those images had to be directly related to which type of bird and canine they were supposed to represent.'

Hunter nodded and offered her a seat by indicating the sofa. She took it and reached for her briefcase.

Hunter pulled one of the pine chairs by the breakfast table, turned it around and sat down with the backrest between his legs.

'OK, so while you guys were out I went to work,' Alice continued. 'I searched the net for all different types of canines and medium-sized "chunky" birds. Like you suggested – crow, raven, jackdaw, whatever. I compared their images . . .' She paused and corrected herself, 'Actually, their *silhouettes*, to what we had.'

'And what did you get?'

'A whole bunch of stuff.' She opened her briefcase and retrieved a few sheets of paper. 'Well, individually, each one of the animals I checked has several metaphoric meanings. The more I looked, the more complicated it got. When I started looking at different cultures and different time periods, I was simply overrun with symbolisms.'

Hunter's eyebrow arched inquisitively.

'For example,' Alice placed a sheet of paper down on the coffee table between them, 'to several Native American Indian tribes, coyotes and wolves could mean anything from a god, to an evil being, or even the devil himself. It's no coincidence that from cartoons to serious works of art, most drawings of demons – Satan, Beelzebub, Azazel, or any devilish creature you care to name – resemble canine figures.'

Hunter reached for the sheet and skimmed through the information on it.

'In Egyptian mythology, Anubis is a jackal-headed god associated with mummification and the *afterlife*.'

Hunter nodded. 'In the Old Kingdom pyramid texts, Anubis was the most important god of the dead. Later substituted by Osiris.'

It was Alice's turn to look at him inquisitively.

Hunter shrugged. 'I read a lot.'

Alice carried on. 'Several cultures around the globe believe the raven to be a creature that comes from darkness, just like the bat. As such, it symbolizes mystery, confusion, anger, hate, aggression or anything that's usually associated with the dark side.' She placed a second sheet of paper on the coffee table.

Hunter reached for it.

'A common meaning associated with the raven or the crow is . . .' she paused like a schoolteacher to raise her students' curiosity, '. . . death. Some cultures used to send a crow or a raven to an enemy to indicate that they had been marked for death. Sometimes the entire bird, sometimes just their heads.' She took a deep breath. 'In South and Central America some still do.' She indicated the passages on the sheet in Hunter's hands.

Hunter acknowledged it and had another sip of his Scotch. He finished reading the rest of the document in silence.

'Before I move on I need to ask you something,' Alice said.

'Shoot.'

'Why in the world would the killer create that sculpture and the shadow puppets? I mean, if he's trying to communicate, why not just leave a message written on the wall as he did for that poor nurse? Why go to all that trouble, risk the amount of time it takes to create something like that, just to leave us a clue?'

Hunter slowly rotated his neck from left to right. Even after the shower and a couple of drinks, his trapezius muscle still felt stiff.

'*Usually*, when criminals deliberately leave a clue behind, it is for one of two main reasons,' he said. 'One: to taunt and challenge the police. They believe they are too smart. They believe they can't be caught. To them, it's like a game. The clues up the stakes, make it more challenging.'

'They believe they are God?' she asked, remembering what her arts expert friend had told them.

'Sometimes, yes.'

She chewed on those words for a moment. 'What's the second main reason?'

'To confuse, to throw the police off the scent, so to speak. The clues will have nothing to do with anything, but *we* don't know that, and they know that if they leave something apparently significant behind, the police will have to investigate. It's protocol. Valuable time *will* be spent trying to decipher whatever bogus cryptic clue they left behind.'

'And the more cryptic, the more time is lost by the police.'

'Yes.'

Alice read Hunter's expression. 'But you don't believe that theory applies here, do you?'

'Not the second one, but there's a chance that this killer is delusional enough to think he's invincible, to think he can't be caught. To think he's God.'

'But you're not convinced.'

'No,' Hunter said without hesitation.

'So what's on your mind?'

Hunter looked down at his glass, and then back at Alice. 'I think this killer is leaving clues behind because it's important to him. Because the sculpture and the shadow puppets have a specific and very important meaning in all this. We don't know what it is yet, but I just know they do. Something directly related to the killer, the victim, the act itself, or all of it. The sculpture and the shadow puppets weren't created just for fun, just to challenge the police or to throw us off course. They weren't created just to show us how clever the killer is. They were created because without them the act wouldn't be complete. Not to the killer.'

Alice shifted on her seat. Something about that statement made her really uneasy.

'So what else have you found out?'

Alice placed a third and final sheet of paper on the coffee table. 'Something very interesting. And I think it might be the answer we're looking for.'

Hunter leaned forward, his eyes scanning the sheet.

'I remembered that Derek was into mythology. He was always reading about it. And he never missed an opportunity to make an analogy, or quote a mythological passage, be it in a regular conversation, or during a statement in a court of law. So I took a shot in the dark.'

'And ... ?'

'I found out that the *coyote* shares many traits with the mythological figure of the *raven*,' Alice said, 'speed, cleverness, stealth ... but when both figures are combined, that most commonly means ...' She indicated on the sheet.

Hunter read the line.

'*The figure of the coyote, when paired with that of the raven, mainly symbolizes a trickster, a liar, a deceiver ... a creature or person who betrays.*'

Thirty-Two

A police siren wailing in the distance disrupted the eerie silence that had taken over Hunter's living room. Alice tried her best to read Hunter's face, but failed.

'The killer has got to be telling us about his feelings for Derek,' Alice said. 'He has to be telling us that he considered Derek to be a liar, a deceiver, a betrayer.' She lifted a hand before Hunter could respond. 'I know what you're going to say. Derek was a lawyer, and many people consider lawyers to be deceivers and liars by trade.'

Hunter said nothing.

'But Derek Nicholson wasn't your regular, everyday liability or personal-injury lawyer. He was a state prosecutor. He had *one* client, and *one* client only – the State of California. His job was to prosecute criminals who'd been apprehended by the LAPD or the California State Police. And his fee didn't depend on a win or a loss, or on how much he could bleed out of the counterpart.'

Hunter still said nothing.

Alice was getting animated. 'The point is, I don't think the killer is alluding to himself as a deceiver. He's got to be referring to Derek, but not simply because he was a lawyer. It's got to be because of something else. Something that we haven't found out yet.'

'Did you get anywhere with the list of criminals Nicholson prosecuted over the years?' Hunter asked.

'No breakthroughs yet,' Alice said, getting up. 'Nothing about the ones who've been released or the relatives of the ones who are still inside suggests that they'd be capable of anything of this magnitude. But if they're out there, I'll find them. Do you mind if I grab another beer?' She pointed to the kitchen.

'Make yourself at home.'

Alice opened Hunter's fridge and frowned at how empty it was. 'Wow, what do you live on? Protein drinks, Scotch and . . .' she quickly scanned the kitchen, '. . . air?'

'The diet of champions,' Hunter replied. 'How about the ones Nicholson didn't send to prison? The ones who escaped being sentenced because of a technicality or whatever? How about the victims of the accused? The ones who felt the state didn't perform its duty. Could any of them be capable of retaliating? Has anyone ever directly blamed Nicholson for losing a case?'

Alice poured the new beer into her glass and returned to the living room. 'I must admit I haven't had the time to check that yet. But trust me, if there is a link between Derek's murder and any of his cases, I'll find it.'

Hunter's gaze stayed on Alice. Something about the natural, self-assured way she talked told him that her confidence wasn't just cockiness and bravado, which was surprising, given that she worked for the cockiest, most self-glorifying law-enforcement office he knew in all of California – the district attorney's office. No, her confidence wasn't just shallow words. It was exactly that; confidence in herself and what she knew she could do.

'The second victim . . .' Alice asked, sipping her beer. 'Was he also a lawyer, a prosecutor?'

Hunter got up and moved towards the window. 'Worse. He was an LAPD cop.'

Alice's eyes widened in surprise as her brain already started measuring the consequences.

'His name was Andrew Nashorn,' Hunter said.

'Was he a detective?'

'He was until eight years ago.'

She paused midway through a sip of her beer. 'What happened?'

'Nashorn was shot in his abdomen while pursuing a suspect in Inglewood. That resulted in a collapsed lung, a month in hospital and six on sick leave. After that, he couldn't be out in the field anymore. He chose to stay with the South Bureau's Operations Support Division.'

'And how long was he a detective for?'

Hunter could see she was catching on quick. 'Ten years.'

Alice's face seemed to sparkle with the same thought Hunter had had hours earlier.

'He and Derek could be case-related,' she said. 'Or even more than a single case. Ten years is a long time catching criminals.'

Hunter agreed.

'Derek was a prosecutor for twenty-six years.' Alice's thoughts were now on full flow. 'Chances are he did prosecute at least one perpetrator that . . . what's his name again?'

'Andrew Nashorn.'

'That Nashorn apprehended.'

Hunter agreed again.

'That could be our first real link. Maybe even a breakthrough. I'll cross-reference it and see what I get.'

Hunter checked his watch. 'Yes, but not now. We both need to get some sleep.'

Alice nodded but didn't move. Her eyes were fixed on Hunter. 'You said there was a second sculpture.'

Hunter stayed silent.

'Did you have a chance to check it? Did it also cast a shadow puppet onto the wall?'

'Alice, did you hear what I said? We need to get some sleep. And *you* need to disconnect for at least a few hours.'

'It did, didn't it? We've got something else now. A new clue from the killer. A new shadow puppet. What is it?'

'We don't know yet,' Hunter lied.

'Sure you do,' Alice challenged. 'Why don't you wanna tell me?'

'Because if I do, you're going to go back home, you're going to get on your computer and you're going to search the net until you come up with something. And *we need to get some sleep*. That means *you* too. Drop it. Give your brain a few hours' rest or else you *will* burn out.'

Alice paused in front of a sideboard in Hunter's living room where a few picture frames were neatly arranged. She reached for the one right at the back – a young and smiley Hunter in his college graduation gown. His father was standing next to him. The expression on his face told the whole world that on that day no one was a prouder dad than he was. She smiled at it and placed it back on the sideboard before facing Hunter again. 'You don't remember me at all, do you?'

Thirty-Three

Hunter didn't flinch, didn't say a word. His stare was chained to Alice. His mind was chasing a memory but he had no idea where to find it.

The first time he saw her yesterday morning, something about her had struck him as familiar, but he couldn't place her. Things had happened so fast yesterday that he'd never had a chance to check her out. He played it as calm as he could.

'Should I remember you?'

Alice flicked her hair to one side.

'I suppose not. I've never been very memorable.'

If she was looking for sympathy or pity, Hunter gave her none.

'You were a prodigy kid,' she said. 'You went to Mirman, a special school for gifted children. If I remember correctly, the words that were used were "his IQ is off the charts". Even for a prodigy kid.'

Hunter leaned against the window and felt the bulk of his pistol press harder against his lower back.

From a very early age it had been easy to see that Hunter was different. He could figure things out faster than most, and while the average student was expected to graduate from middle school at the age of fourteen, Hunter had finished the entire lower- and mid-school curriculum by his eleventh birthday. It hadn't been long before his school principal had referred him to the Mirman School for the Gifted in Mulholland Drive.

'But even a special school's curriculum wasn't hard enough for you. You finished all four years of high school in what, two?'

His memory of her was returning to him. 'You went to Mirman as well,' he said.

Alice nodded. 'I was in your class when you first started.' She smiled. 'But you didn't stay long. In a matter of months you'd completed the entire year's program, and they moved you up to the next grade. You made Mirman's curriculum seem so easy that they found it hard to place you. So for you, four years of high school became two, right?'

Hunter gave her a subtle shrug.

'I know because my father was a teacher there.'

Hunter watched her. Her eyes became melancholic.

'He taught Philosophy.'

'Mr. Gellar?' Hunter said. 'Mr. Anton Gellar?' Suddenly the clear image of this girl – petite, chubby, dark hair, cheeks full of freckles and shiny braces on her teeth came to his mind. He remembered talking to her a couple of times when he was fourteen or fifteen. She was terribly shy, but very bright and sweet.

'That's him,' Alice replied. 'Mr. Gellar, that was Dad. You remember him then?'

'He was a fantastic teacher.'

Alice looked down at her feet. 'I know.'

'You changed your hair.'

Alice laughed. 'I've been a blonde for over fifteen years now.'

'Your freckles are gone.'

She looked at Hunter with a pleased expression, as if saying – *You do remember me!* 'No, they're still here. Only hidden under a tan and expert makeup. The braces are gone forever, though, and I lost quite a bit of weight.' Alice had one more sip of her beer. 'My father was really proud of you. I think you were his best student – ever.'

Hunter said nothing.

'I heard you went to Stanford University on a scholarship and flew through their curriculum as well. You got your PhD in Criminal Behavior Analysis and Biopsychology when you were twenty-three.'

Still silence.

'Now that's impressive, even for a Mirman student. My father used to say that you'd probably become the President of the United States someday, or a scholar of some kind. Definitely someone famous.' She shifted her weight from leg to leg. 'But I guess you preferred the thrill of chasing psychopaths, huh?'

No answer.

'You also passed on five invitations to join the FBI. But your PhD thesis paper became, and still is, mandatory reading at their NCAVC.' She paused and looked at Hunter's graduation photo again. 'When I left Mirman, I went to MIT.'

Most people would've said those words with a massive injection of pride. The Massachusetts Institute of Technology is the most prestigious and famous research university in the USA, and probably the world. Alice seemed almost embarrassed.

'I've got a PhD in Electrical Engineering and Computer Science.'

'I guess you preferred the thrill of working as a research specialist for the Los Angeles DA, huh?' Hunter said.

Alice chuckled. 'Touché. The truth is I got tired of hacking into systems for the government. That's who I worked for before.'

'Special branch?'

It was Alice's turn to be silent. Hunter didn't push.

'Don't kid yourself,' he said. 'You still work for the government.'

'I guess I do,' she admitted. 'But the cause is different.'

'More noble?'

She hesitated for an instant. 'I guess you can say that.'

'But you're still hacking into systems,' Hunter challenged.

Alice tilted her head to one side in a subtle but charming way. 'Sometimes. And I'm sorry. That's how I know so much about you. And about what you did after you left Mirman. When DA Bradley told me I'd be working with a homicide detective named Robert Hunter, all these memories from Mirman came rushing back into my head. I just had to find out what you'd been up to since then.'

'You hacked into the FBI database?' Hunter asked. He knew the fact that he'd passed on precisely *five* invitations to join the FBI wasn't exactly free information.

'Not all their files are kept under the most secure encryption algorithms,' Alice said. 'In fact, very few are. Getting into any system isn't that hard if you know what you're doing. Once inside, it's just a question of knowing how to navigate.'

'And my guess is that you are a pretty good navigator.'

Alice shrugged. 'We're all good at something.'

Hunter finished his Scotch. 'How's your father?'

Her eyes went sad. 'He's not with us anymore.'

'I'm sorry to hear that.'

'It was ten years ago, but thank you.' Her gaze moved to a new picture frame – Hunter as a young kid, maybe ten or eleven years old, she thought. Shorts, skinny legs, white T-shirt, ultra-skinny arms, and straight hair that was way too long. Just like she remembered him. 'You used to be geeky, and as thin as a stickman. Your nickname was . . .'

'Toothpick,' Hunter helped her.

'That's right. Gosh you bulked up like the Hulk.' Her eyes settled on his pecs. 'What do you bench press, the whole gym?'

Hunter said nothing.

'You know,' Alice said, with a slight head movement, 'I'm not surprised by your decision to become a police officer.'

'And why is that?'

Alice had a slow sip of her beer. 'Because you always liked defending and helping people.'

Hunter looked uncertain.

'My best male friend in school was a kid called Steve MacKay. Do you remember him? Thick glasses, blonde curly hair, even thinner and shyer than you were. In school they called him Loose Noodle.'

Hunter nodded. 'Yes, I remember him.'

'Do you remember defending him after school one day?'

No answer.

'He was walking back to his house just a couple of blocks away from Mirman. These three bigger street kids turned up and started pushing him around. They wanted to take his new tennis shoes and whatever money he had on him. You came out of nowhere, punched one of them in the face, and told Steve to run.'

'Yeah, I remember,' Hunter said after a brief silence.

Alice smiled awkwardly. 'They beat the living hell out of you. What were you thinking, that you could take on three bigger and stronger kids just like that?'

'It worked. The plan was to get their attention away from the small kid so he could get away.'

'And then what?'

Hunter looked away. 'OK, I agree. The plan wasn't well thought through, but it still worked. I knew I could take the beating. I didn't think the other kid could.'

Alice's new smile was full of tenderness. 'Steve hid behind a car and watched everything. He said you just wouldn't stay down. They'd beat you to the floor, you'd get up. They'd beat you down again, you'd get up again, bleeding and all. Steve said that after the fourth or fifth time, the bigger kids just gave up and walked away.'

'I'm glad they did. I don't know how much more I could've taken.' Hunter turned his head, showing Alice his left ear, and folding its top half down. 'This scar is from that beating. They almost tore my ear off.'

Alice looked at the lumpy scar that contoured Hunter's ear. 'You were in your senior year and you took a hell of a beating for someone you barely knew. A kid two grades below you. I really don't know anyone else who would've done that.'

Hunter went silent, and Alice couldn't tell if he was embarrassed or not.

'You know,' she finally said. 'Despite the fact that you were geeky, skinny as hell, and dressed like a rock-and-roll reject on a bad day, a lot of girls in Mirman had a crush on you.'

'Did you?' Hunter pinned her down with an interrogating stare.

Alice bit her bottom lip and looked away. 'I guess you're right. We both need to get some sleep.' She finished the rest of her beer in one long gulp, grabbed her briefcase and crossed to the door.

'I'll see you in the office,' Hunter said.

Alice's reply was a simple smile.

Thirty-Four

Captain Blake was standing next to Garcia, her mouth half-open, her unflinching gaze welded to the shadow images on the wall. This was the first time she had seen them.

'This can't be serious,' she said after a long silence.

Garcia said nothing.

'You're telling me that some maniac killer out there broke into a Los Angeles prosecutor's home, butchered him into pieces, bundled his severed body parts together to create some godforsaken artifact, just so he could cast a shadow puppet of a dog and a bird onto the wall?'

'It's a coyote and a raven,' Hunter said as he entered the room. He'd managed just a little over four hours of sleep, which for him was as good as it got.

'What?' Captain Blake turned and faced him. 'What the hell are you talking about, Robert? And does it matter what species they are?'

'Good morning to you too, Captain.'

She indicated the replica sculpture, and then the shadow puppets on the wall. 'Does that look like a good morning to anyone?'

'A coyote and a raven?' Garcia asked, his eyes narrowing at the shadow puppets.

Hunter took off his jacket and fired up his computer.

'How did you find that out?' Garcia insisted.

'I didn't. Alice did.'

As if on cue, Alice Beaumont pushed the door open and stepped into the office. Her hair was back in the same slick ponytail she had the day before, but this time the look was complemented by an expensive-looking pair of designer sunglasses. She was wearing an impeccably fitted light gray suit with a white charmeuse blouse and a dainty white gold necklace.

All eyes shot towards her.

She looked up and paused, feeling the heat of everyone's stare. 'Good . . . morning . . . everyone. Did I do something wrong?'

'I just told them you found out about the shadow puppets being a coyote and a raven,' Hunter said. 'Maybe you should explain the meaning behind them.'

Alice placed her briefcase next to her improvised desk and ran Captain Blake and Garcia through everything she had found out the night before. When she was done, a thoughtful silence enveloped the room for an instant.

'It makes sense,' Garcia eventually agreed.

Captain Blake folded her arms over her chest, still measuring everything.

'The way I see it,' Alice continued, 'if the killer considered Derek to be a liar, then to generate this kind of payback, it must be connected to something that happened during one of his cases. It must've been an alleged lie that caused somebody to lose his or her freedom, or that sent someone to death row. Someone the killer considered innocent. Or even, as Robert suggested, an alleged lie that meant someone *didn't* get the justice he or she felt they deserved. Someone who felt betrayed by the system and by Derek in particular.'

Captain Blake was still pondering everything. 'And do we have any names yet? Anyone Derek Nicholson put away that would fit this theory?' Her stare went back to Alice.

'Not yet,' Alice said, not shying away from the captain's hard gaze, 'but we will before the end of the day.'

'You better make that before the end of the morning,' Captain Blake came straight back at her. 'DA Bradley said you were the best he had, so be the best.' She threw a copy of this morning's *LA Times* on Hunter's desk. The headline read 'SCULPTURE OF TERROR. LAPD OFFICER MURDERED AND CHOPPED TO PIECES'.

Hunter skimmed through the article. It mentioned how Nashorn's boat cabin had been bathed in blood, his decapitated and dismembered body left on a chair facing the door, and his severed body parts used to create some sort of grotesque and sickening sculpture-like arrangement. It also mentioned that loud heavy-metal music was left playing on the stereo. No real details were given.

'The TV edition of that story made the news bulletin late last night and again early this morning,' Captain Blake blurted as she started pacing the room. 'I woke up this morning to find a newspaper reporter together with a photographer pretty much camping out in front of my house. Goddamn it, as soon as I find out which officer at the scene leaked that kind of information to the press, he's on a no return trip to shit-licking duty.'

'I don't think a cop leaked the story, Captain,' Hunter said.

'Who, then? The woman from the neighboring boat who found the body?'

Hunter shook his head. 'She was too distressed to talk to anyone last night. It took me half an hour just to get a few pieces of information out of her. Her subconscious was already starting to block her memory. Pretty much the only thing she remembered was the blood. And there was an officer with her until she was sedated and fell asleep. Reporters didn't talk to her.'

'Well, they talked to someone.'

'Probably the marina security guard on duty last night.' Hunter reached for his notebook. 'A Mr. Curtis Lodeiro, fifty-five years old. Lives in Maywood. In her panic, Leanne Ashman ran back to the marina's security hut after leaving Nashorn's boat. While she called 911, Mr. Lodeiro went over to check it. He had a better look at the crime scene than she did.'

'Great. I had the DA on the phone to me this morning even before I got out of bed. And his call was quickly followed by Nashorn's captain, and then by the Chief of Police. With the press now sniffing around this story like starving dogs, the heat for results in this investigation has just hit DEFCON-1 status. And everybody wants some goddamn answers pronto. If it was attention this killer was looking for, one thing is for sure: he's got every cop in this city thirsty for his blood.'

Thirty-Five

Alice reached for the newspaper on Hunter's desk and read through the article.

'This is all speculation,' she said, breaking the rough silence that had descended onto the room. 'Pure and simple. There are two pictures; one is a shot from the outside of the boat and the other a colored portrait of Andrew Nashorn. There are no witnesses or detectives' statements. No interviews. All the details, if we can call them that, are flimsy at best.'

'Well, thank you for stating the obvious,' Captain Blake shot back, glaring at her. 'Speculation or not, it won't change the fact that a story has hit the papers and the airwaves. It's out there now. Which is all that's needed for people to start panicking. They don't need any proof. All they need is to read it in the newspaper or see it on TV. Now everybody is looking at us for answers, and as always, they want them by *yesterday*.'

Alice had no reply. She knew how right the captain was. She'd seen it many times in courts of law. Attorneys throwing statements at the jurors that they knew would be objected to by the opposing side, sustained by the judge, and consequently struck from the record. But it made no difference. The statement was out there. Struck from the records or not, the jurors had heard it. And that was all that was needed to get their thoughts moving in the direction that suited the attorney in question.

Captain Blake faced Hunter. 'OK, talk to me, Robert. If you're right about those shadow puppets, then it means Nashorn's boat has given us something new.'

Hunter looked at Garcia, who was now standing by the pictures board, organizing the new crime-scene photographs into distinct groups.

'It has,' Garcia replied.

Captain Blake and Alice moved closer, scrutinizing every photo as Garcia pinned them up to the large white board. The prints showed the cabin, the blood on its walls and floors, the body left on the chair, Nashorn's head on the coffee table, and the new sculpture on the tall breakfast bar.

'Jesus Christ!' Alice said, touching her lips with the tips of her fingers. In spite of her horror, she was too transfixed to look away.

Captain Blake's expert gaze moved from picture to picture, drinking in every detail. In her long career, she was sure she'd seen every ugly face crime and murder had to offer, but what she'd seen in the past three days had fragmented that notion to little pieces and pushed the boundaries to a new level. Evil seemed to be able to reinvent itself very easily.

Her attention finally settled on the group of photographs that showed the new sculpture – arms, hands, fingers and feet covered in blood; dissected, and then put back together in a totally incoherent and horrific way.

'Did the killer use wire and superglue again?' Alice asked, squinting at the photo on the far right of the board.

'That's right,' Garcia confirmed.

'But no message on the wall this time.'

'There was no reason for it,' Hunter said. 'The message left on Derek Nicholson's wall wasn't directly related to the crime committed. It was a spur-of-the-moment thing.'

'OK, I can understand that, but why do it?' Alice insisted. 'Why leave such a message? Just to psychologically destroy that poor girl?'

'That message wasn't only intended for the nurse.'

Hunter's words caused Alice to do a double take. 'Excuse me?'

'It was also intended for us.'

'What?' Captain Blake finally turned away from the board. 'What the hell are you talking about, Robert?'

'Determination, resolve, commitment,' Hunter said, but offered nothing else.

'Keep on talking, Big Brain,' the captain urged him, 'I'll tell you when we've caught up.'

Hunter was used to the spikes in the captain's intonation.

'It was the killer's way of telling us that nothing would've stopped him, Captain,' he clarified. 'And if a completely innocent person had walked in on him, and in any shape or form endangered his objective, he would've killed her as well. No remorse. No guilt. No second thoughts.'

'It confirms that there was nothing random about Nicholson's murder,' Garcia took over. 'Robert used the operative word – *objective*. And our killer sure as hell had one: to kill Derek Nicholson and use his body parts to create his morbid piece. The nurse was never part of the plan, and she didn't endanger his goal. She would have, if she'd turned on the lights.'

'And that also tells us a very important thing,' Hunter stepped in again. 'That this killer isn't prone to panicking.'

'How's that?' Alice asked.

'Exactly because he didn't kill her.' He wandered over to the window, stretching his stiff arms and back as he went. 'When the killer heard the nurse walking back into the house that night, he was composed enough to stop what he was doing, turn off the lights in Nicholson's room and wait. Her fate was in her hands, not his.'

'Whereas most perps surprised by a third party would either have panicked and gone for her,' the captain caught on, 'or fled the scene without finishing what they started.'

'Correct. The message on the wall wasn't planned. It was an afterthought. But the killer saw it as a chance to . . . warn us of his resolve, his commitment, despite its psychologically destructive nature.' Hunter undid the latch and pushed the window open. 'We didn't realize that at first, because we had no way of knowing he would kill again.'

'This guy is very confident, and he has no problem boasting about it,' Garcia said, pinning the last photograph onto the board. 'Last night, instead of a written message, he decided to show us that he also has a sense of humor.'

'The heavy metal song he left playing,' Captain Blake commented.

Alice flinched. 'I read that in the article. What's that about?'

'The killer left the stereo in Nashorn's boat on – full blast,' Garcia explained. 'Same song playing on an endless loop.'

'And where's the sense of humor in that?' she asked with a slight shake of the head.

'The song the killer chose is an old song called "Falling to Pieces",' Hunter told her.

'And the lyrics in the chorus say something about someone falling to pieces, and asking to be put back together again,' Garcia added.

Alice paused a beat.

'So he's laughing at us,' Captain Blake said, leaning against Garcia's desk, anger in her voice and a steely glint in her eyes. 'Not only is this perp crazy enough to kill a state prosecutor and an LAPD cop, but he's also bold enough to taunt us with messages written on walls, songs with double meanings, sculptures made from the flesh of his victims and shadow puppets. He's making this his own private goddamn circus.' Her eyes flashed fire. 'And *we* are the clowns.'

No one replied.

Alice had redirected her attention back to the pictures board. 'What did you get when you shone a light on this?' She indicated one of the photographs of the new sculpture. 'I know you're not waiting for the lab to produce another replica to find out. You checked it last night, didn't you?'

'Yes.'

'So what did you get?' Captain Blake this time. 'Shadow puppets of the Four Horsemen of the Apocalypse?'

Garcia walked back to his desk, reached for an A4 brown-paper envelope and retrieved a single photograph from inside. He turned it over and showed it to the room.

'We got this.'

Thirty-Six

Garcia crossed to the pictures board and pinned the new photograph onto it, just below the group containing the images of the sculpture found in Andrew Nashorn's boat.

Captain Blake and Alice both craned their necks and squinted at the same time, as if in a synchronized dance move.

'We used a forensic power light against the new sculpture to cast the shadows onto the wall,' Hunter explained. 'That's how we managed to photograph the shadows. There was no need for a camera flash. It took us a while to find the correct angle. In fact, the killer was the one who showed us how exactly to look at it. He left us a clue.'

Neither Captain Blake nor Alice seemed to be paying attention to Hunter's words. For them, during the past few seconds it was as if the whole world had disappeared, and all that was left was the photograph Garcia had just stuck to the board.

The captain was the first to speak. Her words came out slowly, surrounded by doubt. 'What the hell is this?'

Hunter folded his arms and once again looked at the image that had taken over his mind since he first set eyes on it last night. 'What does it look like to you, Captain?'

She took a deep breath. The way Andrew Nashorn's arms

had been bundled together – inside wrist against inside wrist, hands open outwards as if ready to catch a flying ball, cast a silhouette onto the wall that looked just like a distorted face. The thumbs, broken and twisted out of shape, pointing up, made it looked like crooked horns were growing out of its head.

'Like a goddamn giant monster's head with horns, or something. Maybe some sort of devil.' The captain squinted harder and shook her head, hardly believing her eyes as she stared at the shadow images cast by the four figures that had been created by bundling all the severed fingers together two by two.

The way the killer had expertly carved out the figures – round and chunky at the top, curved at the center, and skinny at the bottom – and then placed them in relation to the light source was mesmerizing. A true work of a sick genius. With the light being shone from that specific angle, the shadows cast by the two upright figures look just like two people standing up, viewed from a profile perspective. The shadows cast by the two lying down figures also resembled two people, lying on top of each other on the floor.

'And what is this devil doing?' Captain Blake asked. 'Staring at four people? Two standing up and two on the floor?'

Hunter shrugged. 'You see exactly the same thing as we do, Captain.'

Captain Blake was getting fidgety. 'Great! And all that crap means what, exactly?'

'Another riddle within a riddle,' Garcia said, returning to his desk.

'We don't know yet, Captain,' Hunter admitted. 'We

haven't had time to analyze and research the image and its connotations. We only got this last night, remember?'

'The shadow that looks like a head with horns could represent the killer,' Alice offered, pointing at the photograph and stealing everyone's attention. 'That's why it's so much bigger than the four other images. The crooked thumbs casting horn shadows and making the whole figure look like a devil's head obviously characterizes evil. Maybe he believes he's possessed by an evil being or something.' She shrugged as she considered the rest of the image. 'And one could maybe argue that the reason he's looking down at four other figures is because they represent his . . .' Her voice trailed off and she shuddered, scaring herself with the thought that swirled around in her head.

'Victims,' Hunter finished the sentence for her.

Captain Blake almost choked. 'Wait up. So you're saying that this new riddle, this new shadow image, could represent the killer and his agenda?' The annoyed edge was still in her voice.

Hunter turned his palms up in a subtle 'who knows' gesture. 'As I've said, we don't know yet, Captain.'

'But it makes sense, doesn't it?' Alice pushed. 'Maybe that's why there are two figures already lying down, look.' She stepped closer and indicated it on the photograph. 'They could represent the two victims we already have: Derek Nicholson and Andrew Nashorn. Maybe he's telling us he's got his sights set on at least two more. You were discussing this just a moment ago, weren't you?' She addressed Captain Blake. 'Saying that this killer was cocky enough to taunt the investigation with messages and songs and sculptures and shadow puppets. So why not be bold enough to tell us that he's going after two more victims? We know he's confident. We know he's big-headed.' She tapped her index finger over the oversized image of what looked like a head with horns. 'We know he thinks he can't be stopped.'

The captain lifted her hand to keep Alice from going any further. 'Slow down a second, Professor Sunshine. Yesterday, with the first sculpture, you were debating whether the killer might be delusional enough to think he is God. Now we think he's changed his mind and he's telling us he's the devil? Evil personified? We're skating all over the rink here.'

'I'm pretty sure I've said this before,' Hunter interrupted, his voice firmer this time, 'but we don't know what the meaning behind those shadow images is yet, Captain. All this is just guesswork based on nothing other than our own imaginations and interpretations. Even what we think we know about the images behind the first sculpture might be wrong. We have no way of being sure.'

'So find a way,' the captain barked as she moved towards the door. 'And get me something more concrete than damn guesswork.' She scowled at Alice. 'And you better get crack-ing on that list of names, Miss DA's-Best-Researcher.' She exited the room, purposefully allowing the door to slam behind her.

A fraction of a second later the phone on Hunter's desk rang and he reached for it.

'Detective Hunter,' he said into the mouthpiece and listened for about ten seconds before frowning so intensely his eyebrows almost touched. 'I'm on my way down.'

Thirty-Seven

The famous Parker Center building had been the headquarters of the Los Angeles Police Department since 1954. In 2009, the entire operation was moved from the old building, located at 150 North Los Angeles Street, to its new, half-a-million-square-feet site just south of City Hall. The new Police Administration Building houses over ten different LAPD divisions, including Vice, Juvenile, Commercial Crimes, Narcotics and the Robbery Homicide Division. It's no wonder that its reception hall is always overflowing with people – civilians and officers alike.

It didn't take long for Hunter to spot her. Olivia Nicholson was sitting in one of the many fixed-row plastic seats near the building's floor-to-ceiling glass entrance doors. Dressed in a conservative black ruffle chiffon dress and black stiletto-heel court shoes, she stood out from the much rougher-looking crowds around her like a bright laser beam. Her oversized sunglasses were perched high on her small and pointy nose.

'Ms. Nicholson,' Hunter said, offering his hand.

She stood up but didn't reciprocate the gesture. 'Detective, could we talk?' Her voice was as steady as she could manage.

'Of course.' Hunter lowered his hand and quickly scanned

the hall. 'If you follow me, I'll find us a quiet spot.' He guided her through the crowd and used his security card to green-light one of the magnetic turnstiles, allowing them deeper into the building. As they stepped into an elevator, Olivia moved her sunglasses to her head, pinning her loose blonde hair back, away from her face. Her eyes were still bloodshot. Hunter identified it as the compound effect of crying and lack of sleep. Her makeup expertly hid the dark circles under her eyes, but she still looked exhausted. Not knowing who her father's killer was was eating at her. Hunter could tell.

Hunter pressed the button for the first floor, where the press-conference and meeting rooms were located. With the pictures board, the replica sculpture, and case files strewn about everywhere, his office was definitely out of bounds. The interrogation rooms on the second floor were too ominous, with their metal tables, bland walls, large two-way mirrors and no windows. Either the main press-conference room, or any of the smaller meeting rooms were a much better choice.

They rode the elevator up in silence and exited into a long, wide and brightly lit corridor. Hunter took the lead, and tried the door to the first meeting room on the right. It was unlocked and empty. He flicked on the lights and showed Olivia inside.

'How can I help you, Ms. Nicholson?' he asked, indicating one of the five seats around the small, oblong-shaped table.

Olivia didn't sit down. Instead, she unzipped her handbag, retrieved a copy of the morning paper and placed it on the table. 'Is this what happened to my father?' Her lower eyelids looked like water dams overflowing with tears, and it was only a matter of seconds before they burst. 'Did the person who killed him use his body parts to create some sort of sick sculpture?'

Hunter kept his hands by his side and his voice even. 'That article isn't about your father's murder.'

'But it's about a very similar murder,' Olivia snapped back like a sharp switchblade. 'A murder that, according to this article, you are investigating. Is that true?'

Hunter held her stare. 'Yes.'

'DA Bradley assured me that everyone was doing everything they could to bring the monster who broke into my father's home to justice. He assured me that the case detectives were the best in the force, and that they were working *exclusively* on my father's murder investigation. So the only logical conclusion is that these murders must be connected.' She searched Hunter's face for an answer. Found none. 'Please don't insult me by saying that those questions you asked me and my sister the other day about sculptures were because you found a metal piece from a broken sculpture in my father's house.'

Hunter's face didn't give anything away, but he knew the game was up. 'Please, Ms. Nicholson, have a seat.' This time he pulled a chair out for her, moving into Stage One in dealing with an individual whose emotions have taken over: take simple, unchallenging steps to reduce their anxiety. If possible sit them down – a seating position is always more relaxing than a standing one – physically and emotionally.

'Please,' Hunter insisted.

Olivia finally sat down.

Hunter approached the cooler in the corner, filled two plastic cups with ice-cold water, and brought them back to the table before sitting down opposite her.

Stage Two was to give the person a drink. This would get the digestive system working, giving the body one more activity to occupy itself with and distract from an approaching panic attack. A cold drink on a hot day cools the body down, which is a very comforting feeling.

Hunter had a sip of his water first, leading the way. Seconds later Olivia did the same.

'I apologize if I gave you the impression that I was lying to you and your sister,' Hunter said, maintaining eye contact. 'It really wasn't my intention.'

'But you did lie about the sculpture piece found in my dad's room.' Her words were shadowed by hurt.

Hunter nodded once. 'Knowing the details of a crime scene, or the exact cruelty used by sociopaths, never helped anyone deal with their grief. It often has the opposite effect. Trust me on this, Ms. Nicholson. I've seen it many times. Me questioning you and your sister that day was already hard enough for you. There was no reason for me to add to your pain. Your answers wouldn't have changed if I'd told you the truth about the sculpture.'

Olivia had another sip of her water, returned the cup to the table and kept her gaze on it, obviously measuring her next words. 'What was it?' she finally said.

Hunter made a face as if he didn't understand.

'What was the sculpture? What was created with my father's . . .' She couldn't finish the sentence. Tears were stalking her eyes again.

'Nothing identifiable,' Hunter replied. 'It was a shapeless form.'

'Was there a meaning to it?'

The last thing Hunter wanted to do was to contribute any more to Olivia's pain, but he saw no way out of it, he had to lie again; he couldn't compromise the investigation, and he had no proof that what Alice had found was the real meaning behind the shadow puppets. 'If there is, we haven't found it yet.'

Thirty-Eight

Olivia was studying Hunter's face. She kept her large green eyes locked on his for five long seconds before deciding that he was telling the truth. She reached for her cup but didn't bring it to her mouth. Just a nervous reaction to keep her hands from shaking. It didn't work.

'I haven't been able to sleep for the past couple of days,' Olivia said, looking away, finding a neutral spot on the far wall and holding it for a moment. 'I'd rather stay awake than close my eyes and deal with what my dreams have brought me.'

Hunter said nothing. He doubted it would be any comfort to Olivia if she knew that he'd been living that exact way for most of his life.

'We knew Dad didn't have long to live, and as hard as it might've been, I thought Allison and I had prepared ourselves for it.' She shook her head and her bottom lip quivered. 'It turns out that we weren't as prepared as we thought. But having to find out details of what really happened this way.' She pushed the newspaper towards Hunter and said nothing else.

'Once again, I'm sorry,' Hunter said, not even glancing at the paper. 'I had to make a decision. And I made it based on my experience in dealing with grieving families of homicide victims.'

Hunter's words were delivered in a tender and non-patronizing tone, and Olivia seemed to pick up on it.

'What happened yesterday . . .' Her gaze quickly moved to the newspaper on the table, and then back to Hunter. 'Is there really a connection?'

Olivia's question simply brought forward something that Hunter had no way of avoiding.

'From what we've been able to gather so far, we believe that both crimes were committed by the same person, yes,' he replied and quickly followed it up. 'You obviously read the article.' He nodded at the paper.

'Yes.'

'Does the name Andrew Nashorn ring any bells?'

'No,' she replied with a subtle headshake.

'You don't recognize him at all from the newspaper photo?'

'When I read the article this morning, I asked myself that exact same question, Detective.' Olivia shook her head and looked away again. 'Neither his name nor his face ring any bells. If my father knew him, I don't recall him ever mentioning him. And I certainly don't recall seeing him anywhere.'

Hunter acknowledged it with a slight tilt of his head.

Olivia finished her water and pinned Hunter down with a pleading stare. 'You don't have much so far, do you, Detective?' She paused for a fraction of a second. 'And please don't lie to me again.' Her voice almost croaked.

Hunter waited, debating what to tell her. The anticipation in Olivia's demeanor was almost electric. 'At the moment we have bits and pieces that we're trying to piece together. But we *are* making progress,' he assured her. 'I can't really reveal much more than that. I'm sorry. I hope you understand.'

Olivia sat in silence for a long, uncomfortable moment. 'I know that nothing will ever bring my father back, Detective, but the thought that the monster who took him is still out there . . . still killing . . . and he might never be brought to justice, makes me sick. Please don't let that happen.'

Thirty-Nine

Mid-morning, and no one had any doubts that today would be another spectacular summer's day. Clear blue skies had paired up with bright biting sunlight, and though it was still early, the heat had built up enough to feel almost oppressive. The A/C in Garcia's car was back on full blast as he and Hunter made their way to the coroner's office. Doctor Hove had finished with Andrew Nashorn's autopsy.

Hunter sat in silence, his elbow resting against the door handle, his chin on his knuckles. Though he seemed to be observing the cacophony of morning traffic, his thoughts were somewhere else. Olivia's heavy words were still ringing in his ears. Her anguish was as real to him as it was to her and her sister.

Just weeks after Hunter received his PhD in Criminal Behavior Analysis and Biopsychology, his father, who worked as a security guard for a downtown branch of the Bank of America, took a bullet to the chest during a robbery gone disastrously wrong. He fought for twelve weeks in a coma. And during that whole time, Hunter never left his side, believing that his companionship, the sound of his voice, or maybe even his touch, could help his father find the strength to fight back. He had been wrong.

Despite two of the robbers being shot dead at the bank,

the three others who made up the rest of the gang escaped. They were never caught.

The bitter taste of knowing that his father's killers were never brought to justice had never left Hunter's mouth. And that knowledge kept the pain alive year after year. He didn't want the same to happen to Olivia and Allison Nicholson.

'Everything OK?' Garcia asked, pulling Hunter away from his thoughts.

It took Hunter a few seconds to drag his eyes from the traffic outside and look at his partner. 'Yeah, yeah. I was just . . .'

'. . . Away somewhere else?' Garcia nodded. 'I know.' He smiled and let the moment settle. 'You know, the longer this killer stays at a crime scene, the higher the risk of getting caught, so I'd say he wouldn't stay a second longer than what was needed.'

Hunter agreed.

'But those sculptures, those shadow images, they are not the work of a beginner. I've never seen anything so intricate. This killer didn't just chop and twist body parts right there and then hope he got it right first time out. He must've practiced, and a lot.'

'I have no doubt he has.'

'Using what? Dummies?'

'Anything, really, Carlos,' Hunter said. 'He could create models out of wire, papier mâché, cast, even regular toy dolls with flexible rubber arms and legs. The kind you'd find in any convenience store.'

'So this guy sits at home, playing with dolls before going out and ripping his victims apart. This city is fucked up, you know?'

'This world is fucked up,' Hunter corrected him.

'Andrew Nashorn's file finally came through. It's on the backseat.' Garcia quickly jerked his head back.

'Have you read it?'

'Yep, reads like any other detective's résumé I've ever read. Nashorn was born in El Granada, San Mateo County in Northern California, where he lived until he was twelve or thirteen or something like that. His parents moved to Los Angeles then. His father was an accountant, and got offered a better job down here. His mother was a church-going housewife.'

They came up to a red traffic light. Hunter leaned over and grabbed the file from the backseat.

'Nashorn was a regular school kid,' Garcia continued. 'Not the best student, but not the worst either. Though he lived in Maywood, he attended high school in Bell. He never went to college. Worked several odd jobs for a few years after high school before deciding to join the force. It took him a while to make detective.'

'Twelve years,' Hunter said, reading from the file. 'Failed the exam four times.'

'He's a widower. No kids.'

Hunter nodded. 'Got married when he was twenty-six,' he said, reading from the file. 'His wife died less than three years later.'

'Yeah, I read that. Some odd heart condition they never even knew she had.'

'Cardiomyopathy,' Hunter confirmed. 'Heart-muscle disease. He never remarried.'

'From what I gathered he was a good cop,' Garcia said, shifting his car into gear and turning left into North Mission Road. 'Put plenty of dirtbags away during his detective years. And then what every cop dreads happened. He got shot on the job, pursuing some lowlife street mugger down in Inglewood.' Garcia shook his head. 'Poor guy. In Brazil they'd say he was born with his butt facing the sun covered in chili powder.'

Carlos Garcia was born in São Paulo, Brazil. The son of a Brazilian federal agent and an American history teacher, he and his mother moved to Los Angeles when Garcia was only ten years old, after his parents' marriage collapsed. Even though he'd lived in America most of his life, Garcia could speak Portuguese like a true Brazilian, and he still visited the country every few years.

Hunter looked at his partner and screwed up his face. 'What? What the hell does that mean?'

'It means he was born unlucky, and in Nashorn's case, I think it applies.'

'Really? So what do Brazilians say if they think someone was born lucky? "He was born with his butt facing the moon covered in sugar"?'

'Precisely.' Garcia looked impressed.

'You're kidding?'

'Nope, that'd be pretty much the exact translation.'

'Interesting analogy,' was all Hunter could say. The next couple of pages in Nashorn's file were a brief of the latest investigations Nashorn had been involved with.

'His captain said that he was a man of habits,' Garcia offered. 'Always took his vacation at the same exact time of year – first few days of summer. Always two weeks by himself out in the sea, fishing. He used all his savings to buy that boat. According to his captain, that boat *was* his retirement plan.'

'No girlfriend, no partner.' Hunter was still reading from the file. 'Next of kin are an uncle and aunt who still live in El Granada.'

'Yep, his captain is getting in touch with them.'

Hunter checked the file for Nashorn's home address – an apartment in East LA. A forensic team had already been dispatched there this morning. Last night, they'd found no cellphone, computer, address book, diary, or anything of that sort in Nashorn's boat, and according to his captain there was nothing at his desk either. No personal files in his hard drive. They were checking his work emails. Hunter was hoping something would turn up from Nashorn's apartment search. He closed the file and returned it to the backseat as Garcia pulled into the County Coroner's parking lot.

Forty

Alice Beaumont printed out another document page and placed it on the floor next to the tens of pages that were already there. With Hunter and Garcia out of the office, she had temporarily turned the place into her own private research haven.

She had a quick stab at finding out what the shadow image created by the second sculpture could mean, but after three quarters of an hour searching the net, she had nothing that even remotely excited her. Unlike the first shadow puppets, she found no mythological meaning that could be attached to the entire image. If she broke the image down, then it was easy to link the distorted head with horns to any devil figure she liked, but that didn't explain the four smaller shadow figures created by Nashorn's severed fingers.

Alice wanted to carry on searching, but she knew that, for now, the investigation's priority was to work on the lists of perpetrators Derek Nicholson had put away over the years. If she could find some sort of link to any case Andrew Nashorn had worked on, either as a detective or as a Support Division officer, that could give them the starting point they were so desperately looking for.

Alice sat on the floor with all the printouts surrounding her and started rereading and regrouping them in lots of two, three, four and sometimes five pages.

She had brought her own laptop in with her this morning. She had a feeling she would be needing a few of the powerful development applications she had in her hard drive. And she was right. Hunter had told her to go back five, maybe ten years in her search for perpetrators who'd been released, had escaped, or were out on parole. That gave her way too many names and files to read through. Couple that with all the new names and files she'd got from Andrew Nashorn's investigations, and also a list of original victims who personally blamed Nicholson for losing their case, and she'd need at least a week to get through them all. But that was where her expert computer skills came in.

The first thing Alice did when Hunter and Garcia left was to write a quick application that would read through text files and search for specific names, words, or phrases. The application could also link files together using a variety of criteria. The problem she had was that not all the files were digitized. In fact, about 50 per cent of them were still on paper only. Getting a simple list of names was easy, even going back twenty-six years. But the actual case files only really started being digitized around fifteen years ago. Older cases were being added to the Los Angeles District Attorney's databank as fast as possible, but the sheer number of them, together with a lack of personnel, made the process laborious and very, very slow. The same applied to the LAPD and Andrew Nashorn's cases.

Alice was doing really well with what she had. Her application had already managed to flag and link forty-six documents, but she had yet to start looking into Nashorn's investigations.

Forty-One

Hunter pulled his surgical mask over his nose and mouth and stood to the right of one of the two examination tables inside Special Autopsy Theater One. Garcia was just behind him, arms folded over his chest, shoulders hunched forward as if trying to protect himself from a freezing gust of wind.

As always, the room felt too cold, despite the hot summer's day outside; too somber, no matter how bright the surgical and ceiling lights were; and too macabre, with its stainless-steel tables and counters, its clinical atmosphere, its honeycomb of human-body freezers, and its soul-chilling display of laser-sharp cutting instruments.

'There's no need for the mask, Robert,' Doctor Hove said, a shadow of a smile playing at the corners of her lips. 'There's no risk of contamination and the body doesn't really smell.' She paused, considering her words. 'Maybe just a little bit.'

Though every cadaver inevitably smells due to its natural breakdown of tissues and the explosive growth of bacteria after death; that odor alone never bothered Hunter. Carefully washed prior to the autopsy examination, the body's smell was usually all but gone.

'You do realize that your sense of smell is as dead as fried chicken, don't you, Doc?' Hunter replied, slipping on a brand new pair of latex gloves.

'My husband tells me that every time I cook.' The doctor smiled again and directed both detectives' attention to the two autopsy tables. Nashorn's dismembered body occupied one of them, and his severed body parts the other. Doctor Hove approached the table containing the body parts.

'The official cause of death was heart failure, induced by severe loss of blood. Just like our first victim.'

Hunter and Garcia nodded in silence. The doctor continued.

'I compared the lacerations to the ones on the first victim. They are consistent. The killer used the same cutting device.'

'The electric kitchen carving knife?' Garcia asked.

The doctor nodded. 'But this time the killer did it a little differently.'

'How so?' Hunter asked, moving around to the other side of the table.

'He took the time to try and properly stop the hemorrhage. The feet amputation carries all the signs of a proper Syme's ankle disarticulation.'

'A what?' Garcia questioned.

'It's an ankle amputation procedure named after James Syme,' Doctor Hove clarified. 'He was a Clinical Professor of Surgery at the University of Edinburgh in eighteen-something. He developed an ankle-amputation procedure that is still used today. Anyway, the incisions we have here were made clean across the ankle joints. In accordance with the Syme's ankle-disarticulation guidelines, the arteries were transfixed, and large veins ligated as much as possible, given that the entire procedure was carried out inside a boat cabin without a surgical team. Usually, smaller blood vessels are electrocoagulated during the procedure, but the killer didn't bother with that. Either because he didn't have the equipment, or . . .'

'Because there was no need for it,' Hunter took over. 'He knew the victim would die in a matter of hours, maybe minutes. He just didn't want him to bleed out and die too quickly.'

'I'd have to agree with that,' the doctor said. 'The feet were certainly the first to be amputated. The killer used a compression dressing of fluffs, contoured over the stump and wrapped in place with a bias-cut stockinet. Nicely done.'

'You mean professionally done?' Garcia asked.

'I'd say so, yes. But first, the wounds were covered in cayenne pepper powder.'

'Cayenne pepper?' Garcia's brow furrowed. He thought about it for a second. 'Jesus!'

Hunter's memory immediately took him back to the boat and the strange, stinging smell he picked up inside its cabin. He knew he'd smelled it before, but he hadn't been able to identify it then. 'The pepper wasn't used to add to the pain,' he said, picking up on Garcia's suspicion, and quickly dismissing it. 'It was used to stop the bleeding.'

'Excuse me?'

'Robert is right,' Doctor Hove noted. 'Cayenne pepper has been used as a natural remedy for years. More specifically – a blood clotter.'

Garcia's focus moved to Nashorn's severed feet on the metal table. 'Like coffee powder?'

'Yes, coffee powder can have a very similar effect,' the doctor confirmed. 'Both powders react with the body to equalize blood pressure, meaning an extra gushing of pressure will not be concentrated in the wound area as it normally would be. Blood will quickly clot when the pressure is equalized. It's an old trick, but it works every time. The bandaging has already been sent up to the lab for analysis.'

'Did the killer use the same level of care for the subsequent amputations?' Garcia asked.

Doctor Hove tilted her head to one side and twisted her mouth. 'Kind of. Arteries and large veins in the arms were also ligated, using a thick thread, but as you'll remember, there was no dressing of the wounds. And unlike the feet amputations, cayenne pepper was never used to try and contain the hemorrhage. But what was done would certainly prevent the victim from bleeding out too quickly.'

'We obviously have no toxicology results yet, right?' Hunter said.

'Not yet,' the doctor confirmed. 'In a day or two. My guess is that we'll get the same result for the heart-rate regulating drugs the killer used on his first victim.'

Hunter had the same feeling, but he noticed something else in Doctor Hove's demeanor. Something seemed to be troubling her. 'Is there something else?' he chanced.

Doctor Hove took a deep breath and tucked her hands inside the large pockets on her long white overcoat. 'You know I've been a pathologist for many years, Robert. And when you are a pathologist in a city like LA, you get to see pretty much the worst human beings have to offer, almost on a day-to-day basis. But I'll tell you now, if there's such a thing as pure evil, or a real demon walking amongst us, then this killer is it. And it wouldn't surprise me if, when you catch this guy, you find he's got devil horns on his head.'

Those words stopped Hunter and Garcia dead in their

tracks, the image of the shadow figure cast by the sculpture found in the boat cabin coming back to them like a recurring nightmare.

'Wait.' Garcia lifted his hand before exchanging a quick, unsettling glance with Hunter. 'Why do you say that, Doc?'

The doctor turned around. 'Let me show you why.'

Forty-Two

Alice finished reading through another file and checked her watch. She'd been at it for three and a half hours and she still hadn't found a path she thought was worth pursuing further. She'd already read through thirty-eight of the forty-six initial documents her application had flagged.

She shook her head disapprovingly as she studied the two untouched case-file boxes on her desk. She had no doubt that this time she'd bitten off a lot more than she could chew. She needed a team of readers, and maybe one or two other programmers, to get through those documents by the end of today. Maybe she should go back to searching for a meaning to the shadow image cast by the new sculpture. Maybe she'd have better luck there.

Alice poured herself a fresh cup of coffee and leaned back against the wall. Her eyes rested on the pictures board for a moment, and the brutality of it all made her shiver. How could anyone be this evil? This disturbed? And still be clever enough to come up with the sculptures and the shadow images? Still be clever enough to walk into someone's house or boat, spend hours torturing them, rip them to pieces, and then walk out without being noticed? Without leaving any clues behind, except the ones he wanted the police to find?

Alice forced herself to look away, trying to shut the images out of her mind. Her attention returned to the documents on the floor. The cover pages carried the case number and the accused or convict's name. She stared at them for a while, her brain throwing thoughts around, rummaging through possibilities. She'd already scanned through several cases where Andrew Nashorn had been the lead detective, and a handful where he'd been involved in the investigation, either in a detective capacity, or as a support officer. Almost all of them concerned gang members, muggers, thieves and petty criminals. Individuals who, in her opinion, didn't have what it took to be this killer. She doubted very much she'd find a relation there. But she hadn't even started on the list of victims who might've personally blamed Derek Nicholson and the State of California for losing their case.

She sipped her coffee too quickly, burning the roof of her mouth. Suddenly she paused as her brain spat out a new idea, instigated by the very lack of relation between the lists of names she had.

Back at her computer, Alice called up the code screen for the application she'd written earlier. All she needed were a few alterations here and there and she'd have a new search-and-compare tool. It took her thirty minutes to make all the necessary modifications. She used her security-clearance password to allow her new application to gain access to the Los Angeles District Attorney's database. Hunter had also provided her with a password that allowed her to connect to the LAPD and the national criminal database.

While the program searched away, Alice went back to the files. The application had to connect to, and search, two different databases in two different locations – she was expecting it to take a while. The first results, using her initial search criteria, came back after thirty-five minutes. Thirty-four distinct names. Alice called up their individual case-summary pages and printed them out. She read through them, jotting down notes in the margins as she went along. As she started reading the summary page for search result number twenty-four, she felt a chill envelop her body. She put the page down and quickly shuffled through the remaining pages, looking for the match her application had indicated.

Alice sucked in a startled breath, and it rushed into her lungs like a cold wind.

'OK, now this is very interesting.'

Forty-Three

Doctor Hove redirected Hunter and Garcia's attention back to the first autopsy table and Nashorn's body parts.

'The head was the last part to be severed from his body,' she said, stepping closer, twisting Nashorn's head around and exposing the large wound to the left side of the face. 'But this was the initial manner in which the killer subdued his victim. A very powerful, single blow to the face. Probably using some sort of heavy metal, or thick wooden weapon, like a pipe, a bat or something.'

Garcia rotated his neck uncomfortably from side to side, as if his collar was bothering him.

'His jaw was fractured in three places,' Doctor Hove continued, indicating the exposed mandibula – the same quarter-inch-wide piece of jawbone protruding through the skin that Hunter had identified back in the boat cabin. 'Bone splinters cut into the inside of his mouth. Some perforated his gums like nails. He lost three of his teeth.'

Without anyone noticing, Garcia ran his tongue over his own teeth and fought off a shudder.

'Forensics did find all three in the boat cabin,' the doctor noted.

'So the blow to the face was what knocked him unconscious?' Hunter asked.

'No doubt about that. But unlike the first victim, who was practically bedbound and could offer no resistance to the killer's sadistic wishes, if awake, this victim could've easily fought back. He was in good physical health, considering his age and the fact that one of his lungs worked on a reduced capacity.' Doctor Hove indicated the disjointed body parts on the table. 'The muscles in his arms and legs were strong enough, consistent with regular physical exercise. He kept active.'

'But there are no visible restraining marks on his wrists, or anywhere on his arms,' Hunter said, bending over and studying the body parts on the table a little more closely.

'That's right,' the doctor agreed. 'Forensics also found nothing that suggested the victim was tied to the chair in which he was found, or to anywhere else for that matter.'

'So what you are saying is . . .' Garcia jumped in, '. . . that the victim was unconscious throughout the entire procedure.'

'That would've been the logical conclusion.'

Hunter sensed hesitation in the doctor's voice. 'Would've been?'

'The blow to the face undoubtedly knocked him out, but without being sedated, as soon as the killer started cutting away, the pain would've woken him up.'

'So he was sedated,' Garcia concluded.

'I would've gone with that until we got the toxicology results, if not for this . . .' She pointed to a small piece of bone of about three inches long, which had been placed on the table next to Nashorn's feet.

Hunter looked at it and cocked his head back, a little worried. 'Vertebrae?'

'Cervical vertebrae,' Doctor Hove clarified.

'What?' Garcia bent over to have a closer look.

'Part of the cervical curve,' Hunter said.

'And that means what?'

The doctor faced Garcia. 'OK, let me try to explain this without launching into a long lecture about the cervical or spinal cord. These are vertebrae C5 through to C7.' She indicated the bone fragments on the table again. 'The cervical cord is made up by vertebrae C1 to C7, and it sits right on the top of the spinal column.' She touched the back of Garcia's neck to show its actual position on the human body. 'C1 being the topmost vertebra, up against your skull, and C7 being at the base of the neck – the beginning of the upper back. It's a very sensitive part of the spinal column, and any damage to it can cause paralysis. But that also greatly depends on which vertebra the damage is located around. The closer to the skull you get, the more sensitive, and the more severe the paralysis. Are you with me so far?'

Garcia nodded like a school kid.

'If the damage is right at the top, around vertebra C1, C2, or C3, it can cause tetraplegia – paralysis from the neck down, and a halt of the nervous system – no feeling below the neck. But it can also easily cause impaired breathing, and without the help of a ventilator, death will come very quickly.'

Hunter felt his heart beat faster as he realized what Doctor Hove was about to reveal next.

'Damage around the C4 vertebra, halfway down the cervical cord,' she touched the back of Garcia's neck again, indicating the location, 'can cause tetraplegia and numbness of the nervous system, but it rarely causes impaired breathing.' She paused, measuring the gravity of her words. 'The reason why we have this small section of his spinal cord is because when the victim was decapitated, the incision was made just after vertebra C7 – base of the neck. When I examined the head and neck, I found out that his cervical cord had been ruptured just below vertebra C4. He had been intentionally paralyzed from the neck down. No feeling throughout most of his body.'

Garcia could feel cold sweat starting to run down his back. 'Hold on, Doc. Are you saying the killer paralyzed him?'

'That's exactly what he did.'

'How?'

'Let me show you.'

Doctor Hove reached for Nashorn's decapitated head and turned it around, bringing everyone's attention to its nape. About three and a half inches from the base of the skull was a fresh sideways cut of around one inch long.

'The killer severed his cervical cord with a sharp knife, inserted at the back of his neck.'

'You *are* joking.' Something tightened in Garcia's stomach.

'I'm afraid not even a little bit. As I said, to me this killer is evil personified – a man-demon. Who in this world would've thought of something like this?'

'A stickman,' Hunter said.

Everyone looked at him as if he was from outer space.

'It's called a stickman,' Hunter carried on. 'It was a technique used by sadistic troops during the Vietnam War. It wasn't as precise as this. During the war, soldiers would simply drive a knife through a victim's back and sever the spine at any position. Sometimes the paralysis was from the neck down, sometimes only of the legs, it didn't matter. It meant the victim couldn't fight back.'

'You're not suggesting this killer is a Vietnam veteran, are you?' Garcia asked.

'I'm just saying that the technique isn't new.'

'Due to the proximity of the spinal cord to the skin surface,' Doctor Hove proceeded, 'the cut doesn't need to be very deep. In the case of our victim, if the knife had penetrated an inch or so deeper, it could've cut through his windpipe, and death would've come almost instantaneously.'

'Wow, so there's no doubt this killer really has medical knowledge,' Garcia said, taking a step back.

'In my opinion, no doubt at all,' the doctor confirmed. 'He knew he had to sever the cervical cord at the C4 vertebra to obtain a neck-down paralysis without compromising the respiratory system. And that was precisely what was done. Add that to the almost perfect Syme's ankle-disarticulation procedure, the ligation of the proper veins after the amputations, and the careful dressing of the leg stumps, and this guy could be a surgeon in a hospital.'

Forty-Four

'The killer paralyzed the victim by rupturing his cervical cord with a knife through the back of the neck?' Captain Blake's voice almost faltered as she read from a copy of the autopsy report Garcia had just handed her.

Hunter nodded.

District Attorney Dwayne Bradley was sitting in one of the two leather armchairs in front of Captain Blake's desk. He also had a copy of the report in his hands.

'Wait a second,' he said, shaking his head at the report. 'According to this, a severed cervical cord would also affect the nervous system, leaving the victim numb and insensitive to pain.'

'That's right,' Garcia said.

'So why the hell do it? If the killer wanted the victim to suffer, why take away his sense of feeling? Why numb the pain before cutting him up? It makes no goddamn sense.' His cheeks were already going slightly pink.

'Because for some reason, the killer wanted the victim to go through a different kind of pain,' Hunter said, resting his elbow against the bookcase on the west wall. 'Psychological pain.'

Bradley hesitated for a moment.

'Imagine having to watch your own body being

disfigured and mutilated, your own blood being splattered around the room without feeling a thing, without you being able to react. Imagine having to watch your own death as if it were a film on a screen. You know you're dying, but you can't feel it.'

DA Bradley kept his eyes on Hunter as he measured his words. 'Well, you sure know how to paint a gruesome picture.'

'How long did this go on for?' the Captain asked. 'I mean, the mutilation, the psychological torture?'

'Hard to say. But taking into consideration the time it would take to severe the body parts and restrict the bleeding in the way that was done; over an hour, maybe more.'

'Goddammit,' DA Bradley let out a whispering breath and flipped a page on the report. 'It says here that the time of death is estimated to have been somewhere between four and seven p.m.'

'That's right,' Garcia agreed.

'And the body was discovered around eight o'clock by a girl from a neighboring boat, right?'

'That's right,' Garcia said.

'Did we get anything from the CCTV system at the marina?' Captain Blake asked. 'People walking in and out?'

Garcia chuckled. 'That's what we expected, but they still use an old system. It records onto VHS tapes, if you can believe it. And it's been busted for over two months now.'

'Typical,' the DA commented. 'How about door-to-door, or in this case, boat-to-boat? No one noticed anyone who looked like he didn't belong, leaving that specific dock around the time the loud music started to blast out of the victim's boat?'

'I don't think the killer is that stupid,' Hunter said.

'Stupid? What do you mean?'

'There's no way we can confirm it, but the stereo in Nashorn's boat has a "wake-up" programing facility. My guess is that the killer set the timer to turn the stereo on at least half an hour after he left. If you add to that the fact that people would only really start getting annoyed with the loud music after it been going on for some time, by the time people started to take notice, the killer was long gone.'

The captain closed the report in front of her and pushed it to the edge of her desk. 'How about the victim's apartment? Did we get anything? Computer, cellphone?'

'Forensics found a laptop computer,' Hunter replied. 'They are working on it as we speak, looking into files, photos, emails, anything they can get. No cellphone, though.'

'Nashorn was ready to go on his yearly two-week vacation,' Garcia added. 'So it's safe to assume that he had his phone with him. We think the killer either took it with him or got rid of it by throwing it into the water or destroying it.'

'We can get his number, contact his provider and go from there,' DA Bradley said.

'We've done it already,' Hunter told him. 'The phone is switched off, so if it hasn't been destroyed, it can't be traced until it's switched back on. But we might be able to get a cell-site analysis of his calls.'

'*Might* isn't an option,' the DA countered. 'Alice will get you the cell-site analysis.' He quickly checked his watch.

'OK,' Hunter said. 'I'm also revisiting Amy Dawson later today.'

DA Bradley and Captain Blake's eyes narrowed and they both responded with a slight headshake.

'Derek Nicholson's weekdays nurse,' Hunter reminded

them. 'I want to show her a picture of Andrew Nashorn and check if he was the man who she said had visited Nicholson in his home, other than DA Bradley. We still haven't identified who that second visitor was. I asked DA Bradley and he has enquired around all branches of the District Attorney's office in Los Angeles County. No one has come forward, so we have to assume that that second visitor wasn't a colleague from the DA's office.'

The DA nodded.

Captain Blake started tapping a pencil against her desk while her thought process shifted into a new gear. 'Tell me something,' she addressed Hunter. 'I know the MO on both murders was the same, but what Dwayne said got me wondering. Why make the first victim suffer physically and the second one psychologically? It doesn't make a lot of sense.'

'It never does, Captain,' Hunter replied.

'OK, but just humor me here. Do you think there's a chance there could be more than one perpetrator? Two people acting together, maybe. One who hated Nicholson and the other Nashorn? Maybe they met in prison. Sent to the same institution, but for completely unrelated crimes. They became friends inside. That could've given them years to come up with a morbid revenge.'

'She's got a point,' DA Bradley agreed.

'That's more than unlikely, given what was actually done to the victims.'

'How so?'

Hunter walked over to the center of the room. 'If you consider the severity of the psychosis manifested in both crimes, and the craziness of the act itself, it would be virtually impossible to have two separate attackers. The crime scenes suggest a compulsion acted out by the killer, down to the tiniest of details. Just look at the sculptures. At a psychological level, that's impossible to share. Killing his victims, dismembering their bodies, and constructing the human-body-part sculptures gives him pleasure. It fulfills something inside him that only he understands. No one else would've had the same level of satisfaction. That kind of psychological disturbance can't be shared. It's the same killer, Captain. Trust me.'

A knock on the door interrupted them.

'Yes,' Captain Blake called out.

The door was pushed open halfway and Alice Beaumont popped her head through. She'd gone back to the District Attorney's office to check on some files she couldn't access over the Internet. Her eyes widened in surprise and she stood perfectly still. She didn't know Hunter and Garcia were back from the morgue, and she'd had no idea DA Bradley would be in the room.

Everyone turned and faced Alice.

Three silent seconds.

'Sorry to interrupt.' Her eyes circled the room, making sure she had everyone's attention. 'But I think I finally got something.'

Forty-Five

DA Bradley motioned Alice into the office as if it were his own. He waited for her to close the door behind her.

'So what have you got?' he asked, throwing the autopsy-report copy on Captain Blake's desk.

'I've spent all morning going through the long list of names of criminals who were prosecuted by Derek Nicholson.' She nodded at Hunter. 'This time I went back fifteen years. I looked for links concerning the two victims. Mainly someone who'd been apprehended by Nashorn, and subsequently prosecuted by Nicholson.' She fetched four sheets of paper from the green plastic folder she had with her and handed one to each person in the room. 'Out of all the criminals Nashorn busted in the twelve years he was a detective, Nicholson prosecuted thirty-seven of them.'

Everyone's attention moved to the names on the list.

'Thirty-seven? There are only twenty-nine names here,' DA Bradley said, his eyebrows rising slightly.

'That's because I did a preliminary check on the initial thirty-seven,' Alice clarified. 'Eight have already died. The problem is, all thirty-seven of them were just your average street criminal – armed robbery, mugging, drug dealing, sex exploitation, aggravated assaults, gang members, that kind of thing. When I checked their background, I got nothing but school dropouts and poorly educated people who came from broken homes and abusive parents. People with explosive tempers who just don't fit the pattern.'

'What pattern are you talking about?' the DA asked.

'The pathologist's report from Nicholson's autopsy suggested that the killer had some sort of medical knowledge,' Alice explained.

'That was further confirmed after Nashorn's examination this morning,' Garcia added.

'So that would back up my argument,' Alice proceeded. 'The criminals on this list don't have the level of education needed to be able to commit the kind of murders we're investigating. They just wouldn't have the knowledge, the patience, or the determination to dismember a victim and create the sculptures.'

'So what you're saying is that none of the names on this list is worth investigating?' Captain Blake said with lilt in her voice. 'So what's the point in handing it to us?' She dropped the list on her desk carelessly.

'No,' Alice shot back in the same tone. 'What I'm saying is that that's my opinion. I compiled the list because that was my job. In all the years I've worked for the DA's office, one thing I've learned is that time is a precious commodity in any investigation. But if you have the resources and the time to investigate all twenty-nine names on that list, then please be my guest.'

DA Bradley smiled like a proud father as he looked at Captain Blake. The only thing missing was the sentence 'That's my girl'.

Hunter saw a muscle flex on the captain's jaw. 'But this isn't what you're excited about,' he quickly intervened. 'You found something else, didn't you?'

A new glint brightened Alice's eyes. 'After I finished going over that list, I had an idea. I thought that maybe we could look at this from a different angle.'

'And which angle is that?' The captain's voice was still dry.

Alice moved over to the edge of the captain's desk. 'What if the person we're looking for is linked to only one of the victims, not both?'

Everyone considered it for a heartbeat.

'But then why kill the other one?' Garcia asked.

Alice lifted her right index finger, as if to say 'That's the key question.'

'Because the link is somewhere else.' She didn't give anyone a chance to question her. 'With that in mind, I quickly wrote an application that would search through the DA's database – specifically cases handled by Nicholson. It would then try and link the results, in any way, to any criminals who had been apprehended by Nashorn over the years.'

'What criteria did you use?' Hunter asked.

Alice subtly tilted her head to one side and shrugged. 'That was my problem. The scope can be quite wide, so I decided to start with something simple, something Robert had suggested before – family or relatives, prioritizing anyone who had been released or paroled recently.' She paused and bobbed her head from side to side. 'Well, not so recently, I went back five years for starters.'

'And . . . ?' Captain Blake placed her right elbow on the arm of her swivel chair and lightly rested her chin on her knuckles.

'And I might've gotten lucky, because a very strong candidate came up.'

Forty-Six

Alice let a subtle smile curve the ends of her lips before retrieving four copies of a printed mugshot from her green plastic folder.

'This is Alfredo Ortega.'

She handed everyone a copy. The photo looked old. Its subject had an asymmetrical face with a squared jaw, a pointy nose, ears that looked too small for his head, crooked teeth, and thick lips – not exactly an attractive man. His hair was midnight black and long, falling past his shoulders.

'OK,' the captain said. 'He's sinister-looking enough. What's his story?'

'Well, Mr. Ortega was an American citizen of Mexican origin. He used to work as a stacker and forklift driver in a warehouse in southeast LA. He was a big guy – six foot four, and two hundred and forty pounds. The kind of guy you don't really mess with. One rainy day in August, he wasn't feeling too good, apparently something he ate. In the afternoon, his boss took pity on him and told him to take the rest of the day off. Ortega had been married for two years then – no kids. He got home earlier than usual to find his wife, Pam, in bed with another man. Actually, a drinking buddy of his.'

Garcia screwed up his face. 'Damn, that can't be good.'

Alice shifted her weight from foot to foot before continuing. 'Instead of freaking out and losing his temper, he left them alone, drove several towns over to his wife's family's house in San Bernardino, killed her mother, her father, her grandmother, and her younger brother. He didn't touch their dog. After the bloodbath, he decapitated them and left their heads on the dining table.'

Four pairs of concerned eyes moved from the photo printout to Alice. She let the suspense stretch for a moment.

'Ortega then drove back to LA and to his friend's house, the one who'd been sleeping with his wife. By then, his friend was back home with his own wife and kid, who was only five.' Alice paused and took a deep breath. 'He killed them all the same way he killed his wife's family – with a machete. Left their heads on the kitchen worktop. After that, he calmly took a shower in their house and had some food from their fridge. Only then did he return home. He made love to his wife before hacking her head off.'

Everyone was staring at Alice almost catatonically.

'Wow ... that's an *inspiring* story,' Garcia said with a deflated breath. 'How long ago was this?'

'Twenty-one years ago. He didn't resist the arrest or anything. When he was caught, he pleaded innocent by reason of temporary insanity. That's why there was a jury court. Derek Nicholson was the prosecutor.'

Stunned silence.

'I remember the case,' DA Bradley announced.

'Was Nashorn the arresting officer?' Garcia asked.

'He couldn't have been,' Hunter said, shaking his head. 'That was twenty-one years ago, Carlos. Nashorn wasn't a detective then.'

'Wait a second.' Captain Blake placed the printout down on her desk. 'You said that in your search criteria you requested people released or paroled in the past five years. Are you telling me that this charmer has been released? How?'

'No.' Alice shook her head. 'The jury was unanimous. Ortega got the death penalty. He was on death row for sixteen years. He died by lethal injection five years ago.'

Puzzled looks all round.

That was the last of Captain Blake's patience. 'Are you fucking kidding me?' She slammed the printout against her desk as she got up, her gaze making rounds between Alice and the DA. 'First a list of names that you think we shouldn't really look into, now a photo of someone who's already dead. What the hell is this, "waste the LAPD's time" day? What sort of morons do you have working for you, Dwayne?'

'The kind that could dance circles around the morons you have in your department, Barbara.' DA Bradley motioned his head in Hunter and Garcia's direction.

'Alfredo Ortega is the link I found on Nicholson's side,' Alice replied in an even voice, not allowing the argument to heat up any further, and fetching a new photo printout from her folder. She handed a copy around to everyone once again. 'Now let me introduce you to Ken Sands.'

The new mugshot looked a lot more recent than the one from Ortega. The man on it looked to be in his mid-twenties. His skin had a golden tone attributed more to heavy sunbathing than ethnicity. His cheeks were pitted like a sponge from acne scars, probably dating back to his teens. His eyes were so dark they were almost black. He had the spaced-out stare of an intravenous drug user, but there was something else in those challenging eyes – something cold and frightening. Something evil. His dark hair was cropped short, and he had the confident smile of someone who knew he'd get revenge some day.

'OK, and what does this Ken Sands bring to the party?' Garcia asked.

Alice smiled a cheeky smile. 'Quite a lot.'

Forty-Seven

'Sands grew up with Ortega in Paramount,' Alice read out of a new document. 'They were best friends. Neither had any brothers or sisters, and that brought them even closer together. They both came from poor families. Sands's father drank a lot, so life in his house wasn't exactly perfect. Sands hated being home. He hated his father and the beatings he used to get from him. He spent most of his time out on the streets and with Ortega. Soon they started getting involved with drugs, gangs, fights – you know the drill.'

The phone on Captain Blake's desk rang and she reached for it. 'Not now.' She slammed the phone back down. 'Carry on.'

Alice coughed to clear her throat. 'Sands and Ortega went to Paramount High School. Ortega was a below-average student, but Sands, despite being disruptive, had better grades than most would expect. Getting accepted into college wouldn't have been a problem if he had wanted, and had the means. But their street life was already escalating into a criminal one, and when they were seventeen they both got busted for auto theft and possession of marijuana. That cost them a year in juvie hall.

'Their quick spell inside rattled Ortega. He decided he didn't really want to carry on with that life. He met Pam soon after he was released. They got married a couple of years later. Though he was still a drug user, he got a job at the warehouse, as I said, and everything indicated that he was leaving the street life behind.'

'But not Sands,' Hunter deduced.

A quick headshake. 'Not Sands. He carried on as a petty criminal for a while after he was released, but in juvie he made quite a few contacts. Before you knew it, he was dealing drugs in a major way.'

'How did you come by all this information so fast?' Garcia asked.

'The DA's office keeps extensive files on everyone we prosecute,' Alice replied, nodding at Bradley and flipping a page on her report. 'One night, Sands got back home drunk and high, had *another* row with his girlfriend, Gina Valdez, and things got out of hand. He lost his head, grabbed a baseball bat, and put Gina in hospital with a beating that left her a breath away from death. She had a few broken bones, a fractured skull, and she lost the sight in her left eye.'

'What a pleasant guy,' Garcia said, leaning against the window.

'You said your application was looking for links between family and relatives,' Hunter cut in. 'How did you manage to link Sands to Ortega?'

'With his wife murdered, Ortega listed Ken Sands as his next of kin after he got the death penalty,' Alice clarified. 'As I said, they were like brothers when young. You suggested that we searched for family members, gang members, anyone on the outside who could seek revenge on someone else's behalf. Well, Ken Sands certainly fits that category.'

'No arguments there,' Garcia said.

'But here's where it gets good,' Alice added. 'Andrew Nashorn was the detective who arrested Sands.'

It felt as if static electricity had been let loose in the room for a moment.

'Sands's girlfriend, Gina, was petrified of him, and rightly so. He'd beaten her up before, many times, it transpired. Nashorn was the one who managed to convince her to press charges when she was well enough. Sands was charged with aggravated battery to a live-in partner with the use of a deadly weapon.

'Which is a felony according to California Penal Code 245,' DA Bradley added.

Alice nodded. 'Add to that the fact that when he was apprehended he was high and carrying over a kilo of heroin, and you get a nine-and-a-half-years prison sentence. He went to the California State Prison in Lancaster.'

'How long ago was that?' the captain asked.

'Ten years. And apparently, after his sentence was read out, and before being taken away by the court officers, Sands had time to look back at Nashorn, who was sitting just behind the state prosecutor, and utter the words – "I'll be coming for you".' Alice placed the report on Captain Blake's desk. 'He was released six months ago.'

Time seemed to halt for several seconds.

'Do we have an address for him?' Hunter asked.

'Just his old home address. Sands wasn't paroled, he served his sentence – clean release, no need to report to a parole officer, or a judge, or anything. No restrictions either. He can even leave the country if he wants to.'

'OK,' Captain Blake said, looking back at the printout on her desk. 'Let's find him ASAP and have a little chat with him.' She motioned for Alice to hand over her folder and the report.

'Until we find him,' DA Bradley said, 'let's keep this as quiet as possible. I don't want any of this leaking to the press, or anyone.' He looked at Hunter and Garcia as if they'd publicize the new finding as soon as they left the room. 'And I mean *anyone*. We've got a prosecutor and a cop murdered. Every police officer, every law-enforcement agency in Los Angeles, is itching to get their hands on any suspect we may have. This gets out, and we're going to have a fucking manhunt on a scale none of us has ever seen before. So not a goddamn word to anyone. Am I clear?'

Neither Hunter nor Garcia replied. They just stared at the DA.

'*Am I clear, detectives?*'

'Crystal,' Hunter answered.

Forty-Eight

After the morning's development, the rest of the day began to drag. Nothing else materialized. Not surprisingly, the address Alice had on file for Ken Sands was out of date, and since he had left prison only six months ago, he hadn't filed for any documents that could help track him down – no driver's license, no passport, no national-welfare registration, nothing. His social-security record still showed the old address.

Hunter had a team trying to track down a bank account, a gas or electricity bill, anything that could point them in the right direction. They were also looking into Sands's old friends. People he hung out with before going to prison, people he met in prison who were now on the outside; anyone, really. But obtaining information from old friends or prison mates was a lot harder than it sounded, and Hunter knew it. In Los Angeles street law, ratting someone out, especially to the cops, was a crime punishable by death. Even his enemies wouldn't talk easy.

Hunter had also requested all the prison-visitation records for Sands and Ortega, but because of California privacy laws it could be a day or two before they got a judge to sanction the request, and another few before they got the files.

Gina Valdez, Ken Sands's girlfriend, whom he had beaten almost to death, had disappeared. Getting your name changed in America wasn't a very complicated process. And in the Internet age, changing your whole identity was getting easier and easier. No one knew if Gina had changed her name, or created a new identity. No one knew if she was still in LA, in California, or even in the country anymore. But one thing was for sure: she didn't want to be found.

As an LAPD detective, Andrew Nashorn had sometimes worked with a partner, Detective Seb Stokes. Stokes wasn't involved in Ken Sands's arrest, but Hunter gave him a call anyway. They arranged to meet first thing tomorrow morning.

Brian Doyle, the head of the LAPD Information Technology Division, had gotten back to Hunter towards the end of the afternoon with what he'd managed to extract from the computer they found in Nashorn's apartment. Hunter and Garcia spent an hour pouring over all the emails retrieved, and what had been compiled from the computer's Internet history. It became obvious that Nashorn was a frequent user of several escort agencies, many of them specializing in fetish, bondage and sado-masochism services. There was also a string of porn websites, and though many of them could be considered hard edge – none were illegal.

The emails gave them nothing suspicious, no threats or anything that could be construed as one. Nor had they made any progress identifying the second person who had talked to Derek Nicholson in his house when he fell ill. What Nicholson's nurse had told Hunter, about Nicholson clearing his conscience and telling someone the truth about something, was still rolling around in Hunter's mind.

Hunter and Garcia spent the rest of the day researching on the Internet, looking for anything that even remotely resembled the new shadow image cast by the sculpture made of Nashorn's body parts. They found nothing that looked like the entire image. The figure of the distorted head with horns could easily be matched to a representation of most devils or demons. And that applied to religions, belief systems and cultures across the globe. But there were also mythological horned gods, like the Greek god Pan, or even Apollo and Zeus, whose early representations were as a horned man.

Devil or God, Hunter thought. *Take your pick.*

Without having a point of reference, it was like looking for a blond hair on a sandy beach.

The second part of the image proved even more elusive. Two figures standing and two lying down, practically on top of each other. Hunter and Garcia found nothing, and Hunter had to start considering the possibility that Alice could be right. Maybe the image had no hidden meaning at all. Nothing religious. Nothing mythological. No parallel connotation. Maybe the meaning was as simple as she had suggested – an evil killer looking down at his victims. Two down, two to go. And that meant he would kill again.

Forty-Nine

It was past dinnertime when Hunter returned to Lennox and parked in front of Amy Dawson's house. Once again, with a polite smile, Derek Nicholson's weekdays nurse showed him into her house, but this time guided him into the kitchen.

The air was sprinkled with the pleasant smell of cooked tomatoes, basil, onions, chilies and spices.

'My husband is watching the game in the living room,' Amy explained. 'He's a big Lakers fan, and when he gets excited, he can be quite loud. You don't mind if we talk in here, do you?'

'Of course not,' Hunter assured her. 'I'll be as brief as I can.'

Amy was wearing a light, floral dress and rubber flip-flops. Her cornrows had been undone, and her hair was now pulled back into a bushy ponytail. She offered Hunter a seat on one of the chairs around the foldout Formica table.

'If you had come a little earlier, you could've had dinner with us.'

Hunter smiled. 'That's very kind of you to say, thank you. But it was probably a good thing. Get me near a nice, home-made pasta dish, and I could eat my bodyweight . . . maybe more.'

Amy paused and skeptically stared at Hunter. 'How do you know I cooked pasta tonight?'

'Umm . . . just a guess judging by the mouthwatering smell in your kitchen.' He shrugged. 'Homemade spicy tomato sauce?'

Amy couldn't hide her surprise. 'That's right. My mother's own recipe. We all like it with plenty of heat.'

'Me too.' Hunter nodded before having a seat. He waited until Amy sat across the table from him. 'I just wanted to go back to that second person you said had visited Mr. Nicholson in his home after he was taken ill.'

'I haven't remembered anything else,' she said, looking sincerely sorry.

'That's OK. What I really wanted was for you to have a look at a photograph, and tell me if there's any chance the person in it is the same person who visited Mr. Nicholson that day.'

'OK.' She leaned forward, placing her elbows on the table.

Screamer, the family dog, started barking just outside the kitchen door. Amy pulled an annoyed face. 'Excuse me for just a second, Detective.' She stood up and opened the door, but didn't allow the dog inside. 'Delroy,' she called out. 'Could you take Screamer and maybe put him outside? I can't deal with him now.'

'I'm watching the game,' a strong baritone voice replied.

'Can you ask Leticia to take him upstairs then?'

'Leticia,' Delroy called in an even louder voice. 'Come get your dog before I strangle it.'

Amy closed the door, shaking her head. 'I'm so sorry,' she said again as she returned to her seat. 'Sometimes that dog drives me crazy. And so does my husband.'

Hunter smiled. 'That's OK.' He placed an A4-sized photograph of Andrew Nashorn in front of Amy. 'This is the person I was talking about.'

She picked it up and studied it hard for a long moment.

'I'm sorry, Detective, that's not him. The man looked younger and leaner, I'm sure.' She returned the photograph to the table.

Hunter nodded, but left the picture where it was. 'How about this person?' He produced a second photograph. This time the mugshot of Ken Sands. He had contacted the California State Prison in Lancaster and managed to get a more recent picture of Sands, taken on the day he was released. His hair was long and messy, and he had allowed a bushy, scraggy beard to grow. None of his facial features were very visible.

'This is the most recent picture we have of him,' Hunter explained. He knew Sands had created that look deliberately. A lot of inmates serving medium to long sentences had a similar appearance. It was a common trick to stop the system from having an accurate, recent picture of them. The long hair and the bushy beard would be gone within an hour of their release. 'I'm sure he won't have so much hair around his face anymore.' Hunter showed her one more picture – Sands's arrest mugshot. 'This is what he looked like ten years ago.'

Amy took the picture from Hunter's hands. She kept her eyes on them for a long instant.

Hunter went quiet, allowing her to study it for as long as she needed to.

'It could've been him,' Amy finally said.

Hunter felt a tingle of electricity run through him.

'But of course, I can't be sure. The man who visited

Mr. Nicholson that day didn't have no beard or long hair. He was dressed in a suit and all.'

'I understand.'

Amy's stare never left the printout in her hands. 'But it could've been him.'

Fifty

The blood had coagulated and dried onto the floor and walls, and as the red blood cells died and started to decompose, the odd, metallic smell had faded, giving way to a much stronger odor – something like rotten meat mixed with sour milk. Many who'd been to a brutal crime scene would argue that that was exactly what a violent death smelled like.

Hunter paused by the door to Nashorn's boat cabin once again. Revisiting crime scenes, alone, in the dead of night, had become almost an obsession with him. It gave him a chance to look around uninterrupted, to take his time, to try, if only for a split second, to adopt the same frame of mind as the killer. But how could anyone make sense of the senseless?

Hunter had read and reread the forensic team's crime-scene report. The many shoeprints he'd seen around the cabin's floor the day before were very inconsistent and couldn't be matched to a specific shoe size. There was so much blood covering the floor that, as soon as the killer moved his foot, more blood seeped back to obscure its outline. That made the forensics analysis a lot more difficult. Mike Brindle, the forensics agent who led the team that attended the scene, told Hunter earlier in the day that he'd found something odd about the shoeprints. The distribution of weight from each step seemed to be unequal. That suggested that the killer either walked with an asymmetric abnormality – as if he had a limp, or had deliberately worn wrong-sized shoes. It was a trick that Hunter had encountered before. Forensics couldn't identify a sole pattern, either, which suggested that the killer had covered his shoes with a thick plastic cover, or something on those lines. That would also explain the lack of bloody footprints outside the cabin.

Brindle had assured Hunter that his team had left the cabin in the exact same state in which they'd found it. The objects that had been removed for forensic examination had been listed in the document Hunter had with him. Everything else was left in its place.

Hunter zipped up his Tyvek coverall and stepped into the cabin. He wasn't worried about contaminating the scene; he just didn't want his shoes and clothes to get smeared with blood, or drenched in that sickening smell. He knew that when that smell found its way into any fabric, no amount of washing or dry cleaning would get rid of it. It was a psychological thing. The brain would associate the clothes with the smell, even after the smell was long gone.

He paused in the center of the room and slowly allowed his eyes to roam the space around him.

Was the killer already on board when Nashorn got to his boat?

The cabin door showed no signs of forced entry, though picking the two locks on it wouldn't pose a great obstacle to anyone with experience.

Hunter went over most of the same movements he and Garcia had gone through the day before, making sure he hadn't missed anything. He walked over to the small fridge and pulled its door open. It had been well stocked – several bottles of water, cheese, cold meats and plenty of beer. He rechecked the trashcan – a candy-bar wrapper and an empty bag of beef jerky. No beer cans. No glasses out in the small kitchen either. If Nashorn had invited anyone on board just before sailing off for two weeks, it probably hadn't been to shoot the breeze.

So what then?

Garcia had suggested earlier that maybe the killer had approached Nashorn outside the boat first with some sort of weapon, forcing him to open the door before striking him across the face. Given both crime scenes, and Doctor Hove's conclusion that the killer's weapon of choice had been an electric kitchen carving knife, Hunter found that theory very unlikely. This killer didn't like firearms.

He crossed the room to the far wall, where the largest concentration of blood splatter was located. The chair in which Nashorn's body was found had been taken away by forensics, but its spot was marked by masking tape. Hunter paused at the center of it and looked around. There was nowhere to hide. Anyone attempting to conceal himself would've been spotted straight away, unless he was a midget. From the door, Nashorn would've been able to see the whole of the cabin, with the exception of the bathroom's interior, but only if its door was closed. If the killer had hidden in there, then he would have had two options: wait until Nashorn pulled the bathroom door open and club him across the face with whichever weapon had been used; or pull the door open himself and storm towards Nashorn once he'd entered the cabin.

Hunter immediately saw two problems with that

theory. As in any small boat cabin, the bathroom wasn't very spacious. Doctor Hove was certain that Nashorn had been knocked out with a single, powerful blow to the face, and the blow had come from right to left in a swinging motion. That was impossible to achieve if standing inside the bathroom. There simply wasn't enough space. If the killer had stormed out of the bathroom towards Nashorn, no matter where inside the cabin Nashorn had been, in such a cramped environment, it would've taken the killer at least two to three seconds to get to his victim. That was enough time for Nashorn to notice the attack and assume the most basic of defensive positions – hands up to protect the face. Even though his arms had been severed from his body, there were no defensive wounds to his hands or arms.

Hunter's gaze circled the room again and paused on the small door to the inboard engine compartment. Like most things at that end of the cabin, it was covered in dried blood. With the forensics team in a hurry to start processing the scene last night, Hunter had not had a chance to properly check the engine pit. He crouched down next to it and lifted the door open. The compartment was small, not much bigger than a regular cupboard. The engine itself occupied most of the space. Blood had leaked in through the top of the door and dripped onto the engine and the oil-stained floor of the pit. Hunter was about to close the door when he saw something that caught his attention. A pattern of blood across the center part of the engine. Not dripped blood that had seeped through the door, but splattered blood. Hunter had seen that type of splatter many times – wound-spray, usually caused by a rotating motion, like when an assailant hits a victim across the face. The force of the blow would cause the victim's neck to rotate, and blood from the inflicted wound would fly out in a thin arc.

He reached for the forensics-report folder and quickly flipped through the evidence photographs. As he found what he was looking for, his brain went into overdrive, calculating all the possibilities. He reached down, stuck his head into the pit, and fiddled with the underside of the engine, as if feeling for something. When he pulled his hand out, it was covered in a thin sheet of slimy liquid.

Hunter felt his blood warm inside his veins. 'Smart motherfucker.'

Fifty-One

By 9:00 a.m., the heat reflected off the dusty roads already felt like an oven door had been opened. Hunter sat at one of the outside tables at the Grub café, in Seward Street. The large white umbrella that shot out from the center of the table provided a very welcome shade. The trimmed green hedges peppered in purple flowers that covered the crisscrossed wooden fence surrounding the café gave the place a country feel, despite it being just east of West Hollywood.

Detective Seb Stokes, Andrew Nashorn's old partner, was the one who'd suggested they meet there. He arrived a couple of minutes after Hunter, paused by the door to the outside yard, and surveyed the busy tables. He was a bear of a man. His battered trousers stretched tight around an expanding waistline, and his jacket looked like it could rip if Stokes shrugged or sneezed too hard. His hair was thin, light brown and combed to one side to disguise an undis-guisable bald patch. He had the worn look of someone who'd spent too much time in the same job, and had grown to hate it.

Despite never meeting him before, Hunter recognized him straight away and lifted a hand, grabbing his attention. Stokes walked over.

'I guess I look too much like a cop, don't I?' His voice matched his image, full-bodied, but tired.

'I guess we all do,' Hunter said, standing up to shake his hand.

Stokes looked Hunter up and down, taking his figure and attire in. The black jeans, the cowboy boots, the shirt with its sleeves rolled up around muscular forearms, the broad shoulders and strong chest, the face with its square jaw.

'Really?' Stokes said with a sarcastic grin. 'You look more like the all-American dream gymnast than any cop I've ever seen.' He shook Hunter's hand. 'Seb Stokes. Everyone calls me Seb.'

'Robert Hunter. Call me Robert.'

They both sat down.

'OK, let's order.' Stokes signaled a waitress over without even looking at the menu and ordered the breakfast special. Hunter asked for a cup of black coffee.

Stokes sat back and undid the buttons on his suit jacket. 'So you're the lead on Andy's murder?' He shook his head and looked into the distance before fixing Hunter with his tired eyes. 'Is it true what I've heard? He was cut up into pieces? I mean . . . dismembered? Decapitated?'

Hunter nodded. 'I'm sorry.'

'And his body parts were left on a table, in some sort of crazy sculpture?'

Hunter nodded again.

'Do you think it was a gang hit?'

'Nothing points that way.'

'What? A single perp?'

'From what we have, yes.'

Stokes used the palm of his left hand to wipe the sweat from his glistening forehead and Hunter saw his jaw almost lock in anger.

'That's fucked up. Fucking coward, piece of shit. That's no way for an officer to die. I would kill for five minutes in a room alone with the mother-humper who did that to Andy. Let's see who would dismember who then.'

Hunter kept his gaze locked on Stokes, watching him feed off his emotions.

'You know you have the entire goddam LAPD behind you on this one, right? Whatever you need, from whatever division, just ask. Fucking cop-killer. He's gonna get what's coming to him.'

Hunter said nothing.

'It wasn't a random attack, right? It was personal? I mean, did it look like a payback job?'

'Possibly.'

'For what? Andy hadn't been in the field for . . .' Stokes shook his head and narrowed his eyes.

'Eight years.' Hunter filled in the blank.

'That's right, eight years. He was with the Operations Support division . . .' He paused, suddenly realizing the implications. 'Wait up. You think it was payback for a case that goes back more than eight years, back to when he was on the field?'

'You used to be his partner, right?'

'Well, not exactly partner. We worked several cases together, yes, but when we were with the South Bureau, most of the investigations we were assigned to didn't require more than one senior detective. We did a lot of low-level robberies, muggings, domestic violence, thefts, that kinda shit. Andy and I worked together in a few homicides, mostly gang related. Anything more high profile got sent to you folks down at the RHD.'

The waitress came back with their coffees. Stokes's had so much whipped cream on top it looked like a snow-covered Christmas tree. Hunter waited as Stokes emptied three sugar sachets into his mug.

'You think this scumbag is someone Andy and I put away?'

'At the moment we're looking at every possibility.'

'Wow, that's a bullshit, by-the-book, detective's answer, if I've ever heard one.' Stokes used a small wooden stick to stir his coffee. 'Wait a second. You think this asshole's gonna strike again? Please tell me you're not here to tell me to be careful.'

'No, I'm not here to tell you that, but it wouldn't hurt if you stayed alert.'

Stokes laughed out loud. A gritty, throaty laugh. 'What do you suggest I do, detective? Take some police protection? Buy a bigger gun?' He leaned forward as much as his stomach would allow, and opened his suit jacket just enough for Hunter to see his shoulder-holstered gun. 'Let him come. I'm ready for him.' He sat back and regarded Hunter for a heartbeat. 'I hadn't kept in contact with Andy as much as I should have. I'm not with the South Bureau anymore. Got transferred to the West Bureau, Hollywood Division, after my divorce.'

'When was that?'

'Seven years ago. A year after Andy got shot. But tell me something. Andy was an active guy. He wasn't on the field anymore, and he wasn't as fit as he used to be, the bullet through his lung made sure of that, but he was no pushover. He was also one of those guys who was always on the lookout, you know what I mean? Wary of everyone. And I know he always packed. How did a single perp get to him like that? Ambush him inside his boat?'

Hunter sat back and crossed his legs. 'No. He posed as a mechanic.'

Fifty-Two

Garcia was an early riser. He always got to the RHD before most, but this morning he'd gotten to his desk a lot earlier than usual. He wasn't an insomniac like Hunter, but no one can really control their thoughts, or what their subconscious will throw at them once they close their eyes. Last night, the images that lay hidden behind Garcia's eyelids were enough to scare sleep away for most of the night.

He did his best not to wake his wife up, but despite his lying soundless and motionless, Anna could sense her husband's uneasiness as if it were crawling up her skin. She always could.

Garcia had met Anna Preston as a freshman in high school. Her unusual beauty captivated many boys, but it mesmerized Garcia, and he fell in love with her almost immediately. As a kid, Garcia was quiet and very shy. It took him ten months to gather the courage to walk up to Anna in a school dance and stammer the words – 'Would you . . . umm . . . li . . . like to dance . . . ?'

'Yes,' she replied with a smile that made his legs wobble.

'I mean . . . with me . . . would you like to dance with me . . . ?'

Her smile widened. 'Yes, I'd love that.'

While on the dance floor, swinging awkwardly to a slow song, Anna whispered into Garcia's ear.

'What took you so long?'

Garcia pulled his chin from her shoulder and looked into Anna's hazel-honey eyes. 'What?'

'Five school dances. This is the fifth school dance this year. What took you so long to ask me?'

Garcia tilted his head to one side and said tentatively. 'I . . . like to keep the ladies waiting?'

They both laughed.

They started dating that night.

Garcia proposed three years later, straight after their graduation.

When Garcia became a detective for the LAPD, he made a promise to himself never to bring home any of the grotesque world his profession took him to. To never, ever discuss his day with Anna. Not because it was against protocol, but because he loved her too much, and he would never stain her thoughts with the images and the reality of his every day. He had never broken that promise.

Late last night, while in bed, Anna pulled herself closer to Garcia and whispered in his ear.

'If you ever wanna talk. You know I'll always be here. No matter what.'

He faced her and gently swept a lock of hair from her face. 'I know.' He smiled. 'Everything is fine.' He kissed her lips.

Anna placed her head on his chest and closed her eyes. 'I love you,' she said.

Garcia started stroking her hair. 'I love you too.' Sleep never came.

* * *

Garcia sat facing the pictures board. His attention mostly on the photograph of the shadow image cast by the second sculpture. 'What the hell is he trying to tell us?'

'I asked myself that same question all night long,' Alice said, standing behind him.

Garcia jumped in his chair. He hadn't noticed her entering the room. 'Wow,' he said, consulting his watch. 'You're up early.'

'Or late, depends on how you look at it.' She placed a few folders on her desk.

'Couldn't sleep?'

'I didn't want to sleep. Every time I closed my eyes my brain cooked up a new nightmare.'

Garcia made a face as if he knew exactly how she felt.

She picked up one of the folders she'd brought in with her and handed it to Garcia.

'What's this?'

'Prison files and visitation records for Alfredo Ortega and Ken Sands.'

Garcia's eyes widened. 'Really? I didn't even know the request had been sanctioned already.'

'That's one of the perks of having the DA, the Mayor of Los Angeles, and the Chief of Police so keen to see an investigation resolved. Things move a lot faster. They were faxed to my office at the crack of dawn today.'

'Have you been through them already?'

Alice used both hands to tuck her loose hair behind her ears. 'I have, yes.'

Garcia's eyes dropped to the folders on his lap.

'I read fast.' She smiled. 'I've highlighted a few points.' She thought better of her words. 'Actually, quite a few. Start with the blue folder, Alfredo Ortega's file. As you'll remember, he went to prison eleven years before Ken Sands.'

Garcia noticed a new quirk in Alice's voice. 'And I can tell you've found something.'

'Wait until you read both files.' She sat at the edge of her desk with a satisfied look on her face. 'You'll have to read it to believe it.'

Fifty-Three

Detective Seb Stokes paused midway through a long sip of his coffee and returned the mug to the table. A teardrop blob of cream now sat on the tip of his round nose. An almost perfect fluffy white mustache contoured his top lip.

'A mechanic?' he said, using a paper napkin to wipe the cream off his face. 'You got the fucker on CCTV?'

'No, CCTV wasn't working,' Hunter replied in an even voice.

'It fucking never is when you need it. So how do you figure the killer posed as a mechanic?'

'Last night I found out that there was some sort of oil leak with Nashorn's boat's inboard engine. He was supposed to leave on his usual two-week sailing trip the day he was murdered. My guess is that he probably noticed the problem while doing his final check-through, and knew he couldn't sail off with a faulty engine. Too risky.'

'Yeah, that would be the Andy I know. He was always very thorough. And the one thing he wasn't was careless. Have you checked with the marina? Do they have a register of mechanics?'

'I've checked.' Hunter sipped his coffee. 'They don't have a mechanic station. What they do have is a list of mechanics they recommend. Nashorn never contacted the marina's admin office asking for a mechanic's name. But most boat owners already have a mechanic they trust anyway.'

'Did Andy?'

Hunter nodded. 'A guy called Warren Donnelly. I spoke with him last night. He said he was never contacted by Nashorn about any engine-oil leak.'

'So you're thinking that the killer tampered with the engine before Andy got to his boat,' Stokes said, reading Hunter's expression. 'Maybe even a day or two before.'

'Possibly.'

'Then all he had to do was hang around somewhere close, observing, waiting for the right moment to offer his services.'

'That's the theory we're looking at,' Hunter agreed.

'But why not just hide inside the boat cabin and wait for Andy to come in? Why complicate things by going through all the mechanic-scenario crap?'

'I'm not sure,' Hunter admitted. 'Maybe because it was a small boat. The cabin was even smaller. There was no place for anyone to hide. Nashorn would've noticed a stranger's presence even before boarding the boat. The killer would've lost the upper hand – no surprise factor.'

'And Andy was still a cop,' Stokes said, leaning back on his chair and running a hand over his rumbling belly. 'And a good one. At the slightest sign of a problem, he would've reached for his gun and been on high alert.'

Hunter nodded again. 'Nashorn was a big and strong guy, obviously able to handle himself. Maybe the killer knew that getting into any sort of fight with him wasn't a good idea. Things could've gone really wrong. And this killer doesn't take unnecessary risks.'

Stokes started chewing on his bottom lip. 'So the killer

needed to be invited onto the boat. That way Andy wouldn't have been suspicious. Once onboard, an opportunity to subdue Andy would've certainly presented itself.'

'Judging by the blood splatter, and the location where his teeth were found, it looks like Nashorn was crouching down in front of the engine pit. Maybe the killer asked him to have a look at something, or hold something in place while he grabbed a tool from his bag.'

'Teeth?'

'Nashorn received a blow to the face. Shattered his jaw and caused him to lose three of his teeth.'

The waitress returned with Stokes's breakfast. 'Are you sure I can't get you anything?' she asked Hunter.

'No thanks, I'm fine.'

'OK, let me know if you change your mind.' The waitress gave Hunter a charming wink before turning on the balls of her feet and walking away again.

Hunter gently scratched the bullet-wound scar on his right triceps. Though it was over two years old, sometimes it still itched like mad. 'Whoever this killer is,' he said, 'he had a lot of hate towards Nashorn. And that's why I'm here. You worked with him. You were part of the same division. Can you think back to any of the cases you investigated together, anyone who comes to mind who you think would be capable of something like this?'

Stokes cut a piece off his Spanish omelet and held it as if it were a slice of pizza. 'After we talked on the phone last night, I knew that question would be coming my way. I gave it some thought. And the only motherfucker I can think of is Raul Escobedo.'

'Who's he?'

'Serial rapist. Convicted for attacking three women in

Lynwood Park and Paramount in the space of eight months. The truth is, we think he attacked and raped closer to ten victims, but only three testified. Sadistic fucker too. Liked to rough 'em up real good before doing his business. We caught him because he made a mistake without knowing it.'

'Which was?' Hunter's interest grew.

'You see, Escobedo was born right here in LA, but his parents were from a small state in Mexico called Colima.'

'Home to the Colima volcano.'

'That's right. Did you know that already?'

Hunter nodded.

'Huh, I had to look that up. Anyway, Escobedo's parents immigrated to the US before his mother became pregnant with him. They came from a small town called Santa Inés. Though Escobedo grew up in Paramount, in his house they only spoke Spanish. His problem was, people from Santa Inés speak with a distinct accent. I can't tell the difference, but there you go.' Stokes had another bite of his omelet. 'He had never been to his parent's hometown, but Escobedo picked up the Santa Inés accent like a native. And that's what fucked him. His mistake was he liked to talk dirty while raping his victims. The last woman he raped was from Las Conchas, which is the next town along from Santa Inés.'

'She recognized his accent,' Hunter said.

'She did better than that.' Stokes chuckled. 'Escobedo used to work for the US postal service as a cashier. Two weeks after the attack, this last victim was staying with a friend in South Gate. It was the week before Mother's Day in Mexico, so they went down to their local post office to post a card to her friend's mother. Lo and behold, Escobedo was the one who served them. As soon as the woman heard his voice, she started shivering and all, but she did good. She didn't lose her cool. Instead of panicking and scaring him away, she left the post office, found a payphone, and got back to us. We put a sting operation on him and *boom* – three weeks later we caught him red-handed, just about to rape someone else. Andy and I were the detectives who arrested him.' Stokes returned to his coffee and Hunter sensed his hesitation. There was something he wasn't telling him.

'What happened with the arrest?'

Stokes put down the Spanish omelet slice he was holding, brought a napkin to his mouth and assessed Hunter from across the table. 'From cop to cop?'

Hunter gave Stokes a confident nod. 'From cop to cop.'

'Well, we roughed him up a little when we caught him.'

'Roughed him up?'

'You know how it is, man. When everything went down, adrenalin was pumping like bad blood. Andy got to him first. Escobedo had dragged this 18-year-old girl into a disused Salvation Army building in Lynwood. Andy always had a temper on him, and his fuse . . .' Stokes twisted his mouth to one side and followed the movement with his head. 'Simply non-existent. He used to get shit from our captain all the time for losing his head. He wasn't exactly a loose cannon, but he was pretty borderline, you know what I'm saying? When he got to the building, Escobedo had already ripped the girl's blouse off and beat her up pretty good. That was the cue for Andy to transform himself into the Incredible Punching Man, fuck being a cop, you know what I mean?'

Hunter didn't reply, and silence took over for several seconds.

'The truth is . . .' Stokes finally carried on, '. . . the bastard deserved every punch he got. Andy made a mess of his face.'

Hunter sipped his coffee calmly. 'So where's he now? Where's Escobedo?'

'I have no idea. This all happened twelve years ago. Escobedo got ten inside and served every second of it. The last I heard, he was released two years ago.'

Something like an electric charge ran up Hunter's spine.

'And I'll tell you right now,' Stokes moved on, 'if that sack of shit is the one who took Andy down then . . .'

'Where did he go?' Hunter interrupted Stokes, scooting up to the edge of his seat.

'What?' Stokes squinted and pushed back a strand of floppy hair off his forehead.

'Escobedo, which prison did he go to?'

'The state prison in Los Angeles County.'

'In Lancaster?'

'That's right.'

Same prison as Ken Sands, Hunter thought.

'Seriously, if Escobedo did this, I . . .'

'You're not going to do anything,' Hunter cut him off again. The last thing he wanted was for Stokes to leave that café thinking that he had a tip on LA's newest cop killer. That bogus information would leak like water through a sieve, and by lunchtime Hunter would have half of the cops in the city out on a vendetta hunt. He needed to dissuade Stokes. 'Look, Seb, if Escobedo is the only guy you can think of, then we'll look into him, but at the moment he isn't even a suspect. He's just a name on a list. We have nothing to link him to the crime scene – no fingerprints, no DNA, no fibers found, no witnesses. We don't even know where he was the day Nashorn was murdered, or if he possesses the skills to do what was done.' Hunter allowed a couple of seconds for his words to sink in. 'You're a good detective. I read your file. You know exactly how investigations work. If a rumor starts circulating now, this whole investigation will be jeopardized. And when that happens, it gives guilty people a chance to walk. You know that.'

'This motherfucker ain't walking.'

'You're right, no he isn't. And if Escobedo is our guy, I'll get him.'

The conviction in Hunter's voice softened the hard look in Stokes's eyes.

Hunter placed a card on the table and pushed it over towards Stokes. 'If you think of anyone else other than Escobedo, give me a call.' He stopped as he stood up. 'And listen, humor me and stay alert, OK? This guy is smarter than your average perp.'

Stokes smiled. 'And as I said . . .' he patted the bulge under his suit jacket, '. . . let him come.'

Fifty-Four

Garcia had just finished reading the files Alice had given him when Hunter pushed the office door open. The drive back from the Grub café to the PAB took him longer than he expected.

'You've gotta read this,' Garcia said, even before Hunter got to his desk.

'What is it?'

'Alfredo Ortega and Ken Sands's prison files and visitation records.'

Hunter frowned and looked at Alice, who was pouring herself a cup of coffee.

'The captain said get a move on; I got a move on,' she said matter-of-factly.

'You hacked into the California prison-system database?'

Alice gave him an almost imperceptible shrug.

'What?' Garcia chuckled at the question. 'You said that these reports were one of the perks of having the DA, the Mayor of Los Angeles, and the Chief of Police on our side.'

Alice gave him a sideways look followed by a smile. 'I lied. I'm sorry. I didn't know how you would react to the fact that I broke protocol. Some cops are very strict in their ways.'

Garcia smiled back. 'Not in this office.'

'OK then, what have we got?' Hunter asked Garcia.

Garcia flipped back a few pages on the first file. Alfredo Ortega went to prison eleven years before Ken Sands, who, as Alice told us yesterday, was named by Ortega as his next of kin. During those eleven years between Ortega going to prison and Sands getting arrested, Ken Sands visited Alfredo Ortega no less than thirty-three times.'

Hunter leaned back against the front edge of his desk. 'Three times a year.'

'Three times a year,' Garcia repeated, nodding. 'Because of the heinous nature of Ortega's crime, he was what is called a "Condemned Grade B" prisoner, and that means that they may only receive non-contact visits.'

'All "Condemned" visits take place in a secured booth and involve the prisoner being escorted in handcuffs,' Alice explained.

'Visits to death-row inmates are restricted to availability; usually one visit every three to five months,' Garcia carried on. 'They can last from one to two hours. We have Ortega's entire visitation history here. Every time Sands visited him, he stayed for the maximum duration.'

'OK, anyone else visited Ortega?' Hunter asked.

'When it got closer to Ortega's execution date, then he got the usual visitors – reporters, members of capital-punishment abolishment groups, someone wanting to write a book about him, the prison priest . . . you know how it goes.' Garcia flipped another page on the report. 'But during his first eleven years of incarceration, Sands was his only visitor. Not a single other soul.' Garcia closed the file and handed it to Hunter.

'We could've guessed Sands would have visited Ortega,'

Hunter said, leafing through the pages. 'From Alice's research we knew they were like brothers, so that was expected. Is that all we got?'

'Ortega's visitation files simply serve to confirm that Sands kept in contact with him for all those years,' Alice said from the corner of the room, sipping her coffee. 'Visitations are supervised, but the conversations are private. They could've talked about anything. And no, that's not all we got.' She moved her gaze from Hunter to Garcia as if to say 'show him'.

Garcia reached for the second file and flipped it open.

'This is Ken Sands's prison file,' he explained. 'And here is where it gets a lot more interesting.'

Fifty-Five

Garcia pulled a new A4 report sheet out of the second folder and handed it to Hunter.

'Sands's prison-visitation file is pretty unimpressive. He received four visits a year during the first six years of his jail sentence, all by the same person.'

Hunter checked the report. 'His mother.'

'That's right. His father never visited him, but that isn't surprising given what their relationship was like. During the remaining three and a half years of his prison term, Sands had no visitors whatsoever.'

'Not a very popular guy, huh?'

'Not really. His only real friend was Ortega, and he was in San Quentin.'

'Cellmates?' Hunter asked.

'Yep, a hard-as-nails guy called Guri Krasniqi,' Alice replied.

'Albanian, kind of a big ringleader,' Hunter said. 'I've heard of him.'

'That's him, all right.'

Garcia chuckled. 'Well, we have a better chance of stepping on unicorn shit on our way out of the office than getting an Albanian crime lord talking.'

Despite the joke, Hunter knew Garcia was right.

'Sands's life received a double hit during his sixth year of incarceration,' Alice said. 'First, Ortega's sentence was carried out and he was executed after sixteen years on death row – lethal injection. Sixth months later, Sands's mother passed away from a brain aneurysm. That's why the visits stopped. He was allowed to go to her funeral under a heavy guard escort. There were only ten people there. He didn't say a word to his father. And apparently he showed no emotions. Not a single tear.'

Hunter wasn't surprised. Ken Sands was known as a *tough guy*, and to tough guys, pride is everything. He would never have given his father, or his guard escorts, the pleasure of seeing him crying or hurting, even if it was over his dead mother. If he cried, he did it on his own, back in his prison cell.

Garcia stood up and moved to the center of the room. 'OK, all that's very interesting, but not as interesting as this next part.' He nodded at the report in his hands. 'You do know that the state penitentiary, as a rehabilitation institution, provides its inmates with courses, apprenticeships and work experience when possible, right? They call it *educational/vocational programming*, and according to their mission statement, it's designed to encourage productivity, inmate responsibility and self-improvement. It never quite works that way, though.'

'OK.' Hunter folded his arms.

'Some inmates can also, by request, and if approved, take a correspondence course. Several US universities have joined this program, offering inmates a vast choice of higher-level degrees.'

'Sands took one of those courses,' Hunter deducted.

'He took two, achieving two university degrees while inside.'

Hunter's eyebrows lifted.

'Sands obtained a degree in psychology from the College of Arts and Sciences, part of the American University in Washington DC, and . . .' Garcia stole a peek at Alice, holding the suspense, 'a minor degree in Nursing and Patient Care from the University of Massachusetts. No practical experience with patients is needed to graduate, but the course would've allowed him to request medical study books. Books that weren't available in the prison library.'

Hunter felt a tingle run through him.

'Remember . . .' Alice asked, '. . . when I said that Sands's school grades were much better than one would expect from such a disruptive student?'

'Yeah.'

'He aced both courses. Honorable mention at the conclusion of his psychology degree, and outstanding grades throughout his nursing degree.' She started fidgeting with the silver charms bracelet on her right wrist. 'So if it's medical knowledge we're looking for, Sands sure as hell fits the bill.' Alice sipped her coffee while holding Hunter's stare. 'But that still ain't all.'

Hunter questioned Garcia with a look.

'Spare time in prison . . .' Garcia read on, returning to his desk, '. . . is very rarely spent at an inmates' own leisure. They are all encouraged to do something useful with their time, like reading, painting or whatever. Several –' Garcia made quotation marks in the air with his fingers – '"personality-enhancing activities" are organized by the California State Prison in Lancaster. Sands read a lot, checking books out of the library on a regular basis.'

'The problem is,' Alice joined in, 'the library-book

register isn't online, and frankly that doesn't surprise me. But it means that there's no way I can get that list by hacking into the system because it doesn't exist in electronic form. We'll have to wait until Lancaster sends it to us.'

'Sands also spent a lot of time in the gym,' Garcia said, returning to the notes. 'But when he wasn't reading or studying for one of his long-distance courses, he was dabbling in his hobby. One he picked up inside.'

'Which was?' Hunter crossed to the water cooler and poured himself a cup.

'Art.'

'Yeah, but nothing to do with painting or drawing,' Alice noted, her demeanor urging Hunter to take a guess.

'Sculpting,' he said.

Both Garcia and Alice nodded.

Hunter kept his excitement at bay. He understood California's psychological approach to its rehabilitation institutions very well – encourage every inmate to guide their negative emotions into something creative, something constructive. Every prison in California has an extensive arts program, and they urge every inmate to take part. The truth is, the great majority does. If nothing else, it helps pass the time. The three most popular arts activities in Californian prisons are painting, drawing and sculpting. Many inmates take up all three.

'And we still have nothing for a possible location on Sands?' Hunter asked.

Alice shook her head. 'It's like he's vanished since he left prison. No one has a clue where he is.'

'There's always someone who knows something,' Hunter countered.

'That's for sure,' Garcia said, clicking away at his

computer. The printer next to his desk kicked into life. 'This is the last list you asked for,' Garcia said, retrieving the printout and handing it to Hunter. 'All other inmates housed in the same facility block as Sands during his entire prison term. There are over four hundred names in that list, but I'll save you the trouble. Have a look at the second page. Recognize anyone?'

Alice threw Garcia a surprised stare. 'When you read through the list earlier you never told me that you recognized a name.'

Garcia smiled. 'You never asked.'

Hunter flipped the page and his eyes sped through the names, stopping three quarters of the way down. 'You are kidding.'

Fifty-Six

Thomas Lynch, better known as Tito, was a scumbag, small-time junkie, who got busted seven years ago after a grocery-store armed robbery went terribly wrong, producing two fatalities – the store owner and his wife.

Though neither masked men's faces were ever uncovered during the whole robbery, when analyzing the CCTV footage, Hunter and Garcia had identified a slight, nervous head movement from one of the men. A tic brought on by stress. It took them three days to get to Tito.

Tito was just a petty criminal. That had been his first armed robbery. He was talked into it by the second man, Donnie Brusco, a lost-case crack-head, who'd already killed twice before.

It took Garcia less than an hour to get Tito talking. From the CCTV footage they knew Tito hadn't pulled the trigger. In fact, he'd even tried to stop the second masked man from shooting the old couple. Garcia convinced Tito that if he cooperated, because it had been his first serious offence, they could plea with the DA for a reduced sentence. If Tito didn't cooperate, he would certainly get death.

Tito talked, and Donnie Brusco was arrested and sentenced to death by lethal injection. He was now sitting in San Quentin's death row, waiting on his execution date.

Tito got ten years for armed robbery and accessory to murder. Hunter and Garcia kept their side of the bargain and pleaded with the DA, who recommended early parole. After serving six years of his ten-year sentence, Tito had been released under the supervision of the California Probation Department and a parole officer eleven months ago. He served his time in the California State Prison in Lancaster – Inmate Facility A. The same facility where Ken Sands had served his sentence.

Fifty-Seven

The fact that he was under the supervision of the California Probation Department meant that Tito wasn't hard to find. His registered address was a small apartment in a public housing project in Bell Gardens, East LA. His probation officer told Hunter over the phone that Tito was as good as they got when it came to paroled inmates. He was always on time for their scheduled meetings, held a steady job at a warehouse, and he hadn't missed a single weekly group session with the assigned psychologist.

Hunter and Garcia's first stop was at Tito's workplace, a privately owned warehouse in Cudahy, southeast Los Angeles. The owner, a short and very round Jewish man who never stopped smiling, told Hunter that Fridays were Tito's day off, but he would be in tomorrow, if they cared to come back. Saturdays he worked the nightshift, from nine in the evening to five in the morning.

Tito's housing project was a redbrick, square-box monstrosity just west of Bell Gardens Park. The building's metal entrance doors clanged like prison gates behind Hunter and Garcia as they stepped into the dingy ground-floor hall. The small space smelled heavily of urine and stale sweat, and there wasn't an inch of wall that wasn't graffitied. There were no elevators, just a set of dirty, narrow stairs going up five floors. Tito's apartment was number 311.

Graffiti followed Hunter and Garcia all the way up, as if the stairwell was a colorful psychedelic tunnel. As they reached the third floor, they were greeted by an even more sickening smell than the one at the entrance hall – something like sour milk, or old, dried-up vomit.

'Damn,' Garcia said, bringing a hand up to cover his nose. 'This whole place stinks like a sewer.'

In front of them, a long and narrow corridor in semi-darkness. Halfway down it one of the few working tube florescent lights that ran along the ceiling was malfunctioning, disco dancing on and off.

'All we need is some music,' Garcia joked. 'And a whole cleaning squad with disinfectants and air fresheners.'

The door to apartment 311 was directly under the flickering light. They could hear Spanish dance music coming from inside. Hunter knocked three times. Instinctively, both detectives positioned themselves to the left and right of the door. There was no reply. Hunter waited about fifteen seconds and knocked again, placing his right ear closer to the door. He could hear movement inside.

A couple of seconds later the door was opened by a five-foot-three Latin woman with dark hair and in her early-twenties. She was beyond skinny. Her olive-tanned skin clung to her bones as if they were the only things left to cling to. Her pupils were dilated to the size of coffee beans, and her stare was distant and dopey. She was naked except for an ill-fitting Chinese-style robe draped over her scrawny shoulders. She didn't bother closing it.

'Oh, sexy visitors,' she said with a Spanish accent, before Hunter and Garcia could introduce themselves. 'We like visitors. The more the merrier.' She gave them a cigarette-stained smile and pulled the door fully open. 'Come in and let's partyyy.' She blew Hunter a kiss and started swinging to the sound of the music.

'What the fuck are you doing, bitch?' Tito stepped out from the bedroom, wearing nothing but a pair of lacy purple panties. 'Get back in here and . . .' He choked mid-sentence when his eyes rested on the two new arrivals. 'What the fuck?' He tried covering himself up. Hunter and Garcia were already inside the apartment, both staring at Tito – a six-foot-one, two-hundred-and-ten-pound man with a pear-shaped body, wearing a pair of women's panties.

'That's not right,' Hunter whispered.

Garcia's headshake was barely noticeable. 'So, so wrong.'

'We've got some more people for our party, Papi,' the woman said, closing the door. 'Let's get naked and daaance.' She let her robe drop to the floor and reached for the buttons on Hunter's shirt. He gently moved her hands away.

'No, unfortunately we're not here for the party.' He collected her robe from the floor and helped her back into it.

'*Ai, chingado*. Stupid bitch, get back in the room,' Tito said, walking over and pulling the woman by her arm before wrapping himself in a white bath towel.

'Thank you for covering yourself, Tito,' Garcia said. 'I was starting to feel queasy.'

'Tito, waz going on up in there?' a new female voice called from the bedroom. This one sounded very young.

'Nothing, girl. Shut the fuck up.'

Garcia kept a smile locked. 'How many people have you got in there, Tito?'

'None of your goddamn business, cop.'

The Latin woman seemed to sober up instantly. 'They're cops?'

'What do you think, you dumb ho? They sure as hell ain't pizza-delivery boys. Now get back in there and stay there.' Tito pushed her into the bedroom and slammed the door shut. 'What do you guys want? And why are you inside my apartment without a warrant?'

'We don't need a warrant,' Garcia replied, looking around the room. 'We were cordially invited inside by your ... girlfriend.'

'She ain't my girlfriend ...'

'We need to talk, Tito,' Hunter cut him short. 'Right now.'

'Screw that, cop. I don't need to talk to you. I don't need to do shit.' He opened a drawer on the wooden sideboard next to him and quickly reached inside for something.

Fifty-Eight

In a blink of an eye, both detectives sprang into synchro-nized action, Hunter moving left and Garcia right, widening the distance between them, and drawing their guns at the same time. Both of their aims dead on Tito's chest. They moved so fast that it made Tito freeze in place.

'Easy there, lacy panties,' Garcia called out. 'Let me see your hands, nice and easy.'

'Hey, hey,' Tito jumped back and lifted his hands high up in the air. He was holding a stereo remote-control unit. 'Holy shit, homes. What the hell is wrong with you all? I just wanted to turn down the music.' Almost imperceptibly he jerked his chin towards his left shoulder. The same nervous tic that gave him away in the CCTV footage from his armed-robbery adventure seven years ago.

Hunter and Garcia thumbed their safeties back on and holstered their weapons.

'What the hell is wrong with *you*?' Garcia replied. 'You should know better than to make sudden moves like that in front of cops. You're gonna get yourself killed.'

'I've done OK so far.'

'Tito, sit down,' Hunter said, pulling a chair from the round wooden table that occupied the center of the small living room. Tito's lounge/diner was dull and dark, decorated by someone with no taste and probably half-blind. The walls were a dirty shade of beige, or maybe they were white once. The laminated wooden floor was so scratched it looked like Tito wore ice-skates in the apartment. The place reeked of pot and booze.

Tito hesitated, trying to look hard.

'Tito, sit down,' Hunter repeated. His tone didn't change, but his gaze demanded obedience.

Tito finally had a seat and slouched back on the chair like an angry schoolboy. His flabby bare torso was covered in tattoos, as were his arms. His shaved head displayed several scars. Hunter guessed he'd acquired most of them in prison.

'This is bullshit, man,' Tito said, nervously fidgeting with a yellow plastic lighter. 'You guys have no right to be here. I'm as good as gold. You can ask my parole officer. He'll vouch for me.'

'Of course you are, Tito,' Hunter said, staring directly at him and softly tapping the tip of his nose three times. 'White gold, you mean.'

Tito pinched his nose then looked at his thumb and fore-finger. A white powder residue clung to them. He quickly re-pinched his nose four or five times, snorting with each pinch to clear away what was left. 'Oh man, that's horse-shit. We were just having a little fun in the room, you know what it is? Nothing heavy, man. Just something to liven us up. It's my day off. We were just letting off some steam, you feel me?'

'Relax, Tito. We're not here to bust your balls, or spoil your little party,' Garcia said, tilting his head in the bedroom's direction. 'So just secure that hard-on for five minutes. We really just want to talk.'

'You *must* be tripping, homes. If I had a hard-on I'd tip

this table over.' He nodded, smiling. 'That's right, homes, I've got more game than a pheasant hunt.'

'OK, whatever, King Ding-a-Ling,' Hunter said, standing directly across the table from him. 'We just need to ask you a few questions and then we're out of here.'

'Questions about what?'

'About another inmate from CSP in Lancaster.'

'Fuck, homes, do I look like information services?'

Garcia clapped his hands once, bringing Tito's attention to him. 'Pay attention, *homes*, 'cos I'm not saying this again. I said we're not here to bust your balls, but I can easily change my mind. I'm sure your parole officer would love to hear about these little drug-fueled parties of yours. How would you like to spend the remaining three and a half years of your term back inside?'

'More than that,' Hunter said. 'If you get busted for possession and possibly distribution of drugs, that'll add at least a couple of years to your sentence.'

Tito bit his lip. He knew he was fighting a losing battle.

'Look, Tito, we just need to know if you know where we can find a guy called Ken Sands.'

Tito's eyes widened like a shark's jaw. 'You gotta be shitting me.'

'I take it you know him then,' Garcia said.

'Yeah, I know him. Everybody in Facility A knew him. He was a bad mother, man. And I mean *real* bad, you dig? Did he escape?'

'No, he was released six months ago,' Hunter said. 'He served his term.'

'And he's already got the cops after him again.' Tito chuckled. 'I'm not surprised.'

'So you guys were friends inside?'

'Screw that, man. I knew who he was, but I stayed the hell away from him. The guy had a temper like an atomic bomb. Hated the world. But he was smart. Every time the guards were around the guy acted like a pussycat. Real polite and respectful. He barely ever got into trouble in Lanc. And he was always surrounded by books. The guy read like a champion. Like a man with a mission, you get me? But he sort of had a reputation, and people just didn't mess with him.'

'Reputation?' Garcia asked.

Tito's head jerked again. 'There was this guy who dissed him once. You know the type, big-muscle gorilla who thinks he's king ass-kicker. Well, this guy dissed Ken right in front of everyone. Ken did nothing for a while. He just waited for the right time. He was patient like that, you know? Never rushed anything. Well, the right time came and he got to the guy in the showers. The guy never saw Ken coming.

'No one saw it happening. So much time had passed between the initial dissing and the attack that it was hard to link the two things together, you know what I'm sayin'? Ken never got heat for it.'

Hunter and Garcia knew that stories like that were common inside prisons.

Tito shook his head and started fidgeting with the plastic lighter again. 'That guy doesn't ever forget, man. If he's got a beef with you, you're positively screwed in red, white and blue with fifty stars, you feel me? Because one day he'll come for you.' Tito coughed like a sick man. 'I was in the yard on the day big gorilla-man dissed Ken. I saw the look in Ken's eyes. A look that I'll never forget. It made *me* scared, and I wasn't even involved. It was like bottled hate, you get my meaning? Like he had a devil inside him, or something.

'I haven't heard his name since I left Lanc. And if I never

hear it again, that'll be too soon. That guy is bad news all the way, homey.'

'Well, we need to find him.'

'Why are you asking me for? You're the detectives, aren't you? So detect.'

'That's what we're doing, genius.' Garcia walked over to the open-plan kitchenette. The smell of pot mixed itself with that of rancid milk. The old-fashioned sink was piled high with dirty dishes. The counters awash in paper plates, takeout containers and empty beer cans. 'I like what you've done with the place,' Garcia said, pulling the fridge door open. 'Do you wanna beer?'

'You're offering me my own beer?'

'I'm trying to be nice here, but you're spoiling it, big time.' Garcia slammed the fridge door shut and stepped on the pedal for the flip-top trashcan. As the lid came up, so did the overpowering smell of cannabis. 'Damn!' Garcia took a step back and screwed up his face. 'Are those joint butts? There must be over a hundred of them.'

'Hey, what the hell, man?'

'Tito,' Hunter sat down in front of him – a much less intimidating position, and he wanted Tito to relax a little. 'We really need to find Sands, do you understand?'

'How the hell would I know where he is? We weren't even friends.'

'But you were friends with others who might know a thing or two.' Hunter observed Tito's eye movement. He was searching his memory. Seconds later the eye movement stopped and his stare became fixed and a little distant. Hunter knew he had thought of someone specific.

'I don't know who to ask, man.'

'Yes you do,' Hunter hit back.

Tito and Hunter locked eyes for an instant.

'Listen, man.' Garcia circled the table to the other side. 'The only thing we want is some information. We need to know where we can find Sands, and that's very important. In return, you get to avoid a visit from your parole officer and a few of our friends in vice squad in the next hour. I'm sure they'd love to search these premises, especially that room with your two young friends.'

'Ah, this is bullshit, homey.'

'Well, it's the only deal we're selling.'

'Shit.' One more nervous tic followed by a heavy sigh. 'I'll see what I can find out, but I need some time.'

'You've got until tomorrow.'

'You've gotta be kidding me.'

'Does it look like we're kidding?' Garcia asked.

Tito hesitated.

Garcia reached for his cellphone.

'OK, homey, I'll see what I can find out, and I'll get back to you tomorrow. Can you leave now?'

'Not yet,' Hunter said. 'There's someone else too.'

'Oh, no way.'

'Another inmate – Raul Escobedo. Heard of him?'

On their way to Tito's house, Hunter had told Garcia all about his meeting with Detective Seb Stokes and his mention of Raul Escobedo.

'Who?' Tito's eyes narrowed.

'His name is Raul Escobedo,' Hunter repeated. 'He was a guest at Lancaster as well. A sex offender.'

'A rapist?' Tito cocked his head back.

'That's right.'

'Nah, man, are you high or something? Are police donuts made of hash these days?'

'I don't like donuts.'

'Me neither,' Garcia added.

'I was in Facility A, man, which houses real bad mothers and the Seg – the Segregation Unit. There's no way in God's creation they'd put a rapist with us, you feel me? Unless the police wanted him dead. He'd be gang-raped and dead within the hour.'

Tito wasn't lying. That was the way prisons in California worked and Hunter knew it. Every inmate, no matter which crime they'd committed, hated rapists. In prison, rapists were viewed as something lower than scum – as cowards who didn't have the guts to commit a real crime, and who weren't good enough to get their own women without the use of force. Plus, every inmate in the country had a mother, a sister, a daughter, a wife, a girlfriend – someone who could easily have become a rapist's victim. Rapists were usually placed in a separate prison ward or block, away from all other inmates, otherwise they'd surely be given a dose of their own medicine, before being brutally murdered. That had been proven many times over.

Fifty-Nine

Alice Beaumont was getting more and more frustrated. She had spent the entire day researching images on the Internet and waiting for the California State Prison in Lancaster to send her the information she was after. Despite the many phone calls and the urgent requests, they seemed to be in no hurry to oblige.

Her image research had hit a dead end every time. She'd spent hours poring over mythology and cult websites, but she'd found nothing new to add to what she'd found previously.

Alice wasn't the kind of woman who'd sit on her hands and wait for things to get done around her. She needed to be involved, and she sure as hell was tired of waiting.

The drive from the Police Administration Building to the California State Prison in Lancaster took her just over two hours. She had called DA Bradley, explaining what she needed. Two phone calls and less than fifteen minutes later he had everything arranged. Warden Clayton Laver said that Alice was welcome to go over and gather together the records she needed herself. They could do it themselves, as the warden had said, but they were understaffed, under-funded and overworked, and it could still be a day or two, maybe more, before they got around to it.

Alice parked in the second of the two large visitors' parking lots and made her way into the reception. She was greeted by Prison Officer Julian Healy, a black, six-foot-four mammoth of a man built like a water dam.

'Warden Laver sends his apologies,' Healy said in an unrecognizable southern accent. His vowels were long and drawn out, and there was a laziness about his voice, as if it was too much of an effort to talk quickly. 'He's tied up in something else at the moment and is unable to meet you. I was instructed to take you wherever you need to go.' He smiled while slowly looking Alice over. She was wearing a navy-blue business suit, complemented by a light-gray silky blouse. Its top button was undone, exposing her neck and a delicate white gold chain with a diamond pendant. 'You'll have to button up your blouse. And I suggest you button up your suit jacket as well.'

'It's Africa-hot in here,' Alice said, handing him her handbag for inspection.

'That's nothing compared to the kinda heat you'll get if any inmates lay their eyes on you and that thin blouse of yours.' He looked down at her shoes. 'Good thing you're not wearing open-toe shoes.'

'What's the problem with open-toe shoes?'

'You'd be amazed at the number of inmates who have a thing for women's feet, especially their toes. Double special if they are painted red or any shade of it. It drives them crazy. You might as well be naked. To avoid a libido explosion in general population, visitors aren't allowed to wear open-toe shoes.'

Alice didn't know what to say. She said nothing.

'It says here you wanna check our library?' Healy asked, reading from the sheet he had with him.

'That's right.'

'Any particular reason?'

Alice regarded him for a heartbeat.

'None of my business, right?' Healy smiled. 'OK. Follow me.' He guided Alice out of the visitors' reception area through the back door and across a three-lane road. They were inside the prison compound now. Behind them, the north wall stretched half a mile, with heavily armed guard towers every two hundred yards. The CSP in Lancaster had a design capacity of 2,300 inmates, but a total institution population of more than double that number. It housed both level-I and level-IV prisoners – level IV indicating maximum security, the highest level found in California institutions other than death row. Guarding the CSP in Lancaster was a very demanding job.

They reached the first building in the compound, a rectangular steel-and-concrete block two stories high. Healy swiped his security card at the front door and keyed in an eight-digit number. The heavy metal door buzzed loudly and clicked open. Inside, more armed guards. All of them looked like they were built to withstand a magnitude-8 earthquake. They moved through the building in silence, Healy gently nodding every time they came across another guard. They exited that first block and proceeded through an open-air walkway.

'The library is in the basement of building F,' Healy said. 'There's a much faster way of getting there, but that involves walking through the internal grounds, and there will be prisoners around. I'm just trying to make things easier for both of us.'

They walked for about three minutes. Healy repeated the process with his security card and keypad as they reached building F and the heavy door buzzed open. Inside, light came only from long florescent bulbs inside metal meshes that ran along the ceiling. They turned left into a long corridor. An inmate dressed in an orange jumpsuit was mopping the floor by the staircase. His tanned, muscular arms were covered in tattoos and scars. He paused and moved to one side, clearing the way for Healy and Alice. The whole corridor sparkled with such a shine that Alice couldn't help but wonder if the inmate went back to the other end and started all over again as soon as he'd finished mopping the floor, repeating the process from sunrise to sunset.

'Mind the floor, boss, it's a bit slippery,' he said with his head low, keeping his eyes on the floor.

The library was bigger than Alice expected, occupying the entire basement floor. Healy nodded at the armed guard at the front door and guided Alice into a small side room.

'Please have a seat in here while I go get the librarian. He'll help you with whatever it is that you need.'

Sixty

The room was a bland, ten-paces-by-six squared box – no windows, one heavy door. There was nothing there but a metal table bolted to the concrete floor, two plastic chairs that would have looked more at home on a patio, and the strong smell of thick bleach. Smell aside, the space reminded Alice of the interrogation rooms she'd seen at the PAB, minus the big two-way mirror mounted on one wall.

A full minute went by before Healy opened the door again. He was accompanied by a man half his size and twice his age. The little white hair he had left on his head was cropped short and neat. His face carried deep, sad wrinkles, testimony to a life spent mostly behind bars. Reading glasses balanced at the tip of a nose that had been broken several times. His eyes looked as though they had once carried a hard, mean look, but now were tired and resigned. He was wearing an inmate's orange jumpsuit.

'Our librarian called in sick today. This is Jay Devlin, our assistant librarian,' Healy announced. 'Has been so for nineteen years. He knows everything there is to know about this library. If he can't help you find what you need in here, no one can.'

Devlin nodded politely but refrained from shaking Alice's hand. He kept his arms by his side and his gaze low.

Healy turned and faced Devlin. 'If she needs to go to the library floor, call Officer Toledo to escort her, you hear? I don't want her out there by herself.'

'No problem, boss.' Devlin's voice was a notch louder than a whisper.

'If you need to use the john,' Healy addressed Alice again, 'Officer Toledo will accompany you and make sure it's empty before you enter it. We don't have women's facilities in here, only in the visitors' block. When you're done down here, Jay will call up and I'll come and get you.'

'Yes, boss,' she replied with a nod, almost giving him a salute.

Healy's eyes narrowed and he gave her a look that could sour milk. 'I hope you find our library to your liking,' he finally said before exiting the room and allowing the door to slam behind him.

'He's not a man for jokes, is he?' Alice said.

'No, ma'am,' Devlin replied, his posture timid. 'Guards here don't really care for jokes unless they involve us prisoners.'

'I'm Alice.' She offered her hand.

'I'm Jay, ma'am.' Again, he refrained from shaking it.

Alice took a step back. 'What I need is quite simple. I just need a list of all the books an ex-inmate checked out from this library.'

'All right.' Devlin nodded, his gaze now moving back to her face. 'That should be easy enough. Do you have the inmate's number?'

'I've got his name.'

'No problem, we can work from that. What's the name?'

'Ken Sands.'

Devlin's eyes fluttered for an instant.

'I take it you know him.'

Devlin nodded and quickly ran a hand from his mouth to his chin twice. 'I know every inmate that comes in here, ma'am. I've been here long enough. Since this library opened, really. Every different prison block here has an allocated day and time during the week when they can use the library. Not a good idea to mix inmates from different blocks, you know what I mean? But very few ever take advantage of what we have here. A pity, really. Ken, on the other hand, pretty much never missed an opportunity to sit and read. He loved his books. He loved studying. He visited this library more than any inmate I ever knew.'

'That's good. So we shouldn't have much of a problem.'

'Well, how long do you have, ma'am?'

Alice cocked a smile. 'Did he read that much?'

'He read a lot, but that's not the problem. The problem is our system. It only started being updated and digitized at the beginning of the year. And that process is going real slow. Until its completion, we still have to use the old library-card system to catalogue our books. No computers.' Devlin bobbed his head from side to side. 'Which is a good thing for me. When the new system takes over, I'll have to find something else to do. I'm not very good with them computers, ma'am.'

As part of the District Attorney's office, Alice understood well why the digitization of prison libraries was moving at a snail's pace. Everything the state's government did was linked to a budget. That budget varied every year, and its allocation was supposedly directly related to prioritization. With so many reforms due to take place inside the California Department of Corrections and Rehabilitation, the prisoners'-library-system automation, Alice guessed, was pretty low on that priority list.

'We use a library card for each inmate,' Devlin continued after a brief pause. 'Every time they check a book out, the book's catalogue number gets added to the inmate's library card together with the checkout date. The inmate's number gets added to the book's catalogue card. No names are used.'

Alice's eyes widened. 'So you're telling me that I'm gonna get Sands's library card, and all it'll have on it is a whole bunch of numbers, no book titles?'

'That's right. You'll then have to cross-reference that number with the book card to find the title.'

'But that's a crazy system. It will take anyone forever to find anything.'

Devlin gave her a shy shrug. 'Time is the one thing we all have to spare in here, ma'am. Ain't no use doing nothing fast. You just end up with more time on your hands and nothing to do with it.'

Alice couldn't argue with that. 'OK.' She glimpsed at her watch. 'Let's get to it then. Where are all the cards and book lists kept?'

'In file cabinets behind the checkout counter, ma'am, on the library floor.'

'Let's call the guard then. If that's the system you guys use, I can't do anything from here.'

Sixty-One

Officer Toledo was a whole foot taller than Alice and as wide as a wardrobe. He had a thick, peppered mustache over thin lips, a shaved head, and sideburns to rival Elvis. He accompanied Alice and Devlin out onto the main library floor and took position to the left of the book-checkout counter – four paces from the main door. There was something in the way his gaze kept reverting back to Alice that made her feel really uncomfortable.

The main library floor had enough seats for a hundred inmates, but at that time there were only a handful of them, scattered around the many Formica desks and tables. Like a scene from an old western movie, they all stopped what they were doing and lifted their heads at the same time to stare at Alice. A quick murmur followed, and it moved around the floor like a Mexican wave. Alice had no interest in finding out what they were saying.

'What kind of books do you carry in here?' Alice asked Devlin.

'A little of everything, ma'am, except crime. We have no crime books of any sort – no crime fiction, no true crime, nothing at all.' He chanced a smile. 'As if that would make a difference. We have a big department on religious and school books, you know – math, history, geography . . . all that. Anyone could learn how to read, or complete their lower or high-school diplomas in here . . . if they wanted to. Not many do. We also have a large and up-to-date law section.'

'What sort of books did Ken read?'

Devlin chuckled and scratched his chin. 'Ken read everything. He was a fast reader too. But he liked them study books a damn lot. He took them correspondence courses – advanced, college stuff, you know. He had a smart brain on him. Because of them courses, he was allowed to request extra books for his studies. Books we didn't have here. But because the state bought them, we got to keep them after he was done with them. No one else has ever checked them out.' Devlin paused, screwed up his face and ran a hand through his short-cropped hair. 'And then there are the books he read in here, sitting at the corner over there.' He pointed to a desk at the far end of the hall. 'The ones he didn't check out. If books are only read in here, then they won't go onto an inmate's card either.'

Alice nodded her understanding.

Devlin showed Alice how the library cards were organized and where they were kept – a long wooden cabinet that ran along the entire back wall. In her mind, Alice was already starting to prioritize things. 'Do you have a medical-books section at all?'

'Yes we do,' Devlin answered. 'A small one. Let me show you.'

They left the book-checkout counter and moved onto the main library floor. Officer Toledo was never more than three paces behind them. Once again, every pair of eyes in the library looked up. Murmurs came from every corner, but again Alice made a point of not hearing any of it.

They carried on towards one of the bookshelves at the back.

'This is our medical-book section,' Devlin announced, indicating a small segment on the top shelf. It was comprised of twenty-four books. Alice made a mental note of its numeric range. 'The only reason we have all those books is because they were part of one of Ken's courses,' Devlin said.

Alice asked to be shown two other book sections – psychology and art. She made a mental note of their numeric ranges as well.

'OK, I just need some pen and paper and I can start.'

'I can get you a pencil.'

'That'll do.'

They returned to the front of the library. Once back behind the checkout counter, Devlin handed Alice a few sheets of paper and a pencil, showed her the drawer in which she would find Ken Sands's library cards, and left her to her task.

Ken Sands had ninety-two library cards, all of them packed full of book-catalogue numbers. He must've been one of those who could read a book a day. As Devlin said, time was something that every inmate had to spare, and it looked like Sands spent every spare second he had reading. It would take her forever to thoroughly check every card. Alice paused for a moment, her brain pondering the easiest and fastest way to work through them. She had an idea, and started jotting down catalogue numbers.

An inmate with a shaved head, who had been sitting quietly at the table closest to the checkout counter, approached Devlin and handed him a book.

'This is a good book, Toby. I'm sure you'll like it.' Alice was way too busy writing down numbers to notice Devlin furtively inserting a slip of paper between the book's pages. If anybody could get a message to someone outside Lancaster Prison, Toby could.

Police officers weren't the only ones who looked after their own.

Sixty-Two

Many connoisseurs will say that the true lover of whisky will drink it with a little water, better still, spring water. Adding a little water to whisky before drinking will prevent its strength from numbing your senses and reducing your enjoyment. Water will also enhance the aroma and flavor of a whisky, bringing out its hidden characteristics. It is widely said that you should dilute your whisky with a fifth measure of water. Connoisseurs also frown upon those who add ice to their Scotch, since reducing its temperature will only freeze its aroma, and dull its taste.

Hunter couldn't care less for what others said, connoisseurs or not. He enjoyed his single malt with a little water, not because it was considered the correct way of drinking it, but because he found that some whiskies were truly too intense to drink neat. Sometimes he enjoyed his Scotch with one, perhaps two cubes of ice, welcoming the coolness of the liquid as it slipped down his throat. Garcia drank his whichever way it came. Tonight, each had a single cube of ice in their glass.

They were sitting at one of the front tables inside Brennan's, on Lincoln Boulevard – a dive bar famous for its turtle racing on a Thursday evening, and its jukebox's classic-rock collection.

Hunter needed a break from his claustrophobic office, not to mention its morbid decoration of bloody crime-scene photographs and the replica body-part sculpture.

Hunter and Garcia both drank their whiskies in silence, each having his own rollercoaster of thoughts to deal with. Hunter had spoken with Doctor Hove on the phone. The toxicology-test results for Andrew Nashorn were in. Their prediction was correct. Traces of propafenone, felodipine and carvedilol were found in his blood, the same cocktail of drugs that was used to reduce Derek Nicholson's heart rate.

A tall, long-haired blonde with a dancer's lithe body and a walk that was as charming as it was sexy entered the bar. She was wearing skin-tight blue jeans, light-brown stiletto shoes, and a cream-colored shirt tucked in at the waist. Her surgically enhanced breasts stretched the thin cotton fabric so much the buttons were almost popping off. Hunter's gaze followed her short walk from the entrance to the bar counter.

Garcia smiled at his partner but didn't say a word.

Hunter had one more sip of his Scotch before stealing another peek at the tall blonde.

'Maybe you should go talk to her,' Garcia said, quickly tilting his head in the direction of the bar.

'Sorry?'

'Well your eyes are about to pop out of your head. Maybe you should go and say "hi".'

Hunter studied Garcia's face for a quick second before subtly shaking his head. 'It's not what you're thinking.'

'Of course not. But I still think you should consider talking to her.'

Hunter placed his glass down and stood up. 'I'll be right back.'

Garcia looked on, surprised, as Hunter made his way towards the bar and the tall blonde, who had already attracted plenty of male attention. Garcia wasn't really expecting Hunter to make a move so quickly, if he made a move at all. 'Now this should be interesting,' he whispered to himself, shifting on his seat to get a better viewing position before leaning forward and placing both elbows on the table. He'd have given anything to have bionic ears at that moment.

'Excuse me,' Hunter said, coming up to the woman at the bar.

She didn't even glance at him. 'Not interested.' Her voice was cold, monotone and a little snobbish.

Hunter paused a fraction. 'I'm sorry?'

'I said, I'm *not interested*,' she repeated, taking a sip of her drink. Still not even a glance in Hunter's direction.

Hunter smiled to himself. 'Well, neither am I. I just wanted to call your attention to the fact that you have sat on some gum, which is now stuck to the back of your jeans like a big blob of green gunk.' He tilted his head to one side. 'Not such a great look.'

The woman's gaze finally met Hunter's for a split second before moving down. She twisted her body awkwardly, trying to look at the back of her jeans.

'On the other side,' Hunter said with a nod.

She twisted her body the other way, her hand shooting straight to her bum. The tips of her carefully manicured fingers touched the gooey mess of gum that ran from her bum cheek down to the top of her leg.

'Shit,' she said, pulling her hand away and looking at it with disgust. 'These are Roberto Cavalli jeans.'

Hunter had no idea what difference that made. 'They're nice jeans,' he said sympathetically.

'Nice? They cost a fortune.'

Hunter stared back at her blankly. 'I'm sure if you take it to a laundry service they'll be able to get it off for you.'

'Shit,' she said again, making her way towards the rest room.

'Well that was subtle,' Garcia said when Hunter returned to the table. 'What the hell did you say to her? All I saw was her grabbing her ass and then shooting straight out into the bathroom like a rocket.'

Hunter had a sip of his whisky. 'Like I said, it wasn't what you were thinking.'

Garcia chuckled and leaned back on his seat. 'You've gotta work on your pick-up lines, man.'

Hunter's cellphone rang in his pocket. He placed his glass down on the table and reached for it. 'Detective Hunter.'

'Robert, it's Terry. I've got some info for you.'

Detective Terry Cassidy was part of the RHD team. Hunter had asked him to find out whatever he could on the whereabouts of the now-released Raul Escobedo, the rapist Nashorn had beat up before sending to prison.

'I'm listening, Terry.'

'Well, this guy you asked me to look into, Escobedo, he's a bona fide piece of shit,' Cassidy began. 'Scumbags-R-us, you know what I'm sayin'? A rapist with a second hard-on for violence. They believe he raped as many as ten women.'

'I know the original story,' Hunter interrupted him. 'What have you got?'

'OK, our friend did some hard time inside. He got ten years for the violent rape of three women, the only three who'd testify. Now get this, during his spell inside, the barf bag repented. He *found God*.' Cassidy paused, either for effect or because he was really insulted by the idea of someone like Escobedo saying that he was now reformed. Cassidy was a real Roman Catholic. 'Inside, Escobedo started reading the Bible day and night, and took the theology program offered by the prison. He graduated with flying colors. Upon his release two years ago . . .' another quick pause, '. . . you guessed it, he started preaching. Thinks he's a reverend now, out there to spread the good word and help others repent. Calls himself Reverend Soldado. Named after Saint Juan Soldado, a folk saint revered by many in northwestern Mexico, where Escobedo's family is originally from.'

'Saint Soldier?' Hunter asked, translating the name from Spanish into English.

'That's right,' Cassidy confirmed. 'I checked it out. The saint's real name was Juan Castillo Morales. He was a private in the Mexican army. Now check this out, if you please . . . Castillo was executed in 1938 for the *rape* and murder of an 8-year-old girl from Tijuana. I shit you not, Robert – rape. His adherents believe that he was falsely accused of the crime, and they appeal to his spirit for help in matters of health, criminal problems, family, crossing the US–Mexico border, and other challenges of daily life.' Hunter heard an uneasy chuckle from Cassidy. 'Believe it or not, Escobedo named himself after a rapist saint. How's that for having balls?'

Hunter made no comment. Cassidy proceeded.

'He runs his own church, or temple, or whatever you wanna call it, in Pico Rivera. Personally, I'd just call it a cult. It's called *Soldiers for Jesus*, would you believe that crap? Sounds like a terrorist group, doesn't it? I wouldn't be surprised if he's now convincing the young women who join his group that they should give themselves to him as an initiation or something, making them believe that it's the will of the Lord, and he's the new Messiah. If he learned anything in prison, it was how to circumvent the law.'

'Did you find out about his whereabouts on those dates and times I gave you?' Hunter asked.

'Yeah. As much as I already hate the guy, he can't be the man you're looking for. On the first date you gave me – June 19th, Escobedo was out of Los Angeles, hosting a service in San Diego. He's planning to expand Soldiers for Jesus. The second date, June 22nd, he spent the entire day recording two CDs and a DVD. He sells them amongst his followers. He has loads of witnesses who'd testify to that. Escobedo is a cesspit of lies, stinky shit, and blasphemy, but he ain't your killer, Robert.'

Hunter nodded to himself. Protocol said he needed to check, but he'd never really considered Escobedo as a real suspect. As a psychologist, and then as a detective for the RHD, Hunter had studied, interviewed and apprehended hundreds of murderers, and throughout the years he'd found that usually there was little to separate a murderer from the regular man on the streets. He'd met killers who were handsome, charming and charismatic. Some who looked like kindly grandfathers. Even some who were voluptuous and sexy. The real difference only surfaced once he started delving into their minds. But there were different kinds of criminals – different kind of killers. Escobedo was a rapist – lowest of the low. True, he was violent, but his only interest was in fulfilling his carnal desires. He'd never stalked his victims, simply randomly picking them from whoever was around on a given night. There was never any planning. Hunter knew that criminals like that very rarely changed their MO. Even if revenge were the motive,

Escobedo would probably have shot or knifed his victims and fled the scene as fast as he could, not spent hours dismembering them and creating those grotesque sculptures – assigning to each one meanings hidden in the shadows. No, Escobedo didn't have the knowhow, the patience, the intellect, or the nerve to commit such crimes.

'Great work, Terry, thanks,' Hunter said before closing his phone and returning it to his pocket. He told Garcia the news and they both finished their drinks in silence. As they got up to leave, the tall blonde came out of the bathroom and approached their table.

'Sorry for earlier,' she said, coming up to Hunter, her voice now charming, with a seductive tone. 'And thanks.'

Garcia's facial expression was a picture. '*You've gotta be kidding me,*' he whispered.

'Not a problem,' Hunter replied.

'I know I came across as being arrogant,' she continued, her smile plastic, rehearsed. 'I'm not always like that. It's just that in places like this a woman has to watch herself, you know?'

'As I said, it's not a problem.' Hunter maneuvered around her. 'Enjoy the rest of your evening.'

'Listen,' she called as he turned to leave again. 'I gotta go home and try to sort this mess out, but maybe we could have a drink some other time.' She very expertly slipped Hunter a folded napkin. 'Your call.' She closed the whole thing with a sexy wink and walked out of the bar.

'You've gotta be kidding me,' Garcia whispered again.

Sixty-Three

Friday night, and The Airliner on North Broadway was pretty much packed to capacity. The spacious up-market dance club and lounge was decked out in a 'don't tax the imagination too hard' airline motif, but certainly served a much finer selection of booze than any US Airways economy flight. With two large and well-equipped bars, a bumpin' dance floor, a plush lounge area and some of Los Angeles' hottest DJs, The Airliner was certainly up there with the best LA clubs, attracting a diverse clientele of Angelinos and tourists alike. And that was why Eddie Mills loved going there.

Eddie was a lowlife, small-time crook, who'd got caught with one-and-a-half kilos of cocaine while driving through Redondo Beach. In prison he met Guri Krasniqi, an Albanian crime ringleader. Krasniqi was never coming out of prison, but he still ran his empire from inside, and got Eddie hooked up with his people when he was released from the California State Prison in Lancaster two years ago.

Eddie was standing by the upstairs bar, sipping champagne. He was so distracted, watching a shorthaired brunette set the dance floor alight, that he didn't even notice the six-foot-one, heavy-set man who'd come up next to him at the bar.

'Jesus!' Eddie almost jumped out of his skin when the heavy hand landed on his right shoulder.

'Wazzup, Eddie?'

Eddie turned and faced the shaved headed man. 'Tito?' He squinted as if he couldn't believe his eyes. 'Goddamn, cuz. Wazzup with you?' Eddie's lips broke into a sparkling, shining white smile and he opened his arms wide.

Tito smiled back and they hugged like long-lost brothers.

'When the hell did you get out?' Eddie asked.

'Paroled eleven months ago.'

'No shit?'

'No shit, homey.'

'So how you doin', dawg?' Eddie took a step back to assess his friend. 'By the looks of you, you're doing well. Where the hell have you been living, in a cake shop?'

'Hey, a man's gotta eat, you know?'

'Yeah, I can see that. A man's gotta stop eating as well, before he bursts.'

'Screw you. At least I don't get to eat that goo they served back in Lanc.'

'I'll drink to that.' Eddie lifted his glass.

'What the hell?' Tito pulled a face. 'Champagne? Really? I guess someone is doing well.'

'Hey man, only the best, cuz. Have some.' Eddie signaled the barman over and asked for a second champagne flute.

'You're looking fly,' Tito said, raising his glass for a toast. 'To being out and staying out.'

Eddie accepted with a head-nod. 'Thanks, man.' He ran a hand down his tie. 'This is Armani, you know?' He nodded at his suit. 'I make this shit look good, don't I?'

'Yeah, very slick,' Tito agreed.

They shot the breeze for an hour or so, reminiscing about their time in the slammer. Eddie told Tito that he was working for a foreign outfit, being as evasive as he could. Tito had no intention of pushing it. To disguise the real reason he was at The Airliner, Tito kept dropping names sporadically, asking Eddie if he knew what became of certain inmates – *Do you remember such-and-such? How about so-and-so?* That sort of thing. Tito knew Eddie used to hang out with Ken Sands when he was inside. Slowly, Tito moved towards the subject.

'Say, Eddie, how about Ken?' He could swear he saw Eddie tense for an instant.

Eddie finished the rest of his champagne, his eyes fixed on Tito. 'Ken? The dude got out, didn't he? No parole, served the long run too.'

'Did he?' Tito played dumb.

'Yeah, got out about six months ago.'

'That guy was the epitome of a bad motherfucker.' Tito laughed nervously. 'Have you been in touch?'

'Nah, man, I just heard he was out. He's got his own issues to deal with. Things he wanted to get done when he got out, you feel me?'

'Like what?'

'Damned if I know. Maybe he wanted to get back at whoever got him inside in the first place. But I pity whoever it is he's got a beef with.'

'Damn straight. Didn't he use to share with that Albanian badass dude? That Guri character? You know him, don't you? I saw you talking to him a few times.'

'I talked to a lot of people when I was inside, so did you. It helps pass the time.' Eddie played it down.

Tito nodded. 'Do you think Ken is back dealing again?

That's what he used to do before he got busted, wasn't it? Maybe he teamed up with the Albanians. I hear they run a tight operation.'

Eddie reassessed Tito with a doubtful eye. ''Sup, cuz, you looking for a job or something? Or you just looking to score some shit?'

'No, man, I'm good.' Tito ran a hand over his shaved head.

Eddie nodded. 'Uh-huh. So why are you so interested in Ken? Did he owe you money or something? If he did, just let it go, bro. It ain't worth it, you dig?'

'Nah, man, just asking, you know?'

'Yeah, I can see that. But asking too much can get you messed up, you know that.'

Tito lifted his hands up in a surrender gesture. 'Just making conversation, homes, that's all. I couldn't really give a rat's fart for how he's doing.'

Eddie said nothing, but looked a little out of his comfort zone. Tito was sure he knew more than he was letting on, and that was good enough for him. He'd pass that information on to those two damn cops who crashed his party. Let them bring the heat onto Eddie. That was the best he could do.

'Let's have another bottle,' Eddie said, already beckoning the barman over.

'Hey, man, I never say no to champagne, you know what I'm sayin'? Let me just go to the pisser first.'

As Tito made his way towards the rest room, Eddie was already heading downstairs to the smoking area, the quietest place for a phone call.

Sixty-Four

It was late and Tito had consumed another two bottles of champagne back at The Airliner with Eddie. By the time he got back to his apartment in Bell Gardens, he was well on his way to hangover hell in the morning.

Tito stumbled through his front door. Champagne had a strange way of getting him drunk very fast, but the truth was he enjoyed being drunk. And getting drunk on expensive champagne paid for by someone else felt even sweeter. His tongue was feeling a little furry, though.

He opened the door to his fridge in the kitchen, poured himself a large glass of orange juice and downed it in one. He returned to the living room and dumped his heavy body onto the old maroon sofa that smelled like an ashtray. He sat there for a minute or two before deciding that he needed a little pick-me-up, something to get the blood flowing again. Tito got up and approached the sideboard by one of the walls. He opened the bottom drawer, took out a small silver box together with a square, frameless mirror, and brought it all over to the dining table. From the box he took out a hand-folded paper envelope. He tapped out a generous amount of white powder onto the mirror and made a long, thick line of it using a razor blade. That was special stuff, finely cut. Premium Colombian powder that he never shared with any of the skanky, second-rate whores he brought back to his place. No, this was for his pleasure, and his pleasure alone.

Tito checked his pockets for a crispy bill he could use. He only had one five-dollar note, not that crispy, but it would have to do. He was too drunk to go looking for something else instead. He rolled up the bill into a tube as best he could, and snorted half of the line up one nostril and the other half up the other one.

He slumped back on his chair; eyes closed, pinching his nose tight.

'Yep, that's what I'm talking about,' he murmured between clenched teeth. That was just what he needed. He threw his neck back and sat there for a moment, his eyes still closed, enjoying the crazy effect as the drug and the alcohol in his blood collided against each other.

Tito was so absorbed in his trip that he never heard the sound of his front door being opened. He'd been too drunk to remember to turn the key in the lock.

Still with his head tilted back, Tito finally opened his eyes, but instead of the ceiling, he saw a face looking down at him. And he had seen those eyes before.

Sixty-Five

In the morning Hunter sat at his desk, checking the overnight emails. He'd gotten to his office early, just five minutes after Garcia. Neither had had a good night's sleep.

Hunter had pulled his attention away from his computer and had started looking through a few notes when Alice knocked at the door. She didn't wait for a reply, pushing the door open and stepping inside. Her tired eyes told everyone that sleep hadn't come easily to her either. She walked straight up to Hunter's desk and placed a three-page printed list on it. Hunter's eyes moved to her face.

'The list of books Sands checked out from Lancaster's prison library,' she said in a half-triumphant tone.

Hunter kept his gaze locked with hers.

'I had to go up there and get it,' she explained.

'You what?' Garcia asked.

'Their system isn't automated, nothing is computerized yet, and there's no book database. Their library uses the old library-card system, and they have their own bizarre way of archiving things. If I hadn't gone up there, it could've been days, maybe even weeks before we got this.'

Hunter said nothing, his expression posing the question.

'I was getting a bit fidgety here yesterday,' Alice admitted. 'You guys were out all day. I got tired of researching on the

Internet and finding nothing. I made a few calls, and DA Bradley arranged with the prison warden to let me check the library. It took me several hours to get this.'

Hunter finally reached for the list.

'Ken Sands pretty much read Lancaster Prison's entire library,' Alice said. 'But there were several books he checked out more than once. Some *way* more than once. I concentrated on those.'

Hunter started skimming through the list. Alice followed his gaze.

'You'll notice that the first twenty-four titles are all medical,' she said. 'Out of those, half of them are only in the library because they belonged to Sands. They were part of his Nursing and Patient Care degree. I spent some time going over their topics. At least five of them have extensive sections on how to contain severe hemorrhages, with detailed explanations and diagrams on transfixing of arteries and ligation of large veins, including the brachial and the femoral arteries.'

Hunter's gaze returned to Alice.

She shrugged. 'I read the autopsy reports.'

Garcia left his desk and moved over to Hunter's. 'That's nothing new, though. We already knew that Sands had medical knowledge,' he said.

'That's right,' Alice agreed. 'But this confirms that he more than likely had the specific knowledge required to carry out the amputations that were performed on both victims, and to properly minimize the bleeding.'

Hunter was still silent, still reading the list of book titles.

'In my view,' Alice moved on, 'if Sands is our man, then he obviously started developing his revenge plan while inside. But that wouldn't have happened straight away. A plan like that takes a while to solidify in anyone's mind. And if this was really retaliation not only for himself, but for Alfredo Ortega as well – who, you will remember, was the closest thing to a brother Sands ever had – then the plan would've only started taking real shape after Ortega's death penalty was carried out, five years ago.'

'It makes sense,' Garcia agreed after debating it in his head for a moment.

Hunter looked over the books' checkout dates before flipping back the page.

'There are no checkout dates on the more-advanced medical books,' Alice said, anticipating what Hunter was looking for. 'The reason is because those books didn't belong to the library at first. They were the prison's concession to Sands, to help him with his studies. He put in a request for them, and was allowed to keep them in his cell until he completed his degree. Upon his release, the books were taken by the library. And if you remember from my previous report, he only started both of his long-distance college degrees after Ortega's execution.'

Hunter carried on reading through the list.

Alice was still tracking his gaze. 'The next bunch of books are all on psychology – his other degree. Again, a concession from the prison warden to allow Sands to conclude his studies. But one book in particular grabbed my attention. Something that hadn't even crossed my mind until I saw it.'

Hunter's eye movement paused halfway down the page. She knew he had recognized it.

Sixty-Six

Standing behind Hunter, Garcia was reading as fast as he could, but nothing stood out. 'OK, what am I missing?'

Hunter tapped his finger over a title – 'Principles of Rorschach Interpretation'.

Garcia pulled a face. 'Pardon my dumbass question, but what's Rorschach?'

'Hermann Rorschach was a Swiss Freudian psychiatrist and psychoanalyst,' Hunter said. 'He's best known for developing a psychological projective test – the Rorschach *inkblot* test.'

They could almost hear Garcia thinking. 'I'll be damned. Isn't that that crazy test when you get shown a white card with just a big ink smudge on it? They ask you to tell them what you think you can see. A little like looking at clouds' shapes in the sky.'

'In a nutshell, that's the test, yes,' Hunter agreed.

'And in a *not*-nutshell way, what *is* the test?' Garcia pushed.

Hunter left the list on his desk and leaned back on his chair. 'The official test consists of ten cards. Each of the blots on them has near-perfect bilateral symmetry. Five inkblots are of black ink, two are of black-and-red ink and three are multicolored. But over the years psychologists have modified the test, creating their own cards with their own inkblots. Some even completely disregard the original bilateral symmetry of the blots.'

'OK, but what the hell is it for? What does it test?'

Hunter's head tilted slightly to one side as if not totally convinced. 'The test is *supposed* to measure a multitude of personality traits and psychological ills like sense of self-worth, depression, inadequate coping, problem-solving deficits . . .' He gestured with his hand to indicate that the list went on and on. 'Basically the test tries to assess an individual's intellectual functioning and social integration.'

'From an inkblot?' Garcia questioned.

Hunter shrugged and nodded once. He completely understood his partner's skepticism.

'Yes, but forget what the test is supposed to measure,' Alice cut in, 'and think of what we have. The shadows cast by the sculptures could be seen as Sands's own inkblot type of test.'

Hunter shook his head firmly. 'The killer is testing us, that's for sure, but not with inkblots.'

'How can you be sure?'

'As Garcia said, the inkblots are exactly that, blots, smudges with no real shape. What the killer has given us has perfect shape. A coyote and a raven on the first one, and though we're still not entirely sure of the meaning of the second image, it certainly isn't a shapeless blot.'

'OK, I'll go with that, but it still comes down to interpretation, doesn't it? What we think we can see,' Alice countered. 'Most people would never have known that, mythologically, a coyote and a raven together mean a betrayer, a liar.'

'We didn't know that either,' Hunter said. 'Until you looked it up, remember? To a certain extent, most images are open to interpretation. The way someone looks at a piece of art might well be very different from what the artist intended.'

'That isn't art, Robert.' Alice pointed at the replica sculpture.

'To us it isn't, but to the killer . . . ?' He left the sentence hanging in the air for a second. 'It's his work, his creation, his art, gruesome or not. And I bet you he saw something completely different from what we are seeing when he put that thing together. Different frame of mind makes you see different things.'

Alice stared at the sculpture. 'Different frame of mind?'

Hunter stood up and approached the pictures board. 'Interpretation is directly related to a person's frame of mind. Looking at the same image, a person could see two completely different things depending on the mood that person is in at the time. And that's the problem with the Rorschach test.'

'How can the same person see two different things?' Alice's gaze had moved to the shadow photograph pinned to the board. 'Every time I look at that, I see exactly the same thing – a devil figure looking down at what might possibly be his victims.'

'Then you're not keeping your options open,' Hunter came back. 'Look, let's say you have a shapeless image that resembles a face with its mouth wide open. You then show it to someone who, at that moment in time, is feeling happy. That person might interpret that image as someone laughing out loud.'

Garcia immediately caught on. 'But if that same person

were in a darker frame of mind for some reason, that same image could be seen as someone screaming in agony.'

'Correct. Your mood alters your outlook. And that's always been the biggest argument against the Rorschach test. Many say that it measures a subject's frame of mind at that point in time more than anything else. But I agree with you, Alice. Whatever the meanings behind those images are,' Hunter pointed to the shadow photograph. 'It has all to do with how *we* interpret it, and that's the key to this jigsaw. If we read it wrong, if we don't figure out exactly what the killer is trying to tell us through those shadows,' Hunter shook his head, 'I don't think we'll ever catch him.'

Sixty-Seven

She had been jittery all night, needing a hit more than she needed food. Regina Campos didn't care what kind of drug she took, she just needed to get high on something – anything. She had no money, but that wasn't too much of a problem. She knew exactly what to do to get her fix. By the age of sixteen, Regina had already learnt that any man would melt like butter if you knew what to do to him in bed.

Regina was only eighteen, and if you asked the few people who knew her, they'd probably describe her as average. She was of average height, with an average body and average looks. In a crowd, no one would give her a second glance. Her hair was neither long nor short, and in high school she'd been an average student, until she dropped out. But she was charming, and she sure knew how to get what she wanted out of people.

Regina had had a string of good-for-nothing lovers and casual encounters. Actually, they were good-for-one-thing lovers – drugs. Her newest good-for-one-thing lover, if she could even call him a lover, was a slob, an ex-convict, who lived in a housing project in Bell Gardens. He was over-weight, had the stamina of a 90-year-old man in bed, and got his kicks by wearing women's panties. Regina couldn't give a dry spit for how he got turned on. All she knew was that he could get her drugs.

She'd called him late last night, desperate, but he told her over the phone he wouldn't be in all night. She could come over in the morning if she wanted to.

It had been a long night of waiting for Regina.

She took the stairs up to the third floor like a marathon runner. By now she was so frantic for a hit she was grinding her teeth like a bunny. She didn't even think twice about the fact that the door to apartment 311 was unlocked, although her lover never left his door unlocked.

She pushed the door open and stepped inside the smelly apartment.

'Hello, babe,' she croaked. She'd been smoking so much crack lately it'd started damaging her vocal cords.

There was no response.

She was about to start searching the apartment for him when she saw something that was much more appealing – a silver box sitting on the small dining table. Next to it was a square mirror, and on it Regina could see residues of a white powder. Her little brown eyes lit up like a 4th-of-July sky.

'Babe?' she called again, with a lot less enthusiasm this time. Who cared where he was when her payment was already there, waiting for her?

Regina approached the table and ran her middle finger along the mirror, collecting all the leftover residue. She quickly brought the finger to her mouth and rubbed it against her gums before licking it, as if it'd been dipped in honey. Instantly her gums went numb and she shuddered with delight from the strength of the drug. That was very good stuff. She opened the box and looked inside. There were five hand-folded paper wraps. Regina knew exactly what was in them. She'd seen plenty of those before. Her lips spread into a huge smile.

For once Christmas had come early.

She grabbed one of the wraps, unfolded it and tapped some of its white powder onto the mirror. Her eyes searched the table for something she could use as a snorting tube.

She found nothing.

Regina took a step back and looked around. Under the table she saw a rolled-up five-dollar bill.

This was turning out to be a fantastic day.

She picked it up, tightened the roll-up, and brought it to her nose. She didn't care for arranging the powder in a straight line or anything, she just needed some of it to reach her bloodstream, and fast. Closing one of her nostrils with her finger, Regina sucked in a deep breath through her nose.

The drug-high hit her almost instantly.

'Wow.'

That was the best thing she had ever tried. No stinging or burning effect, just pure bliss.

She moved the rolled-up bill to the other nostril and sucked in a second deep breath.

This had to be what paradise felt like.

She put the bill down on the table and stood still for a moment, simply enjoying heaven.

Outside the day was already hitting 86°F. Regina felt beads of sweat starting to form at the top of her forehead. The drug had also bumped her body temperature up. She undid the top button of her shirt, but she needed to splash a little cold water on her face. She turned around and made her way to the bathroom. As she reached the door, she was engulfed by a strange sensation, like something crawling up the back of her neck. It made her shudder on the spot.

Her hand paused momentarily over the doorknob and she looked around herself, almost feeling a second presence.

'Babe, are you in here?' she called, moving her face closer to the door.

Again, no reply.

The tingling sensation at the back of her neck quickly ran down her spine, spreading through her whole body.

'Wow, that really was some good shit,' she whispered to herself.

Regina twisted the handle and pushed the door open.

Paradise became hell.

Sixty-Eight

By the time Hunter and Garcia got to apartment 311 in Bell Gardens, the forensic team's investigation was in full swing. Four people dressed in hooded white coveralls were stepping over each other inside the tiny flat, doing their jobs. In the living room, a young forensic agent was dusting a wooden sideboard for prints. A woman armed with a hand-held vacuum was collecting fibers and hairs from the floor. An older agent with a spray bottle and a portable ultraviolet light was looking for blood droplets on a silver box that was sitting on the dining table. All the while, the official crime-scene photographer was snapping away at everything.

Detective Ricky Corbí and his partner, Detective Cathy Ellison, were standing in the corridor just outside the apartment. Another three uniformed police officers were busy conducting the standard door-to-door.

'Are you Detective Corbí?' Hunter asked, coming from the badly lit stairwell.

The tall black man turned around and faced Hunter. He was around fifty years old, with a scowling face topped with tight-cropped hair sprinkled with just a little gray. He wore horn-rimmed glasses, a brown suit, and, judging by his physique, he'd probably played football when younger, and was still very physically active.

'That'd be me,' he said in a baritone voice. 'And by the looks of you two, you're Homicide Special.' He offered his hand. 'Detective Hunter, I presume.'

Hunter nodded. 'Call me Robert.' Corbí's handshake was firm and strong. His palm was slightly tilted downwards, which Hunter knew from experience was usually a sign of an authoritative person or a controlling personality. From the word 'go' Corbí was indicating that he was the one in charge there. Hunter had no intention of opposing that authority.

'Call me Ricky. This is my partner, Detective Cathy Ellison.'

Ellison stepped forward and shook Hunter and Garcia's hand with almost the same firmness as Corbí. She was about five feet six in height, trim but slightly stoop-shouldered, with short dark hair, cut in a textured, graduated style. Her eyes carried the intensity of someone who took her job very seriously. 'Call me Cathy,' she said, quickly studying both detectives.

'As I told you over the phone, the reason why I called you is that we found this in the victim's living room,' Corbí said, making a slight head movement towards the apartment, and handing Hunter a business card. 'It's one of yours, right?'

Hunter nodded.

Corbí reached inside his breast pocket for his notebook. 'Thomas Lynch, better known as Tito. He was out on parole from Lancaster. Been out for eleven months. According to his record,' Corbí faced Garcia, 'you were the arresting officer seven years ago, and the one who got a confession out of him.' He paused and reassessed his words. 'Or should I say, you convinced him to cut a deal. If I had to venture a guess, I'd say that since he was released he became some sort of informer for you guys.'

'Not really,' Garcia said.

Corbí looked at him with a penetrating stare. 'Friend?'

'Not really.'

Corbí nodded, taking off his glasses, breathing on both lenses and using the tip of his blue tie to polish them. 'Care to shed some light on how he came by one of your business cards? A very-crisp-and-new business card.'

The last sentence was delivered with a slight lilt in his tone.

Garcia held Corbí's gaze. 'We contacted him recently, looking for some information – but he wasn't an informer,' he added, before Corbí had a chance to retort. 'He was just someone who showed up in a list of names.'

Ricky Corbí was experienced enough to know that Garcia wasn't being stubborn. He was simply giving him all the information he was prepared to give at that time. Pursuing it further was pointless. He gave Garcia a barely noticeable nod.

'Could you tell us when you saw him last?' Ellison asked.

'Yesterday afternoon,' Hunter said.

Corbí and Ellison exchanged a quick look.

'According to the ME, your boy was murdered sometime last night,' Corbí took over again, returning his glasses to his face. 'Or most probably in the very early hours of the morning. They are just getting ready to take the body away, if you guys would like to have a look first . . .'

Hunter and Garcia nodded.

'I have no idea who he pissed off last night,' Corbí

added, handing the detectives a pair of latex gloves each, together with shoe covers. 'But whoever it was, he did a job on this Tito character. We have a real work of art in there.'

Sixty-Nine

Corbí and Ellison stepped into apartment 311, followed by Hunter and Garcia. Together with the four forensic agents, the already-crowded living room became a sardine can.

'What's in the box?' Hunter asked, nodding at the silver box on the dining table.

'Now, nothing,' Corbí said. 'But it did contain drugs – cocaine, to be more precise. A very fine cut. Probably very high-quality stuff. The lab will confirm it. Initial signs indicate that whoever whacked him took the drugs.'

'You think this was a drugs hit?' Garcia asked.

'Who knows at this stage?' Ellison replied.

'Who called it in?'

'Some terrified girl. Didn't leave a name. She sounded very young.'

'When was this? When was the call made?'

'This morning. We checked the recording. The girl said that she came to visit a friend. Most probably she came here to score some drugs. From the door-to-door so far, no one knows who this young *friend* could be.' Ellison's eyebrows arched. 'Actually, people barely knew the tenant in this apartment. No one is talking. And in a project like this, I'd be more surprised if they ever did. But forensics has already retrieved several sets of prints. Who knows, we might get lucky.'

Hunter's eyes swept the room in a matter of seconds; no blood anywhere. The living room looked a mess, but no different than it had the day before, when they'd paid Tito a visit. No visible disturbance. The chain lock and the inside doorframe were also intact. Nothing indicated a forced entry.

'Are you guys through in there?' Corbí asked the lead forensic agent, indicating the tiny corridor that led to the bathroom and bedroom.

'Yeah, we've got everything. You're clear.'

They crossed the living room.

'There's no way all of us will fit in there,' Corbí said as they got to the bathroom door. 'I thought there couldn't be a smaller bathroom than the one in my house. I was wrong. You guys go ahead. We've seen it.' Corbí and Ellison stepped back, allowing Hunter and Garcia to take lead.

Hunter slowly pushed the door open.

'Oh crap.' The words dribbled out of Garcia's lips.

Hunter said nothing, his gaze taking everything in.

The floor, the walls and the sink in the tiny bathroom were splattered with blood. Arterial spray from a knife being swung across someone's throat or body. Tito was naked, sitting on the floor inside the blood-soaked shower cubicle. His back was against the tiled wall, his legs stretched out in front of him, his arms loosely slumped by his side. His head was tilted back, as if he was looking at something on the ceiling. The problem was, he had no eyes. They both had been pressed back into his skull until they sunk in. One of them seemed to have busted in its socket. What looked like blood tears had run down the corners of the sockets, past his ears, and down the side of his shaved head. His mouth was opened, and half filled with thick, clotted blood. His tongue had been ripped from his mouth.

'We found the tongue at the bottom of the toilet,' Corbí offered from the door.

Tito's throat had been slit the whole length of his neck, and blood had cascaded down his torso and onto his lap and legs.

'According to the forensics guys,' Ellison said. 'There are no visible traumas to the body, which means he wasn't beat up. He was simply brought to the bathroom and slaughtered like cattle. No blood was found anywhere else in the house.'

'Drugged?' Garcia asked.

'We'll need to wait for the autopsy for confirmation. But it wouldn't surprise me if he was as high as my captain's ego when this happened. There's coke residue on the small square mirror on the table in the living room.'

'The bedroom is a damn mess,' Corbí took over. 'And it stinks of dirty clothes, unwashed body parts and pot. But judging by the rest of the apartment, I don't think that was a disturbance. I think he lived like a pig out of choice. We also found marijuana in the bedroom, a kilo of it, together with a few crack-cocaine pipes. If whoever did this was after something, that something was probably inside that silver box in the living room, drug or not.' He waited for Hunter and Garcia to exit the bathroom. 'I'm not gonna ask you what kind of information you requested out of this Tito character. That's your business, and I know better than to butt in into another cop's investigation, but is there anything you can tell us about the victim that might facilitate *our* investigation?'

Hunter knew he couldn't give Corbí and his partner Ken

Sands's name. Corbí would start searching for him, asking around. The heat on the streets to find Sands would increase, and so would the chances of him hearing about it and disappearing. Hunter couldn't risk that. He had to lie.

'Unfortunately there's nothing I can give you,' he said.

Corbí studied Hunter's face and demeanor and saw nothing that belied his answer. If that was a poker face, it was the best poker face Corbí had ever seen. A moment later his gaze reverted back to Ellison, who shrugged.

'OK,' Corbí said, adjusting his tie. 'I guess there's nothing else I can show you here.'

Seventy

Outside the sun was baking people and cars alike. Garcia reached for his sunglasses in his shirt pocket, and ran his hand around the back of his neck. It came back soaking wet. Standing by the driver's door, he looked at Hunter over the roof of his Honda Civic.

'Well, if Sands was the one who got to Tito, then it doesn't look like he's our killer, does it?'

Hunter stared back at him. 'And why is that?'

'Completely different MO, for starters. OK, he ripped the victim's tongue out, but compared to the savagery of the amputations in our last two crime scenes, what happened up there looks like a holiday camp. And we've got no sculp-ture and no shadow puppets.'

Hunter placed his elbows on the car's roof and interlaced his fingers. At that specific moment in time he was inclined to agree with Garcia, but there were still too many loose ends and something was telling him that discarding Ken Sands as a suspect right now was a big mistake. 'From what we gathered so far, don't you think that Sands is intelligent enough to change his MO on an unrelated crime?'

'Unrelated?' Garcia deactivated the central-locking sys-tem and got into his car.

Hunter followed.

Garcia unlocked the engine and switched on the A/C unit. 'What do you mean, unrelated?'

Hunter leaned against the passenger's door. 'OK, for a moment let's assume that we've been right in everything so far, and that Ken Sands really *is* our killer.'

'OK.'

'One of our assumptions is that Sands is going after his victims for revenge, not only for himself, but for his childhood friend as well, Alfredo Ortega, right?'

Garcia nodded. 'Yep.'

'OK, so where does Tito fit into his revenge plan?'

Garcia looked pensive for an instant.

'Remember, Tito said that they never even talked while inside. So there was no bad blood between them from their time in Lancaster.'

Garcia pinched his bottom lip. 'He doesn't fit.'

'No, he doesn't. If Sands is our man and he came after Tito, it wasn't because Tito was part of his original plan. It was probably because Tito went asking about him the wrong way, or to the wrong person.'

'But killers don't usually change their MO, unless they're escalating.' He pointed to the building. 'That's exactly the opposite. He's gone from absurdly grotesque to . . .' he tried to think of a word, '. . . plain nasty, I'd say.'

'And again, it goes back to the fact that Tito wasn't part of his original plan. Think about it, Carlos. To our killer, his MO is *extremely* important – the way he dismembers his victims, the way he carefully puts their body parts back together, constructing a sculpture to cast a different shadow onto the wall each time. To him, all that is mandatory, not a choice, not something he's doing for fun. It's as important as the killing act itself, and the choice of victim. It's part of his revenge. And I have no doubt there's a direct relation between the sculpture, the shadow, and each specific victim. There's a reason why he chose a coyote and a raven for Nicholson, and a devil-like image looking down at four other figures for Nashorn.'

'And Tito wasn't part of that at all,' Garcia said.

Hunter agreed in silence.

'But we're still not sure what the real meaning behind those shadow images is,' Garcia went on. 'And if you're right, and each image has a direct link to each specific victim, then there's something that isn't making any sense in my mind.'

'And what's that?'

'In the first shadow image, the killer paid very close attention to detail, specifically carving the victim's body parts so as to not leave us a lot of doubt. You said so yourself, the curved, chunky beak on the bird image ruled out a lot of possibilities, leaving us with just a few alternatives. And the same was done to the coyote image. But for the second shadow image, the attention to detail wasn't nearly so careful. It's hard to tell properly if we have a human face with horns, a devil, a God, or some sort of animal. The two standing figures, together with the ones on the ground could be people or not. Why would the killer do that? Be so specific with the first shadow image, but not with the second?'

Hunter rubbed his face with both hands. 'I can only see one reason – relevance.'

Garcia pulled a face and turned both of his palms up. 'Relevance?'

'I think the reason why our killer paid so much attention to detail on the first shadow image, is because it *mattered*.

He didn't want us to make a mistake in identifying what it was. He didn't want us to think that he gave us a dog and a dove, or a fox and an owl.'

Garcia thought about it for a heartbeat. 'But it didn't matter as much on the second one.'

'Not as much,' Hunter said. 'The details of the second image are less important to its meaning. It probably doesn't matter if the face with horns is human or not. That's not what the killer wants us to see.'

'So what *does* he want us to see?'

'I don't know . . . yet.' Hunter looked out the window at all the police cars parked in front of Tito's project building. 'But I do think Ken Sands is smart enough to change his MO just to throw us off his scent.'

Seventy-One

As the day drew to a close, Nathan Littlewood sat at his desk, listening to the recording of his last patient's session and jotting down some notes. His psychology practice was located in Silver Lake, just east of Hollywood and northwest of downtown LA.

Littlewood was fifty-two years old, five eleven in height, with classic good looks and a trim physique, kept that way by a good diet and three gym sessions a week. He was good at his job, very good in fact. His patients ranged from teenagers to over-sixties, singletons to married and live-in couples, and from everyday people to a few B-list celebrities. Every week tens of patients would pour their hearts and minds out to him.

His last patient of the day had left half an hour ago. Her name was Janet Stark, a 31-year-old actress who was having terrible problems with her live-in boyfriend. They'd been fighting a lot recently about the most mundane of things, and she was sure he was sleeping around behind her back. The problem was, she suspected he was sleeping around with another man.

Janet herself had slept around with plenty of women, and she still did. She wasn't afraid to admit it, but in her view, female bisexualism was acceptable, male wasn't.

She'd had six sessions with Littlewood so far. Two a week for the past three weeks, and the flirting had started almost immediately. After the first session, Janet had started dressing more provocatively – shorter skirts, low-cut blouses, mega-cleavage bras, sexy shoes, anything to grab his attention. Today she had turned up in a short summer dress, black, open-toed Christian Louboutin ankle boots, 'I-desperately-want-you-now' makeup, and no underwear. As she lay down on the couch, her dress hitched up over her thighs, and she positioned her legs in such a way that absolutely nothing was left to the imagination.

Littlewood loved women, and the sluttier and kinkier they were the better, but he knew better than to have affairs, or even flings, with patients. Things like that never stayed undercover. And in a city like Los Angeles, all that was needed was a flicker of a rumor for the crap to spread like wildfire. In LA, a good rumor had the power to destroy careers. Littlewood was smarter than that. He got his kicks elsewhere, and he paid good money for it.

Littlewood was divorced. He got married in his mid-twenties, but the whole thing lasted less than five years. The problems started pretty much straight after the ceremony. After four and a half years of arguments, discordances and great sexual frustration, their marriage fell into such deep depression that severe psychological damage was caused to both of them. Divorce was the only way out.

They'd had only one son, Harry, who was now studying Law in Las Vegas. After his marriage experience, and the lengthy and arduous divorce process, Littlewood promised himself he would never get married again. Since then, the thought of breaking that promise had not once crossed his mind.

A buzzer screeched on Littlewood's desk. He paused his Dictaphone and pressed the intercom.

'Go ahead, Sheryl.'

'Just checking if there's anything else you need from me today.'

Littlewood consulted his watch. It was way past office hours. He'd forgotten that Janet Stark liked her sessions to start as late as possible.

'Oh, I'm so sorry, Sheryl, you should've gone home over an hour ago. I lost track of time.'

'It's OK, Nathan.' Littlewood had insisted that Sheryl call him by his first name. 'I don't mind. Are you sure you don't need me to stay behind? I can if you want me to.'

Sheryl had been Littlewood's office manager/secretary for just over a year, and the sexual tension between them could probably light up a small town. But he reserved for her the same courtesy he gave his patients, despite the clear attraction that existed between them. Sheryl, on the other hand, would have dropped all professionalism and jumped into bed with Littlewood faster than anyone could say *guacamole*, given the opportunity.

'No, I'm fine, Sheryl. I'm just catching up on some notes. I'll be leaving soon. Half an hour max. Go home, and I'll see you tomorrow.'

Littlewood returned to his recording and his notes. It took him another thirty-five minutes before he had everything organized the way he wanted. By the time he got to his office building's underground garage, there were only three cars left. His was parked in the far corner, under a faulty light.

Despite his psychology practice doing well enough, Littlewood drove a silver, 1998 Chrysler Concorde LXi. He called it a classic, but his friends teased him that just because it was old, it didn't make it a classic.

He used the key to unlock the door and got into the driver's seat. He was desperately hungry, and he could certainly do with a stiff drink. The day's effort in dodging sexual innuendos also left him wanting something else, and he knew just where to go to get it.

He turned the key in the ignition. His engine stuttered and coughed like a dying dog but it didn't come to life. Sometimes his old Chrysler could be temperamental.

'C'mon baby.' He patted the dashboard.

Littlewood pumped the gas pedal three times and tried again. More coughing and rattling – no success.

Maybe it was time to upgrade to a newer model.

One more time.

'C'mon, c'mon.'

Nothing.

'Give me a goddamn break.'

More pedal pumping.

Chu, chu, chu, chu, chu.

Littlewood slammed his clenched fists against the steering wheel and cursed under his breath before closing his eyes and leaning back on his seat. By the looks of it, it would have to be a taxi tonight.

That was when he felt something like he'd never felt before. A sixth-sense warning that came from deep inside him, almost freezing his blood in his veins and making every hair on his body stand on end.

Instinctively his eyes shot up, searching for the rearview mirror.

Looking back at him, from the darkness of his backseat, was the most evil-looking pair of eyes he'd ever seen.

Seventy-Two

Hunter sat alone in total darkness facing the pictures board in his office. It was late and everyone had gone home. In his hand he held a flashlight, which he kept flicking on and off at uneven intervals, in an attempt to trick his brain.

As light enters the eye and hits the retina, the eye's photographic plate, the image that is formed is inverted, but is interpreted the right way up by the brain. If you allow that image to be projected onto the retina for just a split second before cutting off the light source, the brain then has to interpret only what it can remember, drawing from what modern medicine calls the 'immediate' or 'flash' memory.

If the image is a shape well known to the brain, like a chair, the minor details the brain failed to register due to the short light exposure, are automatically compensated by the long-term memory – the brain thinks 'it looked like a chair', so the brain pulls a chair image from its memory bank. But if the shape is unknown to the brain, then it has nothing to fall back on. It then compensates by working harder in trying to identify details from the original image. That was what Hunter was trying to do, force his brain to see something it hadn't seen before.

So far, it hadn't worked.

'Is this your idea of disco lights?'

Hunter turned in the direction of the voice and switched on his flashlight. Alice was standing by the door, holding her briefcase.

'I didn't know you were still here,' he said.

'What, you think you're the only workaholic in this place?' She smiled.

Hunter shifted in his seat.

'Do you mind if I switch on the lights?'

'Go ahead.' He flicked off his flashlight.

Alice hit the light switch before nodding at the board. 'Got anything new?' She knew what he was trying to do.

Hunter rubbed his eyes with his thumb and forefinger while shaking his head. 'Nothing.'

Alice placed her briefcase on the floor and leaned against the doorframe. 'Are you hungry?'

Hunter hadn't thought about it the whole day, and as he did his stomach rumbled. 'Starving.'

'Do you like Italian?'

Seventy-Three

Campanile was a rustically elegant restaurant on South La Brea Avenue, reminiscent of a little Mediterranean village, complete with a bell tower, a fountain-accented courtyard, and a tiny bakery.

'I didn't know you liked this place,' Hunter said as he and Alice took a table in the courtyard.

'There's a lot you don't know about me.' She looked at him with a faint smile on her lips, but not wanting Hunter to dwell on her words, she quickly followed them up. 'I used to come here a lot. I love Italian food, and the chef here is fantastic. Probably the best around this part of town.'

Hunter couldn't disagree. 'So you don't come here a lot anymore?'

'Not as much. I still love Italian food, but I'm not getting any younger, and I really have to watch what I eat. Shifting any excess weight isn't as easy as it used to be.'

Hunter unfolded the cloth napkin and placed it on his lap. 'I don't think there's any shifting to be done.'

Alice paused and looked back at him in a peculiar way. 'Was that you paying me a compliment?'

'Yes, and at the same time telling you the truth.' Alice pushed her hair back behind her ears and swept it around over her left shoulder. A self-conscious and slightly flirtatious move.

It went totally unnoticed.

'Shall we order?' Hunter asked.

'Why not.' The reply came in a less than enthusiastic tone.

They both ordered spaghetti. Hunter had his with primavera sauce, and Alice had hers with the chef's special spicy meatballs and sundried tomatoes. They shared a bottle of red wine and tried as best as they could to keep the conversation away from the investigation.

'How come you've never married, Robert?' The question came at the end of the meal, as the waiter poured them both the rest of the wine. 'As I said, in school most of the girls I knew had a thing for you. I'm sure you had plenty of opportunities.'

Hunter studied Alice while he had a sip of his wine. She had real interest burning in her eyes, almost like a reporter digging for a new scoop. 'There are certain things that just don't go together. What I do and married life are two of them.'

Alice pursed her lips together and twisted them to one side. 'That's a lame excuse, if I've ever heard one. Many cops are married.'

'True, but a large number of them eventually get divorced due to the pressures that come with being a cop.'

'But at least they tried, without hiding behind a pretty bad excuse. What happened to the old saying *better to have loved and lost than never to have loved at all*?

Hunter shrugged. 'I never heard that expression.'

'Bullshit.'

A ghost of a smile betrayed him.

'How about Carlos?' Alice said. 'He is married. Are you saying that his wife will eventually leave him because of his job?'

'Some people are very lucky, or at least lucky enough to find that one person in life they're meant to be with. Carlos and Anna are one such example. I don't think you'll ever find a better-suited couple. No matter how hard you look.'

'And you never met that person? The one you're supposed to be with for the rest of your life?'

In a flash Hunter's memory was inundated by images of one face . . . the sound of one name. He felt his heart warm in his chest, but as the memories progressed at hyper speed, it grew ice cold.

'No.' Hunter didn't shy away from her stare. But he was sure that something in his eyes gave him away.

Alice did see it. First something tender, then something hard and arctic, something very painful, and in spite of her curiosity, she knew she had no right to ask any more questions.

'I'm sorry.' She broke eye contact and changed the subject before the silence became too awkward. 'So you got nothing new from the second shadow image?'

'Nothing.'

'Tell me something, do you think we got the first one right? I mean, the interpretation of it – that the killer was telling us that, to him, Derek Nicholson was a betrayer, a liar.' She lifted a hand to stop Hunter from answering too quickly. 'I know that we'll never know for sure until we catch the killer. But does it ring right to you?'

Hunter could already see where she was leading. 'Yes.'

'But still, you have doubts about our interpretation of the second shadow image.'

'Yes.'

Alice sipped her wine slowly. 'You, Carlos and I have spent countless hours studying that human sculpture and the shadow image it casts, trying to make some sense of its meaning. I don't think there's anything else there, other than what we've been seeing from the start. Even the captain agrees. Why do you think we're wrong this time? Why can't the killer be using the image to tell us that he's going after two more victims?'

The waiter came over to clear their table. Hunter waited until he moved away, balancing all the dishes up his arms.

'In my view, that interpretation is too much of a leap from the first one. It doesn't make a lot of sense.'

Alice's eyes widened. 'Sense? What in this case makes sense, Robert? We have a maniac out on an ego trip, chopping people up and creating human-flesh sculptures so he can give us crazy clues to a jigsaw puzzle. Where the hell is the sense in all that?'

Hunter quickly scanned the surrounding tables to see if anyone else had heard Alice's comment. Her voice had risen a few decibels with excitement. Everyone seemed much more interested in their own food and wine than in their conversation. His attention returned to Alice.

'It doesn't make sense to us because we haven't figured it out yet. But to the killer, it makes perfect sense. That's why he's doing it.'

Alice measured those words in silence. 'That's what you've been trying to do, isn't it? To think like the killer. To see the sense that only he can see.'

'Well, it's been exactly a week, and so far I've failed miserably.'

'No you haven't.' She placed one hand on the table, and the tips of her fingers brushed against the back of Hunter's hand. 'So far you've done a better job than anyone would've expected. If it weren't for you, we'd all still be looking at those sculptures, trying to figure out what they meant.'

Hunter paused and looked at Alice. 'Was that you paying me a compliment?'

'No, just stating the truth. But what did you mean when you said it was too much of a leap from our interpretation of the first one.'

'Would you like to see the dessert menu?' The waiter had come back to the table.

Alice didn't even look at him, simply shaking her head. Hunter gave him a sympathetic smile.

'I think we overdid it on the main course. We've got no space left for anything else, thank you.'

'Prego,' the waiter replied and went on his way.

'What leap?' Alice insisted.

'If we're right in our interpretation of the first shadow image, then the killer gave us *his* opinion of Derek Nicholson, right? He considered him a liar.'

Alice sat back on her chair, things starting to connect in her head.

'But if we're also right in our interpretation of the second image, then the killer didn't give us his opinion of Andrew Nashorn.'

Alice saw his point. 'If we're right, he gave us his opinion of *himself* – an angry devil looking down at his victims.'

Hunter nodded. 'Yes, and I can't see a reason why he would do that. It seems wrong. This killer wants us to see something through his point of view. He wants us to understand why he's doing what he's doing. Why he's killing these people. Telling us that he thought Nicholson was a liar, that he was maybe betrayed by him, makes sense.'

'But telling us that he's an angry devil out for revenge, doesn't?'

'Does it to you?'

Her eyebrows arched for a second. 'No,' she admitted. 'So you think he's trying to tell us something about Nashorn with the second image?'

'Maybe.'

'Yeah, but what? That he considered Nashorn the devil? A man with horns? And how about the other four images, two figures standing and two down? What the hell do they mean?'

Hunter had no reply.

Seventy-Four

His eyelids fluttered like butterfly wings – very damaged butterfly wings. They felt as if they weighed a ton, and it took Nathan Littlewood several seconds and tremendous effort to half open them and keep them that way. Shards of light seemed to rip through his eyeballs. He took a deep breath and his lungs burned as if the air were sulfuric acid. Whatever drug was injected into his neck, it was now wearing off.

His chin slumped down to his chest, his head feeling too heavy for him to lift it back up. He stayed like that for several seconds. Only then he realized that he was naked, except for his sweat-soaked striped boxers clinging to his skin. It took him another moment to understand his position. He was sitting down on a comfortable leather office chair. His arms were pulled back behind him, around the chair's backrest. His wrists were bound together by something hard and thin that was cutting into his flesh. His feet were also pulled back and tied together under the chair's seat, about an inch or so from the floor. His whole body hurt as if he'd been at the receiving end of a massive beating, and the pain inside his head was eating away at his sanity.

Something was pulling against the corners of his mouth, and all of a sudden he was overwhelmed by a desperate gagging sensation. Coughing erupted from his chest with incredible force, but the air was half-blocked by the tight cloth gag in his mouth, and that served only to intensify his desire to retch. Littlewood tasted bile mixed with blood, and the coughs quickly escalated into a struggle not to choke to death.

Breathe through your nose, was the only thought that came into his head. He tried to concentrate on that, but he was too scared and drunk on pain for his brain to muster any discipline at that moment. Littlewood needed more air, he was desperate for it, and instinctively he drew another deep breath through his mouth. The mixture of bile and blood that was sitting just under his tongue was sucked back into his throat, blocking the oxygen passage even more.

Total panic.

His eyes rolled back into his head and the contents of his stomach exploded inside him, shooting up through his chest and esophagus like a rocket, though to him everything happened in slow motion. His body started to go limp. Life was quickly draining away from him.

He felt the acid taste of vomit take hold of his mouth a fraction of a second before it was flooded by warm, lumpy liquid. At that exact moment, his gag gave in, dropping from his mouth as if someone had snipped it off at the back.

He threw up all over his lap. But the good news was he could now breathe.

After a battery of dry coughs and spits, Littlewood started taking desperate gasps of air, trying to fill his lungs with oxygen and at the same time calm himself down. He started shaking, convulsing with two realizations – one: he had just come within an inch of death; two: he was still tied to a chair, and he didn't have a clue what was going on.

Movement came from his left. Startled, Littlewood's head snapped in that direction. Someone was there, but the shadows didn't allow Littlewood to see.

'Hello?' he said, in such a weak voice he wasn't sure it'd been audible to anyone but himself.

A few more desperate breaths to steady himself.

'Hello?' he tried again.

No answer.

Littlewood looked around himself. He saw a large book-shelf crowded with leather-bound volumes, a floor lamp by the side of a large desk across the room from him – the room's only source of light. His eyes moved right and he saw a comfortable brown leather armchair. A few feet in front of it he recognized the psychologist's couch – his psychologist's couch. He was back in his office.

'By the look on your face, I can see you've figured out where you are.' The phrase was delivered in an even voice. Someone had come from the shadows, and was now standing about five feet in front of him, leaning against his desk.

Littlewood's gaze refocused on the tall figure as even more confusion settled in.

'This is your office. Four floors up from the road below. Thick windows. Thick walls. And your window faces the back alley. Outside your door there's a large waiting room, and only then do you reach the door to the outside hallway.' A pause and a shrug. 'Scream if you like, but no one will hear a peep.'

Littlewood coughed again to try and clear the vile taste from his mouth. 'I know you.' His voice was croaked and weak. Fear cloaked every word.

A smile and a shrug. 'Not as well as I know you.'

Littlewood's head was still too fuzzy for him to put a name to the face. 'What? What's all this?'

'Well, what you don't know about me is that I am . . . an artist.' A deliberate pause. 'And I'm here to make you into a work of art.'

'What?' Littlewood finally noticed that the person in front of him was wearing a clear, hooded, thick plastic jumpsuit and latex gloves.

'But I guess that what I am does not matter. What matters is what I know about you.'

'What?' The fog of confusion was getting denser, and Littlewood started wondering if all this wasn't just a bad dream.

'For example,' the artist continued. 'I know where you live. I know about your awful marriage all those years back. I know where your son goes to college. I know where you go when you want to let off some steam. I know what you like when it comes to sex, and all the places you go to get it. The dirtier the better, isn't that right?'

Littlewood coughed again. Spit dribbled down his chin.

'But best of all . . . *I know what you did.*' Pure anger found its way into the artist's voice.

'I . . . I don't know what you're talking about.'

The artist took a step to the left and the light from the pedestal lamp reflected on something that'd been laid out on Littlewood's desk. Littlewood couldn't make out what it was, but he realized that there were several metal objects lying there. Shuddering fear traveled through every inch of his body.

'It's OK. I will remind you as the night goes on.' An irreverent chuckle. 'And for you, it will be a long, long night.' The artist grabbed two objects from the desk and approached Littlewood.

'Wait. What's your name? Could I have some water, please?'

The artist stopped directly in front of Littlewood and chuckled sarcastically. 'What, you want to try your psychology crap with me? What would that be? Let's see . . . ah yes . . . *Appeal to the assailant's human side by asking for the simplest of things, like water, or going to the bathroom. Sympathy for those in need is a natural sentiment to most human beings.* You want to call me by my name? Who knows, maybe I'll call you by yours – *which would humanize the victim in the eyes of the assailant, transposing the victim from a simple victim to a person, a human being, someone with a name, with feelings, with a heart. Someone who the assailant could maybe identify with. Someone who, outside the given situation, could be just the same as the assailant, with friends, and family, and everyday problems.*' A new chuckle. '*Appeal to their human nature, right? It's supposedly harder for people to hurt someone they know. So try to strike a conversation. Even a simple one can have a massive effect on the assailant's psyche.*'

Littlewood looked up with horror in his eyes.

'That's right. I read the same books as you did. I know hostage-situation psychology as well. Are you sure you want to try your bullshit with me?'

Littlewood swallowed dry.

'The building is empty. We've got until tomorrow morning before anyone even walks past your door. Maybe we can chat while I work, what do you say? Want to give it a try? Maybe spark some sympathy inside me?'

Tears filled Littlewood's eyes.

'I say let's make a start.'

Without any more warnings, the artist pinched and

twisted Littlewood's exposed nipple with a pair of metallic medical forceps, pulling it away from his body so hard that the skin almost ruptured right there and then.

Littlewood let out an agonized cry. He felt vomit starting to rise up in his throat again.

'I really hope you don't mind pain. This knife isn't very sharp.' The other instrument the artist had retrieved from the desk was a small, serrated knife. It looked old and blunt.

'Feel free to scream if this hurts.'

'Oh God, pl . . . , pl . . . , please, don't do this. I beg you. I . . .'

Littlewood's next words were abruptly substituted by a soul-chilling scream as the artist slowly started sawing off his nipple.

Littlewood almost passed out. His mind was struggling with everything. He desperately wanted to believe that whatever was happening to him wasn't real. It couldn't be real. He had to be inside the absurd world of some crazy dream. It was the only logical explanation. But the pain that shot up from his blood-and-vomit-soaked chest was very real.

The artist put down the blunt knife and watched Littlewood bleed for a while, waiting for him to catch his breath, to regain some of his strength.

'As much as I've enjoyed that,' the artist finally said, 'I think I want to try something different now. This might hurt more.'

Those words sent Littlewood tumbling down a rabbit hole of such intense fear that his whole body tensed. He felt the muscles of his arms and legs cramp so hard it paralyzed him.

The artist moved closer.

Littlewood closed his eyes, and though he wasn't a religious man, he found himself praying. Seconds later he noticed the smell. Something unbearably strong and intrusive. Something that immediately made him want to be sick again. But his stomach had nothing else to throw up.

The smell was instantly followed by excruciating pain. Only then did Littlewood realize that his skin and flesh were burning.

Seventy-Five

The call came through on Hunter's cellphone mid-morning, just as he was getting back into his car. He'd just revisited both crime scenes – Nicholson's house and Nashorn's boat, still looking for something he wasn't even sure was there.

'Carlos, what's new?' Hunter said, bringing the phone to his ear.

'We've got another one.'

By the time Hunter got to the four-story office building in Silver Lake, it looked like a music concert was about to take place. A large crowd had gathered around the police perimeter, and no one was prepared to move an inch until they got at least a glimpse of something morbid.

Reporters and photographers were sniffing around like a pack of hungry wolves, listening to every rumor, collecting whatever information they could gather, and filling in the holes in their stories with their own imagination.

Police vehicles were scattered on the street and on the sidewalk, causing traffic chaos. Three officers were frantically trying to organize things, urging pedestrians to move along, telling them there was nothing to see, and signaling cars to drive on as they slowed down to take a peek.

Hunter rolled down his window and flashed one of the

policemen his badge. The young officer took off his hat
while squinting against the glare of the sun, and used his
hand to wipe the sweat from his forehead and nape.

'You can go around the side and park down in the building's underground garage, Detective. Forensics and the
other detectives parked their vans and cars there. No
offense, but we don't need any more cars up here.'

Hunter thanked the officer and drove on.

The underground garage was spacious enough, but very
dark and gloomy. As Hunter maneuvered to park next to
Garcia's car, he identified three faulty light bulbs. He also
saw no CCTV cameras anywhere, not even at the garage's
entrance. He parked, stepped out of the car and quickly
studied the ample space – nothing but a cement box with
pillars, parking lines on the ground, and dark corners everywhere. At the center of it, a square block with a wide metal
door that led to the underground landing. From there one
could choose to take the elevator or the stairs up. Hunter
took the stairs. On his way to the fourth floor he passed
four more uniformed police officers.

The stairwell door dropped Hunter at the end of a long
corridor, alive with movement – more officers, uniformed
and plain-clothed, and forensic agents.

'Robert,' Garcia called from just over halfway down the
hallway, as he pulled down the hood on his white coverall.

Hunter walked over, frowning at the number of people
crowding the scene. 'What's all this? Are we having a party?'

'We might as well,' Garcia replied. 'This whole thing is a
mess.'

'I can see that, but why?'

'I just got here, but the initial call didn't come to us.'

Hunter started suiting up. 'How come?'

Garcia unzipped his coverall and reached inside his pocket for his notebook. 'The victim in question is Nathan Francis Littlewood – fifty-two years old, divorced. This is his psychology practice. According to Sheryl Sellers, his office-manager-stroke-secretary, and the person who found his body this morning, Littlewood was still in his office when she left at around seven-thirty last night.'

'Late office hours,' Hunter commented.

'That's what I thought. The reason was that Littlewood's last patient ended her session at seven. Ms. Sellers said she always stays until the last patient of the day has left.'

Hunter nodded.

'She found the body when she came in this morning to start her working day, at around eight-thirty. The problem is, understandably, she panicked when she saw what's in there. A few people from the other offices on this floor had already arrived to start their day. They all heard the screams and came running. Grotesque or not, our crime scene became an early morning attraction before the cops got here.'

Hunter zipped up his coverall. 'That's just great.'

'As I said, we weren't the first ones called,' Garcia continued. 'Silver Lake falls under the Central Bureau's jurisdiction – northeast division. Two of their detectives were sent over. When Doctor Hove arrived and saw the scene, she called us. Basically we have a platoon of people who've contaminated the scene.'

'Where's the doctor?'

Garcia's head tilted towards the office. 'Inside, working the scene.'

'So is this your partner?' The question came from the man who had come up behind Garcia. He was just under six feet tall, with short black hair, close-set eyes and eyebrows so thick and bushy they looked like hairy caterpillars.

'Yes,' Garcia nodded. 'Robert Hunter, this is Detective Jack Winstanley from the Central Bureau's northeast division.'

They shook hands.

'Hunter . . .' Winstanley said, while his brow creased for an instant. 'You're the guys who are investigating that cop's murder, aren't you? The one at the marina a few days ago. He used to be with the South Bureau, right?'

'Andrew Nashorn,' Hunter replied. 'Yes.'

Winstanley rubbed the point between his caterpillar eyebrows with his index finger. Hunter and Garcia knew exactly what was coming.

'Are we talking about the same killer here? Was he chopped up like the guy in there?'

'I haven't seen the scene yet,' Hunter replied.

'Don't give me that horseshit. If you're here to take over *my* murder scene, then you know what the hell I'm talking about. What's in there is pure evil.' He gestured towards the psychologist's office. 'The victim was chopped up like a casserole chicken. And what the fuck is that sick thing that was left on the desk? Are those his body parts?'

Hunter and Garcia exchanged a quick look. There was no point denying it.

'Yes,' Hunter said. 'It probably is the same perpetrator.'

'Mother of God.'

Seventy-Six

Though the first room was, in essence, a waiting room, it'd been done up to look like a residential living area – a comfortable sofa, two comfortable armchairs, a low, glass-and-chrome coffee table, a fluffy oval rug, and framed paintings on the walls. A receptionist's desk sat half-hidden in the corner, expertly positioned so as not to intrude. Two forensics agents were silently working the room. Hunter noticed that the door wasn't alarmed and it didn't look to have been forced; no CCTV cameras were visible. There were no footprints on the rug or carpet. He and Garcia crossed to the door on the other side, to the right of the desk.

As with the previous two crime scenes, the first thing Hunter noticed once he pushed the door open was the blood – large, thick pools of it that had stained most of the carpet, and thin, arterial sprays that crisscrossed each other on the walls and furniture. Hunter and Garcia paused by the door for an instant, as if the horror of what was before them had produced a force field, keeping them from stepping into the room.

What was left of Littlewood's dismembered body was resting on a blood-soaked, wheeled office chair that had been positioned about five feet in front of a large, rosewood executive desk. No arms, no legs. Just a disfigured torso and head, covered in sticky, crimson blood. His mouth was open, frozen in a scream that no one heard. By the amount of dried-up dark blood that had spilled from his mouth and now caked his chin and chest, Hunter knew his tongue had been taken from him. There were deep cuts all over his torso – clear evidence of torture. His left nipple had been cut off. Through all the blood, Hunter couldn't really tell, but there seemed to be something different about the skin around his right nipple. Both eyelids were open. His right eye looked straight ahead in horror, but there was no left eye, just a mutilated, empty dark hole. Despite the heat in the room, Hunter's blood ran cold.

His eyes slowly traveled the five feet between the body and the executive desk. The computer monitor, the books, and everything else that once occupied it were now on a messy pile on the floor. The desk had become the stage for the killer's new repulsive sculpture.

Both of Littlewood's arms had been severed at the elbow joints and placed at opposite ends on the stage, one facing north, the other facing south. The wrists had been clearly broken, but they hadn't been severed from the arms. The index and middle fingers on both hands had been pulled apart from each other to form a common V-sign. The other fingers, with the exception of the thumbs, had been severed from both hands.

Both index fingers' knuckles had been dislocated, creating a horrible lump, which protruded outward from the hands like a tumor. The wrists were twisted forward, as if the palms were trying to touch the inside of the forearms. On the left hand, the fingers in a V-shape were fully extended, their tips touching the stage. From a distance, it looked just like what kids do when they play 'walking fingers'. The fingers in a V-shape looked like legs, the hand like a body. The left thumb had been dislocated and pushed slightly forward.

On the right hand, the 'walking fingers' were also touching the stage, but their tips had been cut off at the first phalange, making them look like shorter legs. As with the left hand, the thumb looked dislocated and it had been pushed forward, but its tip was obviously broken, as it was awkwardly pointing up towards the ceiling.

Hunter looked up, checking if the disjointed tip was pointing at anything specific. Nothing. There were a few blood splatters on the ceiling, but that was all.

Neither of Littlewood's legs was on the desk, they were both on the floor, by the computer monitor – no feet, just the defaced stumps. Part of the right thigh had been carved out. The legs didn't look to be part of the sculpture on the desk. But this time there was something else, something different. The sculpture wasn't made only of body parts. The killer had used common office objects to complete the work. Just inches from one of the desk corners, about three feet away from Littlewood's left hand, the one with the longer walking fingers, a hardcover book lay flat on the desk. It was a thick volume. Its pages were drenched in blood. Its cover was fully open. Three of Littlewood's severed fingers had been oddly placed inside the book.

Hunter frowned. Something was off.

He started moving towards the desk and realized that it wasn't a book at all, but one of those secret boxes that are made to look like a book. From where Hunter was standing, it was very convincing.

As Hunter approached the desk, he saw that the fingers

that had been placed inside the book-box had been carved and were bent out of shape. Two were hanging out the sides. The other one had been placed at the far end with its tip protruding upwards. The inside of the box was flooded with blood.

At the opposite end of the desk, Littlewood's right arm, the one with the shorter 'walking fingers', had been positioned at a strange angle, facing the bookshelf on the corner. Pieces of his carved-out thigh had been placed a couple of feet away from the hand.

Doctor Hove and Mike Brindle, her most senior lead-forensic agent, were standing to the right of the desk. They had been discussing something in a hushed voice when both detectives had entered the room.

Hunter paused as he came closer to the desk. Just like the previous two sculptures, the mess of body parts and blood made no sense. The use of everyday office props made it all the more confusing. He took a step to his right and bent down to have a better look at the book-box.

'It's the same killer all right,' Doctor Hove said. 'And again, he reserved a whole new treatment for this new victim.'

Hunter kept his eyes on the sculpture.

'What do you mean?' Garcia asked.

The doctor stepped away from the desk. 'With the first victim, the killer pumped him full of drugs to stabilize his heart rate and normalize the blood flow, trying to keep him from bleeding out too fast, but no anesthetizing drug. The killer tried to keep him alive for as long as possible, but due to his precarious condition, death came quite quickly. With the second victim, you will remember, the killer used a new approach.'

'The severed spinal cord,' Garcia said.

'Precisely. The killer deliberately took away the victim's sense of feeling, numbing his pain. His anguish was different – psychological. He was made to watch his own body parts being severed from his body. He could see he was dying, but he couldn't feel it.'

'And with his third victim?' Hunter asked.

Doctor Hove looked away, as if scared to even think about it.

Seventy-Seven

Mike Brindle circled the desk and approached the two detectives. He was in his late-forties, stick thin and doorframe tall, with a full head of peppery hair and a pointy nose. He'd worked with Hunter and Garcia on more cases than he could remember. 'We're very sure that this victim died before he was dismembered, Robert,' he said, taking over from Doctor Hove.

Hunter's stare reverted back to the mutilated torso on the leather chair. 'Intentionally?'

Brindle nodded. 'It looks that way.'

Garcia looked confused for an instant.

'From on-location analysis, it seems the killer made him suffer as much as he could before amputating any major body parts and causing severe blood loss. There are several smaller cuts to his torso and limbs. Deep enough to hurt, but not enough to kill. His left nipple looks to have been sawed off with a not-so-sharp instrument. His right nipple was severely burnt.'

That was what was different about the skin around his right nipple, Hunter realized. The leathery texture of the skin – burn marks, but they didn't look to have been caused by fire.

'Blood spillage suggests that the smaller cuts were all done while the victim was still alive,' Brindle carried on.

'But there is a lot of blood here,' Garcia said, looking around the room. 'This didn't all come from small cuts.'

'No,' Doctor Hove confirmed. 'The autopsy will tell me the correct chain of events, but if I had to venture a guess, I'd say the killer had all the fun he wanted to have before severing the first limb, which looks to have been the right leg. His heart was probably still beating. But if you think back to the previous two victims, the killer went out of his way to contain the bleeding – drugs, natural remedies, tying off arteries . . .' She shook her head as her gaze moved back to the body on the chair. 'Not here.'

'The amputations on the first two victims were very clean,' Brindle said. 'These weren't. Judging by the pattern on the skin, and the little we can tell from examining the bones in these conditions, the amputation incisions were performed brutally, in a hacking manner. The ones to both arms . . .' He paused and ran his gloved hand over his nose and mouth. 'It looks like he cut them almost all the way through, lost patience, and then simply ripped them off the body.'

Garcia's eyes widened a touch.

'I have no doubt the victim was already dead by then,' Doctor Hove added.

Hunter's gaze refocused on the floor and the several footprints. They were mainly by the door. 'Has anything been touched?'

Doctor Hove gave him a timid shrug. 'LAPD has tried to track down every curious office worker in this building who decided to have a peek at this. So far, they've all said they haven't touched anything, and neither have the detectives and officers who have been in here; but it's hard to tell.' She faced the sculpture again. 'We don't really know what this is supposed to be, or look like. We can't tell if anything has been moved out of place since it was constructed.' The expectancy in her tone didn't go unnoticed by Hunter. 'I haven't used a flashlight,' she continued. 'That's your show.'

Garcia looked at Hunter as if to ask, *How do you want to play it?*

Hunter knew they couldn't move the sculpture from that desk without disturbing it. As he had told Alice, the killer had been very meticulous about the first sculpture, but less so about the second one. He had no idea what the killer was aiming for with this third one, and something was telling him they were running out of time – fast. They couldn't wait for the forensics lab to create another replica. 'Do we have a flashlight?' he asked.

'Right here,' Brindle said, handing him a medium-sized Maglite.

'Let's have a look,' Hunter replied, taking the flashlight. He looked back at what remained of Littlewood's body on the chair. In the second crime scene, the victim's decapitated head had been placed in the exact location where the killer wanted the beam of light to be shone from, so that his work could be seen as he intended. One of Littlewood's eyes was missing, but the remaining one was looking straight at the sculpture. That had to be a hint. Hunter checked the floor again.

'Has all this been photographed, Doc?' There was no way he could assume the same position as Littlewood's one-eyed gaze without stepping on some blood, and maybe rolling the chair with the body a little out of the way.

Doctor Hove didn't have to ask. She had followed

Hunter's stare and knew what was on his mind. 'Yes, it's all OK,' she replied.

The window shades were already drawn shut. Brindle killed the strong forensic power lights while Hunter positioned himself directly in front of the body, being careful to level the flashlight with Littlewood's line of sight.

Everyone seemed to take in a deep breath at the same time.

Hunter steadied himself and turned the flashlight on.

Seventy-Eight

Everyone had moved over to where Hunter was standing. Garcia was to his right, Doctor Hove and Brindle to his left. All eyes were on the images projected onto the wall behind the sculpture. Brindle shifted nervously on his feet.

'This is freaky,' he whispered weakly. When Doctor Hove had told him about the shadow images cast by the sculptures, he'd imagined something very creepy; but being there and seeing it with his own eyes was a whole new ball game. It had been a long time since he'd felt that uncomfortable at a crime scene.

Instinctively everyone squinted at the images, but no one had to ask. These were the clearest images so far – no animals, no horned creatures.

Littlewood's 'walking fingers' of the left hand projected an image that looked just like a person standing up. The thumb that had been pushed a little forward created an arm. The dislocated knuckle at the top created a head shape. The combined image was that of a person either walking or standing still and pointing at something in front of him or her. The opened book-box projected a shadow that looked like some sort of large container with its lid open.

Depth is imperceptible in shadow images, so the open book-box, three feet away from the hand, seemed to be directly leveled with it. The composition looked like someone standing in front of a large container, pointing at it.

The twist came with the fingers that had been carved and placed inside the book-box. Their shadows created a new image that, in a strange way, resembled someone else lying inside the container. The shadow of one of the fingers created a head, resting against one end. The other two fingers, sticking out to the side of the box, created what looked like an arm and a leg. The rest of the body couldn't be seen, as if it were submerged inside the box. The image reminded Hunter of someone leisurely lying inside a bathtub, one arm hanging out to one side, one foot up on the edge, head resting against one end.

Garcia was the first to utter a comment. 'It looks like someone pointing at someone else sleeping inside a box, or . . . having a bath or something.'

Brindle nodded slowly. 'Yeah, I can go with that. But why is he pointing at it?'

'That's part of the jigsaw,' Garcia said. 'We not only have to find the right angle to see the image, but we have to interpret it as well.'

'Does it mean anything to you?' Doctor Hove asked Hunter. 'Does it tie in, in any way, with what you already have?'

Hunter kept his eyes on the shadow image. 'I'm not sure, and I wouldn't like to speculate until I've studied this image further.'

'It's quite hypnotic,' Brindle added, tilting his head to one side and then the other, as if trying to look at the image from different angles.

'And I'm sure that was exactly the killer's intention,'

Garcia said. 'OK, we've got to do the same thing we did inside Nashorn's boat and photograph the shadow. We'll need to reposition the forensics lights to where the flashlight is, that way we won't need to use the camera flash.'

'It's not a problem,' Brindle replied and started moving towards the forensics pedestal light in the corner.

'Wait,' Hunter said, frowning. Something wasn't right. He turned off the flashlight and turned around, his eyes roaming the room from floor to ceiling.

'What's up?' Garcia asked.

'It doesn't seem right.'

'What doesn't?'

'The image, it's incomplete.'

Garcia, Doctor Hove and Brindle exchanged intrigued looks. No one seemed to know what Hunter was referring to.

'Incomplete, how?' Doctor Hove asked.

Hunter switched the Maglite on again. The shadow image resurfaced on the wall behind the sculpture. 'What do you see?'

'The same as I saw just a moment ago,' she replied. 'Just what Carlos suggested. It looks like someone standing in front of a container that seems to be occupied by someone else. Maybe a bathtub. Why, what do you see?'

'The same.'

Surprised looks all round.

'So why did you say there's something missing?' Garcia asked. He was used to Hunter seeing things that no one else did – questioning things that no one else questioned. It was like his mind was never satisfied. He just had to keep on digging, even when the images were clear in front of his eyes.

'The image of the container is obviously created by the fake book on the desk, and the image of the person inside it, by the torn fingers.'

'That's right,' Garcia agreed. 'And the image of the person standing in front of it is being created by the hand.'

'OK,' Hunter said. 'But from this angle, we've got nothing from the second hand.'

Everyone looked at the victim's right arm at the opposite end of the large desk. The one with the shorter 'walking fingers'. In front of it the killer had laid several carved out pieces of Littlewood's thigh.

'The two arms are too far apart,' Hunter continued. 'The light beam isn't wide enough.'

'Maybe it isn't part of the sculpture,' Brindle said.

Hunter shook his head. 'I'd agree that the legs and the severed feet aren't part of the sculpture. They've been discarded by the side of the desk, but not the arm. It's on the stage for a reason.' Hunter's gaze was again slowly searching the room. His eyes rested on the bookshelf lined with thick volumes to the left of the large executive desk and he paused. Three shelves from the bottom, about level with the desktop, the killer had carefully placed Littlewood's extracted eyeball on top of a book that was lying flat. The eye was looking straight at the second sculpture from a peculiar angle.

'Two separate images,' Hunter said.

Everyone's gaze followed Hunter's.

'Sonofabitch,' Garcia murmured.

Hunter crossed to the bookshelf, held the flashlight level with the bloody eyeball and turned it on.

Seventy-Nine

It took them less than five minutes to reposition the forensics lights and capture two separate snapshots of the two sculptures – or the two parts of the one sculpture, depending on how one looked at it. The body and severed body parts were already being prepared for removal.

Hunter and Garcia left Doctor Hove and Mike Brindle to carry on with their work and walked over to the next office along the corridor. It belonged to an accountant, but it was now being used by the police. Sheryl Sellers, Littlewood's office manager, who had found his body early that morning, had been sitting in there for over an hour, accompanied by a female police officer. Sheryl still hadn't stopped shaking or crying. The female officer practically had to force-feed her a glass of sugary water.

Sheryl had answered a few questions from Detective Jack Winstanley and his partner when they first arrived at the scene, but since then she'd been speechless, sitting in the accountant's office, blankly staring at a wall. She'd refused the offer to speak with a police psychologist. She said that all she wanted to do was leave that place and go home.

As Hunter and Garcia stepped into the office, Hunter gave the female officer a subtle nod. The officer returned his nod and stepped outside.

Sheryl was sitting on a brown, beat-up, two-seater sofa. Her knees were locked together, her hands clasped around a half-drunk glass of water resting on her lap, her whole body looked tense and stiff. She was perched right at the edge of her seat. Tears had made her eye makeup run down her cheeks, and she hadn't bothered wiping it off. The white of her eyes had completely disappeared, they were so bloodshot from crying.

'Miss Sellers,' Hunter said, crouching down to catch her eye. He was careful to settle just below her line of vision, putting him in a less challenging position.

It took her several seconds to bring her attention to the man in front of her. Hunter waited until their eyes locked.

'How are you doing?' he asked.

She sucked in a long breath through her nose and Hunter noticed her hands starting to shake again.

'Would you like a new glass of water?'

It took her a moment to grasp the question. She blinked. 'Do you have anything stronger?' Her voice was a wavering whisper.

Hunter gave her a quick smile. 'Coffee?'

'Anything stronger?'

'Double coffee?'

Her expression softened a touch. In different circumstances, she would've smiled. She shrugged instead, and nodded once.

Hunter stood up and whispered something in Garcia's ear, who then left the room. Hunter went back to his crouch position.

'My name is Robert Hunter. I'm another police officer with the LAPD. I know you've had to talk to a few today. I'm really sorry for what has happened, and for what you had to witness this morning.'

Sheryl felt the sincerity in his voice. Her gaze moved back to the glass in her hands.

'I know you've done this already. And I apologize for asking you to do it again, but could you run me through the chain of events since yesterday. From Dr. Littlewood's last session to when you got here this morning.'

Slowly and in a quivering voice, Sheryl Sellers recounted all the events she'd already told the first two detectives at the scene. Hunter listened without interrupting. The story was consistent with what he'd already heard.

'I really need your help, Ms. Sellers,' Hunter said when she was done. Her silence prompted him to go on. 'Could I ask you how long you've been Dr. Littlewood's office manager?'

She looked at him again. 'I started last spring. It's been just over a year now.'

'Can you remember if Dr. Littlewood seemed agitated or nervous at all after any of his sessions with any of his patients lately?'

She thought about it for an instant. 'Not that I can remember. He was always the same at the end of a session and at the end of the day – calm, relaxed, funny, most of the time . . .'

'Have any of his patients ever gotten violent or angry during a session?'

'No, never. At least not since I've been working here.'

'Do you know if any of his clients has ever threatened him in any way?'

Sheryl shook her head. 'Not that I know of. If anyone has, Nathan never mentioned anything to me.'

Hunter nodded. 'Inside Dr. Littlewood's office we found a secret book-box. Do you know what I'm talking about?'

She nodded but no fear returned to her eyes, which told Hunter what he already expected. When Sheryl opened the door to Littlewood's office earlier that morning, the first thing she saw was his dismembered body on the chair and all the blood. That was enough to send her into a panic. Everything else around her would've become a blur. Hunter doubted she had even noticed the desk and the sculpture. Instead of entering the office, she ran for help.

'Do you know if Dr. Littlewood had one of those in his office? A black-and-white one bearing the title *Subconscious Mind*?'

Sheryl frowned, finding the question a little odd. 'Yes. He kept it on his desk. But he never really used it as a secret box. That was where he always left his cellphone and car keys when he was in the office.'

Hunter wrote a few notes down in his notebook. 'Am I right in assuming that every patient booking for a new session had to go through you?'

She nodded.

'New clients as well?'

She nodded again.

Their eyes moved to the door as Garcia walked back into the room holding a cup of coffee. He smiled and handed it to Sheryl. 'I hope it's strong enough,' he said.

She took it from him, and without caring if it was too hot or not, had a large sip. The coffee was cool enough not to burn her mouth, but she recognized the powerful taste straight away and looked up at both detectives, surprised.

'One of the guys outside is Irish,' Garcia explained. 'The only coffee he knows how to prepare is an Irish coffee.' He shrugged. 'So I asked him.' He smiled again. 'It calms the nerves like nothing else.'

Her lips spread about three millimeters each side. Under the circumstances, that was the best smile she could give them. Hunter waited while Sheryl had two more sips. Her hands steadied a little and she looked back at Hunter.

'Ms. Sellers, I know Dr. Littlewood was a very busy man. Can you tell me if he was able to accommodate any new clients in the past two, three months?'

She kept her gaze on Hunter, but her focus became distant while she searched her memory. 'Yes, I think maybe three new clients. I need to check my records. I can't be sure. My mind just can't think straight right now.'

Hunter nodded, understandingly. 'I assume your records are in your computer.'

Sheryl nodded.

'It's really important that we find out how many new clients Dr. Littlewood had in the last few months, how many sessions they had, and who they were.'

Sheryl hesitated. 'I can't give you their names. That information is confidential.'

'I know you're a great office manager, Ms. Sellers,' Hunter said in an even voice. 'And I know exactly what you're talking about. I know I don't look like one, but I'm also a psychologist. I understand the code of ethics and what it means. What I'm asking you for will not break that code. You will not be breaking Dr. Littlewood's trust. The proceedings of the sessions are confidential and not our concern. I just need to know about the new clients. It's very important.'

Sheryl had one more sip of her coffee. She'd heard about the code of ethics, but she wasn't a psychologist. She'd never sworn to it. And if she could do anything to help catch whoever it was who had done what she'd just seen to Nathan Littlewood, by God she would.

'I need my computer,' she finally said. 'But I can't go back in there. I just can't walk back into that room.'

'It's not a problem,' Hunter said, nodding at Garcia. 'We'll bring your computer to you.'

Eighty

Captain Blake pushed the door to Hunter's office open just minutes after he and Garcia got back. Alice Beaumont was already in there.

'The victim was a psychologist this time?' the captain asked, reading from a single-sheet printout she had with her.

'That's correct,' Garcia said. 'Nathan Littlewood, fifty-two years old, divorced, lived alone. His ex-wife lives in Chicago with her new husband. They had one kid, Harry Littlewood, who lives in Las Vegas. He goes to college there. Nathan himself was a graduate from UCLA. Been on the board of psychologists for the city of Los Angeles for twenty-five years. His practice was based in Silver Lake. He'd been there for eighteen years. He lived in a two-bedroom apartment in Los Feliz, which we'll be checking later on today. As a psychologist he dealt mostly with regular everyday problems – depression, relationship issues, feelings of inadequacy, low self-esteem, that kind of thing.'

Captain Blake lifted a hand, interrupting him. 'Wait a second, how about police-related work? Has he ever helped the LAPD with any investigations?'

'We're on the same page as you, Captain,' Garcia replied, clicking away on his computer. 'If he did, that could certainly link Littlewood to the previous two victims, strengthening the probability of a revenge motive. We're looking into it, but we've got twenty-five years of records to go through, and obtaining those records isn't as easy as it may sound. We've only just got back from the crime-scene, but I've already got a small team working on it.'

The captain's interrogating stare switched over to Alice. She was waiting for it.

'I was just given that information,' she said. 'I haven't started digging yet, but if Nathan Littlewood was ever in any way involved with a police investigation, I'll find out.'

Captain Blake approached the pictures board and allowed her eyes to slowly go over the new crime-scene photographs. She noticed the difference straight away. 'His body is covered in cuts and bruises. Was he tortured?'

'Yes,' Hunter said. 'We'll need to wait for the autopsy results, but Doctor Hove got the impression that this time the killer took his time with the victim until he died, *before* making any of the amputations.'

The captain's attention moved to Hunter. 'Why?'

'We don't know.'

'But the killer hasn't done that to any of the two previous victims. The amputations *were* the torture. Why treat this one differently?'

'We don't know, Captain,' Hunter reaffirmed. 'His anger could be escalating, but most probably he's individualizing.'

'And that means what?'

'That each one of his victims will inevitably spark a whole new group of feelings inside him. Those feelings can, and will, be altered by the victim's reaction. Some victims will be too scared to talk back. Some might think that, if they cooperate, or try to reason with the killer, it could play to their advantage. Some will try to fight back, scream, do something . . . anything, except give up. But as individuals, we all react differently to fear and danger.'

'And the way this victim reacted might've really pissed the killer off,' Captain Blake concluded.

Hunter nodded. 'If he had a chance, and if he kept his nerve, I'm sure that Littlewood tried to talk to the killer as a psychologist, tried to dissuade him from what he was about to do. If the killer caught a hint of a patronizing tone in Littlewood's voice, it could've set off an anger bomb inside him. We don't know what went on in that room prior to the murder, captain. What we do know is that this crime scene carried a lot more anger than the previous two.'

'More anger?' Captain Blake looked at the two previous sets of crime-scene photographs. 'How's that possible?'

'The cuts and bruises to the victim's body suggests that the killer wanted to extend the victim's suffering. He wanted a very slow death. One that he wouldn't be able to achieve or control if he'd gone for the amputations too early. Littlewood's secretary left the office at around seven-thirty in the evening. We can't confirm it yet, but I'd say the killer got to him not much later than that. He had at least ten uninterrupted hours with the victim.' Hunter pointed to the photograph of Littlewood's body on the chair. 'And he tortured him for most of them.'

'And no one heard a peep?

'It's a small building full of small offices,' Garcia replied. 'Almost everyone had already gone home. The last one to leave was a graphic designer, whose office was on the first floor. He left at eight fifteen. The building has no CCTV security in place.'

'And if Doctor Hove's suspicions are correct,' Hunter carried on, 'the killer changed his MO for the amputations as well.'

'What do you mean?'

'In the first two victims, the amputation incisions were very professional,' Garcia explained. 'But not with the third victim. Doctor Hove said that there were indications of hacking and tearing. A butcher's job, not a doctor's one.'

Captain Blake let go of a worried breath. 'OK, so what the hell does this new sculpture give us? I'm assuming there's a new shadow image behind it.'

'No,' Garcia said.

'What?'

'There are two.'

Eighty-One

Captain Blake looked at both detectives but there was no surprise in her eyes. After what they've already got from this killer, hardly anything would surprise her now.

'We're not sure if the killer left us two different sculptures, or one sculpture in two parts,' Garcia said. 'He also did something else differently this time. He used office objects to complete his work.' Garcia proceeded to explain what they'd found on Nathan Littlewood's desk. While he did so, Captain Blake and Alice studied the new sculpture photographs in silence. When Garcia told them that the killer had extracted one of Littlewood's eyes, seemingly for the sole reason of indicating how one part of the sculpture should be looked at, Alice felt something dislodge in her stomach.

'We looked at this part of the sculpture first,' Garcia said, indicating the sculpture photograph on the board. 'And this is what we got.' He pinned the first shadow-image photograph onto the board, directly underneath the one belonging to its corresponding sculpture.

Captain Blake and Alice stepped closer to study the picture.

'So what the hell is this now?' the captain said, irritation peppering her words. 'Someone watching someone else having a bath? Has the killer gone perv now?'

'Or someone inside a box,' Hunter said.

'That's what I was about to say,' Alice suggested, addressing Hunter. 'I understand what you said about the level of detail of the second sculpture being lower than the first, but it was still high.' She pointed to the photograph of the new shadow image. 'This isn't a bathtub. There's a lid.' She compared it to the photograph of the actual sculpture. 'If the killer wanted us to think it was a bathtub, he could've easily ripped the lid from the original box off.'

Those had been Hunter's exact thoughts. If it was part of the image, there was a reason for it.

'So it looks like someone staring at someone else lying inside a box,' the captain corrected herself. 'Any clues as to what this might really mean?'

'Not yet,' Hunter replied.

'So it's just another meaningless clue. Another piece of this endless puzzlebox?'

Hunter said nothing.

The captain stepped back, fidgeting. 'So what's the second image we got?'

With the use of the crime-scene photographs, Garcia explained that the sculptures had been placed at opposite ends of the desk. By positioning the victim's head and his extracted eye at the appropriate spots, the killer had guided the light beam that would reveal the shadow images, like a movie director.

'This is what we got from the second one.' Garcia pinned the second shadow image photograph to the board.

Since the second hand sculpture was very similar to the first one, it was no surprise that the shadows cast by them were almost identical. No one had any doubts that it also depicted a person, but this time, because the killer had severed the 'walking fingers' at the first phalange, it looked like that person was either very short, or kneeling down. The way the thumb had been positioned – forward, with its broken tip pointing up – it looked like the person had his or her arm raised, pointing at the sky. On the floor, directly in front of the figure, there were large pieces of something unrecognizable. Their shadows were created by the carved out pieces from the victim's thigh.

'What the hell? He's fucking with us, that's what he's doing,' Captain Blake said, after an uneasy silence. 'What the hell is all this now? A midget? A child? Someone kneeling down? Praying? Pointing at the sky?' Her attention went back to the previous shadow-image photograph. 'So we have someone staring at someone else inside a box . . .' She stabbed her finger against the newest picture on the board, '. . . and a midget, a child, or someone kneeling down as if worshiping something. What does any of that have to do with this new victim?'

Everyone knew it was a rhetorical question.

'I'll tell you what . . .' the captain carried on, giving no one a chance to reply anyway, 'nothing. He's playing us, giving us animals, horned monsters, wall messages, rock songs, and now this crap. He's wasting our time, because he knows we'll spend hours and hours trying to figure out what all of this junk means.' She waved her hand in a circular motion to indicate the entire pictures board. 'Meanwhile, he's walking the streets, planning his next murder, staking out his next victim, and laughing at us all. Shadow puppets? We are the puppets here, and he's manipulating us in whatever way he likes.'

Eighty-Two

During the afternoon, together with Garcia and Captain Blake, Hunter had faced a press conference that seemed more like a firing squad than anything else. Reporters had talked to everyone in Nathan Littlewood's office building, and the stories they'd got ranged from dismemberment and decapitation, to ritualistic, real-voodoo-doll creation and cannibalism. One woman had even mentioned the word *vampire*.

Hunter, Garcia, and Captain Blake did their best to persuade the reporters that none of the stories they heard was true. But one thing was for sure: the news of a new serial killer was about to break.

After the press conference, Hunter and Garcia got to work on the names Littlewood's secretary had given them. In the past three months, due to his already full roster, Nathan Littlewood had only been able to taken on three new clients – Kelli Whyte, Denise Forde, and David Jones.

Kelli Whyte and Denise Forde both started their therapy sessions last month, and each had had four in total. David Jones had called enquiring about a consultation two weeks ago. He had come in for his first ever session at the beginning of the week. Sheryl said that Jones was a tall man, maybe six two, six three, with broad shoulders and an average body. She wasn't able to tell Hunter very much about his looks, though. She said that Jones had turned up for his only session a few minutes late, clearly concerned about concealing his appearance. He was wearing sunglasses and a baseball hat pulled low on his forehead; according to Sheryl, though, this wasn't uncommon among clients, especially the Hollywood types.

Hunter found out that Kelli Whyte was a 45-year-old recent divorcee who lived in Hancock Park. She managed a stock-trade company based in downtown LA's financial district, and since her divorce six months earlier, she had been struggling to cope with life in general.

Denise Forde was a 27-year-old computer analyst who lived alone in South Pasadena, and worked in a software company in Silver Lake. All they'd found out about her so far was that she was very shy, lacked confidence, and didn't seem to have many friends.

Neither Kelli nor Denise struck Hunter as possible suspects. David Jones, on the other hand, had proven to be an enigma so far. The address Sheryl had for him on file was wrong. It turned out to be a small sandwich shop in West Hollywood. The cellphone number on file rang indefinitely without being answered. And David Jones was too common a name for its owner to be easily traced. A quick search showed that in downtown Los Angeles alone there were over forty-five of them. In any case, Hunter had no doubt that the name was false. He was sure the killer had visited Littlewood's office before the day of the murder. This killer was too thorough not to have done any reconnaissance. The killer knew that Littlewood's office building was deserted at night. He knew that the building had a very low security level, with no night watchmen and no CCTV. He knew that gaining access to the building was child's play. But most of all, he knew he didn't have to bring a small box to complete his sculpture. He knew Littlewood kept that secret book-box on his desk. This killer was too bold, too arrogant. He would've wanted to sit face to face with Littlewood in his office before the day he killed him. Maybe just for the fun of it. And what better way to do it than to pose as a client? Anonymity would be a very easy thing to accomplish. Maybe Captain Blake was right – the killer was playing everyone like a puppet.

Eighty-Three

It was late when the phone on Hunter's desk rang. He reluctantly dragged his attention away from the pictures board and reached for it.

'Robert, I've got a few results for you,' came Doctor Hove's tired voice.

Hunter consulted his watch and was surprised at how late it was. Once again he had lost track of time. 'You still working, Doc?' He gestured for Garcia to pick up his extension.

'Yeah, you should talk. And I bet Carlos is still in the office as well.'

'Yeah, I'm here,' Garcia said, pulling a face.

'You won't catch this guy by frying your brains, Robert. You know that.'

'Yeah, we were just about to pack it all up for the day here, Doc.'

'Of course you were.'

Hunter smiled. 'So what have you got for us?'

Hunter and Garcia heard the sound of pages turning. 'As we expected, all the cuts and bruises to the victim's torso were done while he was still alive. I put the time of death somewhere between three and five in the morning.'

'That would've given the killer at least three hours to create his sculpture,' Hunter said.

'That's right,' Doctor Hove agreed. 'Like the previous two victims, this one also died from major-organ failure, mainly heart and kidneys, induced by severe loss of blood. The victim also had burn marks to his right nipple, torso, arms, genitals, and to his back. I am positive they were made with a hair iron.'

'What?' Garcia asked.

'Some call them hair straighteners.'

'Yes, I know what they are, Doc. Are you sure?'

'As positive as I can be. The burn-marks are very uniform, with asymmetric straight-line edge. The ones to his nipple were what gave it away. The nipple tip isn't burnt. The marks start just a few millimeters to each side of it, as if the nipple had been pinched away from the body, and then clamped through the side with a pair of red-hot clampers.'

Garcia ground his teeth and crossed his left arm over his chest.

'The burn-marks were made by three-centimeter-wide plates, give or take a millimeter or two, which is pretty standard for several hair-iron brands. When the killer was done torturing the victim, he moved on to the amputations. The left leg was amputated first. The victim was still alive, but I'd say barely. That answers the question of why there was so much blood at the crime-scene. As I said, this time the killer wasn't concerned with containing the hemorrhaging. There was no tying off or clipping of major arteries or large veins and vessels. The killer was happy to allow the victim to bleed out, and for that reason I don't think we're going to get much from toxicology this time. Or at least no heart-rate reducing drugs.'

'But maybe some other type of drug?' Hunter asked, picking up on Doctor Hove's uncertain tone.

'Maybe. I found a needle prick bruise to the right side of the victim's neck. It looks like the killer injected the victim with something, we just don't know what exactly, yet.'

Hunter scribbled a few notes on a piece of paper.

'We were also correct about the killer's lack of concern with the quality of the amputation incisions this time,' Doctor Hove continued. 'The instrument used was the same . . .'

'An electric kitchen knife,' Garcia said.

'Uh-huh. But this time he used it more like a butcher, hacking and twisting it as if carving a roast. Also, I found no visible incision-line marks as on the previous two victims. The killer wasn't worried about a correct cut point.'

'He's started enjoying this too much,' Garcia commented.

'We also found ligature marks on the wrists, forearms and ankles. Unlike the previous two, this victim was restrained. And that constitutes yet another departure from the initial MO. We didn't find the restraining rope at the crime scene.' More pages turning. 'The wire used on the sculpture was the same as used on the previous two, and so was the bonding agent – superglue. As expected, forensics found several sets of latent prints in the office and reception room.'

'The office cleaner came twice a week,' Hunter said. 'Last time was two days ago. She was due back tomorrow, early morning. We'll run the prints anyway, but I'm sure they will belong to legitimate clients.'

Doctor Hove sighed. 'That's all I can tell you from the autopsy examination.'

'Thanks, Doc.'

'Any progress with the new shadow images? Any links with the previous two?'

'We're still studying them, Doc,' Hunter replied. This time his voice sounded tired.

'Just out of curiosity, let me know if you get something, will you?'

'Sure thing. By the way, Littlewood's secretary told me that he used that secret book-box for his car keys and cell-phone when he was in the office. Did forensics find them?'

'Give me a sec.' Fifteen silent seconds went by. 'No, it's not in the inventory. I'm looking at it right now. But they did find his last few cellphone bills. He kept them in a drawer in his desk.'

'That could help. Could you send them over?'

'No problem, you'll have them first thing in the morning. OK, I'm going home now to a much-needed rest and a nice glass of wine,' Doctor Hove said.

'That sounds like a great idea to me,' Garcia replied, while fixing Hunter down with a stare.

'Yeah, you're right, Doc,' Hunter agreed, nodding at Garcia. 'We need some rest before we fry.'

'I'll email you the autopsy results right now, and any lab results as soon as I get them, but you know the drill, it might be another day or two, even with an urgent request.'

'That's fine, Doc. Thank you for giving this high priority.'

Eighty-Four

Eleesha Holt woke up with the first rays of sunlight. No alarm needed. Her mind's clock was as fine-tuned as a precision Swiss timepiece. But this morning, instead of getting up straight away as she always did, Eleesha lay in bed for an extra ten minutes, staring at the ceiling of her small bedroom. Thoughts of the long day ahead raced through her mind, and all of a sudden she was engulfed by terrible sadness and a feeling of helplessness. Slowly, she dragged herself off the bed, into the bathroom, and into a warm shower.

After the shower, Eleesha wrapped a towel around her head and slipped into her pale yellow bathrobe. She cleared a circular patch on the misty mirror and stared at her reflection for a long minute. Her sunken eyes, tired skin and weak gums were the result of a young life eaten away by drugs and alcohol. The scar on her left cheek was the result of sleeping with so many men and women – some of them could, and would, get violent. Her black skin did a great job of naturally disguising the dark circles under her eyes. Her hair had lost a lot of its natural shine and life, but with some effort, and a very hot hair iron, she could still make it look nice when she needed to.

Eleesha took a step back from the mirror, undid her

bathrobe and let it fall to the floor. She tentatively ran a hand over her stomach, allowing the tips of her fingers to caress the three stabbing scars on it. Tears started to form in her eyes and she quickly reached for her bathrobe again, shaking the memories of her early life away from her mind.

After a quick breakfast, Eleesha returned to her bedroom, applied some light makeup, got dressed in jeans, a long-sleeve shirt, and comfortable, everyday shoes, before making her way to the subway station. From Norwalk, where she lived, it was only four stops to Compton, with a subway-line change at Imperial/Wilmington.

At that time in the morning, Norwalk Station wasn't busy yet. Eleesha knew that if she tried to leave her apartment around the morning rush hour, she would have to endure a hell of a journey – overcrowded station, over-crowded train, and not a chance in hell of getting a seat. No, Eleesha would rather get to her job half an hour earlier than venture into the city's transport system at rush hour. There was always something to do at her desk anyway.

Eleesha had never gone to college. In fact, she'd dropped out of school midway through eighth grade, but her earlier life made her an expert in what she did. Eleesha was part of the Specialized Supportive Services branch of the Los Angeles Department of Public Social Services. The Specialized Supportive Services was created to help anyone dealing with domestic violence, substance abuse, mental-health problems, violence against women, and broken families.

Eleesha dealt exclusively with women struggling with substance abuse and domestic violence, and street workers who wanted to get out of the game. Her days were tough, long, and filled with sadness, frustration and other people's suffering. There had been so many women she thought she'd helped, for whom she thought she'd made a difference, only for them to fall straight back into their old life just a few months later. But every now and again, Eleesha would succeed in getting someone off the streets and keeping her off. She had seen a few of the women she had helped go on to find a good job, raise a family, and start a brand new life, away from all the suffering and the addiction. Those moments made her job worthwhile.

Eleesha got into the train and grabbed a seat towards the back of the car. An attractive thirty-something man sat two seats to her right, wearing a navy-blue suit and holding a paper coffee cup that could probably hold a gallon. He nodded a cordial 'hello' as he boarded. Eleesha returned the gesture, and followed it with a smile. The man started to smile back, when he caught a glimpse of the scar on her left cheek. He quickly looked away and pretended to be searching for something inside his briefcase.

Eleesha's smile faded. She had lost count of how many times she'd been through that exact situation. She pretended she didn't care, but deep inside her battered ego, another scar was created.

In Lakewood, the next stop along, several people boarded the car. A woman of about twenty-five sat directly in front of Eleesha. She was wearing a light-brown trouser suit and beige, suede flat-heeled shoes, and carrying a lawyer's leather briefcase. The man to Eleesha's right had already finished his gallon of coffee, and after adjusting his tie gave the young woman his best smile. The woman never even noticed him. She took her seat and retrieved a newspaper from her briefcase. Eleesha smiled internally.

As the woman sat back and started reading her

newspaper, something on the front page caught Eleesha's attention. Her eyes narrowed. The headline read 'SCULPTOR SERIAL KILLER CLAIMS THIRD VICTIM'. Eleesha leaned forward and squinted even harder at the woman's paper. The first paragraph of the article went on to describe how a new, sadistic serial killer had *torn* the arms and legs off his victims' bodies, only to use them to create grotesque, human-flesh sculptures, left at the scene. The article speculated that acts of cannibalism and perhaps black-magic rituals had also been performed. Eleesha pulled a disgusted face but carried on reading. The next line sent her memory swirling like a tornado.

No, she thought, *it can't be the same.*

Only then did her eyes register the photographs at the bottom of the article. Her heart stuttered as all doubt quickly vanished from her mind.

Eighty-Five

'Have you seen this pile of shit?' Captain Blake blurted as she stormed into Hunter and Garcia's office, holding a copy of the morning's edition of the *LA Times*.

Hunter, Garcia and Alice Beaumont had all read the article. In keeping with the best practices of shocking journalism, the *LA Times* went on to create its own pseudonym for the killer. It called him, fittingly enough, 'the Sculptor'.

There were four pictures in total. One showed the building where Nathan Littlewood's body was found. The other three were portrait photographs of each of the three victims. The article ended by saying that even after three 'respectable members of the community' (an attorney for the state of California, who had been diagnosed with terminal cancer; a police officer; and a psychologist) had become victims of the most terrifying killer the city of Los Angeles had seen in decades, the LAPD were still chasing their tails like silly dogs. They had no tangible leads.

'Yes, we've seen it, Captain,' Hunter replied.

'Silly dogs?' The captain threw the paper on Hunter's desk. 'Goddamnit. Did they hear a fucking word we told them in that press conference yesterday? This makes us look like incompetent clowns. And the worst of it all is that they are right. Three victims in two weeks and we don't have shit, except shadow puppets.' The captain turned and faced Alice. 'And if you are right about the meaning behind the second sculpture, than that's one more victim off his list. That means he's only got one more to go.' Using both hands she tucked her hair behind each ear as she drew a deep breath. 'Any luck with linking this third victim to the previous two?'

'No,' Alice said, sounding a little defeated. 'I found nothing that linked Nathan Littlewood to any police investigation. He never helped the LAPD with a case. He has never testified in court, nor has he ever been called for jury service. I'm working as fast as I can. Right now I'm trying to find out if he has ever acted as a counselor to any crime victims. I was thinking that maybe he'd helped a victim of a case in which either Nicholson or Nashorn were involved. If so, maybe that case might relate to Ken Sands in some way. But obtaining information on Littlewood's old clients has proven a little harder than I'd anticipated. But just because we haven't found it yet, doesn't mean that Nathan Littlewood wasn't in some way related to either Ken Sands's or Alfredo Ortega's case.'

'That's just fantastic,' the captain shot back. 'So if this new victim doesn't tie in with the only theory you guys have managed to come up with so far – Ken Sands's revenge – then we really have diddly-squat.' Captain Blake turned to address Hunter. 'Maybe it's time that big brain of yours cooked up something new, Robert. I just had my ear chewed off by the Chief of Police and the mayor twenty minutes ago. They're sick of this "Sculptor" killer terrifying the city and laughing at us. DA Bradley already considers this whole investigation a fiasco, and I won't repeat what he's been saying about the detectives running it. This article just did it for everyone. If we don't come up with something solid in the next twenty-four hours, we're off the case.'

'What?' Garcia practically jumped off his seat.

'Look. Right now, we're drowning in sewage. It's been twelve days since the first murder, and though we've all been working nonstop, we have nothing solid. If we don't come up with something concrete by tomorrow morning, the DA will be asking the FBI to take over. Our job will simply be to assist them.'

'Assist them?' Garcia said. 'By doing what, wiping their asses for them? Making them coffee?'

Hunter had worked with the FBI on a case once before, several years ago, and he had hated the experience. He kept his mouth shut, but there was no way in hell he would babysit the Feds or hand them his investigation on a silver platter.

'With the story making the news as it did, the Feds contacted the Chief of Police, the mayor, the DA, and myself, offering their assistance. They said, and I quote "Just remember we're here in case you need us". And out of that bunch, I'm the only one who thinks we don't.'

'That's just a great big pile of bullshit, Captain.'

'Find me something concrete or get used to it, because in twenty-four hours we are the ones who'll be neck deep, shoveling that big pile of bullshit for the Feds.'

Eighty-Six

By late afternoon, the sunny blue sky over Los Angeles had given way to dark and menacing clouds. They'd come to announce that the first downpour of the summer was imminent.

Hunter got to Los Feliz, a hilly neighborhood north of East Hollywood, just as the first roar of thunder cracked the sky. Garcia had gone back to Nathan Littlewood's office. He wanted to re-interview a few of the people he'd already talked to, and have another look at the crime scene.

Littlewood's apartment was located on the tenth floor of a fourteen-story building on the corner of Los Feliz Boulevard and Hillhurst Avenue. Hunter had acquired a spare set of keys from his secretary. The building's entrance lobby was large, well lit, and very clean and welcoming. The porter, a black man of about sixty with a carefully trimmed goatee, was sitting behind a semi-circular reception counter. He raised his eyes from the paperback he was reading, as Hunter entered the building and pressed the elevator button.

'Visiting someone?' he asked without getting up.

'Not today, sir,' Hunter replied, displaying his badge. 'Official business.'

The porter lowered his book, intrigued. 'Has there been a

burglary I'm not aware of?' He started rummaging through a few sheets of paper around the confined space where he was sitting. 'Has someone just called 911?'

'No, there's been no burglary, sir. No one has called 911. Just routine.' That was all Hunter offered as the elevator doors slid open and he got inside it.

The corridor on the tenth floor was long, wide, well illuminated, and it carried a nice exotic air-freshener smell. The walls were cream with a light-brown skirting board, the carpet beige with triangular patterns. Apartment 1011 was towards the end of the corridor. His secretary had told Hunter that Littlewood had no home-security alarm. He unlocked the door and slowly turned the handle. It opened onto a dark entrance vestibule.

Hunter switched on his flashlight and checked the small space from outside. There was a medium-sized mirror fixed halfway up the wall, just above a narrow, see-through console table with an empty wooden bowl on it. Probably the place where Littlewood deposited his keys once he got in. To the left of the mirror a set of three wooden coat hooks was mounted on the wall. A gray blazer hung from the last hook.

Hunter pushed the door all the way open, stepped inside and flicked the light switch on. The entrance vestibule led into a small kitchen directly ahead, and an average-sized living room on the left.

Hunter quickly checked the pockets on the gray blazer. All he found was a credit card receipt for a Chinese restaurant. It was dated a week ago. According to the address on the receipt, the place was just a block away.

Hunter placed the receipt back into the blazer's pocket and moved carefully towards the center of the living room, taking everything in. The centerpiece was a large plasma TV on a shiny black module against the south wall. Underneath it, on a shelf, a DVD player and a satellite-receiving box. The space to the right of the DVD player was occupied by a micro-stereo system. The rest of the shiny module was taken up by CDs and DVDs. The module shared the room with a dining table for four, a plush black leather sofa, two matching armchairs, a glass coffee table, a wooden sideboard unit, and a huge bookcase overflowing with books. The room wasn't messy, but it wasn't excessively tidy either. There were no feminine touches to anything, or any overly masculine details. *Neutral*, *average*, were the words that came to mind. The curtains were drawn, filling the space with dark shadows.

In the living room Hunter saw only one photo frame, half hidden in the corner, behind some CDs on the shiny module. The picture was of Littlewood with his arm around a kid no older than eighteen. The kid was dressed in a graduation gown, and he and Littlewood were sporting great big, proud smiles. Hunter had two similar pictures of him and his father back in his apartment – one after his high-school graduation, the other after his college one.

'What the hell are you looking for, Robert?' he whispered to himself.

Eighty-Seven

Lightning lit up the dark sky outside. A monstrous thunder-clap followed just a split second later, with a crash that rattled the building. Rain came pelting down, smashing against the windowpanes.

Hunter spent a few more minutes in the living room, going through a few drawers and bookshelves, but found nothing of any interest. The kitchen gave him nothing special, either – mismatched crockery and cutlery, enough for four people at the most, and a half-empty fridge. A small hallway linked the living room to the rest of the apartment. There was one room on the left, halfway down the corridor, and one right at the end of it. The bathroom was on the right, directly opposite the first room.

Hunter moved deeper into the apartment. He decided to start with the main bedroom. It was large and comfortable, with an en suite bathroom. A double bed with a wooden headboard was pushed up against the wall. There was a small working desk, a built-in wardrobe, and a high chest of drawers. Again, no feminine touches and no picture frames – nothing precious, no memories. Hunter took his time going through everything. The wardrobe was well organized – suits and shirts took up half of the space. There were only four pairs of shoes, two of them sneakers. Ties and belts had their own little corner. Hunter checked the pockets of every suit jacket – nothing.

The rain was getting heavier, hammering the windows like evil ghosts trying to get inside. Lightning zigzagged across the sky every couple of minutes.

Hunter carried on checking the room. The chest of drawers held T-shirts, jeans, sweaters, underwear, socks and two bottles of Davidoff Cool Water cologne.

He checked the wastepaper basket on the floor by Littlewood's desk. There was nothing there but junk mail and a few candy-bar wrappers. The laptop on the desk was password-protected. Hunter wasn't sure if they'd find anything that could help with their investigation in Littlewood's hard drive, but right now anything was worth a shot. He would hand the laptop to Brian Doyle at the Information Technology Division. The bathroom was even less adventurous in its décor than the bedroom.

Hunter stopped by the window and spent a moment watching the rain castigate Los Angeles. Another bolt of lightning split the sky, branching out into five different directions. It didn't look like Hunter was going anywhere for a while.

He left the main bedroom and walked back down the corridor, entering the room opposite the bathroom. It was small but tidy. No doubt it was the guestroom. The main piece of furniture in this room was a single bed with a metal headboard pushed up against a wall. There was a small bedside table to its right. The whole east wall was taken up by a built-in wardrobe. The curtains were also drawn in this room, but they were different from the ones in the living room. These were heavier and thicker. No light or shadows came through them.

Hunter left them as they were and approached the bed, running his hand over the linen. It felt and smelled fresh – recently cleaned. He checked the drawer on the side table. Nothing. Completely empty. Hunter closed the drawer and moved over to the wardrobe, sliding its doors open. Inside, it looked like a mini garage sale. Everything was old – a vacuum cleaner, books, magazines, lamps, a few raggedy coats, an artificial Christmas tree, and a few cardboard boxes.

Wow,' Hunter said, taking a step back. 'It doesn't look like Littlewood threw much away.'

He turned his attention to the cardboard boxes stacked up on the right, pulling the bottom one out. It was relatively heavy. Hunter placed it on the bed and opened its lid. The box was stuffed with vintage vinyl LPs. Out of curiosity, Hunter looked through a few – Early Mötley Crüe, New York Dolls, Styx, Journey, .38 Special, Kiss, Led Zeppelin, Rush . . . Hunter smiled. *Littlewood was a metal head when he was young.*

He paused and thought of something, quickly flipping through every single LP in the box. Faith No More's album *The Real Thing*, which contained the song the killer had left playing inside Nashorn's boat, wasn't there.

Hunter returned to the wardrobe and retrieved another box. This one was packed full of photographs – very old ones. He grabbed a handful and started leafing through them. A new smile split his lips. Nathan Littlewood looked desperately young – late-teens maybe, several pounds lighter, with back-combed hair that went just past his shoulders. He looked like a garage-rock-band reject.

Hunter reached deeper into the box and grabbed another bunch of photographs. This time he came up with a group of wedding pictures. Littlewood was wearing an elegant dark suit, and in every photo he looked genuinely happy. The bride was about three inches shorter than he was, with eyes that made you want to stop and just stare at them for a while. She looked stunning in her wedding dress. She too seemed ecstatic.

The next bunch of photographs Hunter came up with weren't wedding ones, though Littlewood looked just as young. Hunter had flipped through several of them when something grabbed his attention.

'Wait a second.' He brought the picture about half a foot from his face and squinted at it, concentrating hard, his memory racing like a computer, searching through all the images he'd seen in the past two weeks. As he finally made the connection, a rush of adrenalin found its way to every corner of his body.

Eighty-Eight

Thunder ruptured the sky one more time, making Alice jump in her seat. She didn't like rain, and she hated tropical thunderstorms.

'Jesus Christ.'

She clasped her hands together, brought them up to her mouth and started blowing into her thumbs as if they were a whistle. She always did that when she got scared. Something she'd started doing when she was a little girl.

Alice had spent the whole afternoon in Hunter's office, frantically querying databases and unlocking backdoors to restricted online systems, searching for some sort of connection between the three victims. She still hadn't found anything yet. Nor had she had any luck linking Littlewood to Ken Sands. But she'd been doing this type of work for a long time. She knew that just because she hadn't found a connection yet, didn't mean it didn't exist.

Another bolt of lightning snaked through the sky and Alice shut her eyes tight, holding her breath. Lightning didn't scare her, but she knew that after lightning there was thunder, and thunder petrified her.

The rumble of thunder followed a heartbeat later, and this one sounded reluctant to go, stretching for several seconds. There was nothing Alice could do to avoid the memories. Her eyes filled with tears.

When she was eleven years old, while visiting her grandparents in Oregon, Alice got caught in an enormous thunderstorm.

Her grandparents lived in a farmhouse near Cottage Grove. The entire place was gorgeous, just one huge national-park-like area full of woodlands, lakes and tranquility. Alice loved playing outside. She loved helping her grandpa when he was working with the animals, especially when he was milking the cows, collecting eggs from the henhouse, or feeding the pigs. But what she loved doing more than anything else when she was at her grandparents' house was playing with Nosey, her grandma's 3-year-old, black-and-white beagle. Most of her time in Oregon was spent holding, cuddling or running outside with Nosey.

This particular day in June, her parents, together with her grandpa, had driven to town to get a few supplies. Alice stayed at the house with her grandma. While Grandma Gellar was getting things ready for dinner, Alice and Nosey went outside to play. They both loved playing near the *bushy trees*, as Alice always called the distinct group of elms just down the hill from the house. Though her parents had told her many times never to go play there alone, Alice, being the stubborn little girl she was, never took much notice of their advice.

Alice had no idea how long she'd been running around the trees with Nosey, but it must've been a while, because the sky had darkened down to pitch-black with tiny patches of deep blue peeping through. Alice didn't even notice the strong smell of wet soil that had slowly crept up on them.

The first bolt of lightning that colored the sky froze Alice to the spot. Only then did she notice the dreadful wind that had started blowing, and how cold it had suddenly got. When thunder exploded above her head, shaking the ground, Alice started crying and Nosey went nuts, barking like a crazy dog, and running around in all directions like he'd been blindfolded.

Alice didn't know what else to do other than cry and curl up under the first tree she saw. She kept calling Nosey to come to her, but he just wasn't listening. As he rushed from tree to tree, a new bolt of lightning came down like an evil hammer. Its target – the large metal plate on Nosey's collar. Alice had her eyes wide open, her right arm extended, calling the little dog to come to her, but he didn't have a chance. The lightning bolt grabbed hold of Nosey and held him for what seemed like an eternity. The little dog was propelled up in the air like a bouncing ping-pong ball. When he hit the ground again, Nosey wasn't moving anymore. His eyes had gone milky white, and his tongue, hanging lifelessly from his mouth, tar black. Despite the heavy rain, Alice could see smoke lifting from Nosey's body.

It took almost a year for the nightmares to subside; to this very day, Alice was absolutely petrified of thunderstorms. Even camera flashes made her feel uncomfortable. They reminded her of lightning.

Tropical thunderstorms in Los Angeles don't usually last more than forty-five minutes to an hour, but this one was approaching an hour and a half, and it was showing no signs of easing.

Alice had a lot of work to do, but there was no way she could sit at the computer right now, her fingers just wouldn't move. Instead, she decided to try and look through her paperwork. The itemized cellphone bills that the forensics team had found in Nathan Littlewood's office had arrived a few hours earlier. They were the first thing she saw on her desk.

She had spent about ten minutes identifying Littlewood's most-dialed numbers, when she noticed something that made her forget the storm outside.

'Wait just a moment,' she said to herself and started rummaging through the pile of documents on her desk. When she found the one she was looking for, Alice flipped through the pages, scanning every line.

There it was.

Eighty-Nine

The rain had finally stopped about an hour ago. The clouds had scattered away, but the sky remained dark as night took over.

There were too many photographs inside that cardboard box for Hunter to be able to thoroughly go through all of them while in Nathan Littlewood's apartment. One photo had already gotten his heart racing with suspicion. He needed to get back to his office, and the box of photographs was going with him.

Before leaving Littlewood's apartment, Hunter checked the other two cardboard boxes inside the guestroom's wardrobe; they contained several old bits and pieces of Littlewood's past, but nothing that Hunter thought relevant.

Garcia was sitting at his desk when Hunter walked back into his office. Alice was nowhere to be seen.

'Everything OK?' Hunter asked, noticing the aura of tiredness around his partner.

Garcia puffed his cheeks up with air before slowly letting it out. 'I got a call from Detective Corbí from South Bureau.'

'The detective in charge of Tito's murder investigation?'

'The one and the same. And guess what? They just had a

result come back on a DNA test performed on an eyelash they found in the bathroom. Matches Ken Sands's DNA.'

Hunter placed the box of photographs on his desk. 'An eyelash?'

'That's right. And I know that kind of blemishes the theory that Ken Sands could be both Tito's killer and the Sculptor. The Sculptor has given us three messy crime scenes, blood and guts everywhere, but he didn't leave anything behind he didn't want to leave behind. Not even a spec of dust. So how come, if Ken Sands really is both, he acted so carelessly in Tito's apartment?' Garcia didn't wait for Hunter to reply. 'The problem is, he might not have been careless at all. He might have made a genuine mistake.'

Hunter's interest grew.

'Eyelashes don't shed as easily as regular hairs. I checked it,' Garcia explained. 'Humans lose between forty and 120 strands of hair a day, while eyelashes will live on average 150 days before falling out. It's not a contingency most criminals worry about. No matter how careful they are. So unless Tito's killer was wearing goggles, it was a genuine mistake.'

'What did you say to Corbí?'

'Nothing. Still kept him in the dark about the fact that Sands is a person of interest in the Sculptor case. I did ask him to keep me posted about any new developments. But there's no escaping it now. They'll be looking for Sands as well.'

Hunter nodded his understanding. 'Yes, but you remember Tito's apartment, right? It was filthy. It hadn't been cleaned in months. So an eyelash may be good enough to place Sands inside the apartment, but without an eyewitness to testify that he was there on the night of the murder, without a confession, no one will ever get a conviction. All Sands has to say is that he visited Tito any time before the night of the murder.'

Garcia knew Hunter was right.

'Did you get anything from Littlewood's office building?'

Garcia used both hands to pull his hair back from his forehead. 'Not a thing.' He looked at his watch and irritably pinched his nose a couple of times.

Hunter understood Garcia's frustration well. 'Where's Alice?'

'No idea. She wasn't here when I got back. What's that?' Garcia nodded at the cardboard box Hunter had placed on his desk.

'Something I got from Littlewood's apartment. Old photographs.'

Garcia cocked an eyebrow.

Hunter left the box and moved towards the pictures board. His attention this time locked solely on the human-sculpture and severed-limbs photographs. For a moment he studied them as if that was the first time he was seeing any of it.

'Anything interesting?'

No answer.

'Robert,' Garcia called again. 'Did you find anything in Littlewood's apartment? Anything in that box?'

Hunter reached for one of the photographs and unpinned it from the board. 'We need to go down to the captain's office before she leaves.'

Ninety

Captain Blake was just finishing a phone call when Hunter and Garcia knocked on her door.

'Come in,' she called, after placing a hand over the mouthpiece. As both detectives stepped into her office, she gestured for them to take a seat.

Neither did.

'Well, I don't care how you deal with it, Wilks, just deal with it. You've got lead on this, so lead, goddammit.' Captain Blake slammed the phone down and pinched the bridge of her nose while shutting her eyes for just a moment.

Hunter and Garcia waited in silence.

'OK.' The captain looked up at them and exhaled a weighted breath. 'Tell me we've got at least a sniff of something new.'

He reached inside his breast pocket and retrieved an old six-by-four-inch photograph, placing it on the captain's desk.

'What is this?' she asked.

'A sniff of something new,' Hunter replied with no sarcasm in his voice. 'I found it in Nathan Littlewood's apartment.'

Garcia stepped forward, craning his neck.

Captain Blake picked up the photo and stared at it for

several seconds. 'What the hell am I looking at here, Robert?'

'Could I have a look, Captain?' Garcia asked, extending his hand.

She handed him the photo and sat back on her swivel chair.

The picture wasn't of fantastic quality, but it clearly showed a skinny man barely in his twenties, standing outside by a tree, holding a bottle of beer. It was a bright sunny day and he had no shirt on. His hair was dark and curly. He was smiling. The beer bottle in his right hand was angled towards the camera, as if he was toasting something. It didn't take Garcia long to place him.

'A very young Nathan Littlewood,' he said.

Captain Blake look at Hunter, unimpressed. 'Hardly surprising since you found that picture in his apartment.'

'Not him,' Hunter replied. 'The other person in the picture.'

Captain Blake stole another peek at the photograph in Garcia's hands, and then looked back at Hunter as if he'd lost his mind. 'Are we talking about *this* picture? 'Cos if we are, you might need to see an eye doctor, Robert. There's only one person in it.'

Garcia was already searching the picture's background for any secondary characters. He knew Hunter well enough to know that he'd seen something that most people would've missed. But there was no one. Littlewood was standing by that tree alone. There was nothing in the background but empty space.

'Look closely,' Hunter said.

That was when Garcia noticed part of someone's left arm at the right-hand edge of the picture. Due to its proximity to the camera, it was out-of-focus, but it was easy to tell that the arm was bent at the elbow. Most of the forearm was out of shot.

'The arm?' Garcia asked.

Hunter nodded. 'Stay with it.' He watched as Garcia concentrated on the picture again. His stare went from confusion, to doubt, to surprise, and then finally it clicked.

'I'll be damned,' Garcia said, his eyes darting towards Hunter.

'No, *I'll* be damned,' the captain said, zapping both detectives with a laser stare. Her voice pitch went up a notch. 'Do you see me sitting here? What *about* the arm?'

Garcia stood directly in front of her desk and showed her the picture. 'This isn't just somebody's arm.' He addressed Hunter. 'That's why you were checking the photos upstairs again.'

Hunter agreed and placed the picture he took from the pictures board on the captain's desk. The picture showed a few body parts lying side by side on a stainless steel table. He pointed to one of the two arms in the photograph. Specifically, to a point high up on the triceps.

'See those?' he asked.

The captain cocked her head forward and squinted at it. 'I see them all right; what are they?'

'Moles,' Garcia replied, placing the picture he was holding next to the one the captain was looking at. 'Birthmarks.' He indicated the same cluster of six small, oddly-shaped dark-red moles on the triceps of the person who had inadvertently got in front of the camera. Despite the arm being out-of-focus, there was no mistaking it. They were exactly the same.

Ninety-One

Captain Blake sat still for a while longer, her gaze fixed on the photographs on her desk. She knew that birthmarks were as unique as fingerprints. The odds of two people having the same exact birthmark were about one in sixty-four million. Not even identical twins share them. Two individuals having the exact same six birthmarks, in a small cluster like the one she was looking at, was virtually impossible.

'So that means that this guy was . . .' She stabbed her finger over the out-of-focus arm on the photo from Littlewood's apartment.

'Andrew Nashorn,' Garcia said. 'The killer's second victim.'

Her eyes glint with a new sparkle. 'So they knew each other?'

'It looks that way,' Hunter said. 'Or at least they did a long time ago.'

She turned the picture over – nothing. 'When was this taken?'

'We can send it to the lab for analysis, but judging by how young Nathan Littlewood looks, and the fact that he got married twenty-seven years ago and in that photo he isn't wearing a wedding ring, I'd say that picture is probably twenty-seven to thirty years old.'

Garcia agreed.

Captain Blake leaned back on her chair again, clearly running something over in her mind. She looked up, tilting her body to the right and looking past both detectives towards her office door. 'Where's the DA girl?'

Garcia shrugged.

'I haven't seen her since this morning,' Hunter said.

'Well, it looks like she could be right.' Captain Blake stood up. 'This killer could have a set agenda. That was her reading of the shadow image cast by the sculpture found at the killer's second crime scene, wasn't it? Two victims claimed, two more to go.' She moved around to the front of her rosewood desk. 'Well, he's now claimed his third one. We now know that two of them knew each other. Because of the nature of their jobs, I have no doubt Derek Nicholson and Andrew Nashorn were at least acquainted. Do we have any idea if Nicholson knew the third victim? Was he part of the same group of friends all those years ago?'

Hunter brought his left hand up to his neck to massage it. 'I just came across this information about an hour ago, Captain. I haven't had time to do a lot of digging yet. But we'll obviously be looking into that. I've got a box of old photographs upstairs that might still gives us something else. But we now have a whole new angle to look at.'

'I'd say that's definitely a sniff of something, Captain,' Garcia said.

The captain still looked ill at ease, but Garcia was right, they did have something new. She checked her watch and opened the door. 'Well, get digging then, and let me know the moment you get anything. Right now, I've got to go talk to the Chief of Police and the Los Angeles District Attorney.'

Ninety-Two

Hunter spent most of the night going over every photograph inside that cardboard box. He found more wedding pictures, old holiday snapshots, several photographs of Nathan Littlewood with other friends and family, and a huge collection of photos of Harry, Littlewood's only son – his birth, his first ever steps, his first day at school, his graduation, his first prom. Basically, every important occasion in his life until he left home. Littlewood was certainly a proud father.

After hours of image searching, Hunter was sure that Andrew Nashorn appeared in none of those photographs. That was all they had – an out-of-focus arm at the edge of an old picture, identifiable only by the small cluster of birthmarks on his triceps.

Hunter had examined every face in every snapshot with a magnifying glass. He was fairly certain that none of them was Derek Nicholson, but 'fairly certain' wasn't certain enough. He would contact both of Nicholson's daughters, Olivia and Allison, and check if they had any pictures of their father in his early twenties for comparison. Maybe Nicholson was one of those whose appearance drastically changed as they grew older.

Hunter finally managed to fall asleep just before five in

the morning. He woke up at 8:22 a.m. The scar on the back of his neck was itching like crazy. He had a long shower, hoping that the warm water he allowed to drum down on his nape for five solid minutes would soothe some of that itch.

It didn't work.

When Hunter got to his office an hour later, Garcia was sitting at his desk, shoulders hunched over his keyboard, attentively reading something on his computer screen. He looked up as Hunter placed the box of photographs on his desk.

'Anything?' Garcia asked expectantly, nodding at the box.

'Nope, that was it. I've been through every photograph, every face. That picture in the park is all we got. If Nathan Littlewood also knew Derek Nicholson, there's no evidence of it in this box.'

'Yeah, but that doesn't mean that he didn't. I've got four people on this, digging like demented moles, searching for anything that could link Nicholson to Littlewood, going back twenty-five to thirty years.'

Hunter nodded.

Garcia stood up and walked over to the coffee jug in the corner of the room. 'Just to be one hundred per cent sure, I asked one of the image technicians to compare the birthmarks from the picture you got in Littlewood's apartment and the ones on the autopsy photographs. There is no doubt. Dimensions, distance, pattern, everything, it's all exactly the same. That's Nashorn's arm.'

Garcia didn't need to ask, he could see the lack of sleep in his partner's face: he poured two cups of black coffee and handed one to Hunter.

'Guess what,' Alice said as she stepped through the door, a proud smile on her face.

Hunter and Garcia turned at the same time to face her.

'They knew each other.'

Ninety-Three

Despite the fresh makeup, the neatly combed hair, and the immaculately ironed skirt and blouse, Alice looked tired. Her eyes were what gave it away. The grit that came from lack of sleep was almost visible in them.

Neither Hunter nor Garcia said a word.

Alice placed her briefcase on her desk. 'They knew each other,' she repeated. 'Andrew Nashorn and Nathan Littlewood knew each other.'

Hunter hadn't seen Alice since yesterday morning. She hadn't come back to the office in the afternoon. He knew she hadn't heard the news from him, and judging by how excited she sounded, and the fact that he and Garcia were her audience, it was obvious that she didn't know a thing about the photograph he had found in Littlewood's apartment.

'We already . . .' Garcia started saying, but Hunter interrupted him.

'How do you know this?'

Her proud smile stretched. Alice retrieved two sheets of paper from her briefcase. 'This is part of Nathan Littlewood's cellphone bill.' She handed one of the sheets to Hunter. 'They were delivered yesterday while both of you were out. This one . . .' she passed him the second sheet, '. . . comes from the cellphone records we obtained from Andrew Nashorn.'

Hunter didn't have to search the lists. Alice had highlighted the numbers. The same exact phone number appeared three times in Nashorn's records, and twice in Littlewood's.

'That's the number for an escort girl. Independent, not an agency,' Alice said. 'They both used the same escort girl.'

Doubt colored the face of both detectives.

'Escort?' Garcia asked.

'That's right. She calls herself Nicole.' Alice paused and lifted her right index finger. 'Let me rephrase that . . . "Submissive Nicole". She caters for a specific type of clientele.'

Garcia put down his coffee cup. 'OK, I agree that finding out that Nashorn and Littlewood used the same call girl is something we definitely should look into, but that doesn't necessarily mean they knew each other.'

'She's not a call girl,' Alice corrected him. 'She's a submissive escort. She offers a very specialized service. Her words, not mine.'

'You've talked to her?' Garcia was genuinely surprised.

'Last night.' Alice nodded.

Neither detective was expecting that.

'Look, I knew you were both out chasing new leads. I came across this information late yesterday, and decided to dig a little deeper instead of waiting. It so happened that I managed to meet up with her last night, and we talked.'

'How did you manage to get her talking?' Garcia knew from experience that getting anyone related to LA's illegal sex trade to talk was no easy feat.

'I proved to her I wasn't a cop or a reporter, and

guaranteed her that whatever information she gave me, it would never be detrimental to her.'

'And that worked?'

'Well, I also have different avenues open to me that you, as police officers, usually don't.'

'You paid her,' Garcia concluded.

'It works every time,' Alice admitted. 'How do you think the DA's office keeps its informers, by giving them donuts and hot milk? She's a *submissive escort*. She gets paid to do worse things than simply talk. Getting money in exchange for a conversation was probably her easiest ever job. Plus I gave her a free get-out-of-jail card. I told her to call me if she ever needed a lawyer, and in her profession that's a very attractive proposition.'

Garcia couldn't argue. 'So what did you talk about?'

'You can hear it for yourself.' Alice took a Dictaphone out of her briefcase and placed it on Hunter's desk. 'I've done this kind of thing before.' She gave both detectives a quick wink.

Surprised, Hunter and Garcia approached the desk.

'It's all cued up,' Alice said. 'I had just showed her Andrew Nashorn's picture.' She pressed the play button.

'*Oh yes, Paul, he's pretty much a regular. I see him about once a month. Sometimes more, sometimes less.*'

The voice that came through the tiny speaker was very feminine and sensual, the voice of someone who was probably in her mid-twenties; but there was a hard edge to it, the kind you'd expect from a streetwise person.

'Paul?' Alice's questioning voice came through the speakers.

'*That's the name he uses. Look, I know that none of my clients use their real names. He told me his name was Paul,*'

I call him Paul. That's how it works, lady.' There was a short pause. *'He likes playing rough.'*

'Rough?'

'Yep. He likes to tie me down, gag me, sometimes blind-fold me, slap me about a little . . . you know, play the tough guy.' Nicole chuckled. *'It's all right, I enjoy it too.'*

Hunter guessed that last comment was made because Alice had pulled a shocked face.

'Did he come to you?'

'Sometimes. Sometimes I went to his boat. Sometimes he hired a professional dungeon. There are a few scattered around LA. The equipment is better.'

'And how long has he been a . . . client?'

'A few years.'

'When was the last time you saw him?'

'Not so long ago.'

'Could you be more specific?'

There was a new short pause, soundtracked by the sound of objects being shuffled. Hunter presumed that Nicole had reached into a handbag or a drawer.

'Just over five weeks ago, May 13th.'

'OK, how about this guy?'

Alice paused the recording. 'Right then I showed her a picture of Nathan Littlewood,' she clarified before letting it play on.

'Yeah, I see him too . . . from time to time. Not as often as I see Paul, though. This one calls himself Woods.' A more animated chuckle this time. *'I wouldn't quite put it that way, if you know what I mean, but that's the name he likes, that's the name I call him.'*

'Was he also . . . "rough"?'

Nicole gave a dirty, full-throated laugh that sounded too

old for her. '*All my clients are rough in their own way, lady. That's why they come to me and not some two-buck-an-hour ho from West Hollywood. They get what they pay for here.*'

In the office, Alice subtly shook her head, obviously failing to understand how any woman could subject herself to verbal and physical abuse and other humiliations for money.

'*And when did you see him last?*'

Some more pages flipping. '*Right at the beginning of the month, June 2nd.*'

'*Let me show you one more picture.*' Looking at Hunter and Garcia, Alice mouthed the words 'Derek Nicholson'.

'*Umm, no. I've never seen him before.*'

'*Are you sure?*'

Several silent seconds. '*Yep, positive.*'

'*So he wasn't a client?*'

'*That's what I just said, lady.*'

'*OK, just one more thing. Do you know if Paul and Woods knew each other? Have they ever done a session together with you, or something like that?*'

'*No, I don't do group sessions. Way too intense. And my clients are too greedy. When they book me, they want me all for themselves.*' Another throaty laugh. '*But yes, they knew each other. That's how Woods became a client. When Paul first started seeing me years ago, he said that he had a friend who would probably love to see me too. I told him to pass his friend my number. A week later Woods called me.*'

Ninety-Four

When Alice turned the recording device off, Hunter brought her up to speed on what he'd found in Nathan Littlewood's apartment the day before. She couldn't hide her disappointment that her big discovery turned out to be not so big after all, but Hunter knew it was significant. What he'd found out from the picture he'd got from Littlewood's apartment was that Andrew Nashorn and Nathan Littlewood knew each other about thirty years ago. What Alice had found out was that they had kept in touch ever since, which was a whole new discovery. Hunter knew it was easy to lose touch with old friends – people from school, college, neighborhood, or former workplace. Finding out that Nashorn and Littlewood spent an afternoon drinking beer in a park thirty years ago didn't mean they were friends. Alice's discovery had proved they had been and still were.

'I went through all the phone records,' Alice said. 'There's no direct contact between Nashorn and Littlewood. At least not through that phone. But as you know, many people have more than one cellphone, and sometimes their second phone is the untraceable kind.'

'How about Derek Nicholson?'

'I spent half of the night going over all the phone records we have for him,' Alice said. 'Going back six months prior to him being diagnosed with cancer. Neither Nashorn nor Littlewood's cellphone numbers showed up. His number doesn't show up on their bills either.'

Towards the end of the afternoon, Garcia received a preliminary report from his digging team. So far they'd managed to check school and college records for the victims, together with early addresses. They'd found nothing to suggest that any of the three knew each other from either their neighborhoods or their learning institutions. Garcia told them to keep on digging – gym memberships, social clubs, anything that would've left behind a paper trail; but he understood that even if that paper trail existed at one time, today it would be almost impossible to find it.

The sun had already set, and so had another day coated with frustration.

Sitting at his desk, Hunter let out a weary sigh, placed his elbows on the desktop, and rested his forehead on the palms of his hands. He'd been going over all his notes and the crime-scene photographs for the zillionth time, and right now the puzzle seemed harder than ever. His head was throbbing with a pain that he knew wouldn't go away easily. Questions kept colliding with each other inside his mind, but the answers simply weren't there.

What were they looking at? A coyote and a raven to signify a liar? A devil figure looking down at possible victims – four in total? Someone looking and pointing at someone else inside a box? Was that a coffin? Were those images supposed to represent a funeral? Was that why the next image they got looked like someone down on his knees, praying? Or was that a kid? And how in the world did they relate to each other?

'Drink?' Garcia said from his desk.

'Umm?' Hunter lifted his head and blinked a few times.

'Let's go for a drink.' Garcia checked his watch, already getting up. 'This office is claustrophobic, it's hot as hell, and I swear I saw smoke coming out of your ears about two minutes ago. We both need a break. Let's go get a drink, maybe some food, and definitely some rest. We can start again fresh tomorrow.'

Hunter had no argument against that. If he'd had fuses in his brain, some of them would've burned out a long time ago. He shrugged and started powering down his computer.

'Yep, a drink sounds like a great idea.'

Ninety-Five

With probably the tackiest décor in downtown Los Angeles, Bar 107 sat just a block away from the PAB. Sporting walls redder than Communist Russia, vinyl booths, and a shabby-chic garage-sale theme, the place was a four-room retro drinking spot favored by many for its huge range of cocktails and Scotch whiskies.

Bar 107 was busy, but not excessively so. Hunter and Garcia sat at the far end of the long, varnished bar, and each ordered a shot of 10-year-old Aberlour.

'Great choice,' the female bartender said with an inviting smile. Her blonde hair was done up in a messy bun, but there was something very attractive about the way its edges fell down, caressing her naked neck.

Hunter had a sip of his Scotch and let the dark liquid swoosh around in his mouth, fully enjoying the hint of sherry that had been infused into the Aberlour's taste, enhancing it, but without letting the wine palate take over.

In silence, Garcia watched a well-dressed couple come up to the bar and drink down two shots of tequila each in quick succession. The smile on their lips told him that they were celebrating something. The look on the man's face told him that he really lusted after the woman, but she probably had never given in. Maybe tonight would be his lucky night.

'How's Anna?' Hunter asked.

Garcia dragged his eyes away from the couple. 'Yeah, she's great. She started another crazy new diet. You know – no this, no that, no carbs after seven in the evening.' He pulled a face.

'She doesn't need any of that.'

'I know. I keep on telling her that. But she won't listen to me.' He chuckled. 'She won't listen to anyone.' He paused and sipped his whisky. 'She's always asking about you, you know? How you're doing and all.'

'I had dinner with you guys at your place three weeks ago.'

'I know, but that's how she is. And she knows that if I'm not sleeping well, that means you probably aren't sleeping at all. She cares, Robert. It's in her nature.'

Hunter's smile was full of tenderness. 'Yes, I know. Tell her I'm OK.'

'I do, but she knows better.' Garcia started fidgeting with a paper napkin, folding its edges. 'You know, she can't understand how come you're not with someone.'

Hunter scratched just under his right ear and felt a small, painful lump on his skin. A stress zit was just starting to come up. He left it alone. 'Yeah, I know, she keeps on trying to introduce me to some of her friends.'

Garcia laughed. 'And you keep on sneakily getting out of it. But, you know, maybe she's got a point.'

Hunter looked at his partner funny.

Garcia matched his stare. 'She really likes you, you know? Alice.'

'What?' Hunter had no idea where that came from.

'You know she really likes you, don't you?'

Hunter studied Garcia for an instant. 'And you know this how?'

'Because I've got eyes. Don't even need to be a detective to pick that one up. Don't play the blind man, Robert.'

Hunter said nothing and reached for his glass again.

'Seriously, she likes you. It's in the way she looks at you when you're not looking. It's in the way she looks at you when you *are* looking. It reminds me of school. You know, when you have a crush on someone, but you're just too shy to say something. I know because I was that shy. It took me ages to finally ask Anna out.' Garcia allowed the moment to breathe. 'Maybe you should take her out for a drink, dinner even. She's a nice girl. Attractive, intelligent, determined . . . I can't think of a reason any single man wouldn't like to take her out. And no offense, but Anna is right, you could do with a steady relationship.'

'Thanks, Dr. Love, but I do fine the way I am.'

'I know you do fine. I've seen the way women look at you.' Every time the bartender walked past, her eyes lingered on Hunter for a moment. Hunter and Garcia had both noticed it.

'Look, don't get me wrong, I'm really not trying to play matchmaker here. I suck at it, and your personal life is none of my business. All I'm saying is, take Alice out for a friendly drink. Get to know her out of our work environment – which, I might add, is filled with pictures of dead people. Who knows? You guys might just click.'

Hunter swirled his whisky around in his glass. 'Do you want to hear something funny?' he said. 'We knew each other from before.'

'Who? You and Alice?'

Hunter nodded.

'What? Really?'

Hunter nodded.

'From where?'

Hunter told him.

'Wow, that's a coincidence. So she was a prodigy kid as well? Boy, do I feel like the dumb one in the box now.'

Hunter smiled and finished his Scotch. Garcia did the same.

'I don't want to talk about the case,' Garcia said, ''cos I'm ready to go home here, but do *you* want to hear something funny? I hate puppets, including shadow ones. I have done since I was a kid.'

'Really?'

'I know it's silly, but I always thought there was something evil about them. Nothing would scare me more than a puppet theater. And my fifth-grade teacher made us stage a puppet play every goddamn month. I either had to manipulate them, or sit with the rest of the class and watch.' He chuckled uncomfortably. 'Who knows? Maybe the killer is my teacher and he came back just to haunt me.'

Hunter smiled and stood up, ready to leave. 'I wish. That would make things much simpler.'

Ninety-Six

Hunter felt so exhausted that no insomnia would've been able to keep him awake tonight. Back in his apartment, he had another warm shower and poured himself another shot of Scotch. Against his headache and tired muscles, it worked better than any medicine he could think of.

He kept the living-room lights switched off and headed for the sofa. There was no need for him to see the faded wallpaper, the tired carpet or the mismatched furniture.

Hunter couldn't even remember when the last time was that he'd turned his TV on. He definitely wasn't a TV man, but he knew he needed something to keep his mind occupied, no matter how trivial. Something to keep his thoughts from running away from him and back into the case, at least for one night – he really needed to disconnect. Though he loved reading, books tended to excite his brain, while television simply numbed it.

He searched the channels for late-night sports or cartoons, but without cable or satellite TV his choice of channels was somewhat limited. He settled for a rerun of some old World Wrestling Federation show. Entertaining, but not enough to keep sleep from taking over. Slowly, his body and mind gave up the fight and eased into a restless sleep.

It didn't take long for the nightmares to start. And they

came at him in waves – an empty room, bare brick walls, a single, dim light bulb dangling from a wire in the center of the ceiling, weak enough to keep all the corners in a shadow. Everything was so vivid he could smell the room – damp, moldy, stinking of sweat, vomit, and blood. In his dream he was merely a spectator, watching everything unfold before his eyes without being able to intervene.

First he saw Garcia lying unconscious on a dirty metal table while someone slowly dismembered him with a kitchen knife. No matter how much he tried, Hunter could never see the assailant's face.

In a blink of an eye, the victim on the metal table changed. Garcia was nowhere to be seen. This time, the faceless killer was using his knife on Anna, Garcia's wife. Her terrified screams reverberated through the room in an endless loop.

Hunter twitched on the sofa.

Another change of scene.

This time the victim was Alice Beaumont, and the dismembering started all over again. The floor of the room was thick with blood. Hunter was helpless, watching these people he knew, people he cared for, being slaughtered in front of his eyes, like a second-rate horror film.

Moments later the killer proceeded to use the body parts like Play-Doh, molding and sculpting them into grotesque, shapeless sculptures. All Hunter could hear were the animated laughs the killer let out every so often, like a kid having the best of times with his new toys.

Hunter's eyes shot open all of a sudden, as if somebody had shaken him awake. His forehead and neck were drenched in cold sweat. He was still in his living room, the TV was still on, now showing some black and white film. Somehow, while still locked inside his nightmare, Hunter remembered something Garcia had said to him at the bar, and his brain made a crazy connection.

He jumped up and checked his watch – 6:08 a.m. He had been asleep for close to six and a half hours. Despite the horrendous dreams, his headache was gone, and his brain felt fresh and rested, but he needed to get back to his office. He couldn't believe he hadn't thought of it before.

Ninety-Seven

By the time Garcia arrived at the PAB, Hunter had been sitting in front of the pictures board for about an hour and a half. His mind had run through dozens of scenarios, trying desperately to answer the questions his brain ceaselessly asked. He hadn't managed to answer all of those questions, but one scenario made more sense than all the others, and he wanted to run the idea past everyone.

Captain Blake was the last one to join the group in Hunter's office. Alice had arrived five minutes earlier.

'I've come up with a theory,' Hunter said, drawing their attention to the pictures board. He had repositioned several of the photographs in a different order. 'Please bear with me and hear me out, because it might sound a little crazy at first.'

Captain Blake pulled a face. 'We've got a killer who dismembers his victims and uses their body parts to create sculptures and shadow puppets, Robert. Any theory behind those actions, truth or not, has got to be at least a little crazy. I don't think any of us is expecting a lot of reason here. What have you got?'

'OK,' Hunter began. 'We all know how much effort we've put into trying to understand and identify the meaning behind those sculptures and shadow images. Since we got our third victim four days ago, and consequently, our third sculpture and shadow image, we've been trying every combination we could think of to make any sense of this mess. Carlos and I even tried looking at the images as a group, instead of individually.'

Garcia nodded. 'We thought that maybe the images linked into each other in some way to form something else, maybe a larger image. This whole thing felt like a jigsaw from the beginning. So maybe that was what the killer wanted us to do. Slot the pieces he'd given us into the correct position to complete the puzzle.'

Captain Blake cocked an interested eyebrow.

'We got nothing, Captain,' Garcia said, curbing her enthusiasm with a shake of his head. 'No matter which way we pieced it together, we came up with zilch. Each sculpture casts an individual shadow image, and that's that. They aren't linked.'

Hunter agreed. 'We came to the conclusion that they were independent from each other, not smaller pieces of an incomplete picture.'

'OK,' the captain said. 'So you went back to try and figure out their individual meanings.'

'Yes,' Hunter admitted. 'But with the discovery yesterday that the second victim, Andrew Nashorn, and the third one, Nathan Littlewood, also knew each other – possibly since their late teens – I started pondering new possibilities.'

'Such as?' the Captain queried.

'Carlos said something yesterday that didn't click until sometime in the middle of the night, but I should've thought of it before.'

Captain Blake and Alice's attention moved to Garcia, who in turn looked back at Hunter.

'What did I say?'

'That you never liked puppets. And you told me about your fifth-grade teacher.'

Captain Blake tightened her stare.

Garcia shrugged as if it were nothing. 'Puppets used to freak me out. They still do, in a way.'

'What about your fifth-grade teacher?' Alice asked.

'He came up with a theater class, and made us stage a puppet play every month.' Garcia scratched his left cheek nervously. 'Boy, I hated that class. I hated that teacher. I hated that whole year.'

'And that's an angle I never considered before,' Hunter said.

'What angle are you talking about, Robert?' Captain Blake said. 'Because I don't think any of *us* see it either.'

'A theater, Captain. A puppet theater.' Hunter positioned himself next to the replica of the sculpture from the first crime scene, Derek Nicholson's house. 'Puppets are used in theaters for one reason only.'

Just a fraction of confusion lifted from everyone's faces.

'To stage a play?' Alice said.

'To tell a story,' Garcia commented a second later.

Hunter smiled. 'Exactly.'

Ninety-Eight

Captain Blake's eyes quickly browsed Garcia and Alice's faces; neither of them seemed to be on the same page as Hunter yet either.

Hunter didn't wait to be asked. 'I think we've been going down the right track all along, we were just knocking on the wrong door. There is a bigger picture here.' He pointed at the board. 'But it isn't one single image. And the shadow puppets were the clue.' Hunter cleared his throat before proceeding. 'I think the killer is staging a play. Just like a puppeteer. He's telling us a story, giving us a scene at a time.'

Stunned silence.

Simultaneously, everyone's uncertain eyes left Hunter and moved back to the pictures on the board. Alice started chewing her bottom lip. Hunter had noticed she did that when she was concentrating on something. He could tell that they were trying very hard to stay with him.

'Let me show you what I mean, starting with the first image we got.' He turned off the lights, switched his flashlight on, and aimed its beam onto the replica sculpture. The dog and bird-like shadow images appeared on the wall behind it once again.

'We identified this first image as being that of a coyote and a raven. I have no doubt Alice found the correct interpretation for those two animals in combination – it means a liar, a deceiver, someone who betrays. I also think we are correct in linking that interpretation directly to the first victim. In the killer's mind, Derek Nicholson was a liar.'

'Yeah, we've all agreed on that,' Captain Blake said.

Hunter turned the lights back on and pointed to the shadow photograph they had obtained from the sculpture left at the second crime scene, Andrew Nashorn's boat. The image showed a large, horned, devil-like face looking down at what looked like two people in a standing position, and two lying on the ground, one on top of the other. 'Now, with this second image, I think there are things we got right, and things we got wrong.' He nodded at Alice. 'I think Alice was right again when she said that the killer probably had an agenda. He's after specific victims. He isn't picking them at random out of the general public. At the time he created this sculpture, he'd killed two people, Nicholson and Nashorn. We thought they were represented by these two figures lying on the ground.' He indicated them in the image. 'And it looked like there were two more names on his list, represented by the two standing figures.'

Captain Blake moved closer to the board. 'And you think that's wrong?'

'Partially. I don't think that these two on the ground represent the two victims who had been killed at that point, as was suggested. But maybe these two standing up indicate that, at the time of the second murder, there were still two more names on the killer's hit list.'

Garcia curled his lips over his teeth, considering. 'So what do you think the two on the ground represent?'

'A fight.'

Silence ruled again for the next few seconds. Everyone frowned and squinted at the picture, trying to process it under Hunter's new light.

'OK, let me walk you through what I think this whole image means,' Hunter said, grabbing everyone's attention again. 'Imagine a group of four friends, and for now let's say that those four are Nicholson, Nashorn, Littlewood and a fourth person who we haven't identified yet. This group of friends go out on a drinking night, or a party night, or something. They get too drunk, they get too rowdy as guys sometimes do, maybe even too high, and they end up in an argument with someone, either an outsider, or someone who was originally part of their group. The argument escalates and turns into a punch-up. Even if it had started as a joke . . .' Hunter indicated the two images piled up on the ground once again, '. . . it didn't end as one.'

Garcia was pinching his chin, following Hunter's every word, slowly stepping into his partner's line of thought. Suddenly the dots connected.

'And they killed him,' he said.

The shadow image that he'd looked at countless times before now took on a whole new meaning in front of his eyes. 'The fight got completely out of hand,' Garcia continued. 'The rest of the group was standing around, watching, or maybe they all took turns punching and kicking. It takes one wrong kick to the temple, a stumble and a head hit against a curbstone, or a wall, or something, and the punch-up ends . . . badly.'

Hunter nodded. 'It probably happened unintentionally, but I think somebody was killed. That's the theory.'

Looking at the picture, listening to Hunter's

interpretation, it was like the image had morphed before Captain Blake's eyes.

'But then we're either missing someone, or we got the numbers wrong,' Alice joined in.

'What do you mean?' the captain asked.

'When we first looked at this shadow image, we knew the killer had already murdered two people, and we believed he was after two more, represented by the two standing up figures. If this image represents two people fighting on the floor with the rest watching, and as Robert is suggesting, one of them accidentally dies, then we're left with three remaining figures. The one that comes out of the fight, and the two standing up.' She lifted three fingers. 'We have three victims now – Nicholson, Nashorn and Littlewood. And that would mean the killer has got them all. His list is complete.'

'You're forgetting him.' Hunter pointed to the largest figure in the image. The distorted head with what looked like horns, looking down at the probable fight scene. 'You thought this figure represented the killer, remember? Like a devil. I don't think it does. I think that with every murder, the killer uses the sculpture and the shadow image it casts to represent *that* specific victim. This was left in Andrew Nashorn's boat for a reason. I think the Devil-like figure represents Nashorn.'

'So why the horns?' Captain Blake asked.

'Maybe to indicate that he was the leader, or the instigator. In every group of guys like that, Captain, there's always one who is the *head*. The one whom everyone follows. Maybe Nashorn was the one who started the fight. Or maybe he was the one who, instead of stopping it, urged the participants to carry on punching.'

Uneasiness took over the room.

Hunter gave everyone time to consider his theory.

'Maybe the person isn't dead,' Alice said. 'Maybe you're right, maybe there was a fight, but instead of dying the victim was physically, or even mentally impaired. Maybe after all these years, that victim is back, and he wants revenge.'

Hunter shook his head. 'No, the victim died.'

'How can you be sure?'

'Because the killer tells us.'

Ninety-Nine

Hunter drew their attention to the last two shadow-image photographs on the board. The ones cast by the two-part sculpture left in Nathan Littlewood's office.

'In the last crime scene, the killer left us two shadow images,' he said, 'but I think we read them in reverse order. This should be the first one of the two.' He indicated the image created by Littlewood's right arm and hand – the one that looked like someone kneeling down with his arm lifted up above his head, maybe praying. In front of the kneeling-down figure were small pieces of something. Their shadows had been created by the flesh sections carved out of Littlewood's thigh.

Garcia shivered. Something that felt like an electric shock started at the back of his neck and spread throughout his body at incredible speed. Hunter didn't have to explain. He saw it himself.

'Oh my God,' he said, slightly tilting his head to one side. 'We never figured out why the killer left us two images in one crime-scene. And we specifically struggled to understand that one. It looked like someone on his knees, praying or something, with several objects scattered around on the floor in front of him. It's not that at all.' He drew a deep breath and held it for a long instant before letting it out slowly. 'That's someone chopping a body into pieces.'

Garcia's words bounced off the walls like a crazy rubber ball.

Captain Blake stood absolutely still. For a moment, she almost lost the ability to blink. 'So you think that this group of friends got into a punch-up, beat somebody to death, and cut the body up into pieces to dispose of it?'

Hunter nodded and indicated the last shadow-image photograph they had – part two of the sculpture found in Nathan Littlewood's office – the one that looked like someone staring at someone else lying inside a box.

'They placed the dismembered body inside some sort of container before getting rid of it!' Alice said, letting out a heartfelt sigh. Both images now made perfect sense together.

Hunter waited, taking in their concerned expressions. Almost a minute went by before Captain Blake spoke again.

'How long ago do you think that happened?'

'Somewhere around thirty years ago, give or take one or two. It must've happened when Nicholson, Nashorn and Littlewood were young, very young – late teens or early twenties maybe, probably before Littlewood got married twenty-seven years ago.'

'So the obvious conclusion is that our killer was related to that victim in some degree, and he now wants revenge,' the captain said.

'Yes,' Hunter agreed.

'But why now?'

'Because our killer didn't know anything about what really happened until a few months ago,' Hunter said.

All of a sudden, all the pieces were slotting into place in

Garcia's mind. 'Nicholson,' he said, returning to his desk, picking up his notebook and quickly flipping through it.

Captain Blake and Alice turned to face him.

'Here it is. Derek Nicholson's nurse told us that he said something about making his peace with God. About telling someone the truth about something. That no matter how much good you do in your life, there are certain mistakes that would haunt you until your dying day.' He returned the notebook to his desk. 'That must've been what he was talking about. The mistake that haunted him throughout his life.' He looked at Hunter. 'The person who visited him in his house. The man we still haven't identified.'

Hunter nodded.

'The nurse also said that Nicholson had only two visitors once he was taken ill,' Garcia clarified, for the captain's and Alice's benefit. 'DA Bradley was one of them, but we've never identified the second visitor. He's got to be our killer. Nicholson finally told him the truth about what had happened. He didn't want to carry that secret to the grave with him.'

'And a few weeks later he was murdered,' Captain Blake said. 'The revenge rampage started.'

'So if you're right,' Alice said to Hunter, as another piece of the puzzle clicked into place for her, 'Derek Nicholson must've been friends, or at least acquainted, with our killer from before. If he asked him to come to his house so he could clear his conscience, he must've known him. And that's why the killer considered him a liar.' She shook her head. 'Better yet, a deceiver. He felt betrayed. Exactly what the shadow image told us.'

Hunter nodded.

'And with the next victim and shadow image,' she

continued, 'the killer depicted Andrew Nashorn as the group or gang leader, the one they all followed.'

Another nod.

'And Nathan Littlewood was the one left with the task of disposing of the body.'

'I don't think he disposed of it,' Hunter disagreed. 'I think he cut it to pieces, and packed them inside some sort of container. I think the person who disposed of that container is the last name on our killer's hit list. The fourth member of the group. The next victim.'

Everyone paused and processed that information in their own time.

'But as I said,' Hunter massaged the back of his neck, 'at the moment this is all just a crazy theory in my head. I have no proof of anything yet.'

'Crazy or not, all the pieces seem to slot into place,' Captain Blake said, returning her attention to the images on the board. 'And that would also explain why our killer is dismembering his victims. It's payback time – an eye for an eye – blood in, blood out.'

She paused for a brief moment while she worked things out in her head. It'd been sixteen days since the first murder, and as things stood, she was inclined to claw at any reasonable possibility. She also hated working with the FBI.

'OK, it's plausible, and it makes more sense than anything else we've got so far. Let's go with it. Let's get a team digging into our three victims' past. If that group of friends really existed, I want to know who that fourth person was. If you need to get in touch with the FBI to dig deeper, do it. I don't like them any more than you do, but they have resources that we don't, and they can get access to things a lot faster than we can. Tell the team already digging into Derek

Nicholson's life to dig harder. We need to find out who visited him by his deathbed. Talk to his nurses again. And let's get one last team looking into any cases where the victim was found chopped to pieces inside a box, a container, a matchbox, anything. I know there's a possibility that the body was never found in the first place, but if it was found, and if you are right,' she addressed Hunter, 'we identify that victim, we identifty our Sculptor killer.'

One Hundred

The next twenty-four hours went by in a blur. Everyone was working as fast and as hard as they could, but so far very little progress had been made.

With her experience in navigating databases, Alice had volunteered to run the searches for bodies found chopped to pieces inside any sort of container, but she hit a wall almost immediately. Her expertise was in the digital world. If any records were stored anywhere online, she would no doubt get to them. But when you're searching for something that dates back years before the use of digital databases, it all becomes a lottery. If some underpaid clerk had, at some point, been given the mind-numbing task of transposing that information from paper to digital, then Alice knew she would find it. But if that information was still packed away inside a dark archive room somewhere, that was exactly where it would stay. Realistically, due to budgeting and a lack of staff, most government organizations would never manage to completely digitize their backlog of paper files.

Hunter and Garcia went back to Amy Dawson's house – Derek Nicholson's weekday nurse. She had seen the newspapers front pages and the photographs of all three victims. She couldn't understand why a serial killer would go after Mr. Nicholson.

Hunter revisited the subject of Derek Nicholson wanting to make peace with God and tell someone the truth about something, but Amy told him that that had been all he'd said. He'd never mentioned anything else or any names. She had no idea what truth he had referred to, and she remembered nothing new about the second person who'd visited Mr. Nicholson that day.

Speaking to Melinda Wallis, Nicholson's weekend nurse and the person who had found his body that morning, was a much more delicate affair. Since the murder, she had moved back into her parents' house in La Habra Heights, a rural canyon community located on the border of Orange and Los Angeles Counties. Even with Hunter's experience, interviewing her proved almost impossible. The trauma caused by what she had seen in that room, and the knowledge that she'd been a breath away from a ruthless killer, and the bloody message he had left on the wall specifically for her, had spread its roots deep into her conscious and subconscious mind. Even with years of psychotherapy, which her family couldn't afford, she would never be the same person again. Sadly, Melinda had become another victim of the Sculptor.

One Hundred and One

Before returning to the PAB, Hunter and Garcia had one more stop – Allison Nicholson's apartment in Pico-Robertson, just south of Beverly Hills.

Derek Nicholson's youngest daughter lived in a luxurious two-bedroom apartment in the much sought-after Hillcrest development, adjacent to the famous Hillcrest Country Club. Hunter had contacted both of Nicholson's daughters by phone earlier in the day. They'd arranged to meet at 7:15 p.m. at Allison's apartment.

The Hillcrest development looked and felt more like a holiday resort than a residential complex. Its residents enjoyed a very large fitness center with a cardio island, dry sauna, two resort-style pools, two beauty spas, towering palm trees, waterfalls, and an outdoor fireplace with lounge area and barbeque grills. After signing in with the security guard at the complex's electronic gates, both detectives were given instructions for finding the visitors' parking lot.

The concierge at Allison's apartment block's entry lobby showed Hunter and Garcia to the elevator, and told them that Miss Nicholson's apartment was located on the top floor.

The luxury that had started right at the electronic gates

reached its peak inside Allison's flat. The living room was almost the size of a basketball court, with Karndean flooring, impressive chandeliers, Persian rugs, and even a granite fireplace. The furniture was nearly entirely antique, and expensive paintings hung on the walls. But the décor was charming, giving the place a very relaxing atmosphere.

Allison invited both detectives in with a polite but sad smile. Her deep brown eyes were sorrowful. Her sadness had undoubtedly taken a bite at her beauty. Olivia looked just as worn out. Allison was still in her work clothes – a perfectly fitting dark suit, complemented by a gray, frilled, V-neck blouse. She'd taken her high heels off, and without them she stood at around five foot five.

'Please have a seat,' she said, indicating a pair of light brown leather Chesterfields.

Olivia was standing by the window, her long hair pulled back and clipped at the edge of her neck.

'We're sorry to disturb you,' Hunter said, taking his seat. 'We'll take very little of your time.' Hunter showed both sisters the photographs of Nashorn and Littlewood that had appeared on the front page of the *LA Times*. Neither Allison nor Olivia could confirm if their father were friends with either of the other two victims. Neither their faces nor their names rang any bells.

'Who are these people?' Olivia asked.

'Friends of your father,' Hunter said. 'From a long time ago. We're not sure if they were still friends.'

Allison looked perplexed.

'A long time ago?' Olivia questioned again. 'How long?'

'Around thirty years,' Garcia answered.

'What?' Allison's gaze moved from both detectives to her sister and then back to Garcia. 'I wasn't even born then. What do my father and some friends from thirty years ago have to do with any of this?'

'We believe these killings aren't random, and that the killer is targeting that specific group of friends,' Hunter said.

'A specific group of friends?' Olivia joined in. 'How many?'

'We believe that there were at least four of them.'

Hunter's words hung in the air for a moment.

'Why?' Olivia moved closer. 'Why is this killer after these people?'

'We're not sure.' Hunter saw no point in telling Olivia and Allison about his theory at the moment.

'And you believe this killer is going to kill again.'

Hunter saw the glint in Olivia's eyes.

Neither detective answered her question.

'So you think this killer is after a specific group of people,' Olivia carried on. 'But you're not sure how many. People who *were* friends thirty years ago, but you're not sure if they *are* still friends. And you're not even sure why the killer is targeting them. You guys don't know much, do you?'

Hunter could see that Allison was getting tearful again. He had noticed a wooden sideboard behind the Chesterfields, which held a collection of picture frames of all different sizes. All the photos were of her family.

'I was wondering if you have a photograph of your father when he was young that we could borrow,' Hunter said to Allison. 'It could really help us. You'll get it back.'

Allison nodded. 'I have an old wedding picture.' She gestured towards the sideboard Olivia was standing next to.

Olivia turned, looked at all the portraits and hesitated for a moment, emotion running through her again. She reached for a frame and stared at it for a second before handing it to Hunter. The six-by-four-inch portrait showed a close-up of Derek Nicholson and his wife, their smiles reflecting how happy they were. Allison looked just like her mother, especially her eyes. Hunter remembered a picture he had obtained of Nicholson a year before he was diagnosed with terminal cancer; other than a receding hairline and the addition of the mandatory age wrinkles, he hadn't changed much.

Back in Garcia's car, just as he turned the key in the ignition, Hunter's cellphone rang – *Restricted Call.*

'Detective Hunter,' he answered.

'Detective, this is Tammy from Operations Crimeline. I have someone on hold who'd like to speak with the detective in charge of the Sculptor investigation.'

Hunter knew that the Crimeline team was trained to filter all bogus calls. Every time a high-profile investigation made the news, they received tens of those a day – people looking for rewards, drunks, druggies, cranks, pranks, tricksters, attention seekers, or simply people who liked to waste police time. If the investigation was related to a possible *serial killer*, the call-volume would multiply tenfold, easily going into the hundreds, sometimes even thousands, every day. Since this investigation had started, this was the first call Operations Crimeline had put through to either Hunter or Garcia. 'She says she has some information,' Tammy said.

'What kind of information?' Hunter asked, signaling Garcia to wait a moment.

Tammy cleared her throat. 'She says she knew all three victims.'

One Hundred and Two

The greasy café sat at the corner of Ratliffe Street and Gridley Road in Norwalk, southeast Los Angeles. All tables but one were taken. Sitting alone, facing the shop's front window, was a black woman in her early fifties. On the table in front of her, a half-drunk cup of coffee had been pushed to one side. Twice now, in the fifteen minutes she'd been sitting there, she'd thought about getting up and leaving. She still wasn't sure if she was making something of nothing, but it seemed like way too much of a coincidence to be *just* a coincidence.

She had clocked them way before they entered the café, as they parked their car outside. She could still tell cops from a mile away. She looked up as both detectives stepped through the door, and Hunter immediately saw a face that, long ago, must have been pretty, but now looked hollowed out and emptied of life. There was a long, thin scar on her left cheek that she made no effort to conceal. They locked eyes for just a second.

'Jude?' Hunter asked, coming up to her table. He knew that wasn't her real name, but it was the name she'd given him over the phone.

The woman nodded as she studied both faces in front of her.

'I'm Detective Hunter and this is Detective Garcia. Do you mind if we have a seat?'

She recognized Hunter's voice from their brief phone conversation less than half an hour ago. Jude's reply was a tiny shrug.

'Can I get you another cup of coffee?' Hunter offered.

She shook her head. 'I need to get up early in the morning, and I already blew my caffeine quota for today.' Her voice was slightly husky, sexy even, but firm. She was wearing a collarless, long-sleeve white shirt with a red rose embroidered over her left breast. There was a delicacy to her perfume, with a base-note of spice, something dry and exotic like clove or star anise.

'What can I get you gentlemen?' an overweight waitress asked, approaching the table.

'Are you sure?' Hunter tried again, sending a smile Jude's way.

She nodded.

'Two black coffees, no sugar, please,' Hunter replied, looking back at the waitress.

The waitress nodded and started collecting the plates from the next table along.

They sat in silence for a few seconds. As the waitress moved back into the kitchen, Jude looked across the table at Hunter and Garcia. 'OK, as I told you over the phone, I don't know if this has any relevance, but it has been bothering me for two days now. I'm not a great believer in coincidences, you know?'

Hunter laced his fingers and rested his hands on the table. He knew that the best thing was just to let her speak, no questions.

'I was taking the subway to work two days ago, as I do

every morning,' she carried on. 'I tend to avoid reading the papers, specially the *LA Times*. It's just too much crap, you know? And I already deal with a lot of that every day. Anyway, the woman sitting opposite me had the morning paper with her. As she flipped through it, I caught the front-page headline.' She pursed her lips and quickly shook her head. 'I didn't think anything of it at first. So there was another killer running loose in LA, what's new, right? But then, one of the pictures made me look again.'

The waitress came back with two cups of black coffee.

'Which picture?' Garcia asked, once the waitress was out of earshot.

'One of the victims.' Jude leaned forward and rested her elbows on the table. 'The guy called Andrew Nashorn.'

Garcia nodded calmly. 'What about the picture? What made you look again?'

'Actually it was the name underneath it. I recognized the name.' Jude picked up on the hint of doubt that had colored Garcia's face. 'When I was in school,' she explained, 'I had this big crush on this kid, Andreas Köhler. His family had immigrated from Germany.' A melancholic smile parted her lips. Her teeth looked stained and damaged. 'Anyway, I thought that I could increase my chances of getting with him if I could speak a little German. So I borrowed a few tapes from the school library. I listened to those tapes for about a month solid. Didn't learn much. It's a difficult language. But one of the things I did learn was the names of animals. And I still remember them.'

Garcia's confusion intensified, but he tried not to show it.

'*Nashorn* means rhinoceros in German.'

'Really?' Garcia looked at Hunter.

'I didn't know that either.'

'It does,' Jude affirmed. 'And that made me take a closer look at the picture. He obviously looked older. His hair was all gray, but I would recognize that face anywhere. It was the same person. And that's when I paid a little more attention to the photographs of the other two victims, and it all came back to me. They were all much older, but the more I looked, the less doubt I had. I knew all of them.'

Hunter hadn't touched his coffee yet. His eyes were studying Jude's facial and body movements. There were no twitches, no rapid eye movement, no fidgeting. If she was lying, she was really good at it.

'Well, I didn't actually know them,' Jude clarified. 'I was beat up by them.'

One Hundred and Three

Those words fell over Hunter and Garcia like slabs of rock, almost knocking the breath out of them.

Garcia shook the surprise off his face. 'You were beaten up by them?'

For the first time Jude broke eye contact with the detectives. Her gaze moved down to her unfinished coffee cup. 'I'm not proud of it, but I'm also not ashamed of my life. We've all done things we wished we never did.' She paused, collecting her thoughts. Hunter and Garcia respected her breathing space. 'When I was a lot younger, I worked the streets down in Hollywood Boulevard, the low end of the Strip.'

The east end of the famous Hollywood Boulevard used to be LA's best-known red-light district.

'I was new to the area. My usual spot used to be around Venice Beach, but back then the Strip was a much more popular place. If you could handle the numbers, you could make some serious cash.' There was no shame in her words. She couldn't change her past, and she accepted that with tremendous dignity. 'Anyway, I was picked up one night by this guy. It was really late, past midnight, I think. He was quite good-looking, and funny. He took me to this place out by Griffith Park, but what he'd never told me in the car was that there were another three guys waiting for us.'

Jude's gaze moved past both detectives and up into the distance, as if she was trying to see what was coming.

'Well, I told them right then that I didn't do gangbangs. Not for any money.' She stopped talking and reached for her cold coffee.

'But they didn't care,' Hunter said.

'No they didn't,' she replied after having a sip. 'They were all high on something, and they were drinking a lot. The problem wasn't really having sex with four drunken men at once. The problem was that they liked it rough.' She paused and thought better of her words. 'Well, two of them did, more than the other two. By the time they were done, I was so bruised I wasn't able to work for a week.'

It was pointless asking Jude if she'd gone to the police. She was a working girl, and the sad truth was that the police would've barely lent an ear to her story. She might even have been arrested for prostitution.

'But things like that happened. It came with the job,' Jude said in a resigned tone, without bitterness. 'And they still do. It was a risk us girls took when we chose to work alone. I was beaten up before, worse than that. The reality is that, out on the streets, you never really know what kind of jerk is going to roll down his window and call you over.'

By 'work alone' both detectives knew Jude meant she didn't have a pimp. Pimps provided protection for their girls. If anyone laid a rough hand on them, or decided they didn't want to pay, they would have their legs broken, or worse. The problem was, the girls had to work for peanuts.

Pimps would take 80 to 90 per cent of all the money their girls made, sometimes more.

'The driver,' Jude continued. 'The one who picked me up and took me to his friends, that was the guy in the picture in the paper. Nashorn, rhinoceros man.'

'He told you his name?' Garcia asked.

'No, but while he was on top of me, slapping my face with his animal hands, I heard one or two of the others cheer him on. First I thought it was a joke or something. That they were calling him rhinoceros in German for fun. But then I realized it couldn't be. I remember thinking that he wasn't the only rhinoceros in that room. They were all animals. But when you hear a name being called while someone is on top of you, beating you up, you tend to remember it forever.'

'And you're sure about the others? I mean the other two victims you saw in the paper – Derek Nicholson and Nathan Littlewood?'

'I never heard their names being called that night. But I remember their faces. I made a point of never closing my eyes. Never giving them the satisfaction of my fear. I know that's what dominant men thrive on, right? The submission. That night I did all I could to not submit to them, at least not mentally. While they were on me, I looked straight into their eyes. Every single one of them.' Jude looked up at Garcia. 'So yes, I'm very sure the other two men I saw in the paper were there that night.'

Hunter was still studying her. There was anger in her words, but it sounded dead, something that was now in the past, something that, just as she'd said, was a risk that came with what she did. And she had accepted it.

'You said that two of them liked it rough more than the others,' Hunter said. 'Which two, do you remember?'

Jude ran a hand through her hair. Her stare returned to Hunter. 'Of course I do. Rhinoceros man and the Littlewood guy. They pretty much did all the beating. The other two joined in for the sex, but they weren't violent. In fact, I think they even asked the other two to take it easy.'

Hunter's eyes dropped to the plastic tablecloth and he thought about Jude's last words. He'd seen that sort of situation many times when young, and countless times in his adult life – *peer pressure*. It happened everywhere, even inside the LAPD. People would do things they didn't agree with, or didn't want to do, simply to be accepted, to feel part of a group. It ranged from common behavior like smoking and bullying, to terrible and damaging acts like committing a crime – even murder.

'How long ago was this?' Hunter asked.

'Twenty-eight years,' Jude confirmed. 'A few months after that, I quit the streets.'

One Hundred and Four

For a long moment they all sat in silence. Jude had just confirmed that Derek Nicholson did indeed know Andrew Nashorn and Nathan Littlewood, and that they all used to hang out together. Further to that, Hunter's theory seemed to be correct when it came to the group having a fourth member.

'Are you sure you can't remember any other names?' Hunter said finally, rupturing the silence.

Jude ran her tongue over her dry bottom lip. 'I've been thinking about it since I saw their pictures in the paper and realized who they were. That was one of those nights you just don't want to remember. And to tell you the truth, I hadn't thought about it for years. As I said, I'd been beaten up before, just never by anyone called Rhinoceros and his gang.' She reached for her handbag. 'That's everything I had to say. I don't know if it will help you any, but at least now the weight is off my shoulders, and I can hopefully get some sleep again.'

'Just one more thing,' Hunter said before Jude got up. 'Did you ever see them again? Any of them?'

Jude stared at her thin hands. Her pale-pink nail varnish was chipped everywhere. 'I saw the rhinoceros man once, a few months after that night. I just told you, I quit the streets later that year.'

'Where did you see him?' Garcia this time.

'Same place, down Hollywood Boulevard. He was picking someone else up.' She paused and gave them what sounded like a suppressed chuckle. 'Huh.'

'Is there something else?' Hunter read her expression.

Jude took a moment, searching her brain for an old memory. She put her handbag back down. 'There was this girl who had just started down at the Strip. Roxy, she called herself. Because she was new, she was easily hustled away from the good spots by the other girls. I told her she could work the corner where I was.' Jude tilted her head to one side and explained. 'I know how hard it can get, especially for the new girls. I was just trying to give her a little hand. She was nice. Not stunning, but attractive enough. Very petite, though. I told her she had to get some more meat on her bones. Men like curves, it's a fact. The problem was, she was way too nervous, and she had no idea of how to stand.'

Neither Hunter nor Garcia said anything. Jude explained anyway.

'Out on the streets we had to sell ourselves, and it's all about the way you stand and the way you look. You stand wrong, you never get approached. That's how it works. Well, after about an hour I took pity on her. I bought her a coffee and decided to give her a few tips. That was her first night on the job. She told me that she'd tried, but she couldn't get a job anywhere. She was desperate, and that was why she'd decided to hit the streets. But she wasn't a junky. I know a user when I see one.'

Both Hunter and Garcia knew that prostitution and drugs were like twin sisters.

Jude looked down at her hands. 'Her desperation wasn't for drugs. At least not the usual drugs.'

Hunter looked intrigued.

'She told me she had a kid who was ill. She needed money for medicine. She was really scared for her kid. She said that she only needed to do it that once, maybe two nights, and she'd have enough for her kid's medicine.' Jude shook her head as if trying to erase the memory. 'Anyway, I gave her a few tips and we went back to my corner spot.'

'OK,' Garcia said. 'What about her?'

'Well, later that night I got an easy job down a back alley – twenty minutes. When I was walking back, I saw her jumping into a car. She waved as they drove past me, and that was when I saw the driver. It was Rhinoceros Man. I tried waving them down, but they were too fast.'

'And what happened?' Hunter asked.

'I don't know. She didn't come back that night.' Jude shrugged. 'She didn't come back any night after that, either. At least not to my corner. I was a little worried. I thought that maybe what happened to me had happened to her. The same four bastards ganged up on her. As I said, it took me a week to be able to hit the streets again after they were done with me, and I was much stronger than she was. I never saw her again. But maybe she quit after that night. I hope she did. She said she only needed to do it that one night. Or maybe she got scared. It happened a lot to the new girls. As soon as they encountered their first rough customer, and inevitably they all did, that was when they figured out that that life wasn't for them. After that, I never saw Rhinoceros Man or any of his friends again.'

Hunter was still intrigued. 'Did this Roxy girl ever tell you her kid's name?' he asked.

'She probably did, but there's no way I will remember it

now. That was twenty-eight years ago.' Jude got up to leave again.

Hunter got up with her and handed her a card. 'If you remember anything else, any of the names of the others in that group, could you please give me a call – anytime.'

Jude stared at Hunter's card as if it were poisonous. After a long, hesitating moment she took it, and walked out of the café.

The only thought in Hunter's mind was that he'd been wrong. The shadow image they'd got from Andrew Nashorn's boat didn't depict a fight. It depicted a sexual attack – a gang rape.

One Hundred and Five

It was past ten at night by the time Hunter got back to his apartment. Sleep didn't come. His brain just wouldn't disconnect. Instead of forcing it, he went back to the box of photographs he'd retrieved from Littlewood's apartment and spread them on the floor of his living room. He checked them against the portrait Allison had given him of her parents. He already knew that the victims knew each other, but if Derek Nicholson were in any of those pictures, then maybe the missing fourth member of the group was too.

After an hour on his knees with a magnifying glass, Hunter had got nothing. He felt tired. His legs hurt and he needed rest. His eyes were burning from fatigue and his neck and shoulders ached. But his brain still wouldn't let go.

He heard the couple next door come back in from another night out drinking, slamming doors and slurring their words.

'I need to get some new neighbors,' Hunter chuckled to himself. He turned his attention to the photographs of the shadow images. All the information he had come across in the past few hours was bouncing around inside his head.

Giggling and moans started coming through the wall. 'Oh, no, no,' Hunter whispered. 'Please, not in the living room.'

The moans got a little louder.

'Damn!' Hunter knew that the banging against the wall would start soon. He laced his fingers and placed his palms on the top of his head while his eyes returned to the images on the floor.

The more he thought about it, the more it made sense. Nicholson, Nashorn, Littlewood and whoever the fourth member of their group was, had sexually attacked somebody. It could've been the girl Jude told them about – Roxy – or some other street prostitute. But what had happened to their victim? Had the attack gone terribly wrong? Was she dead?

The loud noises coming from next door didn't bother Hunter anymore. He was in his own bubble now, mentally reviewing every piece of information relating to the case.

He was so absorbed in his thoughts that it took Hunter a few seconds to register the sound of a phone ringing. He blinked twice and searched the room, as if momentarily disorientated. His cellphone was on the improvised computer desk, by the printer. The phone rang again and Hunter snapped it up without checking the caller-display window.

'Detective Hunter.'

'Detective, it's Jude. We talked earlier today.'

'Yes, of course.' Hunter was surprised, but his tone gave nothing away.

'I'm sorry for calling so late, but I did remember something, and though I thought about calling tomorrow morning, it has been bugging me and I can't sleep. You said that if I remembered anything else, I could call at any time.'

'Yes, of course. It's no problem at all,' Hunter said, checking his watch. 'What did you remember?'

'A name.'

The muscles on Hunter's neck tensed. 'The fourth member of the group?'

'No. I told you, I never heard any of the other names that night.' A short pause. 'I remember the name of Roxy's kid. Remember I told you that she mentioned it once or twice?'

'Yes, yes.'

Jude told Hunter the name and he frowned. Unusual, but at the same time there was something familiar about it.

Jude disconnected, glad to have called, and hoping that her brain would now disengage and allow her to get some sleep.

Hunter placed his cellphone back on the desk. The name Jude had given him was swimming around in his head. He decided to run it against the LAPD database. Maybe that's why it sounded vaguely familiar.

Hunter switched his laptop on, and as he waited for it to boot up, his eyes went back to the mess of photographs and files on the floor. He paused as he felt a cold swirl whip around inside his stomach.

There was no need to search the LAPD database. He'd just remembered where he'd heard the name before.

One Hundred and Six

Hunter didn't sleep. He spent the rest of the night exhausting his memory, searching for more clues. Even the possibility that he was right scared him.

He had to drop by either Olivia or Allison Nicholson's house to obtain one last piece of information, but it was too early to go knocking on anyone's door. He reached for his cellphone and dialed Alice's number. She answered it on the third ring.

'Robert, is everything OK?' She sounded half asleep.

'I need a favor.'

'Um . . . OK. What do you need?'

'Can you hack into the California Department of Social Services' database?'

A confused pause.

'Yeah, that won't be very hard.'

'Can you do it now, from your house?'

'Sure, as soon as I power up my gear.' A new pause. 'You do realize that you are asking me to commit a felony, right?'

'I promise I won't tell anyone.'

Alice laughed. 'Hey, you don't have to convince me. This is what I do best.'

'OK then, here's what I need you to find out.'

*   *   *

Olivia Nicholson was about to have breakfast when Hunter knocked on her door. Without giving much away, he explained that they had come across some new information overnight, and he just needed to ask her a few more questions.

Their conversation was brief, but fruitful. She told him that, as far as she could remember, her father's oldest friend was Dwayne Bradley, the Los Angeles District Attorney.

One Hundred and Seven

It was late afternoon when the phone on Garcia's desk rang. He hadn't seen or heard from Hunter all day, but that wasn't uncommon.

'Detective Garcia, Homicide Special,' he answered, and listened in silence for several seconds.

His expression took on such a deep frown that his forehead looked like a tire print. 'You're kidding . . . Where? . . . Are you sure? . . . OK, stay put, keep your eye on the house, and if anything changes call me straight away.' Garcia disconnected, and ran down to Captain Blake's office. Five minutes later he was dialing Hunter's cellphone number. Hunter answered it on the first ring.

'Robert, where are you?'

'Sitting in my car, waiting, gambling on a hunch.'

'What? What hunch?'

'Too complicated to explain now.' Hunter had already picked up the anxiety in Garcia's voice. 'What have you got?'

'You're not going to believe this. One of our teams hit the jackpot. We've got a solid lead on Ken Sands. Apparently he's been working for an Albanian drug outfit. We have a positive lock on his present location.'

'Where?'

'Somewhere in Pomona. I've got the address here with me.'

Pomona was way out of town.

'We've got a green light from the captain,' Garcia said. 'A search warrant is being pushed through the courts as we speak.'

'How fast can we get a SWAT team in place?'

'Five to ten minutes to get a team deployed. I already have someone getting me all the information on the location, including architectural drawings. We'll probably be able to brief the SWAT captain in fifteen, twenty minutes max.'

Hunter consulted his watch. 'I won't make the briefing, Carlos. I'm on the other side of town, and rush hour started twenty minutes ago. Give me the address in Pomona and I'll meet you there.'

Hunter disconnected, and at that exact moment the car he'd been following all day started moving again.

'Damn,' he said, turning the key in his ignition and stepping on the gas.

One Hundred and Eight

The windowless room was located at the basement of the PAB. Five SWAT-team members were sitting two-by-two in school classroom formation, with the fifth member sitting by himself at the back. They were all wearing black fatigues and bulletproof vests with the word 'SWAT' spray-painted across the back. Their black helmets were resting on their desks. At the front of the room, their captain, Jack Fallon, was standing behind a podium. Garcia and Captain Blake were to his left.

'Listen up, gents,' Fallon said in a commanding voice. The room went absolutely still. He pressed a button and Ken Sands's latest photograph, the one Hunter had obtained from the prison board, was projected onto the white screen to his right. 'This charming individual goes by the name of Ken Sands,' Fallon continued. 'This is the last known picture we have of him, taken six months ago on the day of his release from the California State Prison in Lancaster.'

'Looks like a regular scumbag to me, Cap,' Lewis Robinson, one of the SWAT agents said, causing all the others to laugh.

'That might be,' Fallon said, sucking their attention back to him. 'And that's why we're here. Sands is a major suspect in a multiple-homicide investigation. His record shows that he's very violent, very dangerous, and apparently very intelligent. There's a good chance that he's the Sculptor serial killer we've all read about in the papers.'

An uneasy murmur broke out among the agents.

'Which means I don't even have to tell you how royally disturbed that makes him.' Fallon pressed the button again and the image on the screen changed to the blueprint of a single-story house. 'This is our target's location in Pomona. Our intel tells us he's inside at the moment.'

The blueprint showed a house with three bedrooms, one of them en-suite, a living room, a dining room, a bathroom, and a large kitchen.

'Is he alone in the house, Cap?' Neil Grimshaw, the youngest of the SWAT agents, asked. Grimshaw had joined the team only a week ago. This was his first major operation. He looked tense, but in control.

'It looks like he's got at least one other person in there with him,' Fallon replied and looked at Garcia.

'That's the intel we've got so far,' Garcia explained. 'There's an LAPD detective watching the house as we speak, trying to gather whatever new info he can.'

'Do we know if this other person is hostile?' Robinson asked.

'We don't know,' Garcia replied.

'Are they armed?'

'We don't know.'

'Do we know which room the target is in?'

'We don't have that intel.'

'Fuck, is this guessing day, or what?' Robinson said. 'Might as well walk in there blindfolded. So what *do* we know?'

'All the information we have is in the folders on your

desks,' Fallon cut in. 'That's what we have, that's what we'll work with. That's why we are SWAT. Is that a problem, Robinson?'

'Just a bit worried about walking into any environment with an uncertain number of hostiles, having *zero* intel on their firepower, and next to zero on everything else, Cap, that's all.'

'Oh, I'm sorry,' Fallon said, as if addressing a two-year-old. 'I didn't mean to scare you. Would you like to sit this one out, shaky-shorts? We can call you when we go looking for the marshmallow monster in the cupcake factory. That won't be very dangerous, I promise.'

The room burst out into laughter.

'OK, we all better be on our toes on this one,' Fallon carried on. The room went quiet again. 'Sands has been linked to an Albanian drug outfit, and we all know what that crowd is capable of. We're taking no risks. We're going in guns first. I want three teams of two, double-back formation – usual partners. Grimshaw, you're with me. We've got surprise on our side. Sands doesn't know we're coming for him tonight, so we've gotta act fast. Let's pack it up, gents. We've got a scumbag to take down.'

One Hundred and Nine

Dusk had taken over Los Angeles and the wind had picked up considerably by the time they reached Pomona. The house in question was at the end of an isolated road, in a quiet neighborhood. SWAT, together with Garcia and two other police cars, parked at the top of the road and went the rest of the way on foot. At the moment their most powerful weapon was the surprise factor. The last thing they wanted to do was to give away that advantage by alerting the house occupants to their presence.

On their way to Pomona, Jack Fallon had laid out their assault plan to the three SWAT teams. One team was to enter the house through the back, via the kitchen; one would burst through the front entrance; and the third team would enter through the veranda doors that led to the main bedroom at the left side of the house. LAPD would provide cover from the outside, in case Ken Sands tried to escape through a window.

The detective who'd been observing the house had nothing new to report. All the windows and curtains were shut. They'd been shut all day, which made further reconnaissance impossible. No one had left or entered the house in the past two hours.

There was no sign of Hunter. Garcia had tried calling him twice since they left the PAB but had got no reply.

'*Status check.*' Fallon's voice came through loud and clear in Garcia's earpiece.

'*Team Alpha in position,*' came the immediate reply from the first team. '*But we're blind. There's some sort of obstruction under the door. No way of pushing the fiberscope camera in. We've got no eyes inside.*'

'*Team Beta in position,*' the second team responded. '*And we're as blind as a bat as well. No visual.*'

The same obstruction had been placed under every door. '*OK, we're gonna have to rock and roll blind,*' Captain Fallon said. '*Are the LAPD in position?*'

'We're all set,' Garcia replied, after a quick radio check, his eyes scanning the area for his partner – no Hunter. 'Search warrant has been granted. We've got a green light. Are you sure you want to go in with no eyes?'

Five silent, tense seconds flew by.

'*We have no other option, unless you wanna knock on the door and smile.*'

No reply from Garcia.

'*I thought not. OK, all teams, nothing but your "A" game. Let's stick to the plan. We still have surprise on our side. Check every corner, you hear?*'

'Roger that.'

'*Alpha, Beta, on my one-count: three . . . two . . . one.*'

All three teams were carrying breaching shotguns, which provided a noisier, but much faster, entry to most secure households than enforcer rams.

Garcia heard five loud blasts in quick succession, and then all hell broke loose.

All three teams entered the house almost simultaneously. Lewis Robinson and agent Antonio Toro were team Alpha. They were at the rear.

The back door led directly into the kitchen. Toro blew the locks off the door with the breaching shotgun. A fraction of a second later Robinson kicked the door in and blasted through into the house. He was immediately faced with a big, brawny man who had been sitting at a square table in the center of the room. He had a mountain of small plastic packets filled with white powder in front of him, and an Uzi submachine gun by his side. The door blast caught him completely by surprise, but despite being initially startled, he was already halfway off his seat. He had already scooped up the Uzi and its muzzle was on its way up, searching for targets. His fat finger solidly hugging the trigger.

'*Qij ju,*' he yelled in Albanian, as he saw the first figure in black come through the door. There was no way he would go quietly, and surrender was simply not in his vocabulary.

Robinson was about to yell at him to put down his weapon, but he recognized the threat straight away. The Albanian's eyes were full of anger and determination.

Shoot or get shot.

Without hesitation, Robinson squeezed the trigger of his Heckler & Koch MP5 submachine gun. It coughed twice. With a sound-suppressor and subsonic ammunition, the noise was no louder than a baby's sneeze. Both shots hit the Albanian directly in the chest. He stumbled backwards, blood spurting from his wound, and quickly coloring his white T-shirt. The muscle spasms that took over his entire body made his face contort with pain, and his finger tightened on the Uzi's trigger. A blast of uncontrolled gunfire spit out of the Uzi's muzzle, violently smashing against the wall and the ceiling behind and above Robinson and Toro's heads. One of the bullets missed Toro's forehead by just a few millimeters.

The SWAT agents had carefully studied Ken Sands's photograph on their way to Pomona. Despite his long hair and beard, they were each certain they'd be able to identify him in the house.

The man in the kitchen wasn't him.

One Hundred and Ten

SWAT-team Beta was comprised of Charlie Carrillo and Oliver Mensa. They had entered the house through the front door. Mensa was the one who had used the breaching shotgun, so Carrillo was the first to blast through the door. The living room was large but sparsely furnished – an old sofa, a four-seater table, two armchairs, and a TV on top of a wooden box. Sitting on the sofa facing the door was a tall skinny blond man. He looked half stoned. On the sofa next to him was a Sig Sauer P226 X-Five semi-automatic pistol.

The man jumped in his seat like a donkey rejecting a mount as he heard the noise. His gaze seemed distant and totally lost for an instant, and then, as if somebody had waved a magical sobering wand, his eyes refocused with incredible intensity and he went for his gun.

'Nuh-uh,' Carrillo said, aiming his MP5 red laser target beam directly at the man's forehead. 'Believe me, buddy, you ain't fast enough.'

The man paused with his hand mid-air, considering his options. He knew he was one sudden movement away from having his brains splattered all over that living room. His eyes burned with rage.

From the door, Mensa had moved like lightning, and while his aim searched the room for any new threats, he was already by the skinny man's side, and had retrieved the Sig Sauer P226 from the sofa.

'On the floor with your hands behind your back, now,' Carrillo ordered.

The skinny man didn't move.

Carrillo moved closer. They had no time to waste by arguing, or repeating orders. He brought the muzzle of his gun inches away from the man's face, grabbed him by the hair, and dragged him to the floor.

With his knee locked onto the suspect's neck, forcing his face to the ground, Carrillo used a special linked zip-tie cuff to tie the skinny man's wrists and ankles together behind his back. The whole process took less than five seconds.

'*Qij ju, ju ndyrë derr!*' the man screamed, as Carrillo released the pressure from his neck. He started struggling on the ground like a fish out of water. No matter how strong he was, he was going nowhere.

Carrillo took one last look at the man's face.

It wasn't Ken Sands.

One Hundred and Eleven

Hunter didn't drive to Pomona. He made a last-second decision to follow his hunch. Since he had come off the phone with Garcia he'd been following it for almost two hours. It had first taken him to Woodland Hills, in the southwestern part of the San Fernando Valley, and then to the grounds of a derelict building on the outskirts of Canoga Park.

The weather had changed again, and Hunter could smell rain in the air. He parked his car way out of sight, and carefully proceeded on foot. Under the darkness of night, it took him four minutes to cover the distance.

He passed a dilapidated iron gate that led him to the weed-strewn concrete forecourt of a dingy industrial building. It looked like an abandoned medium-sized warehouse or depot, but its walls still looked solid from the outside. The few windows Hunter could see were all smashed, but they were high up, by the building's gable roof – too high for anyone to get to without a ladder.

Hunter hid himself behind a rusty dumpster and observed the structure for a few minutes – no movement. He carried on circumnavigating the building from a safe distance. When he reached the back of the building he saw the black pickup truck. The same pickup truck he'd been following all day.

Everything looked absolutely still.

Being as quiet as he could and using the shadows for cover, Hunter moved closer.

When he got to the pickup truck he was able to see the outline of a dark doorway about eight feet wide in the building's back wall. The large, sliding metal doors were open, and the gap was large enough for Hunter to get through without having to push them any further, which was an advantage – he doubted the rusty sliding mechanism would be silent.

He stepped inside and stood still for a moment, listening. The only light came from the smashed windows by the ceiling, but on a moonless night like this it gave Hunter no guidance. The place smelled of urine and decay. The air was stale and heavy, scratching at his throat and nostrils every time he breathed in.

He heard no sound, and decided to switch on his flashlight. As he did, he found himself in a room around seventy-five feet square, with a single steel door set in the middle of the wall ahead of him. The door had a dappled gunmetal look to its surface. The concrete floor was littered with empty bottles, used condoms, broken glass, discarded syringes and other debris left behind by itinerant homeless people and drug users. Taking great care not to step on any of it, Hunter slowly crossed to the metal door. This door was also open, but he would have to push it further to create a gap big enough for him to slide through. Now he saw that a pale white light came from somewhere beyond it.

He switched off his flashlight, gave his eyes a moment to get used to the low light, readied his Heckler & Koch USP .45 Tactical pistol, and steadied himself, ready to push the door open. That was when he heard the ear-piercing mechanical hum of something that sounded like a small chainsaw or an electric kitchen carving knife, followed by a terrified male scream coming from the next room.

The game was up. No more stealth.

Hunter pushed the door open and stepped through, gun first. This room was larger than the previous one, about a hundred feet square. The pale light that lit the room came from two battery-powered pedestal lights positioned about three feet from the back wall, and five apart. Between them, a hospital-style metal chair. Its naked occupant had been tied to it by his ankles and wrists. A man in his early fifties. He had chubby cheeks, a pointy chin and a full head of hair that had already gone gray. He looked up and his sad, pleading eyes met Hunter's.

It took Hunter a second to recognize him. They'd met before at least once. Hunter was sure it was in a function somewhere, probably at last year's LAPD's Purple Heart award ceremony. His name was Scott Bradley, the youngest brother of Dwayne Bradley, the Los Angeles District Attorney. But worse, Hunter also recognized the person standing behind the chair, holding an electric kitchen carving knife.

Despite all his suspicions, Hunter could barely believe his eyes.

One Hundred and Twelve

Captain Fallon and new recruit, Neil Grimshaw, were SWAT-team Gamma. Their task was to enter the house through the large French doors on the veranda that led into the house's main bedroom. With the curtains shut, they had no way of knowing if the room was empty or not, and, if it was occupied, how many were in there, or if they were carrying any weapons. Surprise and speed were their trump cards.

Grimshaw blasted the doors' lock with a single shotgun shot, sending a shower of broken glass up into the air, and splintering the wood. Before the glass hit the ground, Fallon had kicked the doors open and entered the house, his trained eyes taking in the entire room at once. There was a built-in wardrobe on the left, a double-bed mattress on the floor, pushed up against the wall directly in front of him, a small portable TV on top of a sideboard to the right, and a large mirror on the floor with tens of already cut lines of what could only be cocaine. A naked man with a bushy ponytail was on the mattress. His back was towards Fallon. The moans of pleasure from the petite, short-haired blonde girl who had her legs around him quickly became frightened screams. She couldn't have been older than eighteen.

The man didn't even turn. Still with the girl's legs wrapped around his hips, he rolled to the left and reached for the Uzi submachine gun that was resting against the wall.

He didn't get there.

Fallon squeezed the trigger on his MP5, and the gun coughed silently once. The shot hit the back of the man's hand as his fingers were just a couple of inches away from the Uzi. The blast shattered bone and ruptured tendons, sending a red mist of blood into the air and spraying the girl's face.

The man let out a pained cry that sounded like an injured animal's roar. His arm recoiled back towards his chest, spraying more blood onto the girl's body and the mattress.

'Moving isn't such a good idea,' Fallon said, his red laser target beam now locked onto the back of the man's head.

Grimshaw was also in the room by now, his laser target coloring the girl's chest with a red dot. He was concentrating so hard he didn't notice the door to the en-suite bathroom opening behind him.

The blast from the shotgun was deafening, and it was aimed directly at Grimshaw's back. He took the full force of the impact, sending his MP5 flying from his hands, and propelling him forward before he collapsed to the ground.

Fallon had sensed the danger and had started turning before the shot was fired, but he didn't get there in time. In slow motion he saw the plume of smoke that came out of the 12-gauge shotgun, and Grimshaw taking the shot to his back. Everything else came automatically. Fallon was the best close-quarters marksman the LA SWAT had to offer. He'd been through thousands of simulations, and hundreds of real-life scenarios just like this one.

He saw the shotgun barrel start to move again, re-aiming at him. He locked eyes with the shooter for only a millisecond; despite what he saw, there was no hesitation. He squeezed the trigger, and this time his gun coughed twice. Both shots entered the center of the target's forehead almost millimeter perfect, exiting at the back, leaving a hole the size of a small apple, and splattering gray matter, blood and fragmented bone across the wall.

The girl holding the shotgun looked even younger than the one on the mattress under Ponytail Man. She had an innocent, schoolgirl's face, with dimples and freckles on her cheeks. As she fell to her knees, her sad, almost tearful eyes had no more life in them, but they never left Fallon's face, until she slumped forward, hitting the ground.

The man on the mattress took advantage of the distraction and reached for his Uzi for the second time, but his left hand was out of action. That forced him to twist his body and reach for it with his right. He grabbed the gun, but the position he was in was no good. He had to turn his body around the other way to be able to target Fallon. There was no way that would happen fast enough. As soon as he started turning his body back the way he came, Fallon's aim was back on him.

'Drop it,' Fallon shouted, but the man was screaming in anger as he rotated his body, thirsty for blood.

Another squeeze of the trigger from Fallon, another double shot. Both hit Ponytail Man in his right shoulder, fracturing his clavicle and scapula bone before he could aim the Uzi. His arm went limp instantly.

The girl under him, now covered in his blood, let go of a petrified scream that had been gaining momentum in her throat since the girl from the bathroom had hit the floor, and then she became hysterical.

Ponytail Man dropped the gun and collapsed on top of

the blonde girl. She started kicking and jerking, trying to get him off of her.

Without lifting his aim from the man and the girl on the mattress, Fallon moved purposefully towards the en-suite bathroom, stepping over the teenager's body. The bathroom was clear.

'I've got a man down,' he yelled into his helmet-mic.

Two seconds later the door to the main bedroom burst open. Alpha team stepped inside, immediately followed by team Beta, each of their guns targeting a different quadrant of the room.

'The room is clear,' Fallon announced.

'Whole house is clear,' Toro said from the door.

The entire operation had lasted thirty-three seconds, and unfortunately had turned into a bloodbath.

While Robinson and Toro kept their aims on the mattress occupants, Fallon turned his attention to Grimshaw on the floor.

'Grimshaw,' he called, crouching down next to the boy.

No reply. His whole neck was covered in blood.

'Fuck,' he said, holding Grimshaw's bloody head in his hands. 'Why didn't you check the bathroom? I had the room under control, kid.'

Fallon took Grimshaw's pulse.

Nothing.

A 12-gauge shotgun releases lead pellets. They spread upon leaving the barrel. That means that the power of the burning charge is divided among the pellets, and they lose energy as they travel. From a distance, shotguns aren't very useful, but the large number of spreading projectiles make it the perfect weapon for close quarters combat. By chance, the girl with the shotgun had aimed high. Most of the pellets missed Grimshaw's bulletproof vest, hitting him in the back of the neck. They had torn through skin, muscle, artery and veins. Blood was pouring from his neck like an open faucet.

'We need a medic in here,' Fallow shouted down his mic, already starting to massage and pump Grimshaw's heart, refusing to believe what he already knew. There was nothing any of them could do.

'Fuck,' Fallon shouted, still clutching at Grimshaw's lifeless body. His eyes were still open.

Beta team had crossed to the mattress, where the blonde girl was still screaming. Robinson took one look at the bleeding man slumped on top of her.

They had got their man.

One Hundred and Thirteen

'Drop the gun, Detective,' the Sculptor said, staring deep into Hunter's eyes and pressing the electric knife against Scott Bradley's throat.

Hunter didn't move. His aim didn't flinch.

'Are you sure you want to play this game, Robert? 'Cos I sure as hell am ready.' The powerful electric knife was turned on, its whirr reverberating inside the room like a thousand dentists' drills.

Scott was so terrified that only a feeble whimper left his lips. He wet himself.

Hunter still didn't move.

'Suit yourself.' In a super-fast move, the Sculptor grabbed Scott's right hand and swung the knife against his index finger. The blades sliced through skin and bone with tremendous ease. The finger dropped to the floor like a dead maggot. Blood spurted everywhere.

Scott let out a guttural cry and tried to jerk his hand away, but it was all too late. It was already a bloody mess, the finger gone. He looked like he was about to pass out.

'OK,' Hunter yelled, raising his left hand in surrender. 'OK, you win.' He thumbed the safety on, and placed the gun on the floor.

The Sculptor switched the knife off. 'Kick it this way. And make it far away.'

Hunter did as he was told, kicking his gun towards the Sculptor. It slid against the concrete floor until it hit the wall.

'The back-up too.'

'I don't have one.'

'Really?' The knife came back on.

'Noooo!' Scott screamed.

'I don't,' Hunter yelled over the noise. 'I'm not carrying a back-up weapon.'

'OK, then. Strip . . . slowly. Take off your clothes and throw them to the side. You can keep your underwear.'

Hunter did as he was told.

'Now lay on the floor, face-down, legs and arms spread, star position.'

Hunter knew he had to comply. Time was running out for him and Scott.

'Do you know something?' the Sculptor said, wrapping a piece of medical gauze around Scott's hand. 'I had no doubt you would figure it all out. I knew you would manage to piece everything together, to see the real meaning behind the sculptures, to see their shadows, and understand what I was telling you. I just didn't think you would do it this quick. Not before I was done. Not with this last piece still missing. How did you do it? How did you figure it out?'

Hunter placed his chin on the concrete floor and looked straight into her eyes.

Olivia, Derek Nicholson's oldest daughter, had finally moved from behind the metal chair. She was dressed all in black, wearing a jumpsuit made of some impermeable material zipped up to her neck. She pulled the jumpsuit's hood back from her head, and Hunter saw she was wearing a black, silicone swimmer's cap. Her shoes looked a couple of sizes too big for her feet. Hunter remembered what the lead forensics agent had said about the shoeprints found at the second crime-scene, Nashorn's boat – that the distribution of weight from each step seemed to be unequal. That suggested that the killer either walked with a limp, or had deliberately worn the wrong-sized shoes. She was still holding the electric knife in her hand.

'You really had me convinced,' Hunter said, remembering the first day he saw her in her father's house. 'The way you acted . . . the tears . . . the uncontrollable shivering . . . the despair in your voice . . . I bought it all.'

Olivia didn't even flinch. 'So, how did you do it?' she asked again.

Hunter swallowed. He would gain every second he could. 'A friend of your mother's,' he said, and saw those words hit Olivia like a whip.

She paused, anger and sadness slushing around inside her eyes. She took a moment to compose herself. 'Which friend?'

'Someone she knew. I don't have a real name. She called herself Jude.'

'What did she tell you?'

Hunter coughed. 'Nothing much.'

Olivia waited but Hunter said nothing else. 'You better carry on talking or I will start cutting.'

'She came to talk to us about the victims. Your victims.'

'What about them?'

'She was beat up by them, as a group. Just like your mother.'

Hunter saw rage recolor Olivia's face. Her burning eyes

focused on Scott, who was listening attentively, but still looked frightened and in tremendous pain.

'We did figure out the shadow images,' Hunter quickly added, trying to force her attention back to him. 'But we read them wrong . . . partially wrong.'

It worked. Olivia turned and faced Hunter again.

'It took us a little while, but we figured out the meaning behind the coyote and the raven. You were telling us that your father was a liar.'

'He wasn't my father,' she spat out in disgust.

'OK,' Hunter said. 'I'm sorry. You were telling us that Derek Nicholson was a betrayer, a liar,' he corrected himself.

'He was.' Her voice quivered with anger. 'I was three years old when my mother died. I was lied to for twenty-eight years. Tricked like a little dog to believe a lie.'

'I'm so sorry for that,' Hunter said and paused for a moment. His strained neck was starting to hurt. 'But it took us forever to figure out that what you were doing was telling us a story, scene by scene, like in a puppet theater.'

Scott looked confused.

Olivia said nothing.

'But we read your second sculpture and its shadow image wrong,' Hunter continued. 'We went through tens of inter-pretations, and in the end I was convinced that you were showing us a fight scene. A group of guys who used to hang out together, get drunk and high together. One day they got into a fight, things got out of hand and someone died. We also concluded that you were telling us that Andrew Nashorn was the group leader.'

'He was a scumbag,' Olivia said.

'But it wasn't a fight scene you were showing us, was it?' Hunter said. 'You weren't showing us two people fighting on the floor, with the rest of the group watching. You were showing us a rape scene, with the rest of the group watching.'

'They didn't watch. They took turns.' There was a glow burning in her eyes, like a storm building.

'She was a street hooker.' Scott had finally found enough strength to say something. 'Andy picked her up on a dark corner on Sunset Strip. She was looking for it. That was what she did. She fucked people for a living. How was that rape?'

Olivia turned so fast she almost became a blur, and slammed her closed fist into Scott's jaw, rupturing his lower lip and sending a spray of blood across the room.

'You don't get to speak until I tell you to, you sack of shit.'

Hunter twitched on the floor.

'And you better not move until I tell you to.'

'I'm not going anywhere.'

The moment was tensing up.

'I'm listening,' Olivia said. 'How did you figure out it was a rape scene?'

'Jude used to work the streets as well. When she got in contact with us, she told us how she got into the car with Nashorn one night, and he took her somewhere where the rest of the group was waiting for them. They ganged up on her, beat her up, and had their way with her.' Hunter cleared his throat again. 'Then she told us about this woman she met, Roxy.' He looked up at Olivia to assess her reaction. Recognition was written all over her face, but she didn't say anything. Hunter continued. 'Roxy told Jude that she wasn't a street worker. She'd never done it before, but she was desperate. She had a child, who was ill, and she couldn't afford her kid's medicine. Her idea was to work the streets for only one night so she'd have enough money. She was sacrificing herself for her kid.' Hunter looked at Scott. 'So no, she wasn't a hooker, she wasn't looking for it, and she didn't fuck people for a living. She was desperate, out of options, and scared for her kid's health.'

Tears welled up in Olivia's eyes. 'I used to suffer from asthma. I remember having terrible fits when I was a small kid. As I grew older, it all just cleared away.'

'Jude told us that she saw Roxy get in the car with Nashorn one night. She tried to stop her, but she was too late. She never saw Roxy again.'

'Her name was Sandra,' Olivia said. 'Sandra Ellwood. And my name is Olivia Ellwood.' She moved behind Scott's chair again.

Hunter couldn't see what she was doing.

'Tell him,' she said to Scott through gritted teeth, parading the knife before his eyes. 'Tell him how it happened.' Anger was making her tremble.

Scott was looking at her wide-eyed, uncertain.

In a lightning-fast move, before Scott could react, Olivia grabbed his pinky finger and pulled it backwards until it snapped. The bone-cracking sound was loud enough for Hunter to hear it from across the room. Scott screamed in pain and Olivia slapped him across the face. 'Tell him, or I'm going to carry on breaking every bone in your body before I start cutting you.'

One Hundred and Fourteen

Scott Bradley's scared and confused gaze moved from Olivia to Hunter and then back to Olivia. 'Please,' he said. 'I have a family. I have a wife and two daughters.'

Olivia slapped him across the face again. 'I had a mother.'

Scott saw something in her eyes that he'd never seen in anyone else's. Something that scared him like nothing ever had. His cut lip was beginning to swell up. He swallowed a mouthful of saliva and blood, and fought the desire to vomit before speaking again.

'We knew each other from bars and clubs in West Hollywood,' he said. 'You know, back then we were out all the time. We bumped into each other everywhere. Pretty soon we started hanging out together. Andy was the one who came up with the idea the first time. He would get a street hooker and take her to some isolated place somewhere. The rest of us would be waiting and hiding . . .' He looked away.

'Don't stop talking,' Olivia ordered.

'Andy was LAPD, fresh out of cop school. His beat was West Hollywood. He knew the women who had no pimp, no protection.'

Hunter closed his eyes and let out a heavy breath. Without the protection of a pimp there wouldn't be many consequences for the group if things ever got ugly.

'This one night, Andy brought this skinny bi—' Scott stopped himself before saying the word. 'This skinny woman with him. She was pretty. Andy said her name was Roxy. She . . .' He shook his head as he remembered. 'She looked really scared when she saw all of us.' He looked down, avoiding their eyes.

'And you all liked that, didn't you?' Olivia asked. 'You all liked it when they showed how scared they were.'

Scott didn't reply.

Hunter's eyes were tracking Olivia. She was still behind Scott's chair. She had picked Hunter's gun up from the floor, and he saw her flick the safety off. They were all running out of time.

'That night things went wrong . . . really wrong,' Scott continued. 'We all had . . . had our fun, except Derek, Derek Nicholson. That night he didn't want to do it. Maybe it was because he was just about to get married, or maybe it was because this Roxy chick kept on begging us not to hurt her . . .'

Hunter knew that Roxy's pleas would've fed the sadistic flame in all of them. The more scared she got, the more excited they got.

'. . . She kept telling us that she had a daughter who was ill.' Scott stopped talking and silence took over the large room for a moment. And for a moment, each of them was left alone with their thoughts.

'Tell him how bad things got.' Olivia broke the silence.

'We were all high and drunk. Nathan had been really rough with her. We didn't really notice when it happened, but she stopped breathing.'

'Did you beat her up?'

'Derek and I didn't do anything. Andy and Nathan did.'

Olivia's eyes dropped to Scott's hand. She was ready to snap another finger.

'They beat her up, yes, but it wasn't anything too violent. It just added to the excitement for them. Derek and I just watched, I swear. We didn't hit her. We didn't like the beating-up part. It did nothing for us.'

Those had been Derek Nicholson's exact words to Olivia when he confessed to her.

'Maybe she hit her head or something,' Scott continued. 'She couldn't have died from only a few slaps.'

Olivia looked at Hunter before returning her attention to Scott. 'Carry on.'

Scott spit out a mouthful of blood. 'When we realized she was dead, we panicked. We didn't know what to do. No one was thinking straight. Too much booze and acid. I suggested we just left her there and got the hell out, but Andy said that was no good. The amount of evidence the cops would find in that room and on her body would put us all away for good. We could try cleaning it up, but there were no guarantees. Then Andy came up with a plan.'

Hunter felt his stomach tighten. He knew what that plan would be.

'Andy went out and brought back several thick plastic sheets, a meat cleaver, a long, thick chain, padlocks, and a large, square metal toolbox. It was big, but not big enough to fit a body.' Scott paused and looked away.

'Don't stop now,' Olivia said, not allowing the momentum to settle. 'Tell him what you did.'

'I didn't do anything,' he pleaded.

Olivia slapped him across the face. The gash on his lower lip ripped a little more, sending another spray of blood flying across the room.

Scott shivered, taking in quick gulps of air to steady his body.

'Tell him.'

'Nathan had worked part-time in a butcher's shop. He was good with a meat cleaver,' Scott said.

Olivia didn't flinch. She had heard the whole story before.

'Derek and I couldn't watch. We went outside while Andy and Nathan did what they had to do. Derek was messed up. He was freaking out about the bit— ... the woman's daughter – what would happen to her and all. He was more concerned about her than he was about us. Something to do with him having lost his mother when he was really young. He wanted to go to the cops, but he knew that if he did, we would all go to prison for a fucking long time. He was in his last year of law school. He was engaged to get married in a month's time. He didn't want to throw his life away. Besides, if he'd gone to the cops, Andy would've killed him. He would've killed any of us. He told us all that.' He paused for breath. 'When Andy and Nathan were done, all that was left was this chained and padlocked toolbox. My father had a boat, which I had the keys to. So I was left with the job of dumping that box as far off the coast as I could. Andy came with me while the others went home. The box was too heavy. It would've never surfaced.'

The last victim, Hunter thought. *The one who had disposed of the body.*

'Derek was left with the task of getting rid of the woman's purse and all her documents.' Scott's gaze turned to Olivia. 'I guess that was how he found you. He never threw the purse away. He kept her things.'

Olivia said nothing.

'After that night we saw each other less and less, until we just drifted apart. We all moved on with our lives. But we all kept our secret.'

'Not all of you,' Olivia said, slamming the butt of Hunter's gun into the back of Scott's head, knocking him out cold.

One Hundred and Fifteen

Hunter twitched on the ground again and Olivia aimed the gun at his head. 'Don't, Detective. Trust me, I know how to shoot. And from this distance, I won't miss. If there was one thing my fath—' She cleared her throat angrily, 'Derek taught me, it was how to shoot.'

'My neck hurts. I was just stretching it.'

'Well, don't.'

'OK. I won't.'

Olivia moved to the left side of the room. 'You still haven't told me how you got to me. I know you figured out what I was telling you with my shadow puppets, but how did you figure out it was me?'

'After I heard the story Jude told me about what happened to her, things started moving in my head. I suspected I had read the second shadow image wrong. It wasn't a fight, it was a gang rape. I didn't know Roxy was your mother, but I guessed that, if they had done what they did to Jude and Roxy, there probably were others. Others who, like Roxy, also had a child. And that that child had found out about everything. From the first shadow image you left us, I was certain that the only way that child could've found out was through Derek Nicholson. A confession on his deathbed.'

Olivia chuckled angrily. 'He was able to live with it, but not die with it. How ironic is that?'

Hunter knew how common it was for human beings to endure unspoken guilt throughout their entire lives, but to die with it was something few were prepared to do.

'For Derek Nicholson to be able to call that child to his home in order to reveal everything,' Hunter continued. 'It meant that he had to have somehow kept tabs on who and where that child was. I was running through possibilities in my head when Jude called me again last night. She had remembered the name of Roxy's child – Levy.'

Olivia twitched on the spot.

'At first I thought it was a last name, or maybe a male name. It sounded vaguely familiar, but when I looked at the picture your sister had given me of Nicholson and his wife I remembered where I had heard that name before. It was a nickname. Allison had called you by it that day in your house. Not a common nickname for Olivia, but it was *your* nickname.'

Olivia gave Hunter a melancholic smile. 'My mother always called me Levy, never Liv, or Ollie, or anything else. I liked it. It was different. Allison was the only other person who called me that.'

'First I checked your background. You went to medical school.'

Olivia shrugged. 'UCLA, but in the end I decided I didn't want to do it. The knowledge came in handy, though.'

She offered nothing else, so Hunter continued.

'I called someone I know who could access the California Department of Social Services' database. I found out that Nicholson had adopted you during his first year of marriage. An odd choice for a young couple that had no known problem bearing children. In fact, Nicholson adopted you the same year his wife became pregnant with her daughter, Allison.'

'So you know that he adopted me out of guilt for what he'd done.' The anger was back in Olivia's voice. 'Guilt for being part of the group of animals who raped and killed my mother. Guilt for allowing it to happen. Guilt for not telling the police.'

Hunter didn't reply.

'How could I live with all that knowledge, Robert, can you tell me? Because I struggled with it. He called me to his deathbed to tell me that my whole life had been a lie. I was adopted not into a family who wanted to share their love and care for me, but into a family who wanted to bury their guilt.'

'I don't think Derek's wife knew about what happened,' Hunter said.

'*It doesn't matter!*' Olivia spat the words out. 'He convinced her to take me. He told her that my mother was a drug addict who had left me. He told her that I was this poor kid, unwanted, unloved. But I was loved, and I was wanted, until they took her from me. He was the one who didn't want me. All he wanted was to lessen the guilty feeling that was eating him inside. I was his daily feel-good pill. His anti-guilt drug. All he had to do was look at me, and in that sick heart of his he would find some peace. He would tell himself everything was OK because he gave the poor hooker's child a better life. You know what? I never wanted this better life. I was happy. I loved my mother. But he made me believe that she didn't want me. That she had run away. And for twenty-eight years I hated her for walking out on me.'

Hunter understood now where Olivia's incredible violence came from. Displaced rage. Twenty-eight years hating her mother for something that she didn't do. When she learnt the truth, and that she'd been lied to for most of her life, that rage was woken up, gaining a whole new intensity and purpose. Twenty-eight years is a long time to bottle up rage.

A tear ran down Olivia's cheek and her voice croaked for an instant.

'I still remember her – my mother. How beautiful she was. I still remember how we used to play shadow puppets every night when I went to bed. She was so smart at creating them. She could come up with anything – animals, people, angels . . . anything. She didn't have much money, so I never had any real toys. Our shadow puppet theater *was* my toy. We would sit for hours making up stories of our own. Creating silly plays against the wall. All we needed was candlelight and our hands. We were happy.'

Hunter closed his eyes for an instant. That was why she had created shadow puppets from her victims' body parts – a macabre tribute to her mother. Another way to expel her anger.

'He never played with me, did you know that?' Olivia said, shaking her head. 'When I was a kid, he never played with me in the park or anywhere. He never read me a story, or put me on his shoulders, or had pretend tea with me like any father would. I played shadow puppets by myself.'

Hunter couldn't reply.

'After he told me, I went home and cried for three days. I had no idea how I could go on living. My life had been a lie, a good deed to allow my father to sleep at night. I was never loved the way a child is supposed to be loved, except for when my mother was alive. And now I knew that all four people who had mutilated her body and thrown her into the ocean like unwanted garbage had gone on to raise their own families, to prosper in their careers – to live without an ounce of remorse for what they'd done. And worst of all, they had gone on living without ever being punished.'

Hunter knew that very few minds wouldn't break after being faced with what Olivia had been faced with. And the few that didn't break would certainly be damaged forever.

'You know as well as I do that there was nothing I could do with that information that would bring justice to those people. It happened twenty-eight years ago. I had no proof, except for the words of a dying man. No action would've been taken by the police, the DA, the state, or anyone. No one would've believed me. I would just have had to carry on living as I had for the past twenty-eight years.' She shook her head. 'I couldn't do that, could you?'

Hunter thought back to when his father was gunned down inside that branch of the Bank of America. He wasn't a cop then. But he remembered his rage. A rage that was still inside him, dormant somewhere. And cop or not, if he came face to face with the people who had shot his father, he would kill them – no hesitation.

'I came this close to killing myself.' Olivia brought Hunter's thoughts back to the room. 'And then I realized one thing. If I was able to kill myself, then I was able to kill. Full stop. And I decided that, whatever happened, I would have my version of justice. For my mother. She deserves justice.'

For a moment her stare wandered around the room.

'Everything just came to me like in a dream. As if my

mother was there, telling me what to do, guiding my hand. My fath—' Anger was back on Olivia's face. 'Derek Nicholson loved mythology. He was always reading books, quoting passages. It was only fair to make him into a mythological symbol.' She pulled back and released the slide mechanism on Hunter's gun, manually loading a round into the chamber.

It was time for the final act.

One Hundred and Sixteen

Hunter looked up at Olivia again. There was no way he would be able to get anywhere near her without her seeing and shooting him. The room was too big, and she was too far away for him to mount any sort of challenge. Plus, he'd been on the floor, in that star-position for too long now. His muscles wouldn't respond immediately, at least not with enough dexterity.

'Would you like to see the last sculpture?' Olivia said. 'The last shadow puppet? The conclusion to my *justice* play?'

Hunter placed his chin on the floor again and looked up at her and then at Scott, who was still unconscious. 'Olivia, don't. You don't have to.'

'*Yes I do!* For twenty-eight years Derek Nicholson soothed his heart and guilt by taking pity on the poor prostitute's daughter. For twenty-eight years those assholes lived a life without punishment. It's my turn to soothe my heart, while I still have one. Get up,' she ordered.

Hunter hesitated.

'I said, get up.' She pointed the gun at him.

Slowly, with all his muscles and joints aching, Hunter got up from the floor.

'Walk over there.' She pointed to the left side of the room, just past the pedestal lights. 'Place your back flat against the wall.'

Hunter did as he was told.

'See that flashlight on the floor, to your right?'

Hunter looked down and nodded.

'Pick it up.'

He did.

'Hold it about chest height and turn it on.'

Hunter paused, trying to understand what was going on.

'I had to improvise,' Olivia said. 'I had something a lot more gruesome and painful in mind – my grand finale – but given the circumstances, this will have to do. I hope you like it. Turn the flashlight on,' she repeated.

Hunter brought the flashlight to his chest and switched it on.

Olivia stepped out of the way. Behind her, Scott was still out cold on the chair, his head slumped back, exposing his neck. His mouth was open as if he'd fallen asleep in that position and was about to snore. A few feet past him, while he had his face against the ground, Hunter hadn't noticed that Olivia had attached a thin but rigid piece of wire to the second pedestal lamp, about four-and-a-half feet from the ground. It was around two feet long, and it shot straight out horizontally. Attached to its end was Scott's severed index finger.

Hunter was confused for a moment, until he saw the shadow image projected onto the far wall. It showed the silhouette of Scott's head, tilted back, with his mouth open like he was mid-scream. The finger on the wire, a few feet from him, cast a shadow that looked like some sort of crooked cylindrical tube, positioned at an angle. Because of the absence of perceptible depth, it looked like one shadow was right in front of the other. The cylindrical tube was pointing down at Scott's head-shadow – directly at his open mouth.

Right at that moment, the sound of distant sirens reached them. Hunter had called for backup before entering the warehouse, but from the sound, he knew they were at least three-to-five minutes away. Too long.

Olivia looked at Hunter. Her face displayed reassuring calmness. 'I knew they were coming,' she said, pointing the gun at Hunter again. 'But you being alive when they get here will depend on how fast you can figure this last piece out.'

Hunter kept his eyes on the gun.

'Don't look at me. Look at the shadow.'

Hunter concentrated. His first impression was that the whole image looked like someone waiting with his mouth open under some sort of liquid dispenser, ready to drink from it. Was she going to pour something down his throat? Kill him that way? That would be a complete change from her entire MO so far. Confusion was all that was going on inside Hunter's head.

The shot that came out of the gun in Olivia's hand sounded like a nuclear explosion. The bullet hit the wall inches from Hunter's head and he winced defensively, dropping the flashlight.

'C'mon, c'mon, Robert,' she said. 'You're supposed to be the clever one. The experienced cop. Can't you work under pressure?'

The sirens were getting closer.

'The shadows,' she said. 'Look at the shadows. Read them. 'Cos you're time is about to run out.'

Hunter picked up the flashlight again. He was looking but he couldn't see it. What the hell did all that mean?

Bang!

The second shot hit the wall to Hunter's left. This time even closer to his face. Concrete shrapnel flew in all directions. Some of it grazed Hunter's cheek, burning and ripping through his skin. He felt warm blood starting to run down his face, but he didn't let go of the flashlight. His eyes were still on the shadows.

'I promise you, Detective, the next shot *will* find your head.' She took a step closer to him.

Hunter's brain was trying to cope with the threat of dying in the next few seconds, while throwing possibilities around.

From the corner of his eye he saw Olivia aim the gun again.

He couldn't think.

And then he saw it.

One Hundred and Seventeen

'Recording,' he said, as Olivia's finger tightened on the trigger. The image was showing a microphone pointing down at Scott's mouth, not a drinks dispenser. 'You recorded it. While he was telling the story, you recorded the whole thing. A confession.'

Olivia lowered the gun. A smile almost stretched her lips. She raised her left hand, showing Hunter the mini digital-recording device. 'I recorded them all. I made them tell me what happened every time. The stories are all identical. Their voices are all here, telling how they all took turns beating and raping my mother, before dismembering her, shoving her mutilated body into a box, and dumping her in the ocean. All except Andrew Nashorn. His jaw was broken. He couldn't speak. But none of it matters anymore.'

Hunter couldn't think of what to say.

Scott mumbled something incomprehensible and his eyes slowly flickered open.

'Catch,' Olivia said and threw the recording device to Hunter.

He caught it in mid-air. He stared at it for a moment, doubtful, before looking back at her.

'You can keep it,' she said.

'This might help, but I won't lie to you,' Hunter said. 'In

our less-than-perfect justice system, it won't make much difference, Olivia.'

'I know. I already made the difference I wanted to make. I've had my justice.' She gestured towards the recording device in Hunter's hand. 'I thought I would send that to the press, expose the whole thing. Not for me – I know what's going to happen to me – but for my mother.' Olivia wiped a tear from her eye before it could run down her cheek. 'She deserved justice. Do whatever you think you should do with it.' She placed Hunter's gun on the floor and kicked it towards him.

'Arrest that fucking bitch,' Scott yelled from his seat. 'And get me the fuck out of here, you moron.' He started jerking his body in his chair. 'That slut cut my fucking finger off, did you see that? I'm gonna make sure you fry in the chair, you hear me, you motherless bitch. My brother will rip you into little whore pieces in court.'

This time Hunter was faster than Olivia. The powerful punch he threw hit Scott square in the temple. He slumped to one side, knocked out cold for the second time.

'He talks too much,' Hunter said, facing Olivia and shrugging. 'I have to arrest you. It's my duty as a detective. But I won't cuff you.'

This time the confusion was stamped on Olivia's face.

'We're going to walk out of here, and you can hold your head up high.' Hunter looked at Scott Bradley. 'But I *will* cuff this slimeball.'

The rage was gone from Olivia's eyes. 'You are a good man, Robert, and a good cop. But I had this all planned out in my head from the start. There would only be one ending to my story. The director's cut. And it doesn't include an arrest.'

Hunter saw her throw something the size of a nickel inside her mouth, saw her jaw tense, and heard the crunching sound as she crushed it between her teeth before swallowing it down. He dashed towards her, but Olivia was already collapsing. She had taken fifty times the lethal dosage of cyanide.

By the time the LAPD took the warehouse, her heart had long stopped beating.

One Hundred and Eighteen

Hunter spent ninety minutes taking Garcia, Captain Blake, and Alice through everything that had happened since last night.

'I must admit,' Alice said to Hunter. 'When you called me and asked me to get into the California Department of Social Services' database and search for adoption files for Olivia, I thought it was quite a strange request, but her being a suspect never, ever crossed my mind. The only odd thing I found was how fast the whole process took. California adoption laws are very lenient,' Alice explained. 'The only true prerequisite is that the adoptee has to be at least ten years younger than the adopter. Derek Nicholson had just graduated from law school. He'd made many friends in the judicial system and he knew a great many people.'

'Judges,' Garcia said.

'Them too. With his contacts and knowledge of the law, he was able to fast-track everything. A typical adoption process in California can last anywhere from six months to a year. Derek Nicholson got all the documentation and everything approved in less than ninety days, no questions asked, everything seemingly above board.'

'To circumvent the law, one needs to know the law,' Hunter said.

'That's true,' Alice agreed. 'And with powerful friends, anything is possible.'

'OK, but how did you know Olivia would go after the next victim tonight?' Garcia asked.

'I didn't. All I had were suspicions, so I gambled.' Hunter ran the tip of his fingers over the two cuts on his left cheek. He'd refused any bandaging.

'Gambled?' Captain Blake asked.

'I dropped by Olivia's house this morning unannounced, with the excuse that I had some new information, and I wanted to ask her a few more questions. When Garcia and I talked to Olivia and her sister last night, I asked them for a photograph of their father when he was younger. Allison had an old wedding picture, which was on a sideboard in her living room. *Olivia* handed it to me. As she held the frame and looked at the picture, I saw something in her eyes. Some strong emotion, which I'd thought was grief. This morning when I dropped by her house, I handed the picture back to her, and her eyes burned with it again. It wasn't grief. It was something much deeper, much more pained.' Hunter rubbed his eyes for an instant. 'That was when I asked her if her father ever played shadow puppets with her or her sister when they were kids.'

'You were letting her know that we knew about the real meaning behind the sculptures,' Alice said.

Hunter nodded. 'But Olivia played it really cool. She pretended to be surprised by the odd question, but she gave me nothing else. Then I asked her if her mother ever had, and her coolness wavered for just an instant. Her eyes focused on nothing at all, and for a split second her expression softened to something tender, before hardening in a way I hadn't seen before. And that was when I decided to gamble. I told Olivia that during the night we had come across a new development. We were now sure that the killer had only one more name on his list. I told her that we would have that last victim's name in twenty-four hours. And when we did, we would put him under constant surveillance.'

Garcia smiled. 'In other words, if you were right and she was the Sculptor killer, you'd just told her that she had to act in the next twenty-four hours if she wanted to get to the next victim before we did. You forced her to move things forward.'

Hunter nodded again. 'But I had no time to come back to the PAB and file a request for a surveillance team. I had no grounds to justify that request, either. All I had were suspicions and a nickname.'

'So you decided to break protocol again and become the surveillance team yourself,' Captain Blake said; but there was no harshness in her tone.

'For twenty-four hours,' Hunter agreed.

'So what did she do?' Alice asked.

'Olivia didn't leave her house for most of the day.'

'She was probably re-planning,' Captain Blake said.

'When she left, she drove straight to Woodland Hills, where she met up with Scott Bradley in a parking lot. He left his car and jumped in with her.'

Everyone frowned.

'My guess,' Hunter said, 'is that Olivia had already made contact with Scott in the last few days. He is married, but he has a weakness for pretty women, especially if they tell him they are submissive. Olivia knew how to entice him. I'm sure she'd been grooming him for days.'

'And that explains her change in MO,' Garcia said. 'All

the previous murder scenes had been a place where the victim felt comfortable and secure – Nicholson's house, Nashorn's boat, and Littlewood's office. Scott Bradley had a wife and two daughters, which made using his house that much harder. He didn't have a private office either. He was a market broker, working from a large open-plan floor with tens of other people.'

Hunter agreed.

'So all she had to do was call him and tell him she wanted to meet him tonight,' Alice said. 'I'm sure he would've dropped whatever he had planned for the evening.'

'She never intended to walk out of this alive, did she? Even if she hadn't been caught,' Captain Blake said. 'She knew she wasn't going to prison. She knew she wasn't going to carry on living either.'

Hunter said nothing.

'When Derek Nicholson told her the truth,' Alice said. 'He condemned her psychologically, giving her much more than she could cope with. If you were suddenly told you'd been lied to your entire life, that your mother was brutally murdered, dismembered, and disposed of like unwanted trash – if you were told the names of everyone responsible, but knew that they'd never been punished, and that they never would be, what would you do? How could you ever have a normal life again with that knowledge swinging back and forth in your head? For her, to carry on living would've been a torture, in prison or not.'

'Olivia gave up her life so her mother could have justice,' Hunter said. 'A justice that our system would never have given either of them. In the end, those men killed mother *and* daughter.'

Thorned silence spiked the air.

'I know we did what was expected of us,' Captain Blake said, shaking her head. 'But maybe we should've moved a little slower. If Olivia Nicholson had succeeded in taking out all four victims, I wouldn't have minded it. Not in the least. That scumbag Scott Bradley got away easy, minus a finger. He deserves worse. And he's saying that you knocked him out cold.'

Hunter stayed silent.

'Well, the way I see it,' the captain proceeded. 'He was under immense stress. Things can easily get distorted under those circumstances. What happened was that he simply imagined you punching him.' She paused and her eyes moved around the room. 'Yep, that answer sounds great to me.'

Garcia then told Hunter what had happened in Pomona. Ken Sands had been arrested, and Garcia would now contact Detective Ricky Corbí, the detective running the investigation into Tito's murder. Sands was the prime suspect.

One Hundred and Nineteen

It was the middle of the night by the time Hunter finished all the paperwork. He went downstairs and placed everything on Captain Blake's desk, ready for her the next morning.

His cellphone rang in his pocket and he reached for it.

'Detective Hunter.'

'Robert, it's Alice.'

Hunter had been so busy filling out reports, he hadn't seen Alice pack all her things and leave hours earlier.

'I'm just calling to say that it was nice seeing you again,' she said. 'And that it was quite an experience working with you.'

'Yeah, it was great seeing you again too.'

'Even though you didn't remember me at all.'

Hunter was quiet for a couple of seconds. 'Hey, you're not going to be a stranger, are you? You're still working for the Los Angeles DA, right?'

'Yeah, I'm still working for the DA.'

Awkward silence.

Hunter checked his watch. 'Are you busy? Would you like to go get a drink?'

'Now?' The surprise in Alice's voice wasn't due to the late hour.

'Yeah. I'm almost done here. And I could really use a drink.'

Hesitation.

'And the company,' Hunter added.

'Yes, I'd love to get a drink.'

Hunter smiled. 'How about we meet at the Edison in the Higgins Building on 2nd and Main?'

'Yes, I know the place. Give me half an hour?'

'See you there.' Hunter disconnected.

Outside the PAB, Hunter paused at the corner of South Broadway and West 1st Street, and observed the traffic for a moment. He touched the flesh wounds on his cheek, before looking down at the envelope he had in his hands. It was addressed to Michelle Howard, the Chief Editor for the *LA Times*. She'd made the news herself a few years ago when she revealed that she had been a victim of gang rape when she was a teenager. The offenders were never caught.

Hunter hadn't told Garcia, Captain Blake, Alice or anyone else about the recording device Olivia had given him. He retrieved the device from his pocket and stared at it for a long moment before placing it inside the envelope, sealing it, and dropping it inside the postbox he was standing in front of.

Now his job was done.

He started walking towards 2nd and Main.

Coming soon from Simon & Schuster

Robert Hunter is about to face his grisliest case yet.

Available August 2013 in Hardback and Ebook

Hardback ISBN 978-0-85720-305-2
Ebook ISBN 978-0-85720-309-0

Turn the page for a sneak preview . . .

A single shot to the back of the head, execution style. Many people consider it a very violent way to die. But the truth is – it isn't. At least not for the victim.

A 9mm bullet will enter the back of someone's skull and exit at the other side in three ten-thousandths of a second. It will shatter the cranium and rupture through the subject's brain matter so fast the nervous system has no time to register any pain. If the angle in which the bullet enters the victim's head is correct, the bullet should splice the cerebral cortex, the cerebellum, even the thalamus in such a way that the brain will cease functioning, resulting in instant death. If the angle of the shot is wrong, the victim might survive, but not without extensive brain damage. The entry wound should be no larger than a small grape, but the exit wound could be as large as a tennis ball, depending on the type of bullet used.

The male victim on the photograph Detective Robert Hunter of the LAPD Robbery Homicide Division (RHD) was looking at had died instantly – no suffering. The bullet had traversed his entire skull, rupturing the cerebellum together with the temporal and the frontal lobes, causing fatal brain damage in three ten-thousandths of a second. A full second later he was dead on the ground.

The case wasn't Hunter's; it belonged to Detective Terry Radley in the main detectives' floor, but the investigation photos had ended up on Hunter's desk by mistake. As he returned the A4-sized photograph to the case file, the phone on his desk rang.

'Detective Hunter, Homicide Special,' he answered it, half expecting it to be Detective Radley after the photo file.

Silence.

'Hello?'

'Is this Detective Robert Hunter?' The raspy voice on the other side was male. The tone was calm, not too low, not too high. The person spoke slowly.

'Yes, this is Detective Robert Hunter. Can I help you?'

Hunter heard the caller breath out.

'That's what we're going to find out, Detective.'

Hunter frowned.

'I'm going to need your full attention for the next few minutes.'

Hunter cleared his throat. 'I'm sorry, I didn't catch your na...'

'Shut the fuck up and listen, Detective,' the caller interrupted him. His voice was still calm. 'This is not a conversation.'

Hunter went silent. The LAPD received tens, sometimes hundreds of crazy calls a day – drunks, drug users on a high, abusive people, gang members trying to look 'badass', psychics, people wanting to report a government conspiracy or an alien invasion, even people who claimed to have seen Elvis down at the local café. But there was something in the caller's tone of voice, something in the way he spoke that told Hunter that dismissing the call as a prank would be a mistake. He decided to play along for the time being.

Hunter's partner, Detective Carlos Garcia, was sitting at his desk, which faced Hunter's, inside their small office on the fifth floor of the Police Administration Building in downtown Los Angeles. His longish dark-brown hair was tied back in a slick ponytail. Garcia was reading something on his computer screen, unaware of his partner's telephone conversation. He pushed himself away from his desk and leisurely interlaced his fingers behind his head.

Hunter snapped his fingers once to catch Garcia's attention, pointed to the receiver at his ear and made a circular motion with his index finger, indicating that he needed the call recorded and traced.

Garcia instantly reached for the phone on his desk, punched the internal code that connected him to Operations, and got everything rolling in less than five seconds. He signalled to Hunter, who signalled back telling him to listen in. Garcia tapped into the line.

'I'm assuming you do have a computer on your desk, Detective,' the caller said. 'And that computer is connected to the internet?'

'That's correct.'

A very uneasy pause.

'OK. I want you to type the address I'm about to give you into your address bar...are you ready?'

Hunter hesitated.

'Trust me, Detective, you will want to see this.'

Hunter leaned forward over his keyboard and brought up his internet browser. Garcia did the same.

'OK, I'm ready,' Hunter said in a calm tone.

The caller gave Hunter an internet address made only of numbers and dots, no letters.

Hunter and Garcia typed the sequence into their address

bars and pressed the 'enter' key. Their computer screens flicked a couple of times before the web page loaded.

Both detectives went still, as a morbid silence took hold of the room.

The caller chuckled. 'I guess I have your full attention now.'